WESTERN NOVELS BY
G. R. HOWE

No Time to Trust

Dragons of Fire

Crow Woman on Deadman

Short Stories Out of Kane

TEQUILA PROMISES

G. R. Howe

Acknowledgement

Thank you to the following individuals who have contributed so much time and effort in the editing and creation of this novel: Joy Howe, Rachel and Jeff Montgomery, and Martha Howe. These individuals were marvelous and free with their time, generous suggestions, and comments.

For Joy

Prologue

Low Mountain is a barometer of sorts, a theoretical thermometer that measures the ambient temperature of heaven and hell.

In winter, the storms roll in from the west and the clouds hang low on her rocky, barren slopes. It is then that the scrub juniper and cottonwood disappear and vanish in the cold haze. Sometimes the clouds hang so low you can't see the mountain at all. Sometimes Winter takes a notion to explain how it won't be taken for granted any longer, how a man best bring a good heavy coat because it isn't listening to any whining.

"No," the mountain says, "No more, not now." That's when it gets serious and the thermometer bellies out at forty below. That's when it's God-awful cold and Low Mountain disappears altogether. Yes, sometimes she's a barometer, a harbinger of how hell is going to feel to those not given to fire but think ice will, indeed, suffice.

In the early spring, as the days grow longer and look forward to summer and fall, Low Mountain isn't that way at all. On her flat, often rolling, top, the mountain grass turns green, sprouting up through the purple sage; the mountain sheep, elk, and white tail grow sleek and fat. The rock dog plumps up, barking at almost anything, not because he's alarmed, but because he has nothing else to do. In the cool of the canyon whose sheer walls rise straight up a thousand feet, the fish swim through the ice water of Porcupine Creek, Deer Creek, and Trout Creek. If God ever took a vacation, He'd take it there. No one would visit Him. He'd have it to Himself; He'd be alone. "Alone" is something. Some say "alone" isn't what it's cracked up to be; but those folks haven't ever been alone; they haven't ever stood on ground where only God has walked, where the fish jump on the line, begging to be caught; where the bugle of the bull-elk wakes you up to eggs fried over easy in bacon grease, with hashed browns, and apple juice mixed with a shot of tequila. Even God loves "alone" on Low Mountain before the winter winds blow cold and angry and the grey clouds fill the canyons and draws with the snows of January.

Chapter 1

August 1885.

It started in the early 1880s. They did not recall the exact year with any clarity. It simply didn't matter in the stories told or the number of fish caught. Henry Williams and Frank Rodriguez had visited Trout Creek in August for three, maybe four, years running. In August of 1885 they were camped on the south side of Trout Creek when they met the Indian. It was a dicey area, if border, breed, and birth has any weight or meaning. The small, meandering creek was, at best, ten feet across at its widest. One side was Crow Reservation and the other, not so much. It was simply difficult to know where the reservation ended and everything else began.

Getting to the creek was strictly a horse and saddle affair. Staying long meant having multiple mules and pack saddles to carry amenities such as: a cast iron skillet, corn meal, salt, pepper, a box of matches and multiple bottles of well packed, closely monitored tequila. A second mule carried cans of sliced peaches, smoked sardines bathed in mustard sauce, tin cups, chipped but usable porcelain plates, a canvas tent for inclement weather, Mary Carlos' tamales, a butcher knife, and fishing gear. These were small inconsequential items, but they assisted in the enjoyment of life camping on the back side of Low Mountain.

It was late morning when Frank Rodriguez, fishing pole in hand, found himself looking at the big Indian. The fellow was dressed in loose denim pants and a blue plaid shirt that only threatened to cover his expansive belly. He wore no hat; a knife scar ran across his left cheek from the point of his chin to his ear; his jet black hair was long, hanging down in his face, interferring with his vision, yet covering his forehead and cheek bone on the right side; some strands reached his rounded shoulders; he wore huge leather boots whose tops reached half-way up his calves. Those boots had seen better days. His belly partly hid the wide belt that kept his pants up. The Indian was an anomaly: not only was he big in stature, but he was quick on his feet and athletic.

Seeing the Indian standing in front of him barring his path to the stream was odd. Frank had never seen another man on Trout Creek other than Henry.

The Indian said, "Get the hell outta here. This ain't your creek. You ain't got no business fishin' here."

That simple statement drew the line in the sand daring Frank to cross it.

Frank glanced at the bucket of brook trout he'd caught that morning, then back at the Indian whose hands were cocked belligerently on his hips. This massive man stood tall, his chin sticking out. He was fully aware that he was formidable, an immovable object that had to be dealt with.

"You can go to hell," Frank said slowly, staring at the Indian. "This is my fishing hole. I fish here. You don't. And I personally don't care whether this is

4

Reservation or not." Frank deliberately stopped talking, pausing. Then he said, "You the best they got?"

The Indian bolted toward Frank and took a swing with a huge right fist. He missed, but not by much for Frank was quick. He dodged, dropped his fishing rod, and took a swing at the Indian. He, too, missed. They grappled, stumbled, fell, and rolled down the embankment, very nearly falling into the icy water of Trout Creek. After that, it was swing, miss, swing, connect, roll on the ground, wipe the blood from the mouth and nose, and swing again.

Frank was smiling; it was as if he'd never had this much fun, never giving an inch, never backing down. Neither did the Indian. But the Indian was a little surprised. This man he'd picked to knock around didn't seem to be impressed by his size, belligerence, and bravado. What was amazing was that Frank never stopped coming no matter what he did. He hit him hard, yet Frank didn't stay hit. What was even more amazing was this fellow hit back. It took a few minutes, but soon the Indian realized he should have brought a lunch.

After these exchanges developed an intense, living character of their own, Henry Williams, who'd been watching with some interest, pulled his SAA model 1873 Colt revolver from behind his belt buckle, poked the worn barrel into the bright August sky, and discharged a round. The percussion echoed off the mountain side, slamming against the slopes of the grass-covered hills, then drifted into the network of canyons and draws again and again.

The combatants stopped their engagement to stare at him, trying to figure out whether Henry was angry, crazy, or just liked to fire his pistol and listen to the resulting echo. For a few seconds Henry's intentions were a mystery; the Indian readied himself to sprint for cover; Frank considered falling down from exhaustion-- the inevitable result of absorbing the bigger man's swinging blows.

Their alarm was misplaced. Henry stuck the pistol back behind his belt buckle and wordlessly picked up a tequila bottle and two empty tin cups. He handed one cup to each, poured their respective tins full, and stepped back. With a certain aplomb acquired from fistfighting in the morning, they drained their cups, getting little on their fingers. Henry promptly retrieved the tin cups, then stepped back. He looked at both and then motioned for them to get after it. From his safe perch, he wordlessly watched the morning's entertainment.

Four minutes later, Frank had again rolled off the embankment onto the very edge of the creek and was standing, one foot in the water, the other not. The Indian jumped down to where Frank stood and took a swing. Frank stepped back a few inches, causing the Indian to miss, and counter punched the ribs. The Indian turned slightly and went down only to pop right back up again, a look of anger and determination etched in his face. His knife scar and lips had turned purple and red from smeared blood and his pounding heart.

Simultaneously, both of the combatants were again confronted with the disconcerting percussion of Henry's SAA Colt. This time neither considered jumping, running, or falling down. Instead, they accepted the tin cups and held reasonably still while

Henry filled them. Henry watched as they drained the contents.

Henry motioned for them to get after it, which they promptly did, each throwing the other into the cold water of Trout Creek at about the same time. They came up swinging, thrashing about. The Indian had Frank by the throat when Frank slugged him in the belly and tried to knee him in the groin. That failed. Instead, he pushed him hard onto the Reservation side of Trout Creek.

"Now stay over there!" Frank ordered.

But the Indian didn't. On they went.

The pistol report popped against the mountain sides again, echoing down canyon and draw, calling a timeout. Henry stepped across the water, using the exposed rocks of Trout Creek as stepping stones, handed out the tin cups, then poured them full. He watched the combatants drain their cups, retrieved them, and retreated to the south side of the creek. Another six minutes of a slugfest proceeded before Henry pulled out his pistol and called for yet another intermission.

Half an hour passed. The bottle was drained and another opened; neither man could stand without falling down. Undoubtedly, their unsteadiness of foot was due to in part to consumed liquor. It was also directly related to sheer physical exhaustion, exacerbated by the thin air on top of Low Mountain. Six thousand feet isn't high, but it isn't low either.

"What's your name?" Henry asked the Indian as he teetered, off-balance, looking up, his arms braced on his knees.

The Indian stared at Frank, his breath coming in short gasps. He wiped his nose and shook his head in an effort to clear it.

"Fleury," he answered. "It's Fleury."

Henry said, "You put up one helluva fight, Fleury."

Fleury looked at him, hesitating, unsure of how to respond. "Thanks," he finally said.

"Hey, what about me?" Frank said.

"Franko, in order for Fleury here to put up a helluva fight, you musta given him a helluva fight. He can't put up a helluva fight alone."

"Oh."

"In order for Fleury to fight proper, he needs someone proper to fight. That's the way this fightin' business works. There's a balance. Either of you want some corn bread? Some canned, smoked, and dunked-in-mustard-sauce sardines?"

Fleury looked at Henry and nodded. Henry handed him a plate, the porcelain cracked in spots; then he dished the sardines right out of the can he'd opened with his jackknife. Afterwards, Henry offered him a hunk of cornbread, which Fleury accepted.

Fleury sought a pine log and sat down.

"Well, who won?" Frank asked.

"Franko, nobody wins a fight."

"Oh," Frank responded again. "And I thought the last man standing won."

"Do you want some cornbread and sardines?" Henry asked Frank.

"I want some fried fish rolled in cornmeal," he replied.

8

"Do you want some cornbread and sardines whilst I fry you some fish rolled in cornmeal?"

Frank nodded, accepting the plate, the sardine can, and a hunk of cornbread. Frank sat down beside Fleury.

"That's one helluva swing you got there, Fleury," he said.

"I like your head butt. Ever use that in a real fight?"

"That was a real fight," Frank said.

"He did once. We were in Mexico," Henry said. "Not only knocked the guy down, knocked him plumb out. Franko has got a helluva head butt. Fellow was out, layin' on the floor for half an hour. Franko does love to fight."

"'Fight?' He can't fight. That ain't nothin!"

"Nothing? Maybe so, but I'd say you can't see outta one eye, your bruised nuts ain't helpin' ya much, and your jaw ain't workin' right."

"Yeah?" the Indian said. "What about you? You a fighter or just a talker?"

"Not me. I don't like fightin', but Franko, he likes it. That time I was tellin' you about--You see there were these three--Franko had one on each arm---and the third, he was leanin' into Franko tellin' him all the bad things he was gonna do to him. Franko, he leans back and pops him in the noggin with his head. Knocks him to the floor. And he ain't movin'."

The Indian stared at Henry in disbelief. "What were you doing? Why weren't you helping? Three on one!"

"I was helpin'. I pulled my Navy, popped a

round into the ceiling. Made for a fair fight--Franko takin' one at a time. And that fellow on the floor—he didn't move for a half hour. Fight was over 'fore he wakes himself up."

"Musta been something wrong with them, two on one."

"I don't know. Cowhands, *vaqueros*. Pretty salty boys. Knew their way around the *cantinas*. Their faces looked pretty much like yours is lookin'. Nobody even came close to touchin' Franko's face."

Frank smiled. "Mary Carlos did not like me to have a black eye," he said. "Had to keep my handsome face pretty."

"Where you from, Fleury?" Henry asked.

"St. Xavier."

"I'll be damned. A religious Indian. I didn't know there was such a thing."

"Naw. Not so. Not so. I ain't Catholic." Fleury paused, rubbing his jaw. "I'm Absaroke Crow. That's just where I'm from. You two come here and steal fish often?"

"Every year, second week in August."

"I'll have to be here next year. Make sure you don't steal too many."

"Hold your plate out. I'll give you some of those fish we stole. See how you like 'em."

"Maybe we can have a big fight."

"Maybe, if Franko is willing."

"Maybe we can drink some tequila after each round."

"Maybe, if Franko's tequila don't run out."

Fleury held out his plate. Henry slid four fryers

on it from the cast-iron skillet that he'd used to bake cornbread.

"Tequila is a most necessary requirement though," Henry said. "Wouldn't be proper fishin' without several cases of Mexican fire water."

That's how it was for these three miscreants the second week in August when five days became ten, though no one counted; when stealing fish out of Trout Creek was better than pulling the same fish out of Deer Creek. Stolen fish tasted better. The two creeks were a mile apart, one sort of on the Reservation, and the other not. But it didn't matter. Frank Rodriguez never let such a simple thing interfere with a good fight, nor Henry with a good drink, not in mid-August when the fish were biting and the plump rock dog was barking his intruder warning to all who would listen.

That's the way it was, the way it had always been except when it wasn't that way.

Chapter 2

August 1888

The second week in August 1888 Fleury didn't make it; he simply didn't show. Frank didn't say much about it, nor did Henry.

Frank and Henry were regular cowhands, the sort seen anywhere from Fort Worth, Texas to Missoula, Montana. Frank Rodriguez was born about one hundred-twenty miles north of Mexico City to Spanish parents originally from a small town outside of Seville, Spain. Frank had two older brothers: Jesus and Eduardo. He was three years older than Henry. He could read and write and, when pushed, he could sing. He wasn't pushed all that often.

Henry Williams was born in 1844 in a one room log cabin outside of Danville, Illinois. He had a sister named Ellen, a dog named Ring, a mother named Rose, and a drunk for a father called Fleece--no one knew why. Henry called Frank, Franko.

Frank was partial to leather cuffs, high-crowned Stetson hats with drawstrings to keep from losing them in a wind storm, Bull Durham tobacco and Copenhagen chew. He was light-skinned, burned brown by sun and wind. He spoke Spanish and English fluently. He could handle a riata like it was an extension of his right arm, wore boots to the knee--with the legs of his britches tucked inside--with dog ears to pull them on, as did Henry. Frank called Henry, Henry or Hank.

The crown of Henry's Stetson was not as tall as Frank's. He didn't wear leather cuffs. He didn't like Spanish rowls. He didn't like shotgun chaps, did prefer batwings. He could understand Spanish, spoke it a little; did speak bad English. He stood five foot eleven inches tall, which was two inches taller than Frank. He weighed one ninety-five; Frank weighed two hundred and was a little more stocky. Henry didn't smoke or use chewing tobacco. He was known to drink a little tequila when the occasion called for it; Frank, a little more than he. Frank Rodriquez was defined by what he liked, Henry by what he didn't.

Both men came well-heeled. Both carried Model 1873 Winchester rifles: Frank's bored for 30-40 caliber, while Henry carried a 30-30 in a scabbard. Frank carried two Colt SAA 1873 Peacemakers: one strapped to his thigh, the other tucked behind his belt buckle. Henry carried three--he being a little paranoid, having been raised on Navy Colts that were prone to misfiring and took forever to load. Sometimes he didn't have forever.

Pistols, rifles and ropes were as commonplace as ticks crawling on a horse's belly. Western men never went anywhere without shooting irons, but proficiency was another matter. Most didn't take the time; their waking moments were primarily engaged in work. Henry and Frank regularly burned up cartridges aplenty, having seen the disastrous results of not being able to shoot with accuracy. Both considered firearms to be useless and even dangerous if their owners didn't know how to use them with exactness. They did.

Five days into all-the-fish-you'd-ever-want-to-eat, Henry mentioned to Frank that he missed the Indian.

"Didn't he say he was from some Catholic town? St. Xavier, wasn't it?"

"It was."

"Ain't that north of here?"

"It is."

"What do you say we ride over there and see what's keepin' him?"

"All right."

Just before noon, the sun beating down from a blue sky, crickets and locust singing their aching songs, they saddled their horses, stored their remaining provisions in the V of a tall cottonwood tree, and turned their mules loose in a meadow south of Trout Creek. Then they rode for St. Xavier: riding across the Basin Pasture to where Chain Canyon crossed the Big Horn, following the Bad Pass Trail along the west side of the river and riding north toward Fort CF Smith. They arrived two days later at St. Xavier, Montana Territory.

St. Xavier wasn't much; it consisted of a general store; a livery stable and corrals; three log houses; and a fancy Catholic Church with huge carved doors, stained glass windows, and numerous statues. Scattered about and among the cottonwoods were a dozen buffalo skin lodges. The exact number fluctuated weekly. One-hundred-thirty horses ran out on the grass on each side of the river.

"Ma'am," Frank asked a middle-aged Crow woman standing in the Paxton general store, "do you know a big Indian name of Fleury? Do you know where we could find him?"

She looked from Frank to Henry, then without saying a word, walked away, head held high without looking back.

The store clerk was a little more helpful. He said without being asked, "He's in the jail at Fort Smith."

"Jail?" Frank said.

"Yeah. It seems he knocked out the Sheriff's deputy. Hit him in the head with his head. Put him down on the floor for twenty minutes. I'm told it was something to see. Nobody likes that deputy."

"You saw him do that or you didn't?"

"No, I didn't but everyone else did. The Sheriff has him in jail over at Fort Smith. He's waiting on the circuit judge to put him in Deer Lodge for assaulting a peace officer, being drunk, and disturbing the peace."

Henry looked at Frank, scratched his head, smiled--at what it was hard to tell. He said, "Well, Franko, I guess we need to ride back to Fort Smith."

"What are we going to do when we get there?"

"Visit Fleury, I guess. He ain't gonna fish for a long time where he's goin'."

"All right. So we will say our hellos and goodbyes. That it?"

Pretty much."

Fort CF Smith isn't far from St. Xavier: eighteen miles as the crow flies, provided it flies straight and is not given to detours. It doesn't take long to ride that distance horseback: six hours on a walking horse following along the Big Horn River bottom. They rode a quarter of a mile off the river using game trails, and avoiding the thick brush, the cottonwood timber, and the winding river as it bent back and forth on its way to join the Yellowstone. The fort was built in 1866 by the U.S. Army. It lasted two years, maybe a few days more. The other buildings that made up the settlement came later, after the Hayfield Fight, after Fort CF Smith was negotiated out of existence and the Sioux had burned it to the ground in 1868. The settlement was built along the river, for the most part off the flood plain, after the Crow Reservation was again re-established in 1869.

"*Amigo*, isn't that Fleury's horse?"

Frank pointed at a bay horse standing in the heat of the afternoon in an enclosed pasture a mile north of Fort CF Smith. It stood motionless except for the occasional switch of its tail as it brushed off deer flies, horse flies, and an occasional mosquito. It stood with six other horses, not very good--slightly overweight--examples of saddle horses determined by fate to live out their lives on the Reservation. Both Williams and Rodriguez stared at a big bay, noting a blaze on its face, a long white spot on its right foreleg, and a scar on its left flank where the horse had been branded while a colt.

"Gotta be," Henry finally said. "Ain't nothin' uglier." Henry paused, staring at the horse. He said, "Do you think there's a separate breed called Indian--one that is good for nothin' except eatin' hay and grass, and throwin' good riders? I wonder where Fleury got that horse. Look at him. What's he good for? Can't get outta his own way."

It was Fleury's horse. The duly elected Sheriff of Big Horn County was keeping him with the city livestock while Fleury was holed up in jail awaiting trial and sentencing. Frank caught him with his thirty-foot riata while Henry watched--not that Fleury's horse put up any fight. He just stood there while Frank built himself a loop and tossed it around the horse's head.

"What are you gonna do with the Indian's *caballo*?" Henry asked.

"I do not know, but it seems a shame to leave him here. He is not theirs."

"He ain't ours."

"Let's take him and ask the Indian. Best we can do is turn him loose somewhere so he can get some decent grass and get out of the cold when it turns winter. How long do you think they will keep him in Deer Lodge?"

"Don't know. I'm wonderin' if that Sheriff will even let us see him."

"Guess we will have to ask. Cannot hurt."

Henry Williams and Frank Rodriguez tied three horses to the hitching rail in front of the Fort CF Smith city jail. For a few moments they stood on the boardwalk in front of the Sheriff's office, looking the town over. A wagon with three kids sitting on the endgate passed by. A breeze was coming in from the south.

Fort CF Smith was a typical western Reservation town: blacksmith shop, livery stable, and a store that sold everything from needles to garden hoes, hammers and nails to a bolt of red cotton cloth.

The city jail was a two room log cabin; the jail housing the prisoners was in the back, the Sheriff's office in the front. Once every month the circuit judge came from the Crow Agency to dispense justice in the Sheriff's office. Until then, whatever prisoners the Sheriff collected during the intervening days stayed in the jail behind his office. Sometimes it got crowded--especially when the allotment money was distributed to the local inhabitants and they got into the corn liquor they weren't supposed to have. The jail section had no windows, while the Sheriff's office had two: one on either side of the door.

After he'd stretched, Frank adjusted the pistol in his holster, opened the door, and stepped inside. Henry followed, letting his eyes adjust from the bright sunlight by staring into the darkest corner. A big man wearing a red plaid shirt was sitting at a heavily scarred desk. A row of rifles and shotguns hung in a rack on the wall behind him--originally in a locked cabinet, but no more. Something or someone had broken the door and it had been removed. There were three kitchen chairs with high backs, and a coffee pot on a cold wood stove.

In the front corner there were three saddles stacked, as well as two ropes and a collection of spurs dangling from nails pounded into the log wall. A pair of batwing chaps made of thick bull hide was hanging from a wall peg next to them. A deputy was standing, leaning against the south wall, his face deeply bruised and colored a dark purple and green. It looked like he'd been in a recent fight and hadn't won. Henry wondered what the other fellow looked like, for the deputy looked capable, ready to take on a griz and dish out some punishment of his own.

A familiar voice came from the rear of the building.

"Franko, is that you? What are you doin' here? Henry? Henry, what's goin' on?"

At the sound of the Indian's voice, the deputy straightened up, no longer leaning against the wall. "No talkin' to nobody, Mex. Prisoners are off limits," he said. "Hear me?"

"No talking, *amigo*?" Frank said. "No talking to nobody? But I have not said a word."

The deputy took a step forward. "You get the hell out of here, Mex, before I throw you in there with that damn Indian."

On most days it was hard to tell exactly what would set Henry Williams in motion. He could be-- well--a nice guy and then--sometimes he wasn't so nice. In the middle of the exchange--maybe because the deputy called Fleury a "damn Indian," maybe because he called Frank Rodriguez "Mex," maybe because they were both his friends, maybe because he had a short fuse having ridden for two days coming from Devil's Canyon, crossing the Horn at Chain Canyon, and following the Bad Pass Trail--Henry reacted. In that moment, when authority met with Henry's innate concept of right and wrong, the Sheriff and his deputy found themselves looking at the business end of two SAA 1873 Peacemaker Colt Revolvers. They were the sort that Bill Cody carried around to make himself look really good, tough, and mean in the *Wild West Shows* he presented in Paris, France, and New York, New York. That isn't to say Bill Cody wasn't tough and mean, but those pistols certainly helped the image. It also helped that he'd shot Yellow Hand dead with a Winchester carbine for reasons he couldn't remember.

Frank glanced at the drawn pistols, then looked at his companion's expressionless face. "Henry, what are you doing?" Frank exclaimed. "*Estás loco*! My friend, it is not good manners pulling a pistol on a marshal. I think there is probably a rule against this."

"Maybe, Franko, but I figure that if we don't get Fleury outta this hole, we won't be feelin' good the rest of the year knowin' he's in here with these sonstabitches." Henry hadn't taken his eyes off the Sheriff.

"Now, Sheriff," Henry said slowly in a grating, western drawl, "real slow, you stand yourself up and drop that gun belt. I want to hear it hit the floor and I want to see you shove it under the desk."

"Boy, you're makin' a serious mistake," the Sheriff said, staring at him, undoubtedly surprised by the pistols. He certainly hadn't crawled out of bed thinking some fool cow kid from Illinois was going to pull a gun on him today. But there it was and the barrels on those six shooters weren't wavering.

"Not as serious as you're makin', not standin' up and sheddin' that shootin' iron."

The Sheriff obeyed reluctantly, standing up, moving slowly, aware that the situation in his office had turned from mundane to volatile. The men standing in front of him fully intended to break an Indian out of his jail.

An Indian?

The Sheriff was struck by the ludicrous nature

20

of such an endeavor, shaking his head slowly. He tried, but could not remember such a thing ever happening before.

Henry said, "Franko, have that deputy shed his firearm and unlock that iron door."

"What are we going to do here, Henry?"

"Get the Indian outta there."

"Damn right," Fleury said through the bars. "Get me outta here. Please get me outta here."

"Then, what?"

"Well, we sure as hell can't put these two in that cell. Not with all those Indians. Those boys ain't too happy. They'd kill 'em."

"So," Frank said, "let me see. How about we let all these *hombres* out and put the constables in their own little *hacienda*?"

"Right. Right. That's right. We let the folks in there out and put these two in their place."

"So we jail the jailers to save their worthless lives." Frank paused, shaking his head. "*Aye yai yai, compadre*. Have you thought this through?"

"No. Not at all. But we shouldn't get them killed savin' the Indian. But savin' their lives and getting the Indian outta there--that'd be damn nice of us."

"Please, please," Fleury begged. "Please stop bein' so damn nice and get me outta here."

"Now, Fleury, do not hurry us," Frank said. "*Es muy importante*. We have to think our mistakes completely through before we make them."

Frank didn't take long thinking.

"*Hombre*," Frank finally said to the deputy. "You heard the man, *chico*. Drop the irons, open the door, give me the keys. Let those boys out and get yourself in. *Por favor, amigo*. Please."

"You're makin' a mistake, Mex," the deputy said.

"I know, *amigo*."

The deputy grudgingly dropped his gun belt to the floor, voluntarily kicking it toward Frank. He stared darkly at Frank before retrieving the key from the wall peg behind the Sheriff's desk. Grudgingly, he inserted the key in the iron gate and turned it. The mechanism clicked and disengaged. The heavy iron gate swung open, squeaking on its oil-starved hinges. The deputy said, "I'm telling you, you're fixin' to make a big mistake, Mex. You surely are."

"I know, *amigo*. I heard you the first time. That's why I thought it through so carefully."

Fleury was first out, first to the Sheriff's desk to get his pistol, his hunting knife, a Winchester rifle, saddle bags and whatever was in the cotton sack. The rest of the drunks, malcontents, vagrants, the man who had slapped his wife around and had the hell beat out of him by the other prisoners for this activity, and the lone thief of a sack of hard rock candy walked out the door of the jail and the Sheriff's office. The thief, while refusing to pay for the confection, had been inclined to eat the candy; this activity had angered the store clerk.

The cell, once emptied, became the new home for the Sheriff and his beat up and furious deputy. They stood just inside the iron door with no keys and no pistols, wearing their badges prominently on their chests.

Fleury had collected his gear. He looked out the

open door as the ex-prisoners, some running, some walking, moved down the street. "Is that my horse?" he asked.

"It is," Frank replied. "Fleury? What I want to know is did you do that to the deputy? Is this the fellow I hear you head butted?"

"My horse ain't got a saddle," Fleury noted.

"Well, he did not come with one."

"I'll borrow the deputy's. He won't be needin' it. Him bein' in jail," Fleury said. He stopped and looked at the deputy standing in the jail cell, his fingers stuck inside his belt. "I did do that, Franko. I did. He sure is pretty, ain't he?" Fleury shook his head. "But he didn't stay out for thirty minutes, more like fifteen or twenty."

"That is not bad," Frank said. "But I still have the record. So do not get a big head."

"Why are you boys here, anyways?" Fleury asked. "Not that I'm complainin'. I figured it was Deer Lodge for me once they were through."

"Henry got lonely. Nobody to drink with and the fish were not biting. And since you were not there, it was no fun stealing fish out of Trout Creek."

Fleury picked up the deputy's saddle from the corner of the office. The deputy started swearing.

"Now, Richie," Fleury said, "you know I'm just borrowin' your saddle. I'm gonna return it soon as I can get it off my horse. You know that."

"I'll get you. Damn you."

"Well, let's hope it won't be any time soon."

Frank looked at Henry standing quietly in the middle of the room, a pistol in either hand. As he

23

walked by him, he said, "I do not know, Henry, what we have done here."

"Step into the saddle, Franko, while I have a word with these two."

Frank smiled, glancing at the two officers standing in their cell. "Now, Henry, don't you be shooting them, not even to slow them down. That would not be right."

Hearing Frank's exchange with Henry, the deputy backed up against the far wall. The Sheriff, however, stepped closer to the iron door.

"Get goin', Franko," Henry said.

Henry Williams stared at the two men standing in the cell now empty of prisoners.

"Boys," he said, "I don't want to see either of you on my back trail. That'd bother me."

"I'll be on it. You know it," the Sheriff snapped, pursing his lips as he spoke. "I'll get you. I will. And when I'm through you'll--"

Henry pulled back the hammer on one of his SAA Colts. The click echoed in the empty room.

The deputy spoke softly. He said, "Paul, I think he means it. Just shut your mouth."

"Sheriff, if I see either of you, I'm gonna burn your house to the ground, shoot you, shoot your dog, shoot your horse, shoot your cat, then I'm gonna get serious. I might torture you somethin' awful, cuttin' important parts off your body."

The Sheriff grew sullen.

"Do we understand one another?"

The deputy interjected softly, "We understand."

"Good," Henry said, touching the brim of his hat

with the barrel of the pistol in his right hand, seating the hammer. "Just so we do." He paused. "If not, I'll tell you right where I live if you want to know. If you want to discuss this further."

"Tell me!" the Sheriff demanded. "Tell me who you are! Henry who?"

Before Henry could say a word the deputy interrupted him. "No, don't tell us a thing! Damn it, Paul! Leave it be!"

"You're fired!"

"You can't fire me! I quit, you self-righteous son of a bitch! Can't you see he wants to tell you where he lives? He's invitin' you to visit him and he's holdin' a pistol pointed at your chest. You got less brains than God gave a cracker."

The Sheriff stared at his now ex-deputy, then turned to Henry. "Tell me!" he demanded. "Tell me right now!"

The deputy hit his ex-boss from behind, knocking him senseless to the floor of the cell, kicking him in the back of the head where he lay. "You two, get the hell out of here! I don't want to know where ya all live! I don't want to know who you are! Get!" He screamed. "Get out of here!"

Frank nudged Henry. "Let's go, *amigo*. Leave that poor boy alone. He has had a real bad day."

Henry nodded his head in agreement. "Okay," he said, and followed Frank through the door, thinking he hadn't seen anything like that before.

Chapter 3

"I got married," Fleury said.

Both Frank and Henry looked at him.

"Is that good?" Henry asked. "Did you want to get married?"

"Hell, yes, it's good, but you don't know what I had to tell her so's I could come up here. She don't understand fishin' and drinkin' and fightin' and raisin' hell."

"Bring her next time," Frank suggested.

"You crazy? I ain't gonna bring no woman up here." Fleury looked at Frank. "You married, Franko?" he asked.

Henry answered with a straight face, not cracking even a smile. "He is. He married my gal. Stole her from me when I wasn't lookin'."

"No. No, Mary Carlos is not your gal," Frank said to Henry. Turning to Fleury, he explained. "I married his gal's sister. Mary had a sister. Her sister was his gal. He's confused."

Fleury stared at the two in disbelief. "So am I. What happened? I mean, really? What happened?"

Frank shook his head woefully. "Anna Marie? She married someone else. Broke his heart."

Henry rolled his eyes. He said, "Cut it out, Franko. At least get the story right. You mean her father married her to someone else."

"Yeah. That, too. Her *padre*--their *padre*--he got angry at Henry, called him out, wanted to kill him. He found Henry with Anna Marie. Caught them out in the moonlight, kissing, heating the night with *mucha* passion. Embarrassed the old man. Seems he promised her to someone else with more money than Henry. So he starts beating on Henry, slapping him around, pushing on him. Henry just takes it. After all, the old man is Anna's father and Henry did not want to upset her."

"Didn't help none," Henry said. "She still got upset."

"Well, anyway, there we were: Anna Marie trying to get between her father and Hank; the old man pushing her away, trying to slap Henry; and Henry trying not to upset Anna Marie." Frank smiled. "It was awful. It was awful right up to Henry getting knocked on his butt. Then it was really awful."

Henry shook his head and Frank continued, wiping imaginary tears from his eyes as he sat peeling the corn husk from a tamale.

"Hank--he is a little slow," he said. "There he was lying on the ground and it occurred to him that if he did not do something, he was going to get killed. So Henry picks himself up and starts in on Anna's father. Of course, he didn't want to. He throws a fist at the old man's nose, then one in the jaw and knocks the old man into the next world." Frank paused, took a bite of the tamale, and shook his head. "So," he said, "the old man was lying there like he's dead; Anna Marie standing over him crying. Mary Carlos--she is trying to comfort her sister."

27

Henry looked decidedly uneasy as he sat on the log fingering his hat band, more than once knocking imaginary dust from the brim and crown. "What he ain't tellin' ya, Fleury, is that Franko is standing there smilin' like he's the guest at some church social."

Frank smiled, "Ah, yes, Henry, but I'm telling this story." Frank turned to Fleury. "So there we were," he said. "Anna Marie's father flat out on his back, her crying: Mary Carlos consoling her sister: Hank standing there looking down at the old man. At first, Anna will not talk to him. When she finally does she tells him to get out of there. 'You go away,' she says. Maybe five or six times she says this. So Henry picks up his hat, knocks the dust off of it. He looks at Anna Marie and he asks her, 'You sure?' She says, 'Yes, I'm sure. Look what you did to my *papá*. This is not good,' she says. So Hank, he swings up on his horse and rides out of the *hacienda* heading north. He did not wait for Anna's father to come to his senses and discover Henry had beaten him unconscious. You see the old man employed forty *vaqueros*. Every one had a six shooter and maybe a Henry rifle. It would not have been too good for Henry if he stayed. In the end, Anna Marie married the man her father chose. Me and Mary Carlos followed Henry to California. Left in the dead of night. Mary Carlos was very angry at her father for the way he treated her sister--insisting she marry a man she wasn't in love with. It was a family thing. Good for me; bad for Henry."

"Why'd you leave in the middle of the night? You didn't beat on her old man."

"It seems that their father also had some hombre

picked out for Mary Carlos to marry and it wasn't me. Mary Carlos told me we had better go before we cannot go, so we left in the middle of the night."

"How old were you, Henry?" Fleury asked.

Henry looked at Fleury. "Too young. I was nineteen when I got there. I'm forty-five now." He paused, thinking. "Maybe I was twenty or so. That'd be twenty-six years ago: a long time, a lifetime. We were workin' cows, breakin' horses in Mexico. That's where I met Franko."

"Did you ever go back? To see her, I mean? Sweep her off her feet? Take your woman?"

"No. And I don't want to talk about this no more."

Frank smiled. "Let us fish, *compadre. Creo que no quiere hablar de eso, mi amigo*. He does not want to talk about it any more. It is his wounded heart, I think."

Fleury put his feet under him and contemplated standing, getting a drink of water, or maybe some warm coffee. "My wife . . . she's pregnant," Fleury announced.

Henry and Frank turned and looked at Fleury.

"Now don't that beat the hell right outta livin'?" Henry said. He picked up his fishing gear and walked down the rise to the murmuring sounds of Trout Creek.

To hear Frank Rodriquez tell it, he hardly ever drank too much. But it was the cool of the evening; they were on the back side of Low Mountain in August; the rest of the world was baking in hundred degree summer heat. West, across the Bull Elk pasture, the sun was roosting on the crest of the East Pryor Mountain,

29

shining through the tall spires above Layout Creek. It was late. His belly was full of trout, cornbread, and peaches soaked in heavy syrup, eaten directly from the can. Maybe he'd had a tiny bit too much, but Frank would never admit it. Too much tequila on such an evening was akin to having too much money, or a woman being too pretty, or owning a horse who was too fast.

"Henry," he said, "I've been thinking about Anna. *He estado pensando en ella, compadre.*"

"What?" Henry said. "What did you say?"

"*He estado pensando en ella.*"

Henry looked at Franko leaning back, sitting on a flat rock, his feet resting on a piece of firewood, basking in the orange glow of the setting sun and the flickering light of the small campfire.

"Franko, I really don't want to talk about her. It's passed. It's done. It's gone. There's nothin' I can do. It's over: ancient history, over a quarter of a century has past. And I don't want to think about her."

"Yeah, Franko, really," Fleury agreed. "Leave the man alone. He's done lost her, ain't gettin' her back. She sleeps in another man's bed. He needs to forget her."

"No. No. That is not what I meant. I mean that if I die, you got to take care of Mary Carlos."

Both Fleury and Henry stared at Frank. "What's one got ta do with the other?" Henry asked.

"Nothing. Not . . . nothing." Frank paused, his words coming out of his mouth disconnected. "But if I die, you got to take care of my Mary Carlos. You got to promise me. Manny, too."

"You're crazy, Franko," Fleury said, sipping on his beverage. "Really crazy and a little drunk. Who's Manny?"

"Manny is my son." Frank became insistent. "Henry, I do not know what I would do if she was not taken care of. I mean, if I die. And my son, he will need a father."

Henry replied, "Franko, you ain't gonna die. What the hell have you been drinkin'?"

"Tequila. Henry, promise me, Henry. *Por favor, compadre*? I need to rest knowing she is taken care of."

The conversation ceased, falling into dead silence except for the popping of burning firewood and the wind drifting through the needles of a pine forest. In the twilight, somewhere to the north along the upper rim of the Cookstove Basin, some wolves were howling. Further west, on the flat above the Big Horn Canyon, hoot owls talked among themselves, saying the same thing over and over again. On the edge of the Duggan Bench, a string of twenty-three elk ran south in a line heading for the pasture in Hannon's Cooley and the safety of the pine forest. The silence stretched out; nothing filling it until the fabric of the silence became uncomfortable, resting heavy.

"Henry?" Frank said. It wasn't a question so much as it was a pregnant pause: where time stands still, where the sun refuses to go down, and the earth ceases to turn. "Henry?"

"All right, Franko," Henry said. "All right. I promise. You happy now? Go to sleep. I can't stand any more of this dyin' talk."

Henry glanced up. Fleury was lying on his bed

roll staring at him, his hands holding a tin cup that rested on his chest. "What do you want?" he asked.

"You gotta promise me, too."

"What the hell's got into you two?"

"I'm married. My wife's pregnant," Fleury replied. "Ya gotta promise me."

"Are you serious? I don't even know her name."

"Anne."

"You're just sayin' that," Henry said, pausing. Now, both he and Frank were staring at Fleury.

"No, I'm not just sayin' that. Her white man's name is Anne. Her Crow name is She Who Stands Shaking Her Fist." Fleury was staring at the flames of the small fire. He glanced at Henry. "Are you gonna promise me? I need both of you to promise me." Fleury paused, explaining. "I am married and I'm gonna have a baby."

Henry started to laugh, but caught himself, thinking better of it. "Why not, Fleury?" he said. "I promise. Feel better? I'm sure as hell not gonna break you out of jail again." Henry paused. "What's your first name anyway?"

"My Indian name is Blue Spotted Horse. My white name is Ronald. I am told it means--how you say it?--advisor to one who is chief."

"Ronald? That's not an Indian name."

"My mother--she wasn't all Indian, just mostly. She named the part that's not Indian Ronald; the other part, Blue Spotted Horse. Listen, did I tell you what happened to the Sheriff?" Fleury exclaimed as he sat up, looking to fill his cup. "Did I tell you?"

Both Henry and Frank stared at him, waiting.

"They gots themselves fired. The city council, the big chiefs at Fort Smith, didn't believe that everyone just woke up one day and broke outta jail just by walking out the front door. Fired 'em right on the spot 'cause they didn't do nothin'. Nobody was dead. Somebody should have been dead. The way they figured it, it wasn't a real jail break."

Henry nodded. "Where you livin' now, Fleury?"

"Pryor. That's where her people live."

"And her name is Anne, really?"

"Yes. Anne. Anne Fleury. I'm hopin' for a boy."

"Well, how did Anne get to be Anne? That ain't Indian either."

"Nuns in St. Xavier. Ever hear of Saint Anne?"

Henry shook his head "no."

"Well, I ain't neither. She has the other name also, the Absaroke Crow name. She was named by her father's father: She Who Stands Shaking Her Fist."

"I'll be damned," Henry said. "Thought you weren't a religious Indian. Here you're goin' to church."

"How'd you know all this about Saint Anne and Ronald?" Frank asked.

"Catholic nuns. They know these things."

"She Who Stands Shaking Her Fist?" Henry said. "What was her father's father thinking when he named her that? Do people call her both names?"

"I call her Anne," Fleury said. "Just Anne. She has a temper. Gets mad fast."

Fleury looked at his two companions. "This is a good thing," he said. "We promise each other like this. Alone, we are just men; together, we are more than just

33

men. Know what I mean?"

Frank nodded, taking a deep breath, staring into the fire, watching the yellow and orange flames consume the wood. Henry didn't say a word, keeping his thoughts to himself. Above their heads, the night birds darted across the darkening, star-studded sky, plucking insects from the warm air. Henry stared at the heavens, studied the last light fading above Layout and Davis Creek on the East Pryor. His heart was heavy and he didn't know why.

Chapter 4

"Wonder where the Indian is?" Frank said.

Henry looked at Frank. "Last time he didn't show up, he was in jail."

"He would be here if he could. Something has happened," Frank said.

"Maybe he broke his leg."

"That would be bad, Henry. A broken leg? Remember that *vaquero* that worked for the fellow over by that Los Angeles adobe? Horse rolled over on him, broke his leg; bone sticking right out the side. He lay there in that heat all summer; couldn't move, poor boy. Took nearly a year so he could walk."

"I didn't say he had a broken leg. I was just sayin' he could have a broken leg. Maybe his woman whipped him into shape. I think maybe he's scared of her. He complained whilst cuttin' up that elk how she didn't want him up here. Or he could be workin'. Never know. He has a family."

"Working? The Indian? He is funny when it comes to work. He says, 'If you ain't Christian, you don't have to work. Only Christians need "sweat of the brow" to be important. Absaroke don't. Indians just live. Be happy. Eat plenty of good food.'" Frank paused. "He might have a point. Working does not seem to have gotten us anywhere."

"You got a wife and a boy. That ain't all that

35

bad."

"I do. You are right. All from horses, cows, and a rope." Frank studied his hand, showed it to Henry like it was a medal. "Look at these callouses. I earned every one of these. They are mine."

Henry smiled. "So is Mary Sanchez and Manny."

Frank ran the fingers of his left hand across the finger pads of his right.

Henry had pulled a brookie out of the rushing waters of Trout Creek, taken the hook out of its gaping mouth, and whacked its head on a flat, moss-covered rock. He said, "That Indian was sure taken with that baby girl."

"He was," Frank replied. "She Who Laughs. Pretty name. That was all he could talk about." Frank paused. "He is not working, Henry. That's not him. We better go see. Something is wrong. He would be here if he could."

"He gets sidetracked. Last year he shot that damn elk, spent two weeks dryin' the meat. Singin', drinkin', and dancin' all alone whilst we were fishin'. Had them coyotes sneakin' all over the place, looking for a free meal. And those damn magpies." Henry stood, dropped the fish in the bucket and paused, shaking his head. "That damn Indian. Leave it to him to ruin a good fishin' trip." He looked at Frank, then at the East Pryor Mountain lying across the Canyon in the haze. "I suppose we ought to check on him. Franko, you round up the horses. I'll break camp. That damn, damn, damn Indian. Wish he could stay outta trouble in August. That askin' too much? There are eleven other months; he could make use of them."

"Henry, that is five 'damns' and not one hell. You got that out of your system? Getting the Indian out of trouble is always interesting. You got to admit."

"That sure as hell is a fact," Henry drawled.

Frank burst out laughing. "I will get the horses," he said.

"I'll break camp," Henry replied.

The small settlement of Pryor is "to hell and gone" if a man is camped on upper Trout Creek on the back side of Low Mountain. Getting there they crossed the Big Horn at Chain Canyon, headed North on the Bad Pass Trail, turned west when they reached Dry Head Creek, then followed Sage Creek for five miles. Afterwards, they turned north again, made their way through Pryor Gap, following Pryor Creek. At the mouth of the Gap was Pryor: a settlement consisting of a collection of three buildings and a number of lodges that varied with the inclination of the owners. The grass was good. Horses had plenty; buffalo were mostly dead, so they didn't compete for grass. The creek was the home for white tail; the flat north of the settlement had a few antelope, and a herd of elk that hadn't yet been turned into jerked meat for the winter.

Everyone they spoke to seemed to know the Indian, Fleury.

"He lives down on the creek off to the side of the red mountain aways. Not far. You'll see it, you ride that away." They found it right where they were told.

Frank Rodriguez was off his horse knocking at the door. He knocked repeatedly. No one answered. He looked at Henry sitting his horse. "No one," he said. "No one has seen him and no one is here. Got his horse in the corral. Got a goat and a dog. The horse has been fed and watered this morning. So he is around."

Behind Henry, hens were cackling, scratching the dry earth, dusting themselves in the heat of the day; their beaks open, cooling themselves.

"Franko," Henry said.

Frank looked up. Henry nodded, motioning behind Frank. A man was striding toward them from the creek bottom. Frank turned to watch Fleury walking out of the trees below the house. The man's progress brought him to the hardpack. He stared at Frank, then at Henry for a moment, wordless.

"What are you two doin' here?" he demanded.

Frank said, "It is August, Fleury. You did not show up to keep us from fishing Trout Creek. That is not like you. We figured you had yourself a little trouble."

"I ain't got no trouble."

Henry sat upon his horse and stared at the big Indian without speaking. Frank spat and looked at the ground, stirring the dirt with the toe of his boot, then scratched the back of his head. The heat of the day beat down on their shoulders. Insects were buzzing in the trees. Out in the horse corral, the big bay was stamping his hind foot. Magpies complained in the cottonwoods; one took flight, heading south toward Pryor town.

"You both think I'm a damn liar, don't you?"

"You like to fish and drink tequila too much," Henry said. "If you didn't have trouble you'd of been there."

"I said I ain't got no trouble." He paused, screwing his mouth up as if it were full of yellow jackets. He looked at both men, shook his head in disgust. "All right. I gots trouble. But nothin' you can help me with. Despite what you're thinkin', I ain't no damn liar. I ain't." Fleury looked from Frank to Henry and back to Frank. "All right. My wife's gone. My Anne's gone, and my little one. Eight days, I think." Fleury paused. "I'm not sure, but she's gone. All right? There. Now get the hell out of here."

Frank said, "You are not sure how long? What is wrong with you? You do not know when she went missing? She leave willingly or did someone take her?"

"Listen to me, Franko. I don't know. They're just gone: no trail, no nothin'. Vanished like smoke. Nobody knows nothin'. If they do, they ain't sayin'." Weariness crept into his voice. "The old man says it's the ghost people. That's what he says."

Frank stretched, rubbing his back with his hands, yawning. "Eight days," he said. "That is a while. It rain since they disappeared?"

"No, it ain't rained. Not even a mornin' dew."

"Had any wind?"

"No. Why we talkin' about the weather? You got better things to do than stand here in the heat talkin' about wind and rain."

"I do, but you don't. Fleury, you have two chairs? I want to get some shade."

"Two chairs? What are you talking about?"

"Two chairs. You got two chairs?"

"Well, yes."

"Get them. Set them on the porch."

"Why do you need two chairs?"

"Just get them. Stop wasting time."

Fleury went inside, returning with two kitchen chairs, one in either hand. "What do you want these for?" he asked.

"To sit on."

"What if I don't wanna sit?"

"You will."

Frank tied his horse in the shade, climbed onto the porch, and sat down in the chair that Fleury had provided. He pulled a sack of Bull Durham from his shirt pocket and started building himself a smoke. When he finished licking the paper, he hung the cigarette in his mouth, and glanced up at Henry sitting his horse.

Fleury remained standing, staring at Frank.

"What are you doing here?" Frank asked Henry.

"Wait a minute," Henry said, suddenly sitting up in the saddle. "You don't think? No one asked me, Franko. Fleury--he ain't dead. This here's a husband-wife thing. Maybe she's mad at Fleury. Maybe she's comin' back. Maybe she ain't. Maybe she's visitin' somebody--like maybe her mother, her aunt. Maybe she forgot to tell Fleury where she was goin'. Maybe he got drunk and forgot. Maybe he couldn't read a track if it were writ in English. He said, 'he ain't sure.' We can't just be buttin' in on another man's troubles. It ain't right."

Fleury sat down in the other chair.

"What's goin' on?" Fleury said to Frank, puzzled. "What's he talkin' about?"

"Henry is going to find your woman and little

40

girl for you."

Skepticism immediately flooded Fleury's face. "Yeah, sure he is."

"You will see," Frank said.

Henry was shaking his head. "Fleury ain't dead," he said again. "He ain't dead at all."

"What's he talkin' about, Franko?"

"Him and me. There was a time when we were in this *pueblo* in California, just walking up the street minding our own business. This fellow gets thrown out of this *cantina*. Henry is standing there and goes to help him up. This fellow gets all agitated--real hot--and starts pushing Henry. Henry has to pop him alongside his head with his revolver to quiet him down. Turns out that this fellow's brother had thrown him out of the *cantina* and he wants to know why Henry popped his brother on the head. I had to shoot the brother to keep him from shooting Henry and Henry had to shoot the fellow that got thrown out of the *cantina* to keep him from shooting me."

Frank looked at Fleury. "So we are just naturally a little spooked about getting into family troubles. But . . . but, we promised to protect and provide for your woman, if you were dead. Henry is noting that you are not as dead as he would like."

"Well, I ain't dead," the Indian said.

"He knows you are not dead, Fleury. And I know you are not dead, but I am thinking about shooting you myself so as to avoid any further trouble."

"You ain't gonna do that." Fleury stood, staring at Frank, a little unsure.

Frank looked at Henry. "Hank," he said, "just

get to it. You know you are going to have a look around. You know you are going to tell us to sit right here. So here we are."

"Damn it," Henry said, staring at Frank. "Fleury ain't askin' for no help. He might not need any help. Maybe we're just buttin' in."

"I am asking," Frank said. "Besides, didn't I introduce you to Mary Carlos' sister? Who did that? And who kept that *federale* in Senora from sticking that knife in your back?"

Henry did not say another word after that, just sat staring at Frank. "You ain't gonna let that one die, are you?" he finally said.

"Not likely."

"Ah, dammit all." Henry looked at Frank. "I sure as hell shouldn't."

"I know you 'shouldn't.'"

Both men smiled.

"All right," Henry said, still shaking his head. "All right."

"What's goin' on?" Fleury asked.

"Sit and watch," Frank said.

Fleury sat down again in the empty chair and looked at Henry.

Henry stared at the two for the longest time. "All right," he said again, exasperated. "All right." He turned his gaze on Fleury. "Fleury," he said, "since your woman disappeared, who's been here? Which direction did they come from?"

Fleury thought, shaking his head before he spoke. "There's been seven of the best trackers on the Reservation. There ain't none better. They came from

42

Pryor, mostly."

"Seven plus yourself?"

"Yes, but I ain't no tracker. They looked this whole area over plenty good. Took two days. They didn't find nothin'. You ain't gonna find nothin'."

"Your woman--how much she weigh?"

"A hundred-twenty."

"The girl?"

"Maybe thirty, forty. Not much."

"You and your woman--you have a disagreement?"

"No. Not really."

"She talk about goin' somewheres?"

"No."

"She disappear in the mornin' or the evenin'?"

"In the mornin' after I went to do the chores. Had to go to Pryor to get a sack of flour and some salt."

"All right. You two sit here. Don't go movin' from the house. I'll be back. Can't believe I'm doing this."

Henry reined his horse around, pulled his hat down on his forehead, and proceeded slowly down the dirt road that he and Frank had used to get to the Fleury cabin. A quarter of a mile down the road, he started leaning over the left shoulder of his horse, staring at the ground. A mile down the road, he veered to the left and disappeared into the cottonwood trees.

Frank and Fleury had been watching.

"Is this some sort of joke?" Fleury finally said to Frank.

"There was a time when I thought so," Frank said. "Not any more. Hank starts looking at the ground.

No body gets away."

"Why do you keep jabbing him about that woman? That'd get really old."

Frank turned to Fleury. "Henry's a one-woman man who never stopped being a one-woman man, even when he should have, even when I begged him to forget her. So when I want him to do something for me, I bring her up. Gets him every time." Frank paused. "You know that is not it, either. Not really." Frank shook his head slowly. "One time I got myself caught up in a flash flood; came out of nowhere. I was standing on dry ground. Suddenly I'm in over my head. Henry uses a rope; he throws it to me, flat out racing his horse alongside this ravine full of water, me blowing bubbles, drowning, soaked to the skin, going under. He gets the loop around me and pulls me out. If it weren't for him getting that rope around my neck, I would have died." Frank looked at Fleury. "I owe him my life. He owes me his. Trouble is, we do not know who is ahead. I am thinking it is, maybe, him. He is thinking it is, maybe, me. Fact is, if he asks me for something, I'm going to do it. Sometimes I use the woman to convince him even when I know he's going to do it."

Frank smiled. "Hank knows I'm going to bring her up. He expects it. Likes it. So I do. He tells everyone I stole Mary Carlos from him. I didn't. As long as Hank's alive, Mary Carlos is safe."

Fleury stared at Frank, slowly shaking his head. "That's all kinds of crazy."

"It is."

"You think Henry can find what the best trackers could not find? One of those fellows tracked

44

for the Seventh. He and his son are very good and they found nothing at all; not even a partial trail. They looked for two days. They've gone home. 'There is no trail' they said. 'It's the ghost people,' they said, 'the little people that live in the canyons of the Pryors. They took 'em. No tracker can find 'em. Ghost people.'"

"Fleury, those boys might have been good— even real good--but they were not the best. Henry is the best."

"Henry is a white man."

"Yes, he is. Do you have anything to eat? This is going to take a while." Frank looked at Fleury and smiled. He said, "Tell you what, I will bet on Henry finding a trail. Say five hundred?"

"Five hundred? I ain't never seen five hundred."

"Here is your chance. You say Henry cannot track--he being a white man. 'There ain't no way,' you say. So put your money, the money you do not have, right where your mouth is."

"I ain't got no money. But I'll take the bet. Takin' candy. That's what this is. I ain't gonna need no five hundred dollars. You better have it. I don't like no welchin' on a bet."

"Good. Good. Got anything to eat? Something that does not look like fish and does not taste like corn bread? I am a little tired of Hank's brook trout."

Henry Williams returned four and one half hours later. The sun was creeping down the side of the West Pryor, bathing the high-timbered crest in red and orange, sinking into the Absarokas: a bright, red burning circle of fire and heat. He rode into the yard tired and hungry, but did not dismount. He was confronted by two empty chairs. Frank came to the doorway of Fleury's log cabin munching on a baking powder biscuit.

"Henry," Frank said, acknowledging the man on horseback. He stepped to the side of the doorway, leaning against the log wall, his face partially hidden in the long shadows of late afternoon.

Fleury stepped out of the house onto the hardpack, staring at Henry.

"Did you find 'em?" he asked.

Henry shook his head "no."

Fleury turned and started for the doorway. "See?" he said to Frank. "What'd I tell you? You owe me five hundred bucks. And I want it. Remember what I told you. There ain't gonna be no welchin' on no bet."

Frank smiled, the upper part of his face normally covered by his hat seemed more white than normal.

"Fleury," Henry said to Fleury's back. The big Indian stopped, turned, and stared at Henry.

"What?" The weight of the world seemed to bear down on his shoulders; long strands of black hair hung in front of his eyes, covering days of grief and frustration. He was clearly tired and upset.

"A little over five days ago--I'd say, five days and maybe four or five hours--a very small child, a woman, and six men left this cabin. No horses. They walked due west following that outcropping of granite behind your house. They stayed on that rock, walking single file, following it as it circled around to the east. They followed that rise until it reached the creek. They followed the creek, walkin' right down the middle for about three miles; maybe a little less. The woman was barefoot. She favored her right foot--cut it somehow, bled a little. About three miles from here, someone kept some horses, an extra one for the woman. Been there a day. The ground was all chewed up--lots of horse turds. One of the men walked with a limp. One was a big man--wore hobnailed boots with an odd pattern in the right heel." Henry paused. "Don't know if your wife was a willing traveler or not. Doubt it, seein' she was barefoot with an open cut on her right foot. Someone, maybe her, kept dropping small red beads, dress beads. Seems she wanted to be followed."

Henry paused, staring at Fleury. "I didn't find 'em, Fleury. I want to know if you want to find 'em. What I saw on the ground doesn't make a lotta sense. Sometimes I wasn't sure if your woman went willingly or not. Sometimes it seemed she did; other times it felt like she didn't."

Fleury stared at Henry. At first, he was only able to work his jaw. Nothing came out. He was considering the fact that his daughter was wearing a doeskin dress with elaborate bead work: the picture of a fiery sunrise over the Bull Elk Pasture. And his wife was barefoot when he last saw her. Henry would not have known that. He couldn't. The thought was unsettling to Fleury.

"By the way, your tracker friends did a hell of a job destroying the trail. Walked all over it, around it, across it," Henry said. "Once you get farther away from your house, it ain't so bad."

"There you go, Fleury," Frank said, "you do not owe me a thing. I have seen it all before. Not a fair bet--

like taking candy. Know what I mean?" He laughed.

Fleury stared at Henry, full of wonderment, for the moment ignoring Frank's jab.

Frank caught up his horse from under the cottonwood tree at the side of the log house and mounted.

Fleury glanced at him. "Where you goin'?" he asked.

"Do you want to find your woman? If you do, grab that sack I prepared for Henry, saddle your horse. I can tell you, Henry is not in the mood."

Frank looked at Henry. "You in the mood, *compadre*?"

Henry shook his head.

"See Fleury? Henry is not in the mood. If you are coming, catch up. I am interested in seeing this woman of yours." Frank glanced at Henry. "North? Down the creek?" he asked, then without waiting for an answer he urged his mount forward. Turning in the saddle, he said "Fleury, you better hurry. There is not much light left. An hour from now it will be hard to tell where we will be."

Wordlessly Henry reined his horse around and followed Frank.

Behind them they heard Fleury running for the door, swearing. He caught up fifteen minutes later, handing Henry the cotton sack then dropping into line behind Frank, Henry out in front.

He said to Frank, "Nobody will believe this. He's a white man. I don't even believe it."

"I know," Frank said. "Nobody ever does."

Frank glanced at Fleury and reached into his

shirt pocket and found a sack of Bull Durham. "See if you can believe this. We were in a small little town south of Nogales maybe a hundred miles. Henry and I were there picking up thirty head of green horses. There was a celebration going on. So we took our time arranging for the horses; had a *cervesa*, some *mescal,* watched the locals grab chickens by the head, pulling them out of the dirt on horseback. Henry had purchased this white doeskin jacket with long fringe. You know the kind? It was nice. He got it for Anna Marie. Had all these red and blue beads on the back. Shiny silver for buttons. Things like that. He hung it on his saddle horn and we'd gone to watch the bull fights in the local arena, maybe a hundred yards away. We got back and it was gone. Someone had left the horse and the saddle and had stolen Anna Marie's jacket. Henry never said a word. He looked at the ground, walked around his horse, then started off like he knew where he was going. I followed.

"With people walking all around, dust five inches thick, he followed this trail across the street through an alley, through a livery stable, back on the street down a boardwalk, across another alley to the far end of town. A half mile farther, maybe more, there was this *cantina*. He walked in. There at the bar was this girl with Anna Marie's jacket around her shoulders talking to this vaquero. Henry looked at the man's boots, at his pants, then at him, then the girl. I don't know what he saw but he saw something. Henry said to the girl. 'Take it off.'

"The vaquero turns around. Maybe he's thinking he'll talk, maybe kill this gringo slowly; maybe have a

49

little fun. This fellow smiles and finds himself looking at the business end of two Navy Colts. I don't think he was expecting all these guns. Henry didn't want to talk. Henry says, '*Amigo*, you stole my jacket. Have your gal take it off. If there is so much as a drop of *mescal* on it I'm blowin' your head off, I'm killing your dog and I'm burning your house to the ground.' Henry likes to say that.

"I said 'Henry, I don't think he understands English. Henry explains it to him in Spanish. Better than I speak. I didn't know he could do that. Henry tells the girl in Spanish this time to take the jacket off. She does and starts to hand it to Henry. Henry says, '*Chico*' motioning at me. So, I take the jacket. I look it over and tell him there is no *mescal* on it, no spots.

"Henry looks like he's about to go, but instead he wallops this vaquero alongside the head, dropping him to the floor. He announces that the fellow is a thief, not to be trusted. He tells everyone to stay away from him and he starts for the door again. I say, 'Henry, I thought you were going to kick him.' He stops, goes back, and kicks the fellow in the ribs. I think he busted a couple. I tell Henry I was only kidding. He says it sounded like a good idea."

Frank laughed and started looking for some cigarette paper, searching his other shirt pocket. Having found some, he said, "Long story but Henry trailed that fellow across a dusty street, boardwalks, through a livery stable, across two alleys, across a street where hundreds of people had walked, and straight to where this jacket thief was entertaining his girl."

Frank had rolled a cigarette, licking both ends.

He looked at Fleury. "Nobody would believe it. Nobody. I don't believe it and I saw it. I was holding Anna Marie's jacket."

Fleury nodded, glanced at Frank then at Henry's back, wondering if maybe Henry could find them.

They rode until it was dark, following Pryor Creek as it meandered through chokecherry, currant, and buffalo berry stands. The trail left the creek when it was so choked with brush and barranca that it was impossible to get through on a saddle horse or afoot. Henry stopped when he could no longer see the ground. It was quiet except for the coyotes yapping and howling out on the flat.

"I'm gettin' so nervous I can hardly stand it," Fleury said to no one in particular.

"This will get dicey," Henry said. "Your friends are beginnin' to send someone to double back to see if they are bein' followed. They are four or five days ahead, so they ain't aware we're comin'. Not yet. By tomorrow evenin', or the day after, the possibility will arise that they'll see us, especially if they stop and are feelin' safe--thinkin' they got away without bein' followed."

"They ain't my friends."

Henry looked at Fleury. He said, "Fleury, this don't feel right. You got any enemies? Someone that don't like you much?"

"Everyone has enemies."

"Fresh ones. Someone bleeding anger? Someone that wants you to feel pain? Someone that, maybe, just don't want you to forget?"

51

Fleury thought for a moment. He said, "No. Not really. Not that I know. I ain't even been in a fight recently. I don't go to the bars no more. Don't gamble. I stopped. Don't do nothin'. Got a wife and a daughter."

"Your family? How about them?"

"I'm the only one. Got a brother, but he's somewheres up around Hardin. Ain't seen him in a couple of years. Besides, he likes me."

"Your wife's family?"

"That's a different story. Her father is somebody at Crow Agency, not a chief, but someone that likes to throw his weight around. I don't know if he has any fresh enemies, someone that wants to teach him a lesson, or kill him. Her father's people sure don't like me, I can say that. Ain't got the right connections. Don't know nobody. Ain't no agency Indian. Don't line up to get a free blanket and a can of Spam. My dog eats venison, you know what I mean? I ain't got the right blood."

Henry sat in the dark, thinking as he dug around in the cotton sack. He stopped. "Trouble probably comes from her family. Know anyone with a limp? How about someone--a big guy with heavy boots? Another fellow, light, weighs between one hundred-fifty and one-seventy-five? That one--he keeps studyin' his back trail. Last time, he rode back three miles, looked for a good hour. I'd say he's been around. Rides a grey horse. Unshod. Good feet." Henry chuckled. "Your little girl . . . she's still losin' those little red beads. Sometimes, maybe, your woman carries her. Someone does. Maybe not your woman."

"I don't know anyone like that. Nobody."

52

Henry nodded his head and looked at Fleury. "Guess in the next several days we'll find out."

"I will take the first watch," Frank stated. Rising to his feet, he walked off, disappearing through the brush carrying a Winchester rifle, rifled for 30-40 ammunition. "Hell of a fishing trip," he muttered. "I am beginning to think Hank was right. Should have stayed on the creek. Mind my own business. Here I am staying up all night staring into the dark. Sleeping on rocks. Fixing to get myself shot. What was I thinking?"

Chapter 5

The dawn rose up like thunder, exploding off the crest of the Big Horn Mountains across the canyon. The sun was a rust-red, colored by tree smoke suspended in the cool morning air. Somewhere to the west, a forest of pine was burning. Dark underbellies of thunderheads rose high on both sides, framing the sun against the rise of the mountain and the Bull Elk grass on the other side of the canyon.

"Don't suppose we can ride away from this one?" Henry said to Frank Rodriguez. "Know I've said it before. Somethin' just ain't right."

"It is the kid, Henry."

Henry nodded "Probably," he admitted. "Sometimes I wonder if Anna Marie had any--kids, I mean."

"If she did, they would be Manny's age. Some a little older, some a little younger. Probably had six or ten, like any good Catholic girl."

Henry listened. "I suppose," he said absently. "Franko, I think the folks we're followin' suspect we're followin' 'em now. I think they're beginnin' to worry. They ain't seen us, so they don't know. I figure they're feelin' a little anxious. Someone's been doubling back to see."

"You are guessing?"

"There is someone doublin' back. I ain't guessin' 'bout that. The rest is just a feelin'." He glanced at Frank. "But the doublin' back ain't no feelin'."

"That is good enough for me," Frank said and began checking the loads in his two pistols and his carbine, filling the empty chambers. Frank looked at Henry, smiled. "This reminds me of chasing those horse thieves across the back of the Nevadas over in Senora. They kept running. We kept coming. Finally, they just gave us the horses and ran. Got clean away."

Henry smiled, nodding. "We let 'em get away."

"That is so." Frank said, looking at Henry. "Well, *compadre*, let us get to these introductions. The suspense is killing me. I did not sleep all that well. I am really thinking we should be fishing."

Henry laughed and followed Frank's example, checking the loads in his firearms, filling the empty chambers. "You know, Franko, I'm glad we didn't catch those horse thieves. I ain't never liked killin'. Sometimes it bothers me, but I don't like the thought of bein' kilt, neither."

Frank smiled.

"What's with you two?" Fleury asked.

"Gettin' ready for a little shootin' war," Henry said. "Gettin' ready to kill those folks that would bring you grief: hurt a little girl for no reason; make a woman walk with a cut on her foot; make her carry the little one, barefoot and all." Henry looked at Fleury. "Trouble is, Fleury, somethin' ain't right. Anythin' you can remember that'd explain what's goin' on? Anythin' you ain't tellin' me?"

Fleury shook his head, momentarily silent. "No," he said and pulled an old single shot Remington from his scabbard and checked the load. He had no

Colt. Henry, seeing the rifle, its battered stock, scratched and scarred barrel, and worn sight, shook his head in disbelief.

"Does that damn thing work?" Henry asked.

"Whatdya mean does it work?"

"Just that."

"Yes, it works. Works good."

"Where's your Winchester? Your Colt?"

"I ain't talkin' about it."

They caught up with the woman and child two days later. It was a late August day, midmorning. The sky was cloudy, the temperature cool for that time of year. Dew still clung to the stems of drying grass. Everywhere the grass had turned brown. The three men stood their horses in a grove of aspen, looking across a long meadow, the far side bordered against a rounded, treeless hill. At the foot of the hill grew some bull pine. In the trees, almost hidden, a small tendril of smoke rose in the still air, quickly dissipating.

"I reckon that's their camp fire," Henry said.

Each of the men on either side, wordlessly acknowledged his conclusion. Seven horses were picketed on the other side of the camp fire, hidden in some scrub oak in the shadow of the bald hill. Voices carried across the meadow but were indistinguishable. Off to their left, a band of twelve white tail were bounding away, fleeing an unknown enemy. Some of the deer were very small and young and had not yet lost the white camouflage spots they inherited at birth.

"What are we gonna do?" Fleury asked.

Frank answered the question. "Ride right over

there and introduce ourselves. We can ask for your woman, get a cup of hot coffee, go home--that's it."

Henry nodded. "There are six," he said, "not countin' the woman and child. I count seven saddle horses. Should be eight, so we need to be mindful of that. Someone ain't there. The child could be a problem. If she sees Fleury, she might react--make some noise. Gotta expect she will."

"That's a fact," Fleury said. "If she sees me, she'll come runnin'."

No one said anything for several minutes.

"Got a plan?" Fleury asked, repeating himself. "What are we gonna do? How we gonna handle this?"

Henry studied the meadow, the hill rising behind it, the long, waves of waist high grass. "I think we oughta come up along the hill on the north, on the other side of their camp. If we're careful, we won't be seen. Hopefully, we can force 'em into the open if we come in that direction. Once the shootin' starts, we don't want 'em hidin' in those trees. We don't want 'em shootin' at us from that hill. I think we should try and make 'em hide in the grass."

"Then what?" Fleury asked. "What are we gonna do with 'em in the grass?"

Frank answered. "Depends on whether they have your girls or not."

"And which way the wind's blowin'," Henry added. "'Cause if we gots the girls and the wind is blowin' away from the trees, we'll start the place on fire. When they start to runnin', we'll kill 'em. Hopefully, before they kill us."

"That's a plan?" Fleury asked.

Frank was thinking. "Henry," he said, "when we get up next to those trees alongside that hill, you slip off your horse and make your approach on foot. Fleury and I will ride along those trees in plain sight."

"All right," Henry said, nodding. "I can do that."

"You cover our approach in case something ugly happens."

"Ugly? How ugly, Franko?"

"Real ugly, like me getting shot."

Henry smiled. "That would be ugly. Mary Carlos would never forgive me."

"I certainly hope not," Frank said. "I hope she holds you responsible for all my suffering."

Both Henry and Frank laughed.

Fleury stared at them, shaking his head.

One hundred yards from the camp, just outside the quaken aspen and bull pine, the bald hill rising abruptly on his left, Frank reined his horse in, leading Henry's horse, the saddle empty.

"Hello the camp!" Frank yelled.

"I don't see no one," Fleury said in a low voice.

"They are there. They are hiding. Keeping low. Making sure who we are and who we aren't. Someone has a rifle on us. Bet on it. Hello the camp!" Frank yelled again.

"What do you want?" A voice answered.

"Coffee would be nice."

"We ain't got none."

"We got some beans, you got some hot water."

Silence followed, interrupted by a heated discussion. Finally someone yelled back.

"Come on in! Keep your hands where we can see 'em!"

Frank touched his mount with the rowls of his spurs, walking him to the camp's edge, his Winchester lying across the shoulders of his saddle, pistol loose in the holster. Fleury followed two steps behind and to the right side, cradling his Remington single-shot in his arms, his finger laying softly on the trigger guard. His eyes searched the camp, looking for his wife. He didn't see her and began to wonder.

Frank said, "Morning, *amigos. Cómo están?*"

"Where's the third man?" The large, portly man with tall hobnailed boots and a fringe leather jacket asked. "Where is he?" The man moved to Frank's left, on the hill side of the fire, rifle balanced carefully in his hands. His two companions were standing to Frank's left, on the south side of the fire.

Three, Frank thought. *That leaves three. Probably behind me, maybe in the trees, maybe lying in the grass.*

Frank smiled and said, "He is in the trees, his rifle sighted in on the top button of your jacket."

The portly man was suddenly more anxious, a little unnerved. He glanced at the pine trees, then at Frank, then back at the trees. His eyes finally came to rest on Frank.

"You're Mexican. What do you want? Why are you here? Why do you ask for coffee and leave someone in the trees to kill me?"

"I am not so much Mexican as Spanish, *amigo*. My friend here? He is Crow, pure blood Absaroke. He has come for his woman and his young one. If you

59

would be so kind as to release them, we would have no quarrel. I would even make you some coffee over your fire." Frank paused. "Nobody has to die. So give us the woman, the baby. We will be on our way."

The big man continued to stare at Frank, wordless, but the other two looked toward the flap of the canvas tent thirty feet to their left.

Frank smiled. He said, "I can see by that look in your eye that you are not in a mood to give the lady to her husband." Frank paused. "She is in the tent, Fleury," Frank said. "Tell her to get on her belly with the girl and stay there until we sort out this disagreement."

Fleury yelled out the instructions in Absaroke. He heard the squeal of a child's voice followed by the woman's voice saying "hush."

"Well, fatty," Frank said to the big man in the hobnailed boots, "your move. You got something that does not belong to you. We are here to take them. You try to stop us, no matter, you are dead and so is your friend standing behind you. Fleury, you got the fellow in the red shirt. He is easy enough to see; should not be too difficult to kill." Frank smiled. "That is three of you right there, *amigo*. All dead because of a woman."

"He's mine, that one." Fleury said softly.

Frank had removed his right boot from the stirrup.

"You're stupid," the big man said. "Don't you think we ain't got someone with a rifle on you?"

"I know you do," Frank said. "Probably more than one. That is why we sent someone on foot to club him over the head. Really, *amigo*, give us the woman.

60

Have a cup of coffee. You do not have to die on such a fine morning."

"Horse Chaser," the booted man yelled, "you got a bead on this Mexican?"

There was no answer. In that instant, even as the question was asked, Frank threw himself off the right side of his mount, bringing his rifle with him as he fell to the ground and rolled. A micro-second later, a rifle shot whipped across the seat of the empty saddle.

Fleury's horse jumped—reared, trying to avoid Frank. Frank, flat to the ground, moving, brought his rifle to bear on the man in front of him.

A second rifle repercussion slammed against the hill side. Astonished, the big man was shoved backwards even as he was sighting down his rifle barrel at Frank. The man behind him to his left started running, leaping, then crawling on his hands and knees, disappearing into the tall grass. Frank shot the third man through the chest as he tried to shoot him. Behind him, Fleury's horse was crowhopping; then he went straight up, trying to shake Fleury loose from his perch on its back. Fleury obliged him by rolling out of the saddle, the horse's antics saving his life. Behind Frank, someone was firing. Frank was up and running, keeping his horse between himself and the hillside. He was quick: diving, rolling over a log, coming to his feet, crouching low, moving. The big man in the hobnailed boots hadn't been so lucky; he was stone cold still. The man Frank shot from the ground was in a crumpled heap to his right.

Mentally Frank counted two.

A rifle shot echoed off the hillside. Someone

screamed. Silence reigned.

Three. Leaving three.

Frank didn't turn; he was watching the brown grass of the meadow. Nothing moved. But someone was crawling through it, and he was armed. Frank knew that.

Moments later Frank was aware of Henry at his side.

"I'm thinkin' fire," Henry said. "Fire and smoke. We don't dare ride with those boys out there in the grass ready to shoot us."

"I got it, *amigo.*" Frank moved on his hands and knees to the fire circle and returned with a hot tin can half full of burning embers, holding it away from himself by the ends of two smoking sticks. He spread the coals on the ground, blowing on them until fire caught hold. Soon grass was burning in not one place, but three. Smoke began to drift through the grass. Henry waited on bended knee, rifle to his shoulder, surveying the field, searching for any abnormal movement in the waves of grass, any movement at all. He saw no one.

Seconds later, someone swore. Henry held his fire, listening; there was no one to shoot, not yet. Smoke was rising slowly, sifting across the meadow in layers. The flames grew. A small breeze picked up, driving it faster, whipping the smoke in gusts. Henry waited. A man popped up, disappeared and was running low through the smoke. Both Henry and Frank shot at the same time. The man went down.

Four. Frank thought. *Two more.*

"Let's get the hell out of here," Henry said, no

longer interested in waiting.

With Henry studying the grass for movement, Frank looked for Fleury. He was nowhere in sight.

"Henry, I will get a horse for the woman and turn the others loose."

Henry nodded and said, "Careful, Franko, I don't know where the fifth and sixth men are hidin'. Don't know if the sixth man is here. I ain't seen him. Two more, Franko." He wondered if he counted right, if they were just lying flat in the grass, or if they were crawling to get away from the smoke and fire.

"There is at least one in the grass, Henry," Frank said.

"Thanks," Henry said.

Frank started running toward the trees. A child's screech broke the quiet, echoing against the hillside. A man's voice told her to be quiet, to lie flat against the ground. A woman's voice was chattering, clearly agitated.

Henry yelled. "Fleury, catch up your horse. Franko has a horse for the woman! Get 'em out here! Mount up! Get the hell outta here!"

Seconds later, a woman and a child sprang from the tent opening, followed by Fleury carrying the Remington. Fleury glanced first toward the campfire and then at Frank running toward them leading a painted horse. He saw Henry watching the smoke, the orange flames dancing along the edge of the timber, spreading out into the meadow. The blaze had grown into a wave, spreading quickly.

Henry remained low, rifle butt pressed against his shoulder, his eyes searching, moving. Frank grabbed

Anne and flung the young woman into the saddle, handing her the reins of a painted horse.

"Wait!" he yelled. "Follow Fleury soon as he is in the saddle! Stay with him!"

Fleury had caught his horse. He had the reins in one hand, his daughter in his left arm. Fleury set the girl on the shoulders of his saddle and swung up behind her, hoping the bay had worked out his penchant for bucking.

Frank said, "Fleury, ride the way we came. Keep to the edge of the trees. Henry and I will follow. Cover your retreat. Get going. Do not stop. We will catch up."

With that he turned, catching Henry's horse, leading his own. A rifle shot rang out. Frank started swearing, something he seldom did. Henry came to his feet as if prodded by a sharp stick, working the lever of his Winchester, firing as he walked across the smoking, black carpet and into the tall buffalo grass at the edge of the flames. Someone yelled, screaming profanities. Henry kept firing until there was no ammunition left in the magazine. Then he pulled a pistol, firing into the grass and smoke. The yelling and cursing stopped abruptly. Momentarily, Henry stared in the direction of the cursing, peering into the grass, then he turned, hurrying back to Frank.

"You hit?" he asked Frank.

"No, but he shot your saddle dead. Missed your horse. Got my heart beating. For a second, I thought I heard Mary Carlos crying at my funeral. It was all very sad. Lots of flowers, many beautiful girls crying, tamales to eat, tequila to drink--enough to take a bath in."

"One minute, Franko. Hold on. Remember, there's one left."

"I have not seen the sixth one," Frank said.

"Me, either."

"Let's get the hell out of here before he finds us."

"I agree."

Henry reloaded his Winchester, shoving it in the boot, then reloaded his pistol, dropping the spent cartridges onto the ground. Frank was doing the same. Henry glanced at him. "One more minute," he repeated.

"One minute? What are you doing, *amigo*? Taking a *siesta*? Let's get out of here."

"You see what the Indian was packin' for a shootin' iron? He couldn't guard an empty bucket using that Remie as a club. I remember him having something better." Henry picked up the fat man's rifle, ejected a spent cartridge. "Take a look at this. It's practically new. New to me, so it'll be new to Fleury." He pulled the pistol from the man's girth, held it up for Frank to see. "I'm doin' all my serious gun shopping out here on the Reservation. This is one of them double action Colts. Don't reckon this one will be needin' it." Henry glanced at Frank. "All right," he said, "let's get."

Both men mounted and rode at a lope, following Fleury. A mile later they caught up with him as he disappeared into a grove of quaken asp. The child rode on the shoulders of his saddle. Fleury's wife rode out front, her small frame bent over the saddle, her hand gripping the saddle horn as her painted horse trotted. She bounced through deadfall, her butt slapping the saddle seat, moving out into the open, then back into the trees. They didn't stop.

The rest of the day they moved south by southwest riding into the late afternoon. They'd transversed a long meadow with trees on both sides and a small creek wandering through the middle of a valley, brush growing up on both sides of the stream.

In a stand of pine and quaken asp, a rock formation towering above them, Henry stepped down from his bay horse and stared back at the valley they'd just transversed. He was thinking about the sixth man, wondering where he was, what he'd do when he found his friends dead. A breeze picked up, bending the tops of the pine trees, rattling the leaves in the quaken asp. In the very far distance, smoke rose into the afternoon sky. It seemed to be growing.

"Whatdya you think, Franko? Here, good?" Henry said. "Need to give the woman and baby a rest."

"It is good, Henry. Good as any."

Henry and Frank stood in the shade watching Fleury tend to his wife and child.

Frank said, "Say, Fleury, how did that Remmie hold up?"

A sheepish grin crossed Fleury's face.

Frank smiled. "Jammed? Would not fire? Could not get the cartridge in? Could not get it out? What are you doing bringing a single shot bird killer to a shooting affair? You are one crazy Indian."

Henry walked to Fleury's horse and pulled the Remington from the scabbard. He hefted it, shaking his head and, taking it by the barrel, flung it beyond the quaken asp into the rocks. It clattered before coming to a rest. Both men turned to watch Fleury.

"What?" Fleury came to his feet, furious. "What the hell are you doin'? That's mine. That's all I got!"

Henry shook his head. Turning his back, he walked to his horse and retrieved the Winchester 73 he'd collected from the fat man's body. He looked at the now very angry and agitated Indian. "Here," he said, tossing the rifle to him, "in celebration of your birthday."

"What? It ain't my birthday."

"Got you a double action Colt, too."

"I gots my own," Fleury said.

"Where you hiding them?" Frank asked.

"Lost 'em in a card game."

"Fleury, you don't have what you haven't got." A smile came to Henry's lips. Frank burst out laughing.

"What's that mean?" Fleury said. "I was winnin'."

"So was the other guy!"

"He was cheatin'."

"I bet. Ma'am," he said to the woman, "how do you put up with this fellow?" Frank abruptly stopped speaking, glancing quickly from the small girl to her mother. The child was hiding behind the woman, peering at Frank.

Fleury's wife was a slightly built woman, her shoulder length hair straight, curving into her face, framing her high cheekbones. Her features were delicate--not what he normally remembered seeing in a Crow woman--her body thin and angular as if she'd righteously stayed away from fried bread, buttered biscuits, and bacon, living instead on dried choke cherries, currants, buffalo berries, dried venison, tatonka, and elk.

"Ma'am," Frank asked, "who were those men we just killed?"

She glanced at her husband before answering, hesitating.

"I don't know," she answered, her voice soft, her eyes staring helplessly at her husband, Blue Spotted Horse, pleading for help. But Fleury was examining his new rifle, not paying attention to her sudden awkwardness.

Frank watched her. "You see any of them before?" he asked, studying her face. "Know any of them?"

She again hesitated before answering. "No," she said. "I . . ." her voice was low, barely a whisper.

Henry looked at Fleury and took a deep breath, nodding as if understanding some unfathomable thought, something he didn't want to even consider, but did. In frustration, he took up the reins to the bay's bridle, tossing them around the horse's neck, but the horse was trying to graze so the reins slid right off. He picked them up a second time. His horse continued to graze, ignoring him.

In the awkward silence that followed, Fleury took his eyes from the new rifle and saw Henry picking up the reins.

"What? Where you goin'?" Fleury asked.

"Fishin'," Henry said to him. "Your *hacienda*-- it's two days that away." Henry pointed southwest toward the west Pryor. "Fleury, your woman knew those men. I don't know if I want to know who we just killed. I told you somethin' ain't right 'cause somethin' sure as hell ain't right here."

Anne spoke rapidly. "Five of them. Five I never saw before. I did. I saw them but I didn't know them. Five," she said, holding up her hand, spreading her fingers and thumb.

All three men stared at her, not saying anything.

"The sixth . . . that one, he is my brother."

Fleury swore. Henry shook his head.

Frank smiled as if he'd known all along. "And he is not dead?" he asked.

She shook her head. "He went to get my father. He wasn't there."

"Your father?"

"Blue Spotted Horse," she said her eyes on her husband, explaining, "they took the baby. I had to go with them." She paused. "Listen, I kept breaking the bead work, dropping the beads so you'd know. So you'd follow. It wasn't my choice. They took her from me." She looked from her husband to Henry, then to Frank. "Anyway, who are these men?" she asked "They know too much and they don't know anything."

"That damn near sums it up," Henry said, looking at Fleury. "Your Saint Anne here might be telling the truth. This time. I'm guessing, but they probably did grab the baby, so she went with 'em. Maybe they wanted both. So they took the baby. So, what do you want to do, Fleury? Me and Franko are steppin' into a family scrabble. Ain't no rhyme nor reason to it. Why did she lie? Ain't no reason for that either."

Anne responded immediately. "I'm telling the

69

truth." All three looked at her again.

"Who, and how many will your father bring?" Henry asked her.

"I don't know. How would I know that?"

"Will he come?"

She nodded. "He will come," she said, her face turned into a frown. "He doesn't like me living in Pryor. He doesn't like the Sore Lip lodge of my mother. He doesn't like Blue Spotted Horse."

"I thought Pryor is where you're from."

"It is, but not my father. My mother. She is of the Sore Lip Lodge. My father--he is of the Thick Lodge people. Sometimes they do not like each other." She paused, clarifying. "They don't like each other."

Henry took a deep breath. "What do you want to do, Fleury?" Henry asked again.

"I can handle it. I don't need you two. Not now. I will straighten this out."

"Sure you will," Frank said easily, his index finger tapping the wooden grip on the pistol stuck behind his belt buckle. "Let's see, Fleury. You do not know how many you are up against. You do not know which direction they will come from. You do not know when. Now that we have killed five of them, you figure you can handle it?" Frank smiled. "I do not think so, *amigo*. Not today. Probably not tomorrow. You are dreaming if you think you can handle this one alone."

Anne's hands were on her hips. She stood staring at Frank, then she turned to Fleury. "Saint Anne? Why are they calling me Saint Anne? Blue Spotted Horse, what are they talking about? Who are these men, that you listen to them? Send them away.

We don't need them. We can handle my father. Send them away!"

Henry ignored her. "Fleury, if I were you I would prepare for a shootin' war."

"Anne," Fleury said to his wife, "these are my friends and Franko is right." Fleury looked at his wife. "I ain't sending 'em away. Sometimes it is good to have friends. Sometimes trouble is too big for one man and a Remington single shot. Sometimes friends see what needs to be done and do it."

"Friends? You don't have friends. You have men you drink with, men you hunt deer with. They are not friends. What are they talking about?" She paused. "Why does he call me Saint Anne?"

"This one?" Fleury pointed at Frank. "He likes to call you that."

"I don't like it."

"Anne. It's one of those things. Get used to it. It doesn't matter."

"I don't want to get used to it. I want you to get rid of them. Send them away--"

"They'll be coming right up the valley," Henry said, interrupting Anne Fleury. "They won't be likin' the dead men we left behind. They'll be ridin' nervous: angry; lookin' for revenge. Assume there will be a lot of 'em. They'll be followin' our trail. Fleury, I doubt her father puts too much store in you defendin' yourself against those he'll bring. The dead men we left will make him hesitate. He'll be a little cautious if he has any sense. Assume he has some."

Fleury looked at his wife, opening up the breech of the rifle Henry had given him, and started explaining.

"Anne, these are my friends. I fish with them. Their being here is all about fishing and getting drunk on tequila."

"Fishing? Tequila?" Anne paused, looking from Frank to Henry. Henry was studying the valley, looking toward the hills beyond. She said, "These are the men? The ones you fish with in the month of browning grass?"

"They broke me out of jail."

"Jail? I didn't know you were in jail."

"It is a long story, Saint Anne," Frank said. "It is all about fishing and some tequila promises."

She stared at Frank. "I have another name, you know."

Frank smiled. "She who Stands Shaking Her Fist, yes?"

"How did you know this? I don't like being called Saint Anne. I don't know you."

"In August, the fish talk, Ma'am. They say a lot of things."

Henry announced, "I'm gonna go and see if I can round up a fool's hen, a rabbit or two; get us somethin' to eat." Henry paused. "Ma'am," he said touching his hat, turning to Frank. "Franko, maybe you could see to startin' a little fire. I figure those boys'll be comin' up the valley tomorrow. We'll see 'em before they see us. One of us could get up on that rock and watch. Ain't no place for 'em to hide followin' our trail. We made no effort to hide it. Better get ready. The little girl will need somethin' to eat. Maybe we could pull those bed rolls. Get her somethin' to lie on. Probably tired. Ma'am, there's a sack tied to my saddle, has some vittles in there. Might see if the child would like some. I'd look around and find someplace for you and her to hide when the shootin' starts."

Henry paused, looking at Fleury. "I'm sorry this is happenin' to you, *amigo*. You ought to decide if here is where you want to meet your father-in-law. Personally, I think this is as good as any. If I were you, I'd want to get it over. It's up to you. You could run if you think that's best. Franko and me, we'll cover your retreat if that's what you want to do. Suit yourself."

Fleury nodded. "Thanks, Henry. I think so, too. I'll settle this thing once and for all. We'll do it here. I don't like runnin'."

Henry Williams returned with two fool's hens and a jack rabbit gutted and skinned. Frank had built a small fire. Turning from his self-appointed tasks, Frank looked at Fleury and his wife, the baby resting on the saddle blankets.

"Fleury, the grass this way every year? Or is this just a good year?"

"Every year that I remember."

"Sure is a sight." Frank paused. "I think Henry is right. They will come clear to this pile of rocks and these trees. They will be following the trail we left. We should meet them here."

Fleury nodded. "My father-in-law is a hard man to like. He never liked me. I stole his daughter. I mean he really don't like me. I'm not his first choice. I ain't his fifth or sixth choice either. I ain't somethin' he could brag about while he works at the BIA in Crow Agency."

Frank, listening, shook his head.

"Why are you shaking your head?"

"Same thing happened to Hank. A woman. Told you, remember? Anna Marie. Her father did not like him either. Got into a big fight. Henry backed off." Frank stared at the Indian. He said, "The only reason for all of this is her papa. He wants to take Saint Anne and your little one. You going to let him? If not, you are going to have to kill him."

"I've been thinking what can I do? He's her father--my daughter's grandfather. Anne won't like me killin' him, even if I want to. Will you?" He glanced at his wife.

"No," she answered. "It isn't right. My father is a good man."

"I hope you're right."

Frank smiled. "I do not know the man myself. I am guessing. This much fuss? Sending people to get your daughter, your woman? Once his boys had them, they sent word to him. He comes. He is coming with an army. I would say he is planning on killing you. And after what we did to his friends yesterday, he is going to try and kill Henry and me."

Anne Fleury said, "Why would he do that? He won't. He's my father. I know him. He wouldn't do that."

"He can, Ma'am." Frank said.

"You don't know my father. You don't know him at all. I lived with him."

"You are right. I do not know him, but I am guessing. I think he will come to kill us.

"It won't happen that way," Anne said again.

"My father is a good man."

"My guess? Tomorrow he is going to be very dead or we are going to be very dead. Maybe both."

Henry nodded. "You can't get out of it. It's comin' no matter. Here's your chance to clear it up. If he even looks like he's about to open the ball, we should come up shootin'. If we shoot first, men are goin' down, screamin', runnin' all over the place. There'll be a lot of confusion. Maybe we'll have a chance. We gotta be ready. We can't hesitate. Remember we opened up the dance back there. They'll be comin' with blood in their eyes."

"No, no," Anne said. "I will tell my father. I will tell him. He will do as I ask. There will be no trouble. We don't need you."

"Good," Frank said with a smile.

"You think I'm wrong? You both should leave. You should leave right now. Go before anyone dies. If you're not here, there will be no killings. My father will not shoot anyone."

"Nope," Henry said. "I promised Fleury, here. So if your father don't try to kill Fleury, then no one will die. Everyone will live happily ever after. But if he does . . . . Well, if he does . . . ."

"Blue Spotted Horse, send them away! Do it now!"

"Anne, I can't, and I won't."

"You're just being stupid. I might just go with my father."

"Suit yourself, but these are my friends. They ain't goin' nowhere until this is over."

"You're impossible."

"Yes, I am."

It was an uneasy truce that settled on the encampment that evening. Smoke from a small fire twisted into the air; a meadow lark sang, swallows darted about the darkening sky. The baby slept in the stack of bedrolls. Anne repeatedly begged her husband to send his friends away, assuring him that all would be well, that her Father was a good man not given to bloodshed.

Fleury continued to refuse, making her more angry. But the fool's hen was good; the rabbit was good; and the sunset was something to write home about. It covered the western sky like it was burning, a scalding red sky from north to south. Across the canyon on the Bull Elk pastures, a string of elk was moving quickly across the flat, grassy plain at the foot of the big mountain. High in the sky, miles to the north, a flock of buzzards was slowly circling, their wings catching the updrafts as they searched for carrion.

Chapter 6

They came midmorning, riding up the middle of the valley toward the evening's campfire. The ashes had burned down, the embers were cold. Once in a while the riders were obscured by the brush growing along the creek. They were twelve men riding slowly, seemingly not in a hurry. Fifty yards out, they dismounted and eleven continued walking west up a slight incline toward the pile of rocks and grove of quaken asp. One man remained behind holding the reins to a dozen horses. Eleven riders, well armed and expectant, advanced, spreading out on both sides of an older man. Henry guessed the older fellow was Anne's father. *Stands to reason*, he thought. Frank watched, pulling back the hammer on his Winchester, loosening the SAA Colt in its holster, making sure the latch was off the hammer.

Fleury strode out to meet them, his wife by his side, the little girl walking behind them humming to herself, playing *jump, frog, jump* in the tall, brown grass. Fleury stopped. They waited. Except for a meadowlark, everything grew quiet. Magpies no longer argued back and forth. The rock dog, living in the rocks behind Henry, hid in his den, his head popping out now and again to see what was going on.

Anne had insisted over and over, declaring with certainty, that nothing was going to happen. No one was going to be killed. The child was safe. In her frustration, she decided she was leaving with her father. She made her decision after her husband refused to send his friends away. "That's what I'm going to do," she said. "I'm not putting up with this craziness. Not another minute. Why don't you ever listen?"

Henry stood by a log twenty feet to the left of Fleury. Frank Rodriguez was on Fleury's other side, waiting. Both carried a Winchester rifle model 73, stocks butted against their shoulders. Fleury carried a rifle, but the stock wasn't at his shoulder. Anne was sure there was no need. In deference to his wife, he held the rifle in one hand. She was angry, so angry. Still he carried the rifle, even though she was bothered by it.

"Why?" she begged him. "What will it prove? Father isn't going to kill you, especially if you aren't armed. Not like your foolish friends. Father would never do that. A rifle will just lead to trouble. Trouble we don't need. You should have sent these two away like I asked." Fleury did not reply. "That's it," she said, "I'm leaving with my father."

Fleury tried to explain. "There's already trouble, Anne," he said. "They forced you and She Who Smiles from our lodge. They took you and her from me. The men your father sent were armed. They meant to kill me. They wouldn't let you go. Remember?"

She refused to remember. Instead she shook her head in frustration and refused to listen to his explanation.

In the midst of it all Frank had winked at Henry. "See what you are missing, *compadre*? Such delightful conversation?"

Henry could only smile.

78

"Hello, Father," Anne said. "What are you doing? Why have you brought so many men? Why did you take me from the lodge of my husband?"

He didn't immediately answer her, choosing first to look at Fleury, then Frank. Lastly, he stared at Henry standing by the old log, partially concealed behind it, the barrel of his rifle pointed directly at the old man's chest. He thought, *This one will be hard to kill. He takes no chances.*

He turned his attention back to his daughter. "Anne," her father began, "bring the little one. Get behind me. Go beyond where the horses are held. Get yourself low behind the trees."

Anne gasped, a stiff, unyielding realization washed over her like ice cold rain. "No. No. Father. No. They will kill you. Why are you doing this? Let's talk. Nobody needs to die. I've already told them. I said I'd go with you."

"Talk? Someone has already died. These men killed my friends. Burned their bodies like dead buffalo meat. Five men--my friends--are dead."

"But they forced me. They took my baby. You sent all those men . . . for no reason."

"Anne, do as I say! Get behind me," he insisted. "Take the baby. Go to the trees beyond the horses. Did you hear me? Do as I say. Get yourself and the baby low in the trees. Hide yourself."

Henry Williams glanced at Frank, noticed the grin hanging on his face like a sign. His index finger was tapping the trigger guard on his 30-40 Winchester.

Ah, hell's fire! Henry thought. *This is going from not-so-good to I-sure-as-hell-don't-want-to-think-*

about-it!

In that moment Henry began to see the world differently. For him it seemed to slow down. The lips of the old man were moving, but Henry didn't hear what he said. Instead, he saw the small man to the old man's left raising his rifle, moving it ever so slowly. That man had a tick; his eye kept blinking half shut, his fingers clutching at the rifle as it came up even more. The two men to the right of the old man were moving apart, their eyes covered by wide brim hats, rifle butts to their shoulders, a grim set to their jaws. Henry was also conscious of the three that stood ten feet behind Fleury's father-in-law. They moved their heads as if they were trying to see, trying to hear the words falling from the old man's lips.

Henry glanced again at Frank.

Frank was listening, still smiling. He said, "Fleury, *amigo*, tell that little weasel to the left of the old man that if that Winchester comes up a half inch more, I will put a round betwixt and between his eyeballs. Tell him. I want him to understand so he will not be surprised."

Fleury nodded.

Apparently the slender man understood English, because the barrel came down before Fleury was able to translate the message into Absaroke.

Anne, nervous and extremely agitated, started speaking Absaroke, rattling off a string of words neither Henry nor Frank understood. The baby was behind her father, listening. Her face began to pucker up, her lips trembling.

Anne's father stared at Anne. He said, "Take the

baby, get behind me with the horses. Hide in the trees. I am going to take care of these animals who killed my friends. Do as I say. Do it now."

Henry saw something change in Fleury as he listened, surveying the armed men standing before him. Perhaps it was the utter futility of it; perhaps it was the words of Henry and Frank; perhaps it was the realization that he really didn't want to be there. Indecision left him. "Anne," he said loud enough for all to hear, "this ain't goin' to end peacefully. Your father ain't goin' to do what you're askin' him to do. Take our daughter back to the camp fire. Get behind the log where I told you. Tell me when you are safe. Please. The time for talk is over. It's finished."

"Father. Please go away. Please. No one has to die."

"Someone does," her father said. "Someone has to die. I have five dead back where the grass is burning. My friends, all dead."

"But, Father, they gave my husband no choice. They would not release us. You forced this. This is really your fault."

"Anne," Fleury said again, "please. Your father ain't going away."

Henry noted that Fleury didn't have his rifle to his shoulder. He wasn't ready, but everyone heard his thumb pulling back on the hammer of the newly inherited Winchester. It seemed so small in his large hands, the click so loud hanging in the still morning air.

"Anne, please," Fleury begged.

She refused to move. She stepped out in front of her husband, her hands pleading, palms turned outward.

"Please, Father. Please," she begged, "we don't have to do this."

"Franko," Henry began in Spanish. "I'll get the baby. Watch the old man, that strange fellow with the tick, that nervous eye that keeps blinkin'."

"Count on it, *amigo*."

Henry moved quickly from the edge of the rotting remnant of the log, what was left of an old bull pine. He grabbed the baby by one arm as she looked up at him, throwing her to his shoulder. She protested, squealing in fear, trying to struggle. Henry's hand kept her from moving. He retreated, backing up until he regained cover of the log. He rolled the child to the ground, then continued to hold her down.

Henry, speaking in Spanish to Frank, said, "I'm ready. I got the baby. Any time you're ready, open the ball. I got the old man. That fellow standing to his right--I got him, too."

Frank took a step forward, moving to his right, a smile still hanging on his lips. Every eye seemed to follow him. Even Fleury's father-in-law glanced in Frank's direction, trying to determine what Frank was doing.

"Fleury," Frank yelled, "get that woman out of there. Get her out of there before she gets herself killed. I guarantee she will not like being dead."

Henry had never seen the big man move so fast. In one step, using his left hand, he grabbed Anne by her shoulder and literally flung her behind him. Her body was turning in air before she hit the ground. Going down on one knee, Fleury brought the rifle to his shoulder pointed directly at his father-in-law's chest.

82

Behind him Anne screamed as she rolled through the grass. Her body bounced against the sod, hurled through time and space like a sack of potatoes, knocking the wind from her lungs, leaving her sensibilities in total disarray.

Anne's father blinked, obviously surprised at the sudden movement. For an instant no one moved. Then, the man on the old man's left took a step backwards, bringing his rifle to bear on Fleury. Frank shot him through the heart, ejected the cartridge, and, without aiming, fired into the scattering crowd of angry, frightened, running men. No one was sure who shot Anne's father, but he was dead, as were the men who were unfortunate enough to be standing on either side of him. He went down trying to kill Fleury, firing his pistol twice, striking him in the fleshy part of his upper thigh. In the confusion, the men behind him were running, leaping for cover, trying to find someone to shoot: shooting too quickly: seeing no one standing still: trying to avoid shooting their own people. The air resounded with the repeated percussion of rifles, the thunder clap of pistols of various calibers.

From beginning to end, the fight was short. Henry came running past Fleury. Frank was on the other side, rifle at the ready, seeking any target, shooting continually at anything that moved. A cacophony of sound had erupted on all sides, followed by screams of pain, cursing, moaning; men mounting, running, stumbling, falling, getting up again, running for their lives.

Ultimately, Henry was beside Frank, a pistol in either hand. "All right, you sonstabitches ride or come up shootin'!" he yelled. There was no urgency in him. His movement was calm and steady, each shot well placed, nothing forced.

Those left alive were on their feet, backing away, stumbling, practically running. The man holding the horses had released them. For a moment the horses were milling about in confusion, being grabbed, some running away; then, all fleeing down the valley. Three men against twelve: three who were willing, twelve who were not; not in the face of withering gun fire, the screams of wounded and dying men filling their ears and hearts. Courage was absent that day on the ridge overlooking the long valley where a daughter had begged her father for her husband's life and for his.

Frank was smiling, surveying the fallen, the moaning, the running, and those yet to die. He glanced at a wounded Fleury sitting on his butt studying his leg. Anne was trying to sit up behind him. He'd taken a bullet in the leg; blood was leaking down his pant leg. She was doing all she could to scream with barely a whisper crossing her vocal cords.

"And they lived happily ever after," Frank said softly, "in a land of milk, honey, and tequila, so very far away . . . *en España* where the yellow flower grows on the grassy plains of *Sevilla*."

Henry glanced at Frank, shaking his head. "Where do you get that stuff?" he asked.

"*Mi madre, amigo. Mi madre.*"

"You shot?" Frank asked.

"A little."

"Where?"

"Some fool shot my hat dead. Got my head

bleedin' some. Creased my arm. Took one across the top of my shoulder. Nothin' worth cryin' about. You?"

"I am fine. Got a ear nicked. Nobody tried to kill my hat. Shot my holster, though. Got one through my belt. Missed me. How is that for luck?"

"That's good. You always have luck."

The baby was crying, a large piss-ant crawling across her forehead, trying to stand up behind the log where Henry had pressed her so hard against the ground. Her ears ached from the percussion of rifles discharged repeatedly in the morning air.

Anne finally caught her breath and started crying, her shoulders shuddering as she sobbed; her husband hobbled over to comfort her, bleeding leg and all. The baby wailed. She had risen on wobbly legs, her black head of hair bobbing behind the fallen tree trunk. The ant no longer crawled on her forehead.

Silence seeped into their hearts and minds. In that quiet, Henry went to see to the wounded.

Chapter 7

The three met every year after that on Trout Creek, the second week in August. That stopped on September 17, 1912. Henry Williams had turned sixty-eight. He lived in the Neeley Hotel in the small cowtown of Kane, across the river from what was left of the ML Ranch. Once it had run twenty-five thousand head, its graze extending a hundred miles south from the Pryor Mountain to Wind River Canyon, seventy miles east and west, mountain to mountain. Both Frank and Henry had worked for old man Lovell and his handle bar mustache after they'd come north from the desert of southern California. They'd come to the Wyoming Territory and the great Basin, trailing twelve thousand head from Oregon in 1880. Lovell and Mason already had brought twelve thousand head to the Basin. Henry lived in the bunkhouse with the ML hands while Frank built a long log house for Mary Carlos on the west side of the river. They both rode for Mason-Lovell until they rode for themselves, and the mighty ML Ranch shrunk to a footnote in an old Wyoming history book.

"Henry, Henry, wake up. Wake up. Frank is asking for you. Mary Carlos sent word."

Henry appeared a bit groggy, having dozed in his rocking chair on the front porch. Truth be told, his mind was in Mexico. He was riding with Frank. They were sitting their horses on a rise overlooking an adobe, several ranch houses, and corrals. Anna Marie and her sister, Mary Carlos, were standing on the hardpack. They were waving. He and Frank were laughing, riding down off the rise, his heart telling him that nothing could be better.

His sister, Ellen Neeley, shook his shoulder again. "Henry, wake up," she said. Even sitting in the rocker, he favored his left hip. His gruella, spooked by a sage hen, had slammed him into a cottonwood tree, then, throwing a prime fit, had dumped him unceremoniously on the ground, stepping on the same hip. When the weather turned, it hurt like hell on a good Sunday. After that horse stepped on him, most days felt like a good Sunday to Henry Williams; his hip hurt all of the time.

"What's goin' on?" Henry asked, blinking the sleep from his eyes. "What time is it?" He glanced at the sun. It was late morning.

"Frank is asking for you."

"Franko? Lord! It's just a cough, Ellen. Got a little damp, that's all. Caught a little chill. It's just a bad cold. I swear. That's all."

"It isn't a little cough, Henry. The doc thinks it's pneumonia. Both lungs."

"Pneumonia? Really, he said that?" Henry paused, looking up at the thin woman shaking him by the shoulder. "That ain't no good," he said. "That ain't no good at all. Damn it all to hell. That ain't no good at all. Franko's sure got himself into a streak of rotten luck."

"He's asking for you. Manny sent Tomas to get you. He's in the buckboard, waiting."

"Waitin'?"

Henry Williams looked past his sister into the street. Sitting in a buckboard pulled by a pair of young black mares was a Mexican kid. Henry guessed he was about twenty-four.

"I'll be damned," he said. "That boy's all grown up."

Been awhile. Four or five years. Longer.

"Henry?"

"All right, Ellen. All right. I'm comin'. Get my hat, would you?"

A moment later, Ellen was back on the porch handing him a broad brimmed Stetson. He seated it on his head, glanced at her, wearing a look that stated "I'd rather be playin' cards in hell than doing this." Henry had to go because Frank had called for him; so he limped to the edge of the porch and climbed down carefully. The young man, seeing his discomfort, started to get down from his seat above the jockey box.

"Stay put, Tomas," Henry said. "I'll sit on the tailgate so I don't have to climb up there where you're sittin'. Too damn much trouble."

Besides it'll hurt like hell getting up there.

Tomas stared at him, his face full of questions, but he didn't say anything. The old man pulled himself onto the tailgate and waved his hand so that Tomas would know he was ready. Tomas slapped the blacks with the reins; the buckboard lurched forward.

Damn kid, Henry thought, nearly falling over backwards, catching himself with his left hand.

Tomas Carlos Rodriguez drove the buckboard south half a mile along the railroad to cross the tracks at the south crossing, then drove back up on the other side of the tracks to his grandmother's house. His grandmother, Mary Carlos Sanchez Rodriguez, met the buckboard at the front porch. Tomas climbed down to help, but his grandmother was already at the tailgate, her small hands gripping the old man by the shoulder as he slid to the ground, his right foot touching the ground first. Tomas tried to help, but the old woman would not let him, so he stepped back and watched.

He saw the small woman look up at Henry Williams as if she knew him well. The scene perplexed Tomas. Why was his grandfather calling for this white, non-Mexican person--he being so sick? Why did his *abuelo* want him here? He remembered seeing Henry Williams before; he'd been small, a boy doing what his father told him to do. Mr. Williams had been so large then, so strong with his grandfather. *No more,* he thought. *That was a long time ago.*

"Henry," his grandmother said, "Frank does not look good. He has been asking for you for the last hour. The doctor said he has pneumonia, both lungs. He has a terrible fever that will not go away. It has not broken. He keeps getting worse. I am worried, Henry. I am worried."

Henry grunted in dismay. "It was just a small cough, Mary Carlos. It rained. He got a little wet. That's all. Him, me, the Indian."

"It is not little anymore. He can hardly breathe."

"Where's Manny?"

"He is here."

A young man younger than Tomas came outside the long log cabin and stood with his older brother by the buckboard, watching.

Henry looked at him. "Miguel," he said, "how are you this morning? Ain't seen you in a while."

"Fine, thanks, sir. Need some help?" Miguel and Tomas both started forward.

"Got it, thanks. Your father close?"

"Yes, sir. I think he's in the goat pasture. He was fixing some fence in the hog pens. I think he's finished."

"Get him for me? Could one of you do that?"

"Yes, sir."

The old man leaned against Mary Carlos as they walked toward the enclosed porch and the front door of the house. Above their heads the breeze rattled the cottonwood leaves; in the street it picked up dust, swirling it around and around. Somewhere in the limbs above their heads, magpies squawked back and forth. Across the railroad tracks on the westside a dog was having a hissy-fit, barking at something.

As they mounted the first step, a black dog slunk under the porch, whining. "What's the matter with him?" Henry asked.

"Nothing," Mary Carlos said.

"Nothing? Hell of a note, ain't it, Mary Carlos? Get a little wet--I mean just damp--nothin' serious and Franko gets sick. I remember him gettin' snakebit, his leg swellin' up big as a watermelon. He gets on his horse and we go to work. Now he goes and gets a little damp and gets pneumonia. That makes no damn sense."

The old woman didn't reply.

"Tomas." Miguel said, "Is that Henry Williams? He has sure gotten old. He can hardly walk."

"Yeah, Grandfather's friend. He was always with Grandfather when I saw him. The last time we were here, *Papá* stopped at the hotel to see him. They talked a long time. He has been out to the ranch several times. Not recently. Last time, you were in Chicago with the yearlings. He came with Grandfather."

"Grandfather? I hardly remember. I forgot. I remember *Papá* and another man. Maybe it was this one. He looked different. He wasn't so old."

"Ask *Papá*. He will know. He can tell you."

The Rodriguez house was cool and dark when Henry Williams stepped inside. Mary Carlos led him across the living room into one of three bedrooms. The one she led him to was used by her husband and herself. Henry saw two women in the kitchen washing breakfast dishes. Inside the bedroom, Frank laid on a ticky mattress, buried under several winter blankets. It was dark, everything cast in shadows: the pictures on the dresser were covered; the window shades pulled down, the light defused, the room in shadow.

"No wonder he's got a fever," Henry said. "Too damn many blankets. Too damn dark. How the hell can he see?"

Mary Carlos still had Henry by the arm. She grimaced. "It is not what you think, Henry. He said he was cold; has chills real bad. He wanted blankets. The light hurt his eyes, so I covered the windows."

Henry nodded, looking at Frank. He said, "What

the hell's goin' on here, Franko?"

"I am dying, *compadre*." Frank started coughing, unable to stop. The episode visibly weakened him.

"Take it easy, Franko. You look like hell."

"*Muchas gracias, compadre. Por favor, siéntate.* Sit close. I cannot talk. Hardly hear myself. No strength." Frank's breath came in short gasps, wheezing, as if he'd been running and running and couldn't catch his breath, no matter how hard he tried or how long he tried.

Henry complied, sitting on Frank's right side next to the stricken man's bed. Frank lifted his hand. Henry took it, noting that his hand was warm, damp with sweat. Frank didn't say anything for a few minutes, gathering his strength, the only sound in the room the rattling of air as it passed through his tortured lungs. Mary Carlos, a girl, Alejendra Rodriguez, and her mother, Raquel, came into the room and stood on the opposite side of the bed. The girl was staring at the floor, holding her hands in front of her, shifting her weight nervously from one foot to the other.

"Do you need something?" Mary Carlos asked her husband.

Frank shook his head "no" and looked from his wife to his granddaughter, Alejendra.

"*Mi-hija,*" he said to the girl, "you do not need to be in here watching an old man die. Go outside; get some sunshine. I do not want you in here. Find something to do."

His voice was like a whisper played on a rusty washboard; the effort caused him to stop talking.

The girl said "*Mi abuelito*" softly and started sobbing. "I'm so sorry."

Frank motioned for her to come closer, which she did, touching Frank's crumpled blankets with her fingers, not knowing what to do with herself. He took her hand in his, the callouses rubbing against her slender fingers like sandpaper.

"*Mi-hija*," he said quietly, "see this man?"

The girl looked at Henry holding her grandfather's hand, then back at her grandfather.

"When you need me, you go to him. Understand? When you need me, you go to him. He will help you. He will stand with you. *Comprende, mi-hija?*"

"But, *Abuelito*, I . . . "

"*Mi-hija*, I love you. But go. Go to the kitchen. Help your mother. Fix breakfast or dinner. Fix something. Go outside with the boys. Get out of here. Go on." Frank's breath was shallow, his words raspy. "Go," he whispered again.

"Mary," Frank said, pausing, "open up this room, would you? I cannot see Henry. Please? Let the light in. Open the windows. I cannot . . . I cannot see a thing. Cannot breathe."

Alejendra left, hesitating as she passed through the doorway, but her mother, Raquel, lingered, touching the old man's hand.

Frank smiled at her from the pillow that supported his head. "Take care of my son, *mi-hija*, my grandsons, and Alejendra." He patted her hand. "Please, *mi-hija*, you, too. I need to be alone with my friend."

Raquel smiled at him, her eyes brimming; she

bent over the bed and kissed his hot forehead. "We love you, *Abuelito*," she whispered. "We love you."

Henry shook his head. *I don't belong here,* he thought. But Henry Williams, for once in his life, didn't know what do do. Leaving wasn't a possibility, not with Frank holding onto him.

Mary Carlos did as Frank asked. Soon the room was bright; the windows were open. A breeze coming off the river played with the curtains. Mary Carlos returned to her husband's bed, her face drawn, her eyes red but with no tears.

"Thank you, Mary," Frank said softly. "Now, go outside. Be with your granddaughter, with Raquel, your grandsons. Be happy. I will talk with my friend." The last words were barely a whisper. He breathed slowly, coughing.

She nodded. Without saying another word, Mary Carlos left the room, hurrying through the door, closing it behind her, her hands worrying her face and neck.

Frank looked at Henry. "Dying is hard," he whispered. "It is like the very strength of you is leaking out the bottom of your feet; soon it feels like I will have nothing left. Not what I expected."

"Franko, with all of these women bawlin' and makin' over you, I don't see how the hell you can do it. Makes for a helluva reason not to."

Frank turned his head to look at Henry. "Remember your promise, *compadre*. Remember."

"I will remember, Franko."

Frank closed his eyes. Henry started to get up, started to release Frank's hand, but Frank wouldn't let go. As he attempted to move, Frank's eyes opened, staring at his friend. He shook his head "no" and closed his eyes again. Henry sat back, resigning himself.

"Tell that Indian I will not be fishing with him any more."

"I'll tell him."

Henry sat quietly, leaning toward the bed, Frank's hand in his. Sometimes he held his breath waiting for Frank to breathe.

An hour later, Frank began speaking in Spanish, talking with someone not in the room. Sometimes he spoke to his older brother, Jesus Rodriguez; sometimes, his mother. Henry knew both to be dead, but he said nothing thinking that Frank was crazy out of his mind.

A few minutes passed. Frank's eyes opened. He stared at Henry, still grasping Henry's hand. "Remember, *compadre*."

Henry nodded. "I'll remember, Franko," he replied.

Frank looked at Henry, his eyes dark in his head. He said, "Manny is coming. He had trouble with some hog."

"Manny? I forgot about him. I asked Miguel to get him for me."

"He forgot, Henry," Frank whispered, his eyes closed again. "Just told him."

Less than a minute later, Manny was at the door, knocking. Without waiting for an invitation, he came inside the room. He said, "Sorry, *Papá*, I was having trouble. That big boar got out while I was fixing the fence." He glanced at Henry sitting close to the bed, his father's hand in his.

I'll be damned, Henry thought.

Frank looked at his son without loosening his grip on Henry. "*Mi-hijo*," Frank whispered, barely audible. "I have love for you. Very proud. Listen to me. If you need help, you go to this one. Understand what I say. You go to this one, you need anything. He will be there for you."

Manny nodded; his eyes teared up. Henry swore to himself, feeling as out of place as an old brass door knob hanging on a new door. Frank was patting Manny on the shoulder with his free hand. As if on cue, Mary Carlos came into the room and rescued her son, helping the heavy-hearted man out of the bedroom and into the kitchen.

"Come, *mi-hijo*," she said, "you need to eat. You must be hungry."

When she returned, Frank's eyes were closed; he was speaking Spanish, rattling on as though he was in a bar enjoying tequila and guitar music in the *pueblo cantina*.

"He's been doin' that the last several hours, Mary. He won't release my hand," Henry said. "Won't let me move.

"Stay with him. He needs you."

"What's he sayin'? Sometimes I don't understand. Thought I knew Spanish."

"He is talking to his brother."

"I know. His brother, Jesus, right?"

"No. Eduardo. Sometimes he talks to his mother. He is saying something like 'not yet.' Something like that. I heard him say 'go away.' It's crazy, I don't know."

Mary Carlos glanced at Henry. Suddenly the

pressure on his hand increased, holding it fast. Frank's eyes were open, looking directly at him.

"*Compadre*, very bad things are going to happen. Very bad. Remember your promise."

The pressure relaxed; Frank's eyes closed. He breathed slowly until his breathing ceased. The wind blew the ends of the curtains out into the room. It rattled the cottonwood leaves above the house, sounding like ten thousand snakes. From somewhere near the railroad stock corrals, Henry could hear a dog barking. Henry Williams felt heavy and tired but he held Frank's limp hand, held it like it was his job, like letting go would somehow let Frank down, disappoint him in the moment of need.

"You got that right, *compadre*," Henry said. "Somethin' bad has happened."

Chapter 8

The Chicago, Burlington, and Quincy stock train pulled into the yards at Sheridan, Wyoming on April 2, 1913 at 4:15 a.m. It was dark, with only the stars and a sliver of a moon providing light. The old 4503 was on time; the engine running cool, the boiler hot. It was a short stop on a long trip. The cattle cars were loaded with one thousand-sixty-four yearling steers. So far they were standing; not one had gone down to be trampled, injured, or, perhaps, killed by anxious, milling hooves. The 4503 needed to take on water and everyone on the train understood the importance of moving quickly. Soon the yearlings would need to eat and drink. The next holdover was Omaha, Nebraska. There the steers would be unloaded, watered, fed, and allowed to rest for three days before taking the last leg of the journey to the stockyards and processing plants in Chicago. This stop's sole errand was to take on water, to fill the engine's tanks for the purpose of making steam. While she was sitting on the side track, the brakeman would oil the drivers and check each of the couplings and each of the wheels for a hot box. Twenty-five minutes were allotted. Because of the time constraints, the brakeman would not finish his appointed chores before the train was moving once more.

The stock car just in front of the caboose held only one passenger. He stood in a stall, his lead rope tied securely to keep him from moving around, and, hopefully, from being slammed against the walls. This was a distinct possibility, especially likely when 4503's wheels started turning, each car jerking as she got underway. The passenger was Impressive Traveler, a thoroughbred horse colt, a stud horse in the making.

Impressive Traveler was three-years-old going on four. Regardless of when he was born, he turned three on January 1 of his birth year. The actual month of his birth was March 3, 1910 making him an older three-year-old when he turned three. He was big and well filled out. He had the blood lines, the blood, the breeding--the everything that makes a stud impressive and in demand. Somewhere, flowing though his large heart, was a dash of Arabian.

The owner, Gorman O'Neal, knew nothing about thoroughbreds or small dashes of Arabian. He did know he had a winner, that a winner would make him a lot of money, that this stud was indeed different from all the rest. Even as a new three-year-old, Impressive Traveler won races; he won consistently. He won by three, four, five lengths. It was "no contest" as they said in the back bar rooms in Lexington, Kentucky. This one was truly something special. In short, Impressive was impressive.

On April 2, 1913 Gorman O'Neal's chief and only trainer, Bud Oren, had the young stud standing in a stall in the last car just before the weathered, dark red caboose. The caboose accommodated him as well as the conductor, switchman, brakemen and the drovers attending to the cattle. It gave him a few of the luxuries he needed for the trip to Kentucky: a table with cushioned benches, a small Franklin cooking and heating stove, a bunk, a Zane Grey novel entitled *Riders of The Purple Sage*, three decks of worn face cards, and someone to talk to. According to Bud, "it sure as hell was better than riding in the stock car with a damn horse." It also gave him immediate access to the cattle car that carried Impressive Traveler.

Bud Oren took his job seriously: checking on the stud hourly, keeping him watered, his feed bin and manger full of timothy hay, and the once-a-day quart of oats that Oren personally inspected. Each visit was exactly the same: approaching from the same side, patting the horse on the rump exactly the same number of times, talking to Impressive in the same low, loving, reassuring voice. It wasn't by happenstance that Bud Oren was the most sought after trainer on the east coast, or that Gorman O'Neal employed him.

While the engine was taking on water, Oren, with the help of the conductor/flagman, took Impressive out of the cattle car to exercise his legs and get some air in his lungs. He'd already been traveling for eleven hours. Each time they stopped, if there was enough time--even a few minutes--Oren would take the horse outside the cattle car and walk him. If possible, he'd allow him to run, thus, stretching his legs, getting his heart pumping gallons of blood, allowing fresh air to course through his lungs.

In Sheridan, Oren, with the assistance of the conductor, led the horse down the ramp and into the local stockyards. On this occasion, he let him loose in the large cutting pen where cattle and horses were worked, branded, if necessary, and separated into their respective categories--such as heifers, steers, or bull calves--prior to shipping. Once loose, Impressive

Traveler began to run, tossing his head in exhilaration. He ran the full length of the corral, turning and sprinting back to where Oren and the conductor were standing. They were dutifully admiring his lines, commenting on the way he moved, how he held his head, how his eyes seemed to see everything at once. Reaching Oren and the conductor, Impressive Traveler turned left, spewing dirt as the power in his legs pushed him toward the north fence. At that moment in time, the two men had been discussing the intelligent shape of his head, the power generated by his hindquarters as they drove the young stud forward. Oren told the conductor how the three-year-old had won his first race at Bend, Oregon, and his next in Pendleton. His last race had been on March 28.

The first inkling of trouble occurred when Impressive Traveler bolted for an open gate inadvertently left open by Charley Johnston. Charley was the night rider who, last night, had been thinking about his new baby and his wife, Melissa, waiting for him at home. Thus preoccupied, he hadn't double checked the gate latch to make sure it had dropped in place. It hadn't. During the night, the wind running off the flanks of the Big Horn Mountains had pushed the gate open. This was the open gate in the side-fence that Impressive Traveler found on April 2, 1913. It lead to an alley that ran the entire length of the stock corrals. In Oren's defense, the open gate, the plank fence in which it was set, and the plank fence of the alley way created the illusion of one tight corral. Neither he nor the conductor had seen the open gate when he'd turned the horse loose. The horse had.

Once in the alley, Impressive charged forward, gaining speed, feeling the spring in his legs, the power of his expanding chest. Toward the end of the alley, where Impressive would have stopped, especially as he bore down on a closed gate, something spooked him. It was probably Charley's old tomcat, the one that kept the pack rats from setting up housekeeping in the granary and tack room. Impressive was startled and, instead of stopping, he jumped, leaping for safety from the shadow of the cat fleeing for refuge. The jump carried him over the fence at the end of the runway and to more freedom than he'd ever known in his three-year-and-one-month existence. Impressive Traveler saw before him the open expanse of grassland lying between Sheridan and the Big Horn Mountains. No fences. So he ran. In his exhilarating joy, he turned south, the knee-high mountain grass flowing between his knees and cannon bones. He did not stop or slow down until he was mere miles from Buffalo, Wyoming.

The stock train went on without him, as did the conductor, the caboose, and the now empty cattle car that had brought him to Sheridan. Bud Oren stayed. He hired two wranglers from the Bar S Bar outfit to look for Impressive Traveler. It took the horse wranglers a week to find him and three days to catch him. In those ten days, on the northern slopes of the Big Horn Mountains, Impressive Traveler found a mare with no name, no blood lines, and certainly not his muscled physique. But she was a mare; she was a mustang, and she was in heat. And Impressive, though he had never done it before, impregnated the lowly mare.

It was an inadvertent event which Gorman

102

O'Neal had thus far studiously prevented from happening; he wanted his young stud to mate only with the very best of thoroughbred stock, and only when he permitted and supervised it. O'Neal wanted complete control, for control meant money and, given the budding history of Impressive Traveler, a lot of it. Impressive Traveler, though he'd never run in a big race, had not lost a race. The Derby, the Belmont, the Preakness would seal the deal. Afterwards would come the stud fees and Gorman O'Neal's lifetime goal of continuous upward financial mobility and the undying admiration of all thoroughbred owners. With Impressive Traveler, all of this was predetermined, predestined, and inevitable.

Gorman O'Neal knew how to make it so. He'd made several fortunes in shipping and coal. He'd found the horse colt in Oregon, the product of two thoroughbreds who had been bred and raised in Kentucky and then shipped west to grow up. From the moment he first saw the youngster, he knew he had something. He immediately purchased him, paying the owner handsomely to segregate him from the rest of the stock until he could be transported. Gorman also paid the rancher to hide him from prying eyes. There was a secondary reason; Gorman O'Neal wanted the horse colt to grow up in the mountain pastures where his lungs would need to be bigger and have more capacity, a product of running free in the high mountain pastures and thin air. Two years later, he paid for Impressive Traveler to be moved to Kentucky where the big boys lived, raced, and bred the finest mares living, all for a fee.

Gorman O'Neal also, like all good horsemen, wanted to control genetics. The horse's genealogy assisted O'Neal. Impressive's sire was Fair Play and his dam was Sister Sue. Both were championship stock. But that was a secret that he kept close to the vest. He was determined to keep the blood lines pure. Thus, only the best of mares with the finest of ancestry would know Impressive Traveler. Championship horses were created. They weren't the product of happenstance. Everyone, including Gorman O'Neal, was aware of that. O'Neal, however, did not know of Impressive Traveler's tryst with the lowly mustang mare living out her life on the northern slopes of the Big Horns, a horse colt now growing inside her.

The best single act that Gorman O'Neal made on behalf of Impressive Traveler was hiring Bud Oren in the spring of 1912. The exact date was May 27. Oren hadn't even seen the horse at the time. Bud Oren was a master trainer, a lover of thoroughbreds. He had learned from the best--Jason McDougal, himself. Impressive Traveler, when he finally arrived in Kentucky, was literally loved into shape, into being the race horse he was born to be. His training had commenced June 12, while he was a two-year-old, under Bud's supervision on the Oregon high plains. It was early in the horse's development, so early that no one would have believed it if he'd told them.

Later, after he reached Kentucky, Impressive never was kept in the thirty thousand square foot elegant, white barn of Gorman O'Neal. Instead, after a training session, he was allowed to run free. Thus, the wind was always filling Impressive's sails. By the minute, hour, and day, he developed a sense of who he was and what he was; that, first and foremost, he was a horse, a horse born to run. By May 1, 1913, Impressive Traveler was well aware of his own genetics: that, indeed, he was a race horse.

Impressive was born in the high country of Oregon and had been allowed to run free above seven thousand feet. His travels had taken him running over rocks and ridges and across the high plain. He had excellent ankle circulation before there was a Bud Oren in his life. Afterwards, it was even better under Bud Oren's supervision; muscle and joint soreness never was allowed to become a problem.

He was ridden for three and one quarter miles every three days, slowly building strength muscle, muscle tone, and control that would enable him to exert an incredible amount of effort over a mile and a half track. A good morning run with Bud Oren was followed by rest and relaxation. After every session, Impressive received a massage and rub down that would make royalty envious, thus allowing muscles to develop evenly, circulation to increase, and ankle inflammation to be reduced to zero.

A half mile run became a three quarter mile. A three quarter mile run was increased by adding furlongs, building on Impressive's regimen one week after another until a mile and a half was simply a stroll. Muscle memory was catalogued, ingrained, and internalized by a willing and capable horse. Eventually, just before Impressive Traveler turned three, he ran at full speed for short durations.

Over time, Bud had added day to day and week

to week, furlong to furlong. Impressive became phenomenal, his endurance something to behold. The combination exceeded Bud Oren's expectations. The truly athletic horse mastered it all, seemingly without effort. Speed became an afterthought, evolving and blossoming in the stallion's heart, where the expectation was always a reality.

All of this training was administered under the thoughtful care of Bud Oren with the tenderness and forethought of a mother for her newborn. Normally, Bud Oren would not have started speed training this early, but Impressive was well developed for his age. Speed came naturally. In short, he was a prodigy that could not be denied.

Impressive Traveler reached Kentucky on April 13, 1913, mere weeks before the Kentucky Derby was run at Churchill Downs.

Chapter 9

The Kentucky Derby is run on Saturday during the first week in May. It is a Grade I Stakes race, the granddaddy of them all. It is the reason that Colonel Merriweather Lewis Clark, Jr., grandson of William Clark of the Lewis and Clark expedition, organized Churchhill Downs. He had help. The track was donated to him by John and Henry Churchill and he named it after them. It is a race designed to show off three-year-old thoroughbreds.

The Kentucky Derby is the first race of the Triple Crown Stake horse races. The second race is the Preakness Stakes, held in Baltimore, Maryland on the third Saturday in May. The third race is the Belmont Stakes held in Belmont, New York. This third race is the final leg of the U.S. Triple Crown, following exactly five weeks after the Kentucky Derby and three weeks after the Preakness Stakes. Consequently, it is run on Saturday but never before June 5 nor after June 11. The last Stakes race of the Triple Crown is a mile and half. The Triple Crown is the longest of the races.

In 1913 Impressive Traveler was three years old. He arrived on the first Saturday in May at Churchill Downs accompanied by his owner, Gorman O'Neal and his trainer, Bud Oren. He was a virtual unknown. At the beginning, the odds of his winning the Derby and then, the Triple Crown were seventy to one. They improved when O'Neal hired a little known jockey from Great Britain to guide Impressive Traveler to the finish line.

He was little known on the eastern seaboard, perhaps, but in Edinburgh, Scotland he was well known, especially for being in the winner's circle, bedecked with flowers, blankets, and the winner's purse. He was known as "The Turk" for his surly, almost impossible, attitude. O'Neal didn't care. He didn't hire the fellow for his demeanor. He hired him to win. The Turk didn't ride to gain approbation. He rode for the money like his life depended on it. His thoughts on the matter: "winners don't have to be nice to anyone." Those who disagreed with him could do all sorts of mean and nasty things to themselves; mostly they just walked away in a huff.

On that first Saturday in May, Churchill Downs was full of flag-waving patrons. Betting was brisk. O'Neal put twenty thousand dollars down on Impressive Traveler to win, an unheard of amount. The odds at the time he laid his bet were seventy-six to one to win the Derby and the Triple Crown.

The race historians recorded that Impressive started slow, running behind every entry. By the second furlong, he was three lengths behind the second to last horse; he being the last. It was in that moment that everything changed for Impressive Traveler.

The horse was brutal; the jockey was brutal; the race was brutal. Impressive was four lengths behind at the first turn; that was the last time he was ever behind. Impressive had been raced before; he'd never lost. No one in the stands knew that, and on the track the only one who knew it and had witnessed it was Impressive.

O'Neal was about to throw up his breakfast; his horse was so far behind. He shouldn't have been so hasty. It was about then that someone or something told Impressive that he was a horse, that he was in a horse race. His long body began pounding the track. His powerful hips began pushing forward; so powerful was his surge that he nearly dislodged The Turk from the saddle. So impressed was The Turk that he did not strike his charge again. He let the horse run the race. Impressive did just that. Around the last turn he was two lengths ahead. At the finish, he was four.

In the box seats, yards from the finish line, sat an older gentleman of seventy-seven years; he leaned back in his wooden chair, tore up his betting tickets, and threw them in the air in disgust. His prim and proper wife, sitting beside him wearing a large red hat with ostrich feathers and a ruffled blue silk dress, looked at her husband.

"Why are you upset, Raymond?" she asked. "I do believe I won."

"What?" her husband said. "Let me see." He took the betting ticket from her and studied it.

Turning to his wife, he said, "My God, woman, we're rich!"

"I know, dear," she said. "I liked how pretty he looked."

In the owner's box, Gorman O'Neal sat in his chair beside his wife, Evie. He looked at her and shook his fist in delight, throwing his head back, closing his eyes, for he, too, was rich. His horse had not only won, he'd won big.

Two weekends later, Gorman O'Neal, Bud Oren, and The Turk appeared with Impressive Traveler in Baltimore, Maryland for the Preakness Stakes. Impressive was no longer an unknown three-year-old. He was the talk of the town and the countryside.

The Preakness horse race was a mile-and-three-sixteenths track. It had rained all night, so the track was heavy. Impressive won it by six lengths and so did everyone else who bet on him. Surprisingly, even after what he did at the Derby, there were some who bet against him. Those people were not happy.

On the first Saturday in June following the 5th, they appeared in New York City outside the borough of Queens, at the Belmont Stakes. The Belmont track was a mile-and-a-half long. Impressive won it by five lengths. Distance didn't seem to matter to him: a horse race was a horse race and he was a horse. Gorman O'Neal's horse, the one that he'd kept so secret, had won the Triple Crown. Soon afterwards would come the stud fees. They wouldn't be small and the line that would form for his services would not be short.

In 1913 Impressive Traveler entered six more races after having won the Triple Crown, and he won them all running away. Gorman O'Neal, indeed, was a rich man, a man to be reckoned with among those who owned thoroughbreds. He'd reached the pinnacle of thoroughbred horse racing; he was right where he belonged. Everything for Gorman O'Neal was incredibly good.

Chapter 10

On March 12, 1914 Gorman O'Neal stood at his training track watching Bud Oren work with Impressive Traveler. It was at the end of the training session, just before the handlers took over to give Impressive a rub down and massage his muscles. Oren was with O'Neal watching the young colts being put through their exercises.

"What a year!" Oren said to his boss.

"More of a roller coaster ride."

"To think that a year ago, the first of April, Impressive escaped the corrals in Sheridan and ran clear to Buffalo."

"Is that very far?" O'Neal asked.

"I'd guess twenty miles. It took those two cowhands ten days to run him down and catch him."

"Where was he exactly?"

"When I picked him up, he was in the Big Horn Mountains making himself at home. That one fellow said he had a girl friend. That's how they caught him. They penned her up and he hung around until they could get a rope on him. A female led to his downfall."

"A mare? He was with a mare?"

"Impressive was with a mare," Oren replied.

"What happened to her?"

"Those two let her go. Didn't need her after they caught Impressive."

O'Neal's voice intensified. "Was she in season? She must have been for Impressive to hang around."

Bud Oren glanced at Gorman O'Neal. He said, "According to those cowboys, she was. Impressive had some weekend. That's for sure." He paused, and continued. "And he's taken us on some ride himself. I haven't ever seen anything like it. Some horses have ability. It's just in them. Hard to tell where it comes from--"

O'Neal interrupted. "What sort of horse was she?"

"She was a mustang. Had a rather distinctive marking on her left flank. She was a small sorrel looking horse with a white splash, like an egg was busted on her hip."

"You saw her?"

"I did. She was hanging around the corral when I went to pick up Impressive."

"Why didn't you tell me about this?" O'Neal asked, irritated.

Oren glanced at his boss, then back to the two-year-olds being walked on the track. "You never asked," he said, "and it didn't matter."

Gorman didn't sleep that night. At 2:45 a.m. he was still awake, walking the floor in his office. Evie was sleeping deeply. Nothing bothered her--not even a hurricane. "You never asked," he said, repeating Bud Oren's words.

You never asked? What on earth was he thinking? Has he no concept of the importance of keeping the bloodline clean? Especially a Triple Crown winner's bloodline?

O'Neal walked back and forth until the sun brought its warm rays, sending them shining through the trees lining the east paddock. For a few minutes he watched the mares running the length of it, chasing the morning shadows like children running through water spray.

Damn it! This can't be. If someone were to find out, what then?

At 8:45 he had the stable boy saddle his horse. Fifteen minutes later, having eaten toast, fried eggs over easy, and grits, he started his journey to Lexington. He rode all day, getting more and more aggravated with each passing hour. It was ninety miles from the river to Lexington. He made it there late in the evening. He was beat; the horse was beat; but sleep was not in the offing. The next morning he found what he wanted. It involved a forty-five mile horse ride to Clarksville, Kentucky. Having ridden contunally for two straight days, sun up until dark, would have tired most men; not O'Neal. He was driven.

"Name's Gorman O'Neal. I need to talk to someone about a job," he told the bartender at the Dixie Watering Hole in Clarksville, Kentucky.

"A job?"

"Yes, I have a job. I want him dependable. No questions asked. Cash money."

The bartender nodded his head slowly as he tried to digest what he was hearing. O'Neal immediately found him aggravating, so aggravating that O'Neal wanted to smash his face.

"I'll see what I can do," the bartender said.

I'll see what I can do? What does that mean? These people are so damn slow, so damn stupid. This is entirely unacceptable.

113

O'Neal was about to tell the fellow to forget it, to go straight to hell with his "I'll see what I can do" when the slow talking bartender said, "You stayin' here locally? How do I get hold of you?"

O'Neal stared at the skinny man. "I came from Lexington," he answered.

The bartender nodded and finished washing and drying a glass before placing both hands on the polished bar. He spoke slowly, so slowly that O'Neal figured that even the rats hiding in the walls could make out each word with clarity, could spell as well as define them. It all was incredibly annoying for a man used to having his way instantly.

"The Running Stud--you know the place? Just outside of Lexington, going west. Small bar under a large, overgrown magnolia tree."

O'Neal nodded. He didn't, but he could find it.

"Be there in two days, at seven in the evening."

"How'll I know the man?"

"He'll find you."

O'Neal left the Dixie Watering Hole, thankful to be away from the place, not sure he'd accomplished anything. He only knew he did not want to return.

Two days later, O'Neal was in Lexington sitting at a corner table of The Running Stud, thumbing through a local newspaper, a racing rag. A man approached him. He did not expect to reconize him; he didn't. O'Neal didn't expect anything, yet he expected everything. His senses were alert.

Introductions were brief; the stranger was to the point, a quality that O'Neal not only understood, but coveted.

"You're O'Neal?"

O'Neal nodded.

"What do you want?" he asked.

O'Neal stared at the man before answering. "I want you to kill a mare. A mustang, sorrel with a white spot on her left hip and flank. You can find her in the hills west of Buffalo, Wyoming."

"You interested?"

The man nodded.

"So, kill the mare. If you have trouble locating her, you can ask around for two cowhands at the Bar S Bar ranch out of Sheridan. She may either be with foal or have had a foal. As soon as you shoot the mare, verify she's dead, then see if she has a foal. If she has a foal, kill it, too."

The dark man nodded. He said, "Twenty-five hundred dollars."

"Twenty-five hundred? That's a lot."

"You're askin' me to shoot a mare and a colt."

O'Neal nodded.

"That's my price."

"All right. Twenty-five hundred. I'll pay it. I want this job done right away. I want to know as soon as it's done. There can be no slip ups. Mare and colt, if there is a colt. Understand?

The dark man nodded, waiting for O'Neal to count out the bills.

"When will I hear?" O'Neal said.

"As soon as it's done."

"All right. I want you to take care of this right away."

The dark man again nodded his head, took the bills, quickly ran through them, rose to his feet, and left the room. Later, O'Neal realized that if he had to, he couldn't even describe the man.

You're a fool, O'Neal. A damn fool.

He resolved never to handle a matter this serious in this manner ever again.

Three weeks later, he received a short note written on a postcard and posted in Sheridan, Wyoming. It read: "Mare dead. No evidence of a foal." O'Neal read the note twice, stared out the windows of his living room, nodding to himself, a congratulatory expression of relief. He took a deep breath, then let it out slowly. Afterwards, he burned the note and poured himself a drink from a long slender bottle labeled Kentucky's Finest. After draining the glass, he couldn't help but think he'd had better.

Chapter 11

Harry Harris turned fifteen on the ides of February 1914. It was the year that a little known pitcher named Herman Ruth took the mound in Beantown, pitched his first professional baseball game in which he six-hit the Cleveland Naps, and won six to zip. It was also a year known for bloodshed. On July 28, 1914 in Austria, a little known Archduke, Franz Ferdinand, was shot and killed. Thus, commenced the Great War: "the war to end all wars." Unfortunately, for the Harris descendants, it never lived up to its billing.

During the third week in April 1914 Harry Harris and his father, Abraham, a widower named after the 16th President of the United States, traveled on horseback from a small ranchstead thirteen miles west of Meeteetsee, Wyoming. They were headed to the Big Horn Mountains east of Tensleep and west of Buffalo, and camped between Clear Creek and Crazy Woman Creek in Johnston County. It was the wrong time of the year for hunting elk or deer; instead they hunted wild, untamed mustangs. There were plenty. A few miles north, on the Pryor Mountain, hunts were organized with thirty or forty men--sometimes more--armed with rifles; their simple purpose was to reduce the population of wild horses to a manageable level by shooting them.

It took the Harrises the better part of three days to make the journey, and another two days to locate several of the roaming herds. Two weeks later, they delivered forty-three head to the stock corrals belonging to the Chicago, Burlington, and Quincy railroad in Sheridan, Wyoming. They were sold at the auction a day later for three dollars and twenty-five cents a head. The older horses were turned into soap while the younger were purchased for use by the burgeoning armies in France and Great Britain.

"Hey, Pops, look down there. What is that?"

"Looks like a dead horse. It's odd. What would a horse be doing dead on a knoll like that? Let's take a look. We'll need to get a little closer." Abe and his son sat upon their horses in a stand of quaken aspen, studying the lay of the land: the ridge that separated them from the knoll; the creek; the seep springs; the pine trees that crowded the quaken aspen. He took a deep breath, letting it out slowly, getting a feeling that he was being watched, seeing no one. "Let's have a look," he finally said. "Let's be careful. Somethin's rather odd here."

Getting closer was a good idea, except good ideas don't always pan out the way they are supposed to. "Getting closer" forced them to go around the head of Crazy Woman Creek and back down the other side of a small, nondescript canyon flooded in tall pine. Above, looking down, he could see the tall pine and more. The canyon, though small, didn't allow for crossing. Every trail seemed to be blocked by pine forest and canyon walls. They went around those obstacles, too. A short side trip took all morning. The more frustrated they became, the more they insisted on getting where they were going. Besides, burning daylight didn't matter much. Neither had to be anywhere special and they were carrying one hundred dollars and seventy-five cents that they hadn't had two weeks earlier. That was more money than they'd seen all winter. Five dollars would fill the back of a buckboard with enough vittles to last a winter. They got to the mare early in the afternoon. They reached the dead mare early in the afternoon of a cloudless day.

"She's sure dead, Pops. Someone shot her right through the chest. Whatever for, I wonder? She'd have made a nice little saddle horse. She's at least worth three dollars and twenty-five cents." Harry glanced at his father.

"Or a pack horse. Looks like she has a colt. Look at her bag. Her tits have been sucked. The ground around her has been trampled, all churned up." Abe Harris looked up and down the creek, then back in the direction they'd come.

"Listen, boy," he said, "take a look around. See what you can find. Be careful. Somethin' don't smell right. A no-count mustang mare standin' alone don't get shot for no reason. We ain't seen a horse track in ten mile. I'll see what I can find up on that ridge. You take a look around down here. I suggest you follow the creek some."

Harry Harris nodded. He stared at the pine trees that surrounded the knoll where they'd found the dead mare. "Must of taken that shot from up there, Pops, in those rocks. Couldn't have gotten here except through that pass we just used. I didn't see no tracks, either."

"That's what's botherin' me. Whoever shot this horse came for this horse. There ain't another horse in ten miles. No horse tracks. Whoever it was came on

119

foot. I ain't never heard of walkin' into the Crazy Woman to shoot a horse."

After his father left, the tall, skinny teenager stood on a knoll and looked up the side of the mountain. He followed the tree line into the brush and timber that grew along Crazy Woman Creek. His inspection revealed nothing. After half an hour of looking along the creek, he returned to the dead mare to wait for his father. Already he'd searched longer, taking more time than he wanted. If there was a colt, its chances weren't good. Wolves, coyotes, a mountain lion--they all liked horse flesh. An orphan colt would be fair game.

But Pop said there was a colt. The boy studied the carcass, asking himself how long the mare had been dead. *Dead a couple of days at most. She hasn't begun to stink. Not yet. The magpies and vultures haven't started in on her real hard. The ground is churned up, small hoof prints everywhere. Better have another look. He's somewhere, dead or alive.*

Harry found the colt standing in the shallows of Crazy Woman Creek, staring at him. He had probably never seen a human being before. The horse colt didn't move or attempt to run; he just stared. The closer Harry got, the more anxious the colt became. Instead of fleeing, however, he stood in the water tapping the rock bottom, splashing water with his left front hoof. As Harry approached, the young horse colt turned, keeping Harry in front of him. All the time he continued tapping his front foot on the rocky creek bottom, the water spraying.

A few minutes later, Abe joined his son. "Well, lookie there," he said. "Poor little bugger. Must be hungry."

"What'll we do, Pops?"

"He'll die if we leave him. If we try to catch him, he'll run. That's a game we don't want to play. Let's the both of us ride toward his mother. Maybe he'll want company and follow. If not, we'll try somethin' else."

"Pops, did you see a brand on his mother? Was there one?"

"Not on the side that's up. Probably weren't none. There weren't no brands on the herd we took to Sheridan. Look what I found up in those rocks." Abe handed his son a brass casing.

Harry took it, rolling it in his fingers. He said, "A 30-40, Pops. Probably a Winchester."

Abe nodded. "The shooter was afoot, if you can believe it! Wore walkin' boots. That's all he left. I got the impression that he looked at the horse after he shot her. Didn't get too close, though. Went back over those rocks into the canyon. Didn't see if he had a horse somewheres. Had to have one though, clear out here. He'd be in trouble afoot. He ain't here now."

Abe looked at the horse colt. "Tell you what," he said, "let's put a rope on the dead mare's legs and pull her over--see what's on the other side. That'll tell us if she's branded. I'll bet the horse colt will follow us. Let's see." Abe paused. "What's he thrashing that foreleg about, stirrin' up the water like he's doin'?"

"Nervous, I'd guess. Cocky little bugger, ain't he?"

The duo mounted and turned their horses away from the creek, riding in the open, keeping in sight of the horse colt. They rode up the hill, taking their time, returning to the carcass. Magpies were gathering around the dead meat, hopping about on the mare's rib cage. They flew to nearby trees when the riders got close. A hundred yards behind them, the colt came up out of the creek, staring at the riders, tossing his head. Cautiously, he followed. The riders looked back and grinned.

"You ought to want to keep that horse colt, boy," Abe said. "He's got some real blood. You'll have to catch him. Doubt he'll make it all the way home. You could hoist him up into the saddle with you. We'll need to get something in his belly or he'll die. Too young for grass. Looks like he's doin' all right. Long-legged little bastard, ain't he? Got a little blue blood. Thoroughbred, I'd guess. Damnedest thing. Who'd think to find a thoroughbred stud out here? Where'd that mare ever find a stud like that?" Abe paused, watching the colt. "I'd guess he's about four or five weeks old. Got good legs."

"Pops, we ain't got no milk. We ain't even gots a milk cow."

"Let's see if we can use some sugar water; get some in his belly. If we can, maybe that will hold him till we can find ourselves a milk cow. See if you can coax him into a sugar cube. Get him curious. Damnedest thing, I'll tell you."

The horse colt stood and watched as they pulled his mother's carcass over to examine her downside. The dead mare bore no brand. Her colt showed no lack of interest and followed the two saddle horses to their base camp at the head of Crazy Woman. Every time they approached him, he started tapping his left forefoot, but refused to run, giving no ground, moving only when Harry was so close he could practically touch his outstretched nose. Finally, Harry got him to take a sugar cube. After the first one, he developed a sugar tooth that had demands all of its own.

The boy watched him, smiled. "Hey, Pops, I think I'll call him Tapper. He sure likes to do that. It's like he's warning us. Don't mess with me, he's sayin'."

It took the better part of a week to get the colt home. Tapper was a handful, contrary and capricious. At first he didn't like sugar cubes, then that's all he wanted. He didn't like cows' milk, then that's all he drank. He wouldn't eat grass, then that's all he did.

He liked running. He was in continual motion. It took some time for him to get used to the hackamore slipped over his nose and the blanket on his back. Eventually, he didn't mind them, either. He liked Harry and hated having him out of his sight.

The young colt amused Harry's father. "You oughta teach that horse to bark," his dad teased him. "Then you could have a dog as well as a horse to chase a cow."

The horse grew tall--seventeen hands at the shoulder--and began to fill out, eventually weighing sixteen hundred pounds. He was long with hips like steel pistons.

He was gentle. Harry's kid sister, Janille, named after her mother, Jane, and three years his junior, rode Tapper bareback. With Harry leading the horse and Janille patting the horse on his shoulder, she talked to him endlessly. Tapper listened, flipping his ears back and forth; he didn't mind the girl. He liked her even more when she fed him sugar cubes, brought him a bait of oats, curried his glistening coat, and scratched behind his ears. As a result, he followed her around, begging for still more attention. The horse was a two-kid horse on a one-horse ranch.

Chapter 12

In the Spring of 1917, the year the United States entered the Great War to end all wars, Tapper turned three, and all six feet one inches, one hundred and sixty-three pounds of Harry Harris turned 18. At 14 he had stopped attending school; eighth grade was his last year. Now, he was a cowhand; he worked for his father and the neighboring ranchers when they needed help. His work experience was stacking hay, riding the green out of the rough string, gathering cattle in the spring and fall, branding, castrating, marking, and driving yearlings, cows, bulls, as well as horses, to different pastures, and to market. He was a happy-go-lucky boy with hazel eyes, sandy brown, curly hair, carrying the broad shoulders of the Harris people. His legs were slightly bowed. The word "gangly" described his physical appearance and demeanor. He wore his hair on the long side, not because he liked long hair but because he didn't know a barber and wasn't all that good at barbering himself. Curls sticking out from under his hat simply didn't matter to him.

Come July of 1917 Abe Harris, his daughter, and his boy took a buckboard and traveled the thirty-six miles to Cody, Wyoming, intent on celebrating the Fourth of July with their neighbors. They were joined by the riders from the Pitchfork Ranch and folks as far away as Thermopolis, Worland, and Greybull. Harry rode Tapper alongside his Dad's buckboard. It was the first time Tapper had been outside the confines of the

Harris ranch since they had brought him home. Little or nothing was known about him. Only the immediate neighbors had seen the horse and they had no cause to speak of him. Tapper was just Harry's horse. Harry didn't even know what he had. The horse, himself, didn't have any idea of what he was born to do, except eat, and he was good at that.

The afternoon of the July 4th celebration was a mad combination of bare back riding, bull riding, saddle bronc riding, catching greased pigs (if you were into that sort of thing), a chuck wagon race around the rodeo arena, and a horse race. The race track sat on the west side of the Irma Hotel. The track itself was exactly one mile and one-quarter long. A race was set for five o'clock. Those cowhands who thought their mounts could catch greased lightning gathered there to see who was talk and who was real and who was really real. Abe, his daughter, Janille, and his boy, Harry, were at track's end. They sat under the shade of a water-starved cottonwood, in the back of the buckboard, so they could see the winners and the losers. They had no intention of entering the horse race; just watching. Tapper himself was cropping grass and keeping the horse and deer flies at bay. Ben O'Reilly, a cowhand from the Diamond Bar, was a little bit tipsy but still coherent. He stood in the shade of the same challenged cottonwood looking at Tapper and watching him crop grass and fight flies.

"Hey Abe," he said, "why in God's name ain't that horse of yours runnin' with the rest of these scrubs?"

Abe laughed, annoyed at the question. "Same reason you ain't plantin' corn in the spring."

126

"What? No money? What kind of excuse for livin' is that?"

"I ain't wastin' no ten dollars," Abe said. "And it's not so hard not to race when you ain't got ten dollars."

"Ten dollars. I got one dollar right here. One dollar."

"Well, that ain't gonna do it," Abe said. "I'd say that's a little short of not enough."

Ben O'Reilly, uninvited, climbed into the back of Abe's buckboard, nearly falling out, but somehow maintained his balance--mostly because Abe grabbed his arm.

"Who wants to see a real horse race?" he yelled.

People turned to this obnoxious little man teetering in the back of the Harris buckboard. "I need a dollar from each of you," he yelled. "This Harris kid thinks he's got himself a race horse. Need nine more dollars. Come on, you tightwad sonstabitches. Give it up. I need a dollar from each of ya. This here hoss can't win if he ain't racin'. If he ain't racin', he sure as hell can't win."

Folks from up Meeteetsee way knew Abe and his boy. They knew they worked hard and that money was difficult to come by, that they weren't the kind to waste ten dollars, but damn, that boy sure looked grand on the back of that long, grass burning, chestnut horse. He sure was a picture and that freckled face boy was a Harris. If they didn't know him by looking, they knew the Harrises by reputation. Besides, that Harry kid was motherless and somehow, in spite of it, got his hair combed and his shirt buttoned come Sunday morning.

He was one of those deserving people. He lived on the other side of Meeteetsee, up there next to the mountain. Folks knew Harry Harris, so they found a dollar here and there. After all, "he couldn't win if he weren't racin', and if he weren't racin' he couldn't win." Having come up with a dollar, they then came up with five dollars, betting on the boy's horse to win.

The horse race competition was a mixed bunch. There were riders from as far away as Belfry, and across the big mountain to the east, from Sheridan and Buffalo. There was one from as far away as Billings, and one from a place called Big Timber. There were some nice horses, some fast horses, and some able cowboys to ride them. That Meeteetsee boy's horse was just another horse in a group of horses that knew all about racing. They'd done it before.

One dollar? Ben O'Reilly came up with sixteen inside of three minutes. Meeteetsee, small though it was, needed a rider; most of the citizens of that community had no idea what was going to be ridden that afternoon or who was going to do the riding. They just wanted someone to cuss at and yell for: yell when they were ahead, and cuss when they lost. It was about community pride and it didn't make a "damn" bit of difference. As the bareheaded fat man sporting a goatee and a fine-looking mustache said as he sat in the afternoon sun waiting, "why the hell not?"

Abe stared at the sixteen dollar pot in the bottom of Ben O'Reilly's hat, then at his son. "Well, boy," he said, "looks like you're ridin' in a hoss race."

"Okay," Harry said, "I guess I can do that."

Harry saddled the bay, talking to him about

running a race that neither of them had ever run before. Sure, Harry had raced with the boys over on the Greybull River, where it was just a creek and they had nothing better to do. He'd played tag bareback, but that wasn't running a mile uphill, running for one hundred and fifty dollars, and that wasn't against the fastest horses in Northern Wyoming and Southern Montana. Harry didn't even have a proper saddle for that sort of thing. But he lined up with those cowhands in the heat of evening anyway. To get there, he walked the entire mile from the finish line to the starting line. They were moving and Tapper liked moving.

"That is one long horse, you got there," the jockey on his left said.

"Thank you, sir. Tapper . . . I'm hopin' he can run."

The sun burnt red-faced jockey smiled. "First time?"

"Yes, sir."

"Well kid," the older jockey said, "it's a horse that wins or loses a horse race. When the gun goes bang, hit him in the ass with your reins, kick him in the belly, and let him run. You just stay on his back. Let him do the racin'."

Harry smiled. "I think I can do that. Stay on his back, I mean."

Another man to the far right side of the makeshift track was standing in the back of a wagon box. He yelled, "Ready." The restive crowd grew silent. The line of horses was held in, but not too well. "Set." A few seconds later the pistol went off. Thirty-five horses surged from the starting line. All except one. At first Tapper didn't appear to know what was going on. Horses had been milling all around him, lining up on some imaginary starting line. The pistol shot started the line forward. Harry kicked him with his heels, and he moved forward with a lurch, but reluctantly, like he was dragging an anchor. Harry kicked him again and Tapper moved forward faster, already two and a half horse lengths behind.

It must have been seeing all those horse butts in front of him; perhaps Tapper didn't care for eating all that dust; maybe it was the sheer, explosive roar of the crowd as the starting pistol went off; or maybe it was genetic: like father, like son. All of a sudden, as if something yelled in his ear "run, this is your life, this is want you were born to do," Tapper began to run. In sixty-five yards the horse made up thirty-five; in the next thirty-five yards the thoroughbred was running with the three that were in the lead. In the next thirty-five yards he was the lead horse, finishing the course four horse lengths in front of all the other horses. Harry leaped off the bay's back and literally waited for the others to finish.

No one who put up a dollar for Tapper's entry and bet five expected that. The stunned crowd suddenly was wild in jubilation. They'd seen a real horse race that wasn't even a horse race. No one had dared imagine that a freckle faced eighteen-year-old boy riding a never-before-raced horse could finish first, or at all.

"It was the damnedest thing," folks said. "That chestnut horse was a plant," others said. Some contended that "the race was sure as hell, rigged," while others pointed out the simple incongruency of any "good ever coming outta Otto or Meeteetsee." Ben O'Reilly had a drink to all that and enough money in his pocket to plant oats next year.

Abe Harris sat himself down on top of the jockey box of his buckboard and buried his face in his hands. Janille sat patting him on the back asking, "What's wrong, Poppa? Harry won, didn't he?"

Abe was thinking: *a hundred fifty dollars for winning a horse race? Who would have thought it possible?*

No one asked for their money back and Harry Harris was featured on the front page of Caroline Lockhart's newspaper, *The Cody Enterprise*, with a picture that also ran on the front page of *The Greybull Standard*. On July 5 Harry was a Big Horn Basin hero-- not that he wanted to be. He didn't know what to think. He'd never seen that much money in one place in his life.

Afterwards, the Sheriff of Park County thought so little of the horse race that he asked around to see if the horse was stolen. After all, this Tapper horse entered at the very last moment, and all of his drinking friends leaning comfortably against the dark walnut bar at the Irma had just lost a lot of money. They wanted to know "what the hell is goin' on, Harold?" Harold just naturally felt that something evil had happened; he'd lost a hundred dollars, money bet on a sure thing before Tapper even entered the race. All he found out was that no one knew nothin'. "Nobody, Harold, ever seen that damn hoss before." The lingering, unanswered question was "Where'd he come from just like that?"

131

All sorts of things happened to Harry that summer. Harry grew two inches; he raced Tapper in Worland, Thermopolis, Basin City and Greybull; Tapper won walking away. Each time, Tapper's exploits on the race tracks in the Big Horn Basin were recorded front page news. Harry went along for the proverbial ride. Tapper apparently didn't care as long as he finished first. And who knew he was his father's son or even who his father was?

Harry got a job working for the Pitchfork Ranch riding the green out of the rough string for thirty dollars a month, his room, and board. It turned out he was pretty good at that. And for an eighteen-year-old boy doing what came naturally, that was a lot of money.

Chapter 13

The Annual Harvest Box Social was held in Greybull on September 15, 1917 at the Community Hall: a big two-story log building with hardwood floors and multi-paned windows, and a shake shingle roof, pitched high to help the snow slip off in winter. Alejendra's mother wanted her to go and had fixed Alejendra's box lunch with a string of what Miguel called the good stuff: a whole transparent apple pie, the apple slices smothered in brown sugar; deep fried and roasted pheasant (the entire bird); twelve hot tamales wrapped in dried corn husks; and a quart jar of apple juice supplemented with exactly one and one half cups of aged tequila.

"You might find someone you want to impress," her mother said. "You'll be ready. This will do it. I tell you."

Miguel knew who had orchestrated the contents and lamented that Alejendra was his sister *"stupido."* He wished he could legitimately purchase her box lunch, but he knew better. *Mother would kill me for sure*, he acknowledged. Still, he had the thought in mind. Odd as it was to Alejendra, Miguel actually wanted to go to the social. In Greybull everyone liked him, for he'd gone to school there, graduated, knew everyone by their first names, knew their mothers, their fathers, their brothers and their sisters.

Alonso and Miguel were Alejendra's only unmarried siblings. Juan and Tomas were married and had presented their mother with grandchildren. Alonso was in Chicago, but he was coming back. Mother hoped he'd bring "someone" with him. He'd been gone for two years and mother didn't like him being alone. Her father, on the other hand, didn't like him being gone. Mother thought Alonso should be busy making her more grandchildren. That's what she said and she knew what she wanted. In Alonso's absence, she'd turned her attention to Miguel. Certainly something was wrong with Miguel, for he was twenty-three and still unmarried. She said it was "so disgraceful" when anyone asked.

It wasn't as if Alejendra had the only box lunch that gained recognition. Several other girls were known, historically, to pull out all the stops in their box lunch creations. The difference was that Alejendra's mother made hers, and Ruth, Grace, and Mattie created their own. They were no competition for Alejendra's mother when gaining Alejendra suitors was the purpose. It wasn't that Alejendra had "male attention" in mind as the object of the exercise, but her mother did. Alejendra went to the social with Miguel knowing she'd never hear the end of it if she didn't go.

In Alejendra's thinking, guys were okay but so time consuming, so fraught with "don't you like me?" pleas, "come sit with me" requests, and bungled "kissing" on the porch swing--all episodes of awkwardness. Alejendra thought that if you went to a dance, you should dance. A pretty five-foot-seven inch tall girl with long black hair, olive skin, weighing one hundred and twenty-two pounds, slender, full of energy, and a bright smile attracts attention without a box lunch.

She merely has to walk into the room. What more to it was there? The rest was easy; just dance.

The demands of her eleven mares were much different; their adoration was not a cover for wanting something else. Besides, they were so beautiful and she needed a stud horse for them. Of the fifty-six girls and fifty-nine men who went to the box social dance, only Alejendra was thinking about a stud horse for her mares. Only Alejendra had mares, tall, fast, well-conformed and sleek. They were the product of a man who loved his daughter, doted on her, and knew fine horses. She'd raised several from colts, trained them from the time they were tall enough to lead. For Alejendra Rodriguez, they were the reason she got up in the morning, endured Miguel's incessant bantering, paid lip service to her mother's matchmaking efforts, and did the chores before breakfast. Her days always began before first light, long before the sun came up over the Big Horns and settled in the basin below.

Manny Rodriguez may have doted on his only daughter, but he did not shelter her. At round-up she was in the saddle with her brothers and the entire crew, from before sun up until dark. When it was haying time, she ran the stacker, pitched and stacked hay, came in dead tired, worn thin, dirty, hungry and ill-tempered. That was the way of it. That is, for everyone except Miguel. He was always happy, had a running smile, a joke to tell. That was Miguel twenty-four hours a day seven days a week. He never stopped. Alejendra did.

Alejendra loved her brothers, which isn't to say that she understood them. Nothing about them made sense. There was the time that Miguel fell "in love" with Alicia Franklin. She was only five-foot-five, had fine yellow hair, blue eyes, and never ever had grease or dirt under her fingernails. For Alicia, horses were to look at, not ride; she'd rather bat her eyes at Miguel than mark, brand, and castrate yearlings. She loved dresses, couldn't fish, couldn't shoot a skunk stealing eggs from the hen house. What he saw in her was difficult to figure. *Miguel said she could sure kiss. What was that all about? Really!*

Alejendra had heard of Harry Harris. She hadn't seen him and didn't know what he looked like. But more importantly, she had heard that he had a stud horse that was something to see. She also heard he frequented the dances, though he was from the high country west of Meeteetsee and wasn't seen in Greybull much. That's what she heard. Her father had mentioned the Harris stud to her. He'd suggested that she might want to have a look at him for her mares. He said he looked good.

Riding with her brother into Greybull, she was thinking about how she was going to get somewhere west of Meeteetsee. Her brother, on the other hand, was asking her about a girl.

"Alex? Are you listenin' to me? Where's your head?"

"What?"

"I asked you if you know this Karen Colinsky?"

"Karen? You're interested in Karen?"

"She does look fine. I heard she has an eye for me."

"Everybody has an eye for you. The problem is deciding which one."

136

Miguel laughed. "Well, if she's there tonight, I'm goin' to learn all about her." He glanced at his sister. "All right. What's on your mind? If you were any farther away, I'd have to ride all day to get to you."

"*Papá* told me that the Harris stud was something I should have a look at. I was thinking about how I was going to do that."

"Alex, give it a break. There are other things than those mares." He paused. "Do you mean Harry Harris? Is that the Harris?"

"I think that is who *Papá* said. It was something Harris. The Harrises live way west of Meeteesee, up close to the Pitchfork."

"That'd be Harry, all right."

"Do you know him?"

"Everybody knows him."

"Like everybody knows Karen?"

"Easy, Alex. Do you know her?"

Alejendra thought for a moment. "Well, she can ride a horse. I saw her in the Greybull Days parade on a grey mare."

"Geez, Alex, is that all you think of? Horses?"

"What's wrong with that?"

"Nothin'. It's just that you know the color of the horse she was ridin' in a parade. Probably how old it was."

"Six."

"See!"

"I also know she had a crush on that Johnson Teets boy."

"Really?"

"And she likes bitter chocolate, lemon meringue

pie, slow dancing, and that Jay-bird dance thing. She likes to paint her nails fire engine red and she is partial to gingham skirts. She likes white buttons, too. She also thinks it's silly not to kiss on the first date if she likes the guy. She says there's no reason to wait. She said, 'Waiting is silly if you like the guy.' Does that help?"

"Alex?"

"She was in my class, Miguel. I sat right next to her. Oh, and she loves to hold hands between dances 'cause it makes her feel special. Anything else you want to know?"

Miguel smiled at her. "You're somethin', Alex. I'd be careful with that Harry. I haven't seen him much but I've met him. I hear he's more than a handful. Long, tall cow kid. Doesn't really say much. Sort of your type, except I heard he likes himself far too much. I heard he's a fair hand at takin' the starch out of the rough string. I never seen it, but that's what I heard."

"Miguel, I'm not interested in Mr. Harry Harris. I am interested in his stud horse. It's his horse I want to see. I don't really care if he has hair on his chest or not."

"Alejendra, if you want to separate a man from his horse, you have to know the man. He's the first and last piece of the puzzle. Sometimes you don't think."

Surprised at his comment, Alejendra glanced at her brother. "I never thought of that," she said.

"I know. I heard his horse colt is a good one. Tall, fine lines, well-built, really long, maybe fourteen hundred, sixteen hundred pounds. I haven't seen him. I also heard he got him from over the other side of Tensleep on the Buffalo side of the mountain. What I

138

heard was that he and his father were over there huntin' horses, found this mare shot dead with this horse colt standin' over her. Apparently, the mare had no brand so they brought the horse colt home. That's what I heard."

"You hear a lot."

"Not really. I met this guy and that is what he said. Listen, Alex. You know how when you look at a horse standin' in a corral or maybe a field, his head is up; he's watchin' you. Maybe he stamps his foot as you approach; his ears are pointed right at you. The closer you get, the more he's pawin' the ground, movin' sideways a little. He sorta says 'I know who I am but who are you?' He's not really anxious so much as he's defiant. He's sayin' 'you get any closer I'm goin' to kick you to death.' Know the kind?"

"I know. He's telling you you'd better be real careful because he's not liking you much. A real wild one."

"That's right, Alex. And if he wants you out of there, there's no question in his mind why he can't turn you around or kill you. That's the feelin' I get around this guy. It's not somethin' I can put my finger on. I could guess him all wrong. Maybe he just never second guesses himself." Miguel paused, staring at Alejendra. "Listen, just be careful. Sometimes you get so tied up in your horses that you don't look around and you find yourself standin' in horseshit. All 'cause somethin' else has your attention. Know what I mean? Watch yourself."

"Okay, Miguel. I got it. Let's talk about Karen."

Miguel smiled. "Wanna bet I get a kiss tonight?"

"Geez, Miguel, she might not even come to this dance."

Chapter 14

There is something electric about a band tuning up and getting ready to be ready. It commences with the fiddle player running through all the notes that four strings and a bow can develop. Then comes the base fiddle, the drummer, the clarinet; then somehow in the cacophony of sound they get the notes together and from somewhere, somehow, a rhythm begins to develop. After a few minutes, the first fiddle player begins to stomp his left foot, the second joins in, and the three singers begin to hum bar by bar. The lead vocalist steps forward and the first lyrics of "I Dream of Jeannie with the Light Brown Hair" begin to float above the crowd and the night has begun in Greybull, Wyoming. Just as "Jeannie" ends, the three singers inform the crowd there's a "Yellow Rose in Texas." By the third bar, seventh note, everyone has fallen under their spell, enchanted with the music. The hardwood floor fills with swaying dancers, all hoping the night will never end, not for them, not for anyone. After the "Yellow Rose," the "Bunny Hug Rag" is followed by the "Turkey Trot."

"Hello, Ruthie."

"Alex, you're here. It's about time. We were wondering if you were going to show."

"Yes, I am here. *Mamá* would have it no other way."

"Good ol' Mom. Did she do the cooking this

141

evening or do the rest of us have a chance?"

"Couldn't help it, Ruthie. *Mamá* insisted on doing the cooking. I'm sure if she were here, she'd do the dancing, too. She likes to lend a hand."

"So second place is the winner tonight?"

"Depends on the guy. Who's here? Who has lots of money? Who wants to spend it? Who is drinking what? As usual, Ruthie. Anything fun happening?"

"There's the boys from Basin City. There's some that I haven't seen before. Over in the corner by the coat rack are a couple of boys that are kinda interesting. You already taken your box to the stage?"

"Miguel did."

"Ooh, Miguel. Everyone's flame: the heart throb of Greybull."

"Easy, Ruthie. I'll be forced to tell him just who your heart beats for."

"As if it would do any good."

"Never can tell, Ruthie."

"Alex."

Alejendra turned to her brother. "What?"

"He's here."

"Who's here?" Ruthie asked.

"Oh hi, Ruthie. We gonna show them how it's done tonight?"

"Do you know how it's done?"

"You know I do." Miguel turned to his sister. "He's standing with two other fellows. Just came inside the door. Red shirt, double row of buttons, no hat. Well, he isn't wearing it. He's carryin' it. See him?"

"Yes."

"If you're lucky, he rode that stud. He usually

does."

Ruthie glanced in the direction Miguel had pointed. "What are you two talking about?" she asked.

"Alex is looking for a stud horse. Girl," Miguel paused, looking at Ruthie, "shall we? The floor is waiting for you and me."

"Thought you'd never ask."

"I never ask. With you, I beg."

"You gotta work on your lines."

"What do you think I'm doin'?"

Alejendra watched her brother and Ruthie walk onto the dance floor. They were talking animatedly, Ruthie smiling. Both were soon lost from sight in swaying bodies. Alejendra studied the individual that Miguel had described. He was talking to the boy on his left; both laughed. Harry Harris was a head taller than those around him. Broad shoulders. He had his arms folded about his chest, holding his hat. He was clean shaven, wore his hair a little long and combed back over his head. His boots made him a couple of inches taller.

"Alex, it is nice to see you. And as usual, you are stunning."

"Jason," she said, turning to the voice, "you say the nicest things."

"I try," he said. "May I have this dance?"

"You are so lucky," she said, "my dance card is entirely empty."

"Is it luck or did you just get here?" Jason offered her his hand which she took, allowing herself to be led out onto the floor.

"Both," she said. "Miguel and I just got here. And you are lucky. My *papá* says he'd rather be lucky than good, which, according to him, makes you a winner."

They began to slow dance to a tune Alejandra had never heard before. Jason was a good dancer, easy to follow. He had the fresh smell of soap, sage, and pine. His trousers kept their crease. His boots were polished black, matching his belt set off by a white, white shirt. He looked good to her.

"Your hands are calloused. You've been working this summer. I like that. What have you been up to?"

"Same old things," he said. "Cows, horses and timothy hay. That's all I've been doing."

She smiled and they danced through three melodies, chattering about their respective lives.

"Mind if I cut in, Pard?"

Alejandra was surprised. It was the west Meeteetsee boy. And he was tall, very tall. She'd thought about what she might say to him should she chance to meet him, but in a flash that was gone. Before Jason could respond, her mind was a blank.

"I do," Jason said with a smile and Alejandra could tell he meant it. "But I relinquish the lady's hand."

"Jason!" she said amused, suddenly wishing he hadn't been so quick in giving her up.

"Save the last dance for me Alex, please."

"You got it, Jason. The last dance is yours, always." Alejandra turned to look up at a clean-shaven

144

chin and clear hazel eyes.

"Hello," she said. "I am Alex."

"So I heard." He had a drawl but it wasn't southern. It sort of scraped the back of his throat. He, too, smelled like he had just gotten out of a bath tub.

"And you are?"

"Not as formal as you. My name is Harry," he said easily.

"Just Harry? No last name?"

"Pardon me. Harry Harris, Ma'am. I'd like the next dance."

"You're going to make me work for everything, aren't you? Getting information from you is like pulling hens' teeth. You're the Harry Harris fellow with the stud horse. The fellow from Meeteetsee?"

"That'd be me, Ma'am. Folks know more about my horse than they do about me."

"My *papá* told me about you."

"What'd he say?"

"Said you had a stud horse and that I should take a look at him."

"A pretty girl like you needs a stud?"

"I have eleven mares."

"I guess you do. Should we dance?"

The band had started up again. The singer was belting out the verses to "Oh, Susannah." Alejendra smiled and gave him her hand. They danced a fast waltz. Sort of. Harry was hard to follow. It was clear he hadn't done it before, but he tried. Alejendra reminded herself that a lot of guys weren't good dancers and not to be too hard on them.

"Do you know his bloodlines?" she asked.

"No. I know nothing about him other than he's mine. I know that."

"You have a horse that you know nothing about?"

"Yes, Ma'am. I picked him up when I was fifteen. Someone had shot his mother dead. I don't have a clue as to who his pappy might be. His mother didn't look like much, mostly mustang, I'd guess. 'Course she was dead several days when we first saw her. Had to bottle feed Tapper. He was maybe four weeks old. Barely knew how to suck a tit." He paused. "Excuse my language, Ma'am. I don't mean to be vulgar."

"Harry, I know what a tit is. Cows have four. Mares have two. I've seen my share."

"Let's see, a formal girl who is gorgeous, who knows what a cow's tit is, has eleven mares, and wants to find a stud horse--that's quite a combination."

Right there on a dance floor in Greybull, Wyoming, Alejendra Sanchez Rodriquez decided she wanted nothing more to do with Harry Harris. "And you're irritating, Mr. Harris," she said. "As long as you are counting and keeping score, I probably can ride better than you. I probably can shoot the inside circle ten for ten better than you. I'll bet I can rope better than you, stack hay better than you, and carry on a decent conversation better than you. Good evening, Mr. Harris. I don't need to see your horse." Alejendra turned and walked off the dance floor, leaving the boy from Meeteetsee standing alone with a sheepish grin on his face.

"That's a hell of a way to start a relationship," he said aloud, though barely a whisper, still smiling.

146

"And she's sure good looking. Now what do I do?"

If she hadn't promised the last dance to Jason, she'd have left for Crystal Creek that very instant. That fellow, Harry, just plain irritated her. She wanted nothing further to do with him, stud horse or no. Miguel rescued her with a glass of pink punch.

"I'm not sure what's in this," he said to her, "but it might slow your heart down." Ruthie was still with him. That surprised her.

"What did he say to you?" Ruthie asked. "He sure set you off."

"He's just irritating."

"Told you, didn't I?" Miguel said.

"I don't even want to see his horse."

"Well, that horse is another thing. I hear he's a good one."

"He doesn't even know his blood lines."

"He couldn't, Alex. I told you that. They were hunting horses and just picked him up. Carried him clear to Meeteetsee on the back of a saddle horse. Neither his father nor him knows a thing about him. Not a thing."

"Miguel, with my mares? There are already too many unknowns. I don't need to see a horse that no one knows about. I'm not going to use a stud horse that I don't know all there is to know about him."

"Suit yourself, sis."

Alejendra did just that. When it came to blood lines 'care' was the 'watch' word, the 'by' word, and the 'last' word. Exercising it was a must. A person should know who the dam and the sire were and who their dams and sires were. Add to that the muscle and

147

grit standing on the hoof, the latter being just as important. Her father had taught her that. He'd found each of her mares for her. Presently some were three-year-olds; six were coming four. One was six. The rest were coming five. They were a perfect group of brood mares. And they were hers. Two were with foal. They broke the knowledge "know everything" rule. Her father had traded for them while on a trip to northern Montana. Mustang, he'd said. A crap shoot. All her mares were uniform in build, mild in temperament, tall and lank, with intelligent eyes and heads. And they were pets; Alejendra gave each a name and made them gentle to the touch. She had eleven girlfriends who came when she called, ate apples and sugar cubes out of her hand, and thought the world of her. She wasn't taking any chances.

Alejendra excused herself and went outside and found a seat on the porch on a worn and weathered bench. She sat where she could see the street in both directions. It was cooler; the air fresher. Carol waved at her as she walked by. Alejendra returned the gesture and wondered what on earth had gotten into her to dismiss that Meeteetsee boy as she had and in front of everyone. Maybe it was because he was so tall. No, she'd danced with tall boys before. Her interest was in his horse and that interest evaporated with his "I know nothing about him" reply.

Maybe he was trying too hard. He couldn't dance, though he did try. Maybe she didn't have any patience with the "let's get to know each other" ritual. She liked to dispense with all formalities and get right to the main course. She was more into "I like you. You like me. Let's do something." And if it was a dance . . . well, then, let's dance. And for Pete's sake, know how to dance before you ask. I'm not here so you can practice. Find someone else if that's the case. She did not subscribe to "I walk on the bottoms; you walk on the tops." Her feet were too small to have a two hundred pound moron trample all over them while he tried to learn a dance step. If you wanted to impress Alejendra, you'd better know what you were doing.

The band played seven more songs before Walt Lowe, the dance organizer, called everyone to the stage. Alejendra got up and went inside. The band had set down their instruments. A tall slender man, Walt wore a plain, grey jacket and stood on the stage at the east end of the Community Hall. He cleared his throat and, in a high-pitched voice that found every corner and grabbed everyone's attention, began.

"Come hither, come thither, come one and all. It's time to bid on the box lunches. Confections galore. Some good ones we have. Everyone gather. We'll start the auction. Bid one and all, be ye tall, slim, skinny or not so skinny. There's a box lunch for each of you, especially if you have money."

Another fellow, the auctioneer, stood beside Walt. He cleared his throat and started the bidding at ten dollars while Walt held the first box over his head. No one bid. He said, "Let's make everyone a bidder. Do I hear twenty-five cents?" again commencing the auctioneer's babble that no one understood. The first box lunch went for two dollars and thirty cents.

Miguel bid on Ruthie's like his life depended on it but did not win until it reached four dollars and sixty-five cents. Once the auctioneer closed the bidding war, Miguel thrust his arms in the air, threw his head back and let out a victory whoop that echoed through the building. Everyone laughed and cheered. He jumped up on the stage to retrieve the pink ribboned box from Walt, then found the smiling Ruthie in the crowd. Once on the dance floor, he grabbed her by the waist, twirled her around as if he'd won a bull riding event, yelled again, and whirled her out the door, laughing, lunch box under his arm. That single act sent the evening's bidding up a dozen notches. It seemed all the men tried to outdo each other afterwards. The dance charities were well rewarded.

Alejendra's box was sixth from the end and it had a history. Her mother had used that same box over and over again. It was light blue with white polka dots and a white ribbon. Everyone knew whose it was and could readily guess what was in it.

"Five dollars," Jason said as soon as Walt held it above his head.

The crowd awed and wowed, laughed and sighed. For a first bid, that was a lot. From there it went to six and seven, eight and nine before it held on the words, "Going once. Going twice. . . "

"Ten."

Alejendra looked to see who said ten and knew even before she found the voice in the crowd. It occurred to her that the Meeteetse boy probably hadn't said a word all night until right then, not after she'd embarrassed him, leaving him in the middle of the dance floor.

How could he do that after what I've done?

150

"Ten-fifty," Jason volunteered.

"Eleven."

With the last bid it was more than a bidding war, more than just a good cause to finance a dance, a band, drinks, and an evening out. Suddenly bidding mattered. It wasn't as if everyone who was anyone hadn't seen, heard or talked about Alejendra's leaving the Meeteetsee boy standing in the middle of the dance floor, a sheepish grin on his face. Her raised voice had seen to that. Everyone, except maybe the boy from Meeteetsee, knew that Jason was sweet on her and had been since the seventh grade. It wasn't as if everyone didn't know the value of five dollars. Ten dollars was ten days' wages for a thirty a month and found cowhand. Eleven dollars was eleven days of riding the rough string. It wouldn't buy the saddle, but it would come close to buying a decent four-year-old gelding broke to ride, trained to the rein, ever mindful of the rider.

The crowd grew quiet.

"Eleven," the boy from Meeteetsee said, softly repeating himself.

Someone gasped.

Jason shook his head "no." He'd reached his limit. He'd probably reached it when he said five dollars. Few lunches brought more than that even when the bidder was the lover of the lunch maker and someone delightfully wanted to keep them apart, if not for the evening, maybe for thirty minutes. That happened. No one really knew the Meeteetsee boy, but apparently he had money. Whispers abounded. Everyone watched the auctioneer and saw Jason shake

151

his head again when the auctioneer looked at him. Someone offered to lend him a dollar. Another said, "Hey, Jas, I'll lend you two." He smiled. "No," he said and winked at Alejendra. She returned his smile as the auctioneer shouted "sold" and the crowd roared its approval.

Alejendra's stomach turned.

Now what? How's this going to work? What'd I get myself into? What have I done?

The Meeteetsee boy stepped up on the stage to receive the box her mother had prepared. He stopped to thank the auctioneer. Walt was already holding the next box over his head. Alejendra watched Harry walk toward her. He nodded his head as someone congratulated him. He smiled at a comment. His eyes were on her as he approached. With her mother's box under his arm, he touched his hat.

"Ma'am," he said.

It surprised her how sincere he was.

"I am askin' for a second chance at impressin' you. I understand that Alex Rodriguez doesn't give second chances. But I'm askin' for one anyways, seein' how I truly got off on the wrong foot."

His earnest plea made her smile. She wondered how she got that reputation and who had told him about her.

"All right," she said, not sure she had any choice, for he had won her mother's box lunch.

"I thought maybe we could sit on the porch across the street on those steps beside the general store."

"All right," she said again.

"Right this way." Again he deferred to her, opening the door, leading her out of the warm building and across the dirt street. Once across the street, he invited her to sit on the porch steps of the south entrance to the Macon General store. Once she was seated, he set the box beside her.

"Before we get started, I would like to show you somethin', seein' as how third chances are entirely out of the question."

Alejendra stared at him, silently questioning his intent. She was about to tell him he needn't bother, that she'd share her mother's box lunch with him. Certainly she felt guilty, for he'd spent so much. She was going to express her regrets by saying "I'm sorry." Before she could, he'd disappeared into the alleyway. In his absence, she opened the box lunch, took out the tablecloth her mother had provided, and spread it out on the porch. After she smoothed out the cloth, she set out the contents from the box. While doing so, she strengthened her resolve. *I'll apologize but I'm going to get this over quickly,* she told herself. *I'm not leading him on. He's absolutely correct about no third chances. In fact, there was not even a second chance.* Her eating the box lunch with him was a mere illusion that arose from the Meeteetsee boy winning the bid for the box associated with her. This encounter would soon be over.

When she looked up, Harry Harris was standing in the street in front of her but he was not looking at her. Standing beside him was a horse. He stood seventeen hands at the withers. Every muscle defined and rippled as he turned to look at the Meeteetsee boy. He was young, maybe a three-year-old.

153

He held his head high as if he were staring right at her, then turned to Harry Harris and seemed to ask "Who is this girl and why are we bothering?" From tail to cannon bone, he was magnificent. With no effort, the horse took her breath away. If his mother was a mustang, he hid it. Alejendra rose to her feet.

"Thought you'd like to look at the horse you didn't want to see."

"You have a beautiful horse."

"Thank you, Ma'am. Tapper seems to think so himself."

"How old is he?"

"I believe he is three, going on four. I was fifteen when I brought him home. He'd just been born from the looks of him."

"So, you are eighteen?"

"Yes, eighteen, Ma'am."

"You don't have to 'ma'am' me. We're the same age. Harry, you'd better sit down and eat. I'd be careful with the apple drink. *Mamá* put a little tequila in it. It might knock your socks off, if you know what I mean."

"Ma'am."

"I said you don't--"

"I know what you said, but I've been knocked out of the ring once this evening, so I best be on my best behavior."

"Oh, I'm sorry. I didn't mean to hurt your feelings. I was out of sorts."

"You being sorry, I expect don't change things, Ma'am."

"I expect not," Alejendra said in agreement.

"Probably not at all. Out of curiosity, how much would you charge for your horse to service my mares? If I were to change my mind."

"I don't rightly know."

"You don't know? What do you know?"

"I'm skatin' on thin ice, Ma'am. I know that. And I don't know how to skate."

Alejendra smiled. "Well, you best come sit down and eat. Here, take this." She handed him a tamale.

"What is it?"

"It's a tamale."

"A tamale?"

"Yes, unwrap it. Take it out of the corn husk and pop it into your mouth. I'm surprised you haven't heard of a tamale."

"Don't get around much, Ma'am." He took the tamale from her, unwrapped it, and took a bite. "These things are pretty good. Got a little bite to 'em."

"*Mamá* thought you'd like them. She put twelve in there in case you found you couldn't live without them. There's some deep fried pheasant too, an apple pie, and some apple juice laced with tequila. As I said, that drink will stand you on your ear if you don't go easy on it. I assure you, not many can stand at all after they've spent the afternoon sipping on it."

"Yes, Ma'am. How 'bout you? You gonna eat? I don't want to hog all these vittles. Your mother sure is some cook. First, I need to get someone. Someone I want you to meet." He stood up. "Hope you don't mind." He handed her the reins.

Alejendra didn't answer him. Instead. she was

155

staring at the man's horse. Across the street the band was tuning their instruments. She remembered her promise to Jason: the last dance.

Her thoughts were interrupted when he returned.

"Ma'am, I mean, Alex, I'd like you to meet someone." Harry turned to the girl standing behind him. "Janille, come here. Alex, this is my kid sister, Janille. Janille, this is Alex." Harry turned to his sister. "Stay here, sis, while I take care of Tapper. Be just a minute." He glanced at Alejendra. "Hope you don't mind."

Alejendra stood up and offered the younger girl her hand. "Pleased to meet you. I'm Alejendra--my real name, the one my *papá* uses when he wants to yell at me for not feeding the pigs. Come sit with us. Are you having fun?"

"Oh no. I couldn't. Sit with you, I mean. I don't want to mess things up. Harry is tryin' to impress you and I don't want to mess things up. Really. He'll kill me."

Alejendra smiled at the younger girl. "Don't you worry," she said, "he can do messing up all by himself. So far he's doing a real good job. No. You sit with us. There is enough to eat for a crowd. Stay away from the juice, though. It isn't for fun."

"Oh, really!"

"My *mamá* likes to mix tequila with apple juice. She thinks men will be more interested in me if they're drunk. I told your brother to go easy on it 'cause it will stand him on his ear."

"Thanks for the warning. You lookin' at Harry's horse?"

"I was. He's something."

156

"Everybody wants to look at Harry's horse."

"Really?"

"Yeah, really. He's somethin'. He can run, you know. We didn't always know that. We went to Cody on the Fourth. Couple of months ago. This drunk, Mr. O'Reilly--I guess he ain't a drunk, not really--anyway, he gets everyone to pitch in the entry money and Harry ran Tapper in a real horse race. He won by a mile. I mean he won like no one else was runnin'. Know what I mean? Made everyone just furious. Just furious. Said he was a ringer. I didn't know exactly what a ringer was because he's just a horse Papa and Harry found on the mountain, but they were yellin' at Harry like he was some sort of impostor or somethin'. It was crazy. Tapper, he just stands there eatin' grass and watchin' these crazy people. Didn't know he was so famous."

"That's some story."

"We made a hundred fifty dollars. Harry gave it to Papa. I got some new shoes." Janille glanced at her feet, then smiled at Alejendra.

"They're nice, Janille. They look real expensive."

"Thanks. They are. Better than my clunkers to dance in. 'Course I ain't danced."

"You came clear from Meeteetsee to this dance and you haven't danced?"

"Yeah. Harry brought me. Said I should get out. Papa wasn't too excited. Said I was far too young to get out. This is my very first time. I'm sorta nervous."

"Harry's first time, too?"

"Pretty much. He gets out more than me 'cause of that horse. Folks invite him and all."

157

"How old are you?"

"Fifteen."

"So young. You look a lot older. So pretty. And you haven't danced? That doesn't make any sense at all."

"I'm sorta hidin'. Harry said I gotta stop hidin' and have some fun. But it's sorta scary, you know what I mean? Dancin' with a guy and all. I'm not sure I can."

"Did you bring a box lunch? Am I keeping you from some lucky boy?"

"No. Meeteetsee is far. And I don't cook much. There's just Harry and my papa. Can you imagine putting flap jacks and fried eggs in a box lunch? I don't think so. You know what I mean? They don't taste good fresh-cooked. Imagine 'em three days old and growin' mold."

Alejendra smiled. "I don't cook either, Janille" she said.

Both girls looked up when Harry returned.

Janille immediately stood up. "I gotta go," she said to Alejendra.

"No, you don't. You sit down and have something to eat. There is plenty. I insist. I really insist. Besides, Harry paid an arm and a leg for this picnic. Somebody ought to enjoy it. So sit down."

"Really?" Janille glanced at her brother, hesitating.

"Yes, really," Alejendra answered. "Harry and I aren't fixing to rob a bank or get all tangled up sitting here on the porch of the General Store. We don't know each other well enough to giggle. You sit down and eat something."

"I--"

"Harry, tell your sister to sit and eat. Besides, a girl this good looking--you need to keep your eye on her."

Janille looked at Alejendra, still unsure. "Thanks," she said, "for sayin' such nice things."

"Harry?" Alejendra said, looking at him.

Harry smiled. "Janille, please sit down."

"Why does he need to keep an eye on me?" Janille asked Alejendra.

"That's what brothers do. Right now my brother is across the street flirting with Ruthie, probably putting his best moves on her. But really, he's watching me. Making sure I'm all right. It's just what they do."

Harry laughed. "Really?" he said.

"Will he come over here?" Janille asked.

"Probably. Miguel never minds his own business."

"Do you want him to?"

"Of course not. But he won't listen and so I don't bother telling him."

Janille sat down on the edge of the third step. "Okay," she said, "but I don't need nobody watchin' me. You do that, Harry, and I'm gone. Hear me, Harry? Gone."

Harry smiled at her and picked up a piece of deep-fried pheasant.

They finished eating, sometimes talking, sometimes not. Alejendra noted that Harry tended not to talk while he was busy eating. His sister, on the other hand, talked a lot, remarking on the tenderness of deep-fried pheasant, tangy tamales, and how pleasant it was

159

that late summer evening.

Alejendra never mentioned the horse. Finally she said, "Let's put these things away and go inside."

She glanced up at Harry. "Do you want me to put the leftovers in a sack? *Mamá* sent one in case whoever won wanted to do that. She knew there would be lots of leftovers."

"That'd be great," Janille said. "Wouldn't that be great, Harry?"

"Your mother is very thoughtful," Harry said.

"The band has started playing."

Alejendra looked at Janille. "I want you to meet someone."

"You do? I'm not so sure."

"Oh, come on." Alejendra grabbed her arm. "Meeting someone won't kill you."

With Harry trailing behind, his hat in hand, they walked across the dirt road and up the steps to the Community Hall. Alejendra sought out Jason, finding him on the long wraparound porch talking with three other fellows and some girls.

"Jason. Jason, would you come here? Please?" Alejendra said.

He immediately disengaged himself from the group.

"Jason. This is Janille. This is her very first dance. She's fifteen. She has new shoes and she doesn't know a soul. So far she's been hiding her pretty smile in the corner under her big brother's hat. If you can believe that. Would you--?"

"I'd love to," Jason said, smiling at Janille.

"Thanks."

"Oh wow," Janille said. "I mean . . . " Janille glanced at Alejendra. "And he's handsome, too."

"Oh, he is that. And he has a big head. And I've promised him the last three dances. So, please wear your new shoes out and Jason, too."

Jason already had her by the elbow, steering her towards the dance floor, Janille looking back over her shoulder at Alejendra. "Thank you," she mouthed.

Alejendra looked up at the tall cowboy standing beside her. She thought, *Let's get this over with and how do I talk this tall drink of water out of his stud horse for a couple of months without leading him on? Men are so impossible. Maybe he will separate himself from his horse for a pat on the hand, a smile, someone to dance with his sister, and five dollars a mare. Something like that would be nice and the price not too high.*

She said, "Well, Harry, let's dance. My card is full, so we better do it now."

He was staring at her. "Thanks," he said. "Thanks so very much. Janille, she--"

"I know. She's your kid sister and you love her so very much. I've heard it before. I have four brothers and they are all crazy. I can't sneeze without one of them handing me a handkerchief. Should we dance?"

"Sure, but I ain't too good at it."

"I know that but you do have a nice looking stud horse."

"And that's supposed to make up for my clumsy feet?"

"It does. It surely does," she said, thinking *this boy isn't so much. I can do this, big feet and all. It's all*

161

about separating a man from his horse.

"One question, if you don't mind."

"What's that?"

"If you were to have your stud service my mares, what would you charge me?"

"You? Very little."

Alejendra looked up at him, giving him her hand, expecting Harry to lead her onto the dance floor. He took it.

"Please, Harry, I have eleven mares. Some are already pregnant but the others aren't. You have a stud horse. If my father approves of him, I would be willing to pay for his services. How much would you charge me?"

Harry Harris smiled at her. "Well," he said, "how 'bout some of those tamales? I liked them plenty."

"Harry, I'm serious."

He stared at her momentarily. "I am serious," he said.

Alejendra Rodriguez tightened her lips. He made her so angry. They danced the next three dances in silence. Finally, she said, "When you are serious, when you do want to talk about my mares, please get hold of me."

He nodded and smiled. "All right," he said. "You're not taking me serious are you, about those tamales?"

"Harry, you're just a pain. Did you know that?"

"I didn't," he replied.

It was after midnight when she shared the last dance with Jason.

Chapter 15

Janille was trying to keep up with her brother, but her saddle horse was shorter and he kept lowering his head to crop grass, setting her farther behind. They were riding home from Greybull. She said, "I hate the ride back. It takes so long. Meeteetsee is so far. Makes me question whether I should'a come."

"Thought you had fun. "

"Oh, fun. I did. I did have fun. That Jason, he's some character, and he knows everyone, everybody, and he can dance. He can really dance." She smiled to herself, thinking about it.

Janille and her brother had been riding up the Greybull River for most of the morning. The cottonwoods were yellow, having been bitten by the first frost a week before. Skunk brush, currant bushes, and wild roses were red, the grass brown, the sky a pale blue, the air dry and drifting in a breeze.

"He likes the same girl you've taken a shine to. I think he knows her better than you." Janille smiled.

"He should. They went to school together."

"He got her box lunch last year, you know."

"I didn't."

"She'd left work gloves in the box. By accident, of course. But they were in the box lunch, all sweaty and torn, worn around the fingers."

"How do you know that?"

"Jason. He told me."

"Work gloves, huh?"

163

"Yeah. Says something about her, don't you think?"

Harry stared at his sister. "What? You read a lot into nothin'. Probably didn't have a place to put 'em, so she dropped 'em in there and forgot about it. Gloves don't mean nothin'."

"Yeah. Maybe so. But a normal person doesn't put their work gloves in a box lunch that someone else is gonna buy at some dance. Not with the food. You just don't do that. I think it says she doesn't care that much. Maybe she's got other stuff on her mind she thinks more important. The gloves do say she knows how to work; that maybe she likes workin'. Maybe she likes that about herself."

"Maybe. She is hard to take your eyes off of."

"Not for me. I can take my eyes off her plenty easy."

"You know what I mean."

Janille laughed. "I do. I was just teasin' you. Like you're some old stick in the mud. She's way outta your reach."

"You're just as pretty, sis. Notice that after you started dancin' you never stopped the rest of the evenin'. Told you, didn't I?"

"You did. Thanks, Harry. That was a nice thing to say. Really."

"I only said it 'cause it's true."

"You're just my brother. What do you know?"

"I know a pretty girl when I see one. So does everyone else. Those guys last night liked to break their necks gettin' another look at you."

Janille laughed. "Really?"

"Yeah, really."

"Wow! Thanks. Alejendra is good lookin', if you're wonderin'. I'm not sure Jason likes her like you like her."

"What's that supposed to mean?"

"He likes her 'cause she can really dance; that she doesn't take herself half serious. She ain't got time for silliness. Know what I mean? He says you gotta be right up front with her or hold your horses in. You're gettin' nowheres. That's what he says. Gotta say what you want. He says she ain't got time for holdin' hands and blinkin' eyes at some guy. If she wants your attention, she'll ask, and if she doesn't, she'll tell you. She's plenty hard, you don't know what you're doin'. I suspect you don't--not the way she talked to you right out there on the dance floor, everyone a-watchin'. That was awful. Embarassin'. Jason says you oughta just dump her on her head. Look for someone else to be sweet on. Said it would be easier and more fun."

"Yeah, well, he would."

"Not what you think. He's sweet on Karen. Did you know that? She told me. Said they've been holdin' hands and kissin' when nobody was watchin'. Bet you didn't know that, did you?" Janille glanced at her brother, "That's 'cause you ain't watchin'. Got your head all wrapped up in that Alejendra." Janille paused, thinking. "She is nice. I gotta say that. She introduced me to Jason. I mean, she didn't have to do that. How did you get all sweet on her, anyways? It's not like she was hangin' around or nothin'. I didn't even know you knew her and of a sudden you spent a bag of gold on her box lunch. Now that made a statement. Especially after she gave you what for. Never wantin' to see you again. Everyone was talkin'. Mostly everyone thought you were an idiot for puttin' up with her."

"I saw her once before. Bet she doesn't remember." Harry nudged Tapper through the tall grass of the river bottom, turning in the saddle. The horse stopped to crop dried grass. "I was an idiot," he said, "a certifiable, died in the wool, full-fledged, idiot."

"What did you do?"

"Nothin'. Didn't even speak to her."

"Where was that?"

"Greybull. In that store we were in front of last night. She walked by me with an older lady. Probably her mom. I just stood there starin'. Haven't got her out of my head since. Didn't want to. Maybe I should."

"Love by lookin'." Janille paused, urging her horse forward, trying to keep up with the longer legged Tapper. "Well, you're gonna have to do somethin' or forget it," she said.

"I know. I know."

"What are you thinkin'?"

"I got a horse."

Janille looked at him. "Yeah, you do," she said. "You ever even kiss a girl? I mean ever?"

"No, I ain't."

"Well, ain't this gonna be interestin'? Who do you think will get the first kiss? You or that horse? I'm bettin' on the horse."

"Yeah, me, too," Harry replied.

"I'm bettin' he gets the only kiss."

"You ain't no help."

Chapter 16

The Greybull streets were dusty from the trailherds' rambling trek down Main Street to the stockyards and to the auction barn on the north end. The dust made it difficult for the old folks sitting on their green and white verandas to breathe. Inevitably, the dust settled, leaving a skiff on their lemonade, and trouble in their sinuses. The City Fathers, in response to the complaints of its citizens, had passed an ordinance that directed the cattlemen to bring their cows across the flats west of the tracks. It didn't do any good. They brought them down Main Street anyway. The cattle trailed from the east basin used the bridge to cross the Big Horn River and didn't have much choice.

It was the age old issue of which came first: the chicken or the egg. And the cattlemen, for a few weeks in the fall, ignored the ordinance, claiming their cattle took priority. The railroad interest claimed that Greybull, first and foremost, was a railroad town. It was there that the Chicago, Burlington, and Quincy had built its huge repair shops and round table for the service of its massive locomotives. That facility was located up against the hill on the west side. The cattlemen, however, insisted that they were the reason there was a railroad in the first place. The railroad employed nearly everyone who worked in Greybull. If it didn't employ them, the remaining residents serviced those that were so employed, as electricians, plumbers, barbers, store clerks, mercantile and sundries store owners, and hotel people. Even the saloons and bars were supported by the railroad.

The cattlemen, however, were there first, commencing in 1878, when Henry Clay Lovell drove twelve thousand head into the Big Horn Basin. In 1880 another twelve thousand followed. After the ML broke up, the smaller cattlemen who replaced Hank Lovell and Tony Mason, reiterated this statement year after year, bringing the herds to market in Greybull to ride in the cattle cars of the Chicago, Burlington, and Quincy clear to Omaha, Nebraska and Chicago, Illinois.

The Rodriquez clan came to town with their herd of yearling steers and heifers, old cows, old bulls and cripples in the fall of the year, crossing the Main Street bridge, turning and driving the herd north up Third Street to the auction yards. It was the third weekend in September, Saturday the twenty-second, and the streets were dusty and crowded. The bars and saloons were full of patrons; the stores were busy with customers. The auction yards were full of Rodriquez cattle. It was also the day that Abe Harris and six of his neighbors trailed their herd of yearlings from Meeteesee, Wyoming. The auction corrals were bursting at the seams and the cattle cars were lined up for two miles on the side tracks waiting to be loaded.

Harry Harris rode point, bringing the cattle down off the ridge south of the town of Greybull. They'd followed the Greybull River ninety miles from west of Meeteetsee near Franc's Peak before reaching their destination. It had taken the better part of five days. He'd ridden point since he was thirteen years old and each year thereafter, bringing the herd safely into

168

the corrals at the end of Seventh Street past the railroad barns and switching yard.

It was at the corner of Main Street and Seventh that Alejendra saw him riding the stud horse pushing the first thirty head, giving the other weary steers a lead to follow down the street. He was moving them quickly so that the others wouldn't get any ideas and wander off down a side street to stand contentedly on someone's new mowed lawn. Amidst the cacophony of bawling livestock, Alejendra yelled across the street.

"Harry! Harry, when you're through, I'd like my father to look at your stud. Would that be all right?"

The boy touched his hat and rode on, pushing the leads a little faster. Behind him came the main herd, some running, some walking, all hungry and scared. The saloon keeper down the street was glad to see the trail herd as well as the dust and confusion it brought to the small town. Tonight would be a good night for Greybull business men. There would be bar tabs, grocery lists needing to be filled, hotel rooms filled until the "no-vacancy" signs were hung, an overflowing dance hall, as well as money left on the tables at the gambling halls and back rooms of the saloons and liquor emporiums.

A little over an hour later, Harry Harris returned. Alejendra was waiting.

"Thanks, Harry," she said. "I'll get my *papá*. Please wait."

Harry nodded and stepped down from the chestnut stud, stretching, watching Alejendra disappear into Smithie's Mercantile. She found her father, waited while he finished speaking with her mother before interrupting.

She said, "*Papá*, I want to show you the Harris horse--the one you told me about? He's here. He and Harry Harris are out in the street. I asked him to wait so that you could take a look and tell me what you think. Would you come, please? It will only take a minute."

Manny Rodriquez smiled to himself and followed his daughter outside Smithie's onto the boardwalk. The streets were crowded for it was Saturday but it wasn't too crowded for a horse and an eighteen-year-old boy. Harry Harris, however, was of secondary importance to the horse that Manny had been summoned by his daughter to see and judge. Judging horse flesh was not something he took lightly. It was something that he'd learned from those who knew horses. He was very good at it.

"*Papá*, this is Harry Harris. He's the fellow with the horse I was telling you about. And this is Tapper."

Harry dropped the reins and climbed onto the boardwalk, extending his hand.

"Mr. Rodriguez, pleased to meet you."

"Harry."

Pointing at his horse standing in the street, he said, "Here he is, Mr. Rodriguez. See what you think."

It was then that Manny Rodriguez did what he did best. He took a look at a horse. Without another word he stepped into the street and walked away from his daughter, Harry, and Tapper. Turning, he looked at the balance of the animal; how he fit together; seeing heart, girth, hip, neck, shoulder, back and topline. He noted that the horse had the characteristics of a

170

thoroughbred, but not entirely. So he decided to judge the horse as a thoroughbred. It was a place to start.

Stepping farther into the street where he was almost run over by a couple in a black buggy, he viewed the horse from all sides, walking in a wide circle, pausing, paying attention to feet and legs. Mechanically, he ran through his mental checklist. He calculated muscle volume in the chest, shoulder, loin, stifle and gaskin, noting the smooth long muscles, judging him exceptionally high. He looked for a smooth, short coat and good sized feet: not large, not small, but sufficient to carry the horse without difficulty. He looked at the defining characteristics of a stud: muscle, eye, and a well-formed, intelligent head.

Mentally, he reviewed what he knew of thoroughbreds. Most were around sixteen hands. This one exceeded that; he was seventeen. Most weighed somewhere around a thousand pounds. This one weighed thirteen hundred easily, probably sixteen. Most had long smooth muscles; they were defined by the word "long." This one had fine bones, thin skin, and looked graceful just standing in the street. He had a very deep girth with the hind quarters of a quarter horse. There was nothing thin about his hooves, something Manny guessed he owed to his mother who was probably a mustang.

He watched as the horse shook himself, blowing his nose, stamping his front hoof impatiently. Again reviewing, he noted: the long body: hind legs, long: nose a tad longer than he would have liked: neck, long and graceful: withers, well defined: chest, narrow and muscular. Perfect. The horse again shook himself, blowing his nose impatiently; the second time inside a minute. He was impatient. His neck muscles rippled as he turned his head. Tapper looked right at him, his eyes alert as he seemed to study Manny.

"Harry," Manny said, "would you ride your horse up and down the street for me? Please?"

"Sure."

The boy didn't bother with stirrups; he simply grabbed the horn and swung himself up into the saddle, sitting gracefully. Manny noted that Harry talked to the horse, guiding him more with his knees and legs than with any part of his body. *This horse is smart*, Manny thought, *and he is quick.* He remembered Henry Williams advising him to stop overcorrecting his horse because "he is smarter than you." He had said, "Let him be a horse, Manny. Life will be easier." Manny had been seventeen. This was just such a horse.

He watched closely as the horse came at him at a trot, watched him turn and come back, responding easily to the touch of the rein on his neck. Manny smiled to himself. *Quick feet*, he thought. *Quick feet that allowed him to spin on a dime and give you change.* Manny nodded his approval. Manny had spent five minutes. He climbed up on the boardwalk and stood beside his daughter, nodding his head, thinking.

Alejendra said, "*Papá*, remember that Harry doesn't know anything about his lineage. Tell me what you think. Is he good enough for my mares? Should I find another? I'm thinking I should."

"Alex, look at the horse: you'll know his lineage. That is not always so. Some have hidden traits that will surprise you or send you to drinking. But this one wears who he is out in the open. You pretty much see what you get with this one."

Harry had dismounted, listening.

"Alex, look at his length. This horse is thoroughbred, part mustang."

"Is that good, *Papá*?"

Harry had dropped the reins and climbed up onto the boardwalk.

"Nice horse, Harry," Manny said.

"Thank you, sir. What do you think of him as a stud? Is he okay?"

"Interesting word 'okay.' As I was telling Alex, your horse is part thoroughbred and the other part mustang. That lineage appears to work for him. Is he as fast as he looks?"

"He can get out of his own way, sir."

"I heard that."

"Can he follow a cow? That is what you use him for, is it not?"

"Better than me. Sometimes he nearly jerks me out of the saddle, he reacts so fast."

"Your mares, Alex, are mostly quarterhorse. This one is not that, but he is all horse. Personally, I do not think you can go wrong with him. Having said that, I am going to find your mother before she decides I am lost and comes looking for me. Harry, it was nice to meet you. That is a nice stud horse. Has he produced any foals yet?"

"Not that I know of, sir."

"It will be interesting to see what he does produce. Are you going to put him out at stud?"

"Yes, sir. Maybe. I guess so. If the price is

right."

Manny nodded and went inside the store.

"Your father, he don't mess around, does he? He judged that horse in like a minute."

"No. Not really. My father is very good when it comes to looking at a horse. Have you decided what you will charge for your stud to service my mares? I have eleven. Two of them are pregnant--so nine."

"Wow, you have eleven mares? I thought you were kidding."

"I wasn't."

"I can see that." He paused and smiled a wry smile. "You didn't want to take me up on my tamales offer?"

"No, of course not. This is business, Harry. I know you were teasing. I know you weren't serious."

"You didn't think I was serious?"

"No. Not really. I thought you were just talking to hear yourself." Alejendra immediately regretted having said that. "I'm sorry," she said. "I didn't mean to be so rude."

Harry paused, studying Alejendra. "Six dozen tamales," he said. "That's the price."

Harry stepped out into the street, glancing at Alejendra standing on the boardwalk, her hands on her hips. She wasn't smiling.

"Be serious," she said to him.

Harry stepped up into the saddle, reining the horse around, holding him in. For a moment he stared at the eighteen-year-old girl before responding, then touching the brim of his hat, he said, "I am serious. Let

174

me know." Clucking to his horse, he moved down the street. The horse's hooves sent up puffs of dust as they stepped forward at a trot.

Moments later Miguel appeared at her side. To her surprise, Ruthie was with him. She smiled. Alejendra noticed they were holding hands, their fingers entertwined.

"Alex, where is *Papá*? I need to talk to him."

Alejendra stared at her brother. "Men," she said, "they have horse turds for brains. I do not understand them at all. They are so . . . so juvenile. It is ridiculous."

Miguel stared at her, hesitating. "Something go wrong, Alex?" he asked.

"I asked that Harry Harris how much he wanted for his stud to service my mares. Do you know what he said?"

Both Miguel and Ruthie shook their heads.

"Six dozen tamales. That's what he said. Six dozen tamales. Six dozen. I would pay him money but he wants tamales."

Miguel and Ruthie started laughing.

When they stopped, Miguel said, "You've got to be kidding. Six dozen? That's cheap."

Ruthie shook her head. "This isn't about tamales, Alex, or horses. This is about you."

"Me! This has nothing to do with me. I told him I wanted nothing to do with him that way. No. This is about having rocks for brains and wanting to prove that he wasn't kidding. He's just being stubborn. He thinks he's cute. He wants to prove to me he's serious."

"You've got that right," Miguel said. "He wants

you to take him serious. Ruthie's right, though. So what are you going to do?"

"What can I do? I am going to continue looking for a stud. Harris doesn't want to give me a price. Probably because I'm a girl."

"You're right, Alex," Ruthie said. "It is because you are a girl. Take him up on it. That's what I'd do."

"No. I won't give him the satisfaction," Alejendra declared. She looked at Miguel. "*Papá*--he's in there with *Mamá*." She pointed to the Mercantile doors. "She's looking at shoes. What do you want with him?"

"The word is your boy is going to ride Steamboat Two. That horse has thrown everyone that's tried. The Ralley boys have him down at the stockyards. The bet is eight to one that he can't do it."

"My boy?"

"Yeah, Harry Harris is climbing on board this evening at six. I have five dollars on him making the ride to a standstill."

"Five dollars? Are you nuts? You're throwing your money down a gopher hole. What's wrong with you? See what I mean? You're all crazy."

"Tobie Keefer bet the Double X boys that Harry would ride Two to a standstill. Keefer told them to put up or shut up and put down two dollars. The rest of those Keefer riders put up fifty dollars total. Keefer promised to have Harris at the stockyards at six tonight."

"He won't do it. He's stubborn."

"No, he'll do it. Geez, Alex, cut your boy some slack. If he stays on for five seconds, he'll have stayed longer than anyone else ever has. If he rides that horse I'll make forty dollars."

"He's not my boy."

Both Ruthie and Miguel smiled. "We'll see, Alex," her brother said.

"There's nothing to see," she said, following the pair inside.

What a pair of fruitcakes.

"*Papá*," Miguel yelled when he located his father. "*Papá*, oh, excuse me. *Papá*, this is Ruthie. Ruthie, this is my father, Manny Rodriguez. That's my mother, Raquel, trying on shoes."

Manny nodded, but his mother got up, one shoe on and one shoe off and hobbled over to where Miguel and Ruthie were standing. "I am pleased to meet you, Ruthie," his mother said. "Are you from here? Miguel never tells me about his friends."

"Yes, Ma'am. My dad works for Chicago Burlington. He's a mechanic on steam engines."

"*Papá*, Harry Harris is going to ride Steamboat Two at six this evening over at the stockyards. I have five dollars on Harris at eight to one."

"Five dollars?" Manny said, suddenly interested, a smile on his face. "That horse is a mean one. He hasn't been rode. Harry Harris? Isn't that Alejendra's boy?"

Miguel and Ruthie started laughing.

"*Papá*, he's not my boy. I don't have a boy."

"He decide on how much he'll charge for his stud?"

"No, he didn't, *Papá*," Alex said.

Miguel laughed. "Alex, tell the truth. He wants

177

six dozen tamales, *Papá*."

"Six dozen?" Manny chuckled. "*Mamá*," he said, "that Harris boy wants six dozen of your tamales for his stud to service Alex's mares. Apparently he likes them."

"What? Six dozen. Oh my. Who is this boy?"

"*Mamá*, he was only kidding. He wasn't serious." Alejendra stood with her hands on her hips, glaring at Miguel.

"Oh really?" her mother said. "He liked them."

"Yes, *Mamá*, really, and he wasn't serious."

There are events and there are events. Riding a rogue horse that has never been ridden--that is an event. At five in the afternoon the only person in the Big Horn Bar was the bartender. He followed the last patron out and locked the door. In the window he left a sign that read, "GONE TO THE RODEO." That is all it said but everyone knew what it didn't say: He was at the Auction Yards; he was going to be there at six in the evening until he got back. He was betting on the horse. Most everyone was betting on Steamboat Two for he had never been ridden. It was a sure thing, akin to stealing rock candy from a two-year-old child. Nothing could be easier.

To facilitate a huge crowd, the Ralley twins had Steamboat Two in the clearing north of the Auction Bar standing peacefully with a sack over his head. The Bar X crew was keeping the crowd back as far as they could, but that wasn't far. There were folks from as far away as Seattle standing waiting to see Steamboat Two throw another rider. The passenger train for the

Chicago, Burlington & Quincy was standing at the station, going nowhere. The fireman had drawn the short straw so he was minding the engine, keeping the fires in the boiler hot. Everyone else, including the passengers, was at the clearing behind the stockyards.

Even the post office was closed and had been for two hours. A government "holiday" had been declared. A dangerous situation had been discovered behind the mail sorting bins forcing the postmaster to lock down the post office pending a thorough inspection of the mail sacks just received from Billings, Montana. Later, it was discovered that Granny Wilcox's letter contained contraband and had to be burned. Ironically, on being questioned by the Postal Police, Granny didn't even know she had written a letter. The police were forced to let her go with a severe warning because they were unable to prove that she had. The evidence had been destroyed by the postal employees to protect the citizens of Greybull.

Alejendra watched from the top rail of the north fence. Next to her were Miguel, Ruthie, and her mother. She watched as three cowboys walked toward the horse. The middle one was Harry. He carried his hat, the wind blowing his brown hair back across his face. The rider on the left was Tobie Keefer. To her surprise, the cowboy on the right of Harry was her own father.

"Miguel, is that *Papá*?"

"What?" Miguel was standing up on the rail.

Her father had Harry's ear. He was talking with his hands, explaining something. Harry nodded. Manny shook Harry's hand. She thought he must have wished him good luck. She watched as Harry checked the bridle, the cinch. Afterwards, he spoke briefly with Tobie, then Harry mounted the outlaw, pulling his hat hard down around his ears. He set himself in the saddle before taking the single rein from Tobie. The horse didn't even stir. She watched Harry nod his head, his hat rocking back and forth as he indicated he was ready. At the signal, one of the Talley boys released the mustang's ears while the other pulled the blind from his eyes.

Steamboat Two turned his head slightly, eyeing the rider, feeling the looseness of the rein, the weight of the saddle. As if on cue, he arched his back, brought his head down, and kicked out with his hind feet; the saddle popped like a cork. That was the first time Harry Harris came within a millisecond of losing it.

Harry, keeping his eye on the outlaw's head, leaned back, jabbing his spurs into the bronc's shoulders. The mustang went ballistic. Its scream of anger could be heard down Seventh Street. The fireman turned to look out the window of the idling engine. Old lady McGuire came to the door of her two-story house and looked outside. Finding nothing, she returned to what she was doing, folding towels.

The horse sunfished, his belly perpendicular to the hardpack. Coming to the ground, he lit on all fours, jarring the rider to his very core. He started to run, crow hopping. The crowd receded, running for their lives. He went up high, squealing, kicking; a roar of anguish erupted from his tortured lungs. That was just the beginning.

Harry had committed himself to riding the horse to a standstill. A standstill is a lot longer then the customary ten seconds. Over the course of seven long, fateful minutes, Harry did just that, keeping himself balanced in the cat bird seat, holding onto the saddle horn with one hand and the rein with the other. Several times he was within a double split second of being tossed into the blue October sky. But he somehow maintained his balance, keeping his legs straight, his feet in the stirrups, enduring jarring re-entry over and over again. His head snapped. At times he leaned back so far he could feel the horse's hind end on the back of his head. That was when Steamboat was practically vertical, his head between his front legs and his hind end a blur of flexing muscle.

The outlaw came to a standstill, his head down, his entire body pooped, so spent he could hardly move from sheer exhaustion. He may have come to a standstill, but he wasn't quitting. His eyes still danced with fire; it was as if he was preparing for a final exertion, about ready to blow himself up in one final storm of hurricane proportions. He would have, too, except riders came up on each side of Harry, one taking the rein from Harry as he climbed over the horse's rump, jumping to the ground, walking toward the auction corrals and loading chutes.

The crowd was dead silent, then erupted with a roar of approval. They'd just watched two champions going at each other, fighting one another, sparring like hungry mountain cats with all they had. People surrounded Harry, crowding him as though he'd just won the election for President, as if he was Teddy Roosevelt or someone important. Among them were several winners, a lot of losers, and yet, no one was a

181

loser, every spectator forever enhanced by what they'd just witnessed in the yard of the auction barn in Greybull, Wyoming.

The post office did not reopen that day. The train did get started, but was an hour and forty-five minutes late in reaching Casper. No one could figure out why. The record books show it was on time except for the last fifteen miles. Something must have happened: maybe a broken rail, a hot box, a malfunction in the steam lines of the locomotive. It was never explained. The log book indicated a mechanical malfunction ten miles outside of Casper. No one questioned the unstated reason. One letter mailed to the trainmaster in Chicago was perplexing. The letter read: "Thanks for stopping in Greybull, Wyoming. That was the damnedest ride I have ever seen." The trainmaster read the letter three times and handed it to his executive secretary. Eventually, it found its way into a folder, and then a wastepaper basket. It just made no sense to the downtown Chicago crowd.

When he finally made it through the crowd to the fence, Harry found Alejendra Rodriguez standing with her brother and Ruthie McGovern.

"That was some ride," Miguel said, shaking Harry's hand.

"I was really lucky. That horse is everything he's cracked up to be. If he hadn't bounced the way he did, I would have been on the ground, no question."

Alejendra watched him.

You're just good. She thought. *That horse never stood a chance.*

She watched him taking Miguel's praise, Ruthie

patting him on the arm, congratulating him. It was too much for her. Harry Harris was going to be impossible to be around. He already was. He'd have to get a new, bigger hat. She walked away from the trio, heading for the auction barn where her father was talking with several men she'd not seen before. Behind her, her mother shook hands with Harry, speaking to him, smiling. Tobie Keefer was with him when Harry said to her mother, "Mrs. Rodriguez, thanks. I'll have Tapper to you on the first of October, on a Monday. Thank you again. Tell Alex that I am looking forward to meeting with her, seeing her mares."

Chapter 17

Alejendra ran through the house on her way out to the garden. She still had the last of the beans to pick and shell, carrots to pull, turnips to gather, potatoes to dig--the last three to bury in the winter hole where they'd last and last, hopefully until spring. It was nearly evening--four in the afternoon. Her mother had been working in the kitchen--working since late morning. It had never occurred to Alejendra to ask what had her attention for Alejendra had things to do. After the garden chores and gathering the winter squash, she needed to work the mares, inspecting each to determine if they were well, that nothing untoward was cropping up, such as a bruised frog, a loose shoe, or anything else.

"*Mamá*, as soon as I gather the winter squash and cover them with straw, I will be at the Two Grey Hills horse pasture."

"Okay, c*hiquita*."

Alejendra slowed down and hazarded a glance at her Mother's form bent over the table, mixing, humming some tune Alejendra had never heard before. Behind her on the counter were other mixing bowls. She'd been preoccupied with her task since late morning.

"*Mamá*, what are you doing? Are you making bread? Biscuits? Pies?"

184

"Tamales, *chiquita*."

"Tamales?" Alejendra hesitated and then started walking across the floor toward her mother, running through her mind reasons to make tamales: birthdays, Christmas, Easter, anniversaries, (not this month), box socials. "Where's the party, *Mamá*? What's going on?"

"That Harry is coming tomorrow."

"No, he's not, *Mamá*. We never . . . I mean, I haven't made any arrangements. I will have to find another stud horse. You don't have to do all this work, *Mamá*. He's not coming."

"I made arrangements, *chiquita*."

Alejendra, who, up until that moment, had been the perpetual motion girl, stood still, her feet no longer moving, suddenly serious in every respect.

"*Mamá*? *Mamá*, are you saying he's coming here?"

"Tomorrow, *chiquita*."

"*Mamá*?" Alejendra stood in the kitchen staring at her mother, her hands on her hips.

"What?" her mother asked. "*Chiquita*, you should get ready, I think. This boy, he is bringing his big horse."

"*Mamá*, *Mamá*, do you have any idea what that crazy kid wants for the use of his horse?"

"Six dozen tamales."

"You know? You spoke with him?"

"Yes. I spoke with him. He is a nice boy, I think. Very respectful. I shook hands with him. His hands are hard from the work. I was impressed with your boy. He has good manners and no mother. I heard this."

Alejendra slumped down in a kitchen chair next to the table her Mother was using for her work.

"*Mamá*, he's not my boy. He owns a horse, a stud horse. I was interested in the stud horse, but he isn't taking me seriously. Like it's some sort of joke."

"Alejendra, for a boy to ride all the way from the Absaroka Mountains, from Meeteetsee, to bring you a stud horse is most serious. I think he has an eye for you."

"*Mamá*, I don't want him to have an eye for me. I want him to do business with me. There is a difference. I don't want to put on a dress and act all sweet. I don't want to serve him tamales and apple juice to get him to like me. I don't care if he ever likes me. I really do not care for him. He has a swollen head, if you know what I mean. I want to do business. That's all."

"Part of doing business is being nice, *chiquita*. Take the time to be nice and your life will be nice also, I think. It is the thing to do. It is called good manners." Raquel paused, thinking. "*Mi-hija*," she said, "I do not think his head is too big."

"You're welcome to your opinion, *Mamá*. When is he coming?"

"In the morning."

"Oh wow. *Mamá*, I love you but I wish you wouldn't make dates for me. They expect things. They embarrass themselves. At least they should be embarrassed at the things they do and say."

"I don't think this one expects anything. I don't think he knows what he is doing too much."

"Why do you say that?"

"I speak with him. That's how I know this."

"All right, *Mamá*." Alejendra shook her head. "All right. I give up."

"*Chiquita*, this boy--he comes far for to help. Be nice to him. Say thank you. It is nothing, I think. It means much to be happy. Afterwards you will be able to say it: 'I am this nice.' And he will be able to say it: 'I met a nice person.' It is little but it makes for very much."

"*Mamá*, I just want you to please stop trying to find me a husband. I don't want a boyfriend. I don't want you to do this. It is embarrassing."

"What would be embarrassing, *chiquita*, is if we didn't look for you."

Alejendra shook her head slowly, knowing she was getting nowhere with her mother.

"*Mamá*, did you speak to *Papá* about this?"

"No."

"*Mamá*, you should have. If the mares are put with a stud now, they will have colts the first of September. We want April colts. This means they should be with the stud in May. It's just too soon. I wish you had spoken to *Papá*."

"I never thought this," her mother said.

Alejendra rolled her eyes. "Please, *Mamá*?"

"Please, *chiquita*?"

Alejendra stood, forced a smile at her mother, turned on the underslung heels of her boots, and walked out the front door. If she could have screamed and not brought her mother running to her aid, she would have.

Harry Harris arrived at the Rodriguez ranch a little after ten in the morning on Monday, October 1, 1917 riding an Appaloosa gelding, leading Tapper on

187

sixteen feet of rope. The first frost had hit the mountain sides nearly two weeks earlier—the third week in September. The slopes of the mountain were turning red and yellow. Dismounting, he shook hands with Mrs. Rodriquez and said "Good Morning" to her. He did not ask for Alejendra; he did not look for her.

Addressing himself to Mrs. Rodriguez, he touched the brim of his hat. "Ma'am, this is Tapper." He handed her the end of the lead rope.

"Mr. Harris, thank you for your courtesy," Raquel replied. "You've come such a long way."

"I'll be back in four weeks, Ma'am. See if everything is goin' okay. Give my best to your husband. Tell your daughter hello. I hope Tapper does what he's supposed to do. I sure do."

"Would you like to stay a while? Rest? Perhaps have dinner with us?"

"I really would, Ma'am, but I got a job workin' for the Pitchfork so I gotta be goin'. It's a real busy time with roundup and all. I ain't got much time off. Enough to bring Tapper to you. I'm needed pretty bad."

"*Un momento*, please." Raquel left and returned minutes later, handing him a cotton sack. She said, "Take these tamales with you. I will have more when you return."

"Ma'am, you shouldn't have. You are most kind."

Harry Harris accepted the cotton sack with forty-six tamales, some carrots, some onions and four pieces of fried chicken wrapped in wax paper.

He said, "Ma'am, thank you."

Raquel Rodriguez smiled and watched the

young man as he mounted the Appaloosa gelding and rode back in the direction he'd come.

Raquel quietly tied the lead rope to the railing that circled the veranda. She watched the young man as he rode down the road, getting smaller and smaller, riding away without a backwards glance. She smiled, purposefully waiting, taking her time in going back inside. It was a pleasant fall morning. Taking a breath, she sat in the wicker chair thinking, waiting, wondering when Manny would return from moving the sixty head of old cows from the graze on Medicine Mountain to the river bottom. They'd be coming off the mountain soon. It would be getting cold up there. The first snow would soon fall above the timber line. It was coming, maybe soon. It was hard to tell, but she could smell it. The air had changed.

Manny and the boys should be back tomorrow. I'll have something nice for them.

Alejendra came outside wearing a dress. She stared at the stud horse, glanced at her mother, looked at the corrals, and the barn. Finally, she looked back at her mother.

"*Mamá?* Where is he?"

"He is gone."

"Gone. What do you mean gone?"

"He left. He has much work to be done."

"Did you invite him in?"

"I did but he said he was working and had to leave."

Alejendra looked at her mother in frustration. "I got dressed up for this? You would have thought I was going to church."

189

"*Mi-hija*, if you wanted him to stay, you will need to ask him. If you want him to go, you will have to tell him this. I don't think he can read your mind. I cannot." Having said that, Raquel rose to her feet and went inside, a smile on her face.

Alejendra shook her head in disbelief and followed her mother inside to change back into her work clothes. She was clearly annoyed.

And I took a bath for this, she thought, rolling her eyes.

Four weeks passed quickly: twenty-eight days. Alejendra counted them. She watched Tapper. She watched her mares and she waited. Purposely, when the twenty-seventh day arrived, she did not go to the Two Grey Hills pasture and catch the stallion. She waited. She planned it that way. She would go with Harry Harris and he would catch him. She could be "proper." She could thank him. Her mother could "pay" him the tamales. Alejendra purposely prepared other things to use to say thank you. She practiced being gracious, sometimes hating it, sometimes enjoying thinking of what he might say when he discovered an addition to his six dozen tamales. Remembering that he, his sister, and his father lived alone, that he had no mother, she had asked her mother to add to the sum total. She had to think about Harry for a moment, wondering what it was like to live in a two room cabin with one window and no back door. People didn't live that way, she told herself. It was just a story she heard.

Harry Harris arrived on Monday, October 29,

1917 at ten o'clock in the morning four weeks later. There was a cool snap to the air, as fall had turned the grass brown, the trees yellow, the brush on the mountainside a dozen shades of red, leaves falling. Indian summer had held on, the days pleasant. The cows were off the mountain in the fall pastures.

This time Alejendra was waiting. She bade him come inside. He was reticent. She insisted. He complied. He stood in the hallway ill at ease. She took his arm and brought him into the kitchen. Her mother didn't like that so much. She sat him at the table, got him a drink of water, set a plate, and, before he could object, she began filling it with the best food her mother could prepare.

Later, she rode with him to the Two Grey Hills horse pasture. She waited while he caught Tapper. That wasn't too hard, for he just whistled; the horse came running and he slipped the halter around his head.

"Nice trick," she said.

"Thanks."

"I'm so sorry that you had to come all this way. I wish you'd talked to me first."

Harry smiled. "You wouldn't listen, if I did. Your mother seemed to know what she was doing, what she wanted."

"That's just it. She didn't. You see, if the mares get pregnant now they'll have colts in September next year. It would have been better if they'd been with stud in May when they're cycling more consistently. They'd have colts in April. *Mamá* was doing her matchmaker thing. She wanted you to be here with me. I'm sorry about that. I asked her not to. She won't listen. She has a mind all of her own. It's all right, though. I'm grateful."

"Well, I'm here. Guess she got what she wanted."

"She did. I told her it wasn't like that between you and me. She wouldn't listen. Did you ride all the way from Meeteetsee today?" Alejendra was prepared to be amazed if he had.

"No, Ma'am," he said. "I did not. That would be hard. I stayed with Karen Colinsky. Do you know Karen? She said she knew you. She lives down there outside of Greybull a mile or so."

"Karen? You're going with Karen? She's a friend of mine. We went to school together. She sat next to me when I was a senior."

The thought of Harry staying with Karen gave her pause; it was a little risque to begin with. Certainly everyone would be talking. It also made her a little jealous, giving her a twinge in her heart that she couldn't explain and didn't want to. She immediately dismissed it.

"Not going with, not like a steady girl friend or anything like that."

"Well, what then? She's really cute. My brother had a crush on her. Maybe he still does, except now he has something for Ruthie."

"Her mother is my aunt. She and my mom were sisters. My father and I stay there when we come to Greybull with the cows."

Alejendra's hand went to her mouth. She was embarrassed, but Harry didn't seem to mind. She thought she removed her foot from her mouth quite well, if it were possible to do that.

"I am sorry. I thought for a moment that Karen was your girl or something."

"No, Ma'am. I don't have a girl. To tell the truth, other than you, I ain't never talked to girls much. I have talked to Karen but she don't count, her being my cousin."

"You haven't talked to a girl?"

"Well, I've talked to girls. I've said hello. Things like that. But you're the only one I ever asked to dance. The other day was my first time at that. You know how that turned out."

Alejendra smiled, nodding, knowingly. They'd ridden back to the house. *Not too good*, she thought.

He said, "You gotta know there ain't too many gals on the other side of Meeteetsee, and the Pitchfork-- it ain't got any. There ain't too many to talk to. It is hard to get any serious practice doin' that sort of talkin'."

Alejendra laughed. "Come inside. Let *Mamá* fix you up for your trip home."

"Ma'am, I better be goin'."

"Harry, get down off that horse and get inside. Let my mother spoil you. She's been planning it for days. You do not want to disappoint her."

"I. . . ."

"Harry, do what I am telling you to do. You need practice anyway. This will give you the opportunity to talk to a girl. The last time I checked I am one."

"You sure are."

"Thank you. Now get down and open the door

for me. I'm helpless. I didn't know a cow had four tits and a mare had only two. You'll have to explain that to me."

Harry burst out laughing. He stepped down from the gelding.

"Ma'am, let me get that door for you."

"I should say."

Both of them laughed.

Harry spent two hours with Alejendra and her mother. He received a lot of practice talking with the opposite sex as her mother made over the two of them. Alejendra was not interested in him "that way," but she did enjoy herself and she enjoyed watching her mother disappear into thin air so they could be "alone," and she loved her for it. She was grateful that Harry Harris had brought his stud clear to the other side of Greybull, up against the Big Horn Mountain for her and her mares. She verbally expressed her gratitude. She touched his hand, patting it, asking if he'd like more water in his glass. She touched his shoulder and asked if he'd like some more fried chicken.

No. No, he didn't. He was stuffed to overflowing.

When he left, Harry Harris was convinced that Alejendra Rodriquez was a real girl, a nice girl, someone who made him laugh and feel good about himself. The Rodriguez girl was all he could think about all the way home.   Alejendra probably didn't plan on that.

Chapter 18

Gorman O'Neal sat in his overstuffed sofa and stared out the floor to ceiling windows, enjoying the view. The weathered, low-lying frame house at the bend of the Cumberland river in Wayne County, Kentucky sat back from the river on a sloping hillside. It sat overlooking grassland and hay meadows on the north and the river on the south. He could see the fenced pastures where his twenty-seven thoroughbred mares lived, the white barn and paddocks where they foaled, the oval track where, mostly, the two and three-year olds trained. Toward the south, he could see sections of the serpentine river, partially hidden in willow oak, black gum, white pine, magnolia, and other trees he couldn't name. Yesterday, below the white barn, next to a fence line, he'd found a black walnut pushing its now red, frost-bitten leaves through the rails. One thousand forty-six acres, grass and trees: it was his. He relished the fact that it was hidden away like a lost jewel from the eyes of gawkers, ne'er-do-wells, and the freeloaders he so detested.

It was a cool mid-October evening. Indian summer had thankfully dragged on and on. From the house porch, he watched Impressive Traveler going through his paces, running lazily, running full out, trotting, walking, then being led around the track in the red and yellow hues cast by the late evening sun. Earlier, he saw the white pants and red shirt of Bud Oren, watched him wave his arm at a diminutive jockey. The rider had pulled up, waiting while Oren approached him from the left side, talking rapidly, using his hands as he expressed himself. In the heavy evening air, the rider received instructions, nodding, the tall horse tossing his head like an indolent school child; then both moved down the track.

Gorman O'Neal walked the length of the veranda, shoulders slightly hunched, his hands held in a knot of fingers behind his back. His thoughts drifted to Impressive Traveler, to all the time and money he'd invested. *Something needed to be done. No, something had to be done.*

He shook his head at the sheer luck of it, random chance playing its part. In some place called Sheridan, Wyoming, a place he'd never been, never heard of, Impressive had gotten away from his handlers, from Bud Oren. How often did that happen? Never. Not ever. Now it looked like Impressive had fathered a horse colt. The unexpected–something he hadn't planned on. As soon as he found out, he'd hired the mare shot. She'd been a mustang, a horse of no worth, no breeding; nothing to worry about. But no one mentioned a colt; no one had seen a colt. Three years ago, he'd received the report that the mare was dead; thus the issue was taken care of, never to resurface. It frustrated him. His man had used a rifle at five hundred yards, then reported her dead. He'd failed to see she was lactating. The problem was the shooter had been in too big of a hurry. If he'd looked at the corpse, he'd have seen her swollen teats; he'd have realized at a glance that the mare had a colt, and the problem could have been solved with the single pull of a trigger.

Shooting the mare was simple, inexpensive house cleaning, something he did to make sure that nothing existed on Impressive's back trail that could possibly haunt his ever ascending rise to fame and fortune. Bud had told him not to worry about it, that it didn't matter, that it was just a mustang mare of no consequence; it was useless to worry. He'd said that even if Impressive got a dozen mares pregnant in the mountains of Northern Wyoming, there was nothing to tie the pregnancy to Impressive; that even if he had, it simply didn't matter. What's another horse colt in the millions born every year? What did it matter?

Nothing, Gorman supposed. It was just a minor loose end, something to be taken care of, then forgotten. The mare, however, refused to be forgotten. Three years afterwards, there came an innocuous newspaper report from *The Greybull Standard* about some backwoods hayseed from a place called Meeteetsee who had a remarkable horse colt. The boy had found him standing by his dead mother in the Big Horn Mountains west of Buffalo. Standing behind the boy was a hazy newspaper image of a tall horse, the spitting image of Impressive. He had the same sleek, muscular build, the same way of standing, the same way of holding his head, as if he were looking straight through you, asking you just who you thought you were. The newspaper article said the boy and horse took on any takers and won every race they entered. It had pictured a smiling, toothy, shy boy standing with the horse under the caption, "Meeteetsee boy finds a diamond in the rough--a real winner."

There could not be two Impressive Travelers. Absolutely not. That mare, that colt found on the mountain, mattered.

"Mr. O'Neal, you have a visitor. He would not give me his name. Shall I send him away, sir?"

The voice belonged to Jefferson, Gorman O'Neal's manservant, a slender fellow from England who spoke with a distinct English accent that O'Neal enjoyed. Out on the porch O'Neal could hear his wife, Evie, moving around in the kitchen, his young son, Roger, singing to himself in the den as he played with small wooden horses on made up roads.

"No, Jefferson. I'm expecting him. At least, I think I am. Please show him in."

"As you wish, sir."

"Thank you, Jefferson," he said, thinking how dreadful it would be to live without Jefferson at hand to keep him organized.

A brief time later, likely less than a minute by Bud Oren's stop watch, Jefferson showed a hulking stranger through the living room and out onto the veranda. The man wore a dark, nondescript overcoat, a hat like the ones dozens of men wore every day to work. His riding boots were scraped and scarred black but not so much as to call attention to them. They were of the western variety with a pointed toe and an underslung heel. His trousers were dark, worn denim. Although O'Neal couldn't tell for sure, it appeared that the man wore a pistol under his overcoat, maybe more than one. O'Neal might have called the man on it. Better to let sleeping dogs lie, however. He thought how odd it was that the fellow could look like everyone and no one at the same time; he had a talent for

198

anonymity. That was good, just what he wanted.

Three weeks ago, O'Neal had put the word out that he needed someone, someone to take care of a small, growing problem. For three weeks he'd waited. Last week he'd given up and started searching again. The problem wasn't going to solve itself. The horse and boy seemed to land themselves in the newspapers after every podunk county fair. No, the problem wasn't going away. It needed some help.

O'Neal stared at the man, wondering if he could do the job. There was something vaguely familiar about his mannerisms that resonated in his memory. Maybe sometime in the past he'd hired him but he couldn't think when or where. Maybe. He wasn't sure.

There had been a first time--years ago. A shadow in a doorway by a horse barn in Frankfort. "I hear you're looking to clean up a situation," the stranger had said. Back then the man seemed to disappear in shadows, a figure hardly worth remembering. But that long ago task had been taken care of. O'Neal remembered the feeling of satisfaction, though he did not remember what the man's services had involved. *Just as well.*

The man ushered out onto the veranda looked at O'Neal, studying him. He said, "You left a message said you had somethin' that needed takin' care of?"

It was more a question than a statement. Yet it was neither. If there was a definition to the word "nebulous," the man's question personified it. O'Neal, in spite of himself, found the visitor unsettling, leaving him with the feeling that he ought to bar and shutter the windows, a nasty, distasteful, let's-get-this-fellow-out-of-here feeling. *Right man, right place. And to the point. No "howdy, how have you been?" western, small talk.*

"Pardon me," O'Neal said, "I was wondering if you were the man for the job I have in mind."

"What's the job?"

"I need a horse killed."

"A horse? What do you need me for? You got thirteen men standin' around here that could put a slug in the back of a horse's head. They could do it in broad daylight whenever you are of a mind. No questions asked. To make it easier, your horses won't shoot back."

The statement left O'Neal taken aback, almost wordless. It was as if the man didn't like the prospect of killing a horse. *What would be the difference? A man? a horse?*

O'Neal stared at his visitor before responding. He said, "Yes, I could but this isn't just any horse. It's a horse in Wyoming belonging to some kid. It seems that my stud got a mare pregnant. It was a mistake. I had the mare killed but she had a horse colt that I didn't know about. Some kid picked him up and raised him on a bottle. I can't have this. I want all of my stud's unauthorized progeny dead. I don't want him to have any. I want any mare that my horse impregnated without me knowing about it, without me giving permission, dead. That includes any foal that he sired. I want it dead, too. I want it done immediately before it gets out of hand. Frankly, it is already out of hand."

Taking a breath, O'Neal realized he was also amused. His visitor had counted his hired men. He'd

200

looked around before inviting himself into his house. That was impressive.

"You want me to kill some kid's horse?"

"And any mare that that stud got pregnant, and their colts, if any."

"That's a first."

"What do you mean?"

"I've been hired to kill a lot of things, but never a horse. Especially some kid's horse from the backwoods of Montana."

"Wyoming."

"That's what I said, Wyoming."

"You don't want the job, just say so. I'll get someone else."

"Killin' a horse?"

"Most likely several horses."

"Several?" Again, it was a question, then it wasn't. "What's the job pay?"

"Before you jump in, perhaps you should know the parameters. I want the killing of these horses to appear as an accident. What do you charge to kill a man?"

"Depends on the man. If he's real important, hard to kill, as much as ten thousand."

"This is a horse and as you pointed out, a horse doesn't shoot back. Not as dangerous. It should be a lot less."

"Yeah, you're right except the fellow that owns him, he does shoot back. Not two years ago some fellow got himself hanged over in Galveston for stealin' a horse. Come the next mornin', there he was hangin' from a tree, a note pinned to his shirt. It said, 'This here's a dead horse thief.'"

O'Neal tried to study the man, tried to see him clearly for what he was. Even in the shadows at the close of day he seemed to be disappearing in front of him. *That's a rare talent. I like this.*

"So just how important do you consider killing a particular horse? What is it going to cost me?"

"It's you that must consider him important, wantin' him dead like you do."

"I know he may have impregnated as many as eleven mares. All belonging to a man named Manny Rodriquez, some no count Mexican living outside of a place called Greybull. Things could change even as we speak. You'll need to kill the stud first, then the mares. They haven't foaled yet. I don't want them to. Time is very important."

"How do you know this?"

"A week, ten days ago, I hired someone in Wyoming to find out. It seems the stud horse is servicing eleven mares. Been with them since the beginning of October. Not long. I need to control the damage. As I said, I need this done right away. It would be easier while they are together in one place."

It occurred to O'Neal that the man hadn't removed his hat, overcoat, or gloves and yet he was still standing on O'Neal's veranda. In answer to O'Neal's question, he said, "Three thousand for shootin' the stud. Two thousand for each of the mares. Two thousand for any additional foal or mare I come across that needs killin'."

Gorman O'Neal gasped. He couldn't help himself. "That's a lot," he said.

202

"Yes it is. I don't get asked to kill horses every day. That will be up front."

"You haven't done the job."

"And I ain't gonna do the job unless I'm paid up front for the stud and the mares. Damn serious thing killin' a man's horse 'cause he's got the wrong daddy."

"I could get someone else cheaper."

"Yes, you could. I expect you won't."

"You're sure of yourself."

"I know who I am and I know who you are."

"What's that supposed to mean?"

"It means if I agree to the job, it'll get done. I ain't dickerin' here. That's my price and that is the way it is. Killin' a horse is a hell of a lot different from killin' a man."

"That's more than some men make in two lifetimes."

"I ain't some men."

Gorman O'Neal hesitated, resisting. Twenty-five thousand dollars. That was a much higher cost than he had anticipated. Still, he needed the job done, needed it done right, needed it done now. And this man seemed capable. It wasn't as if he didn't have twenty-five thousand. O'Neal decided. He said, "I've already said this. Make the mares' deaths look like an accident. The stud, too. Understand?"

The stranger nodded.

"Wait here. I'll see that you are paid. I'll be a minute." O'Neal stared at the man on his veranda. "The stud and the mare are together right now," he said. "I don't know how long that will last."

The stranger nodded again.

Gorman O'Neal didn't trust the man, yet he left him standing on the porch with his wife in the kitchen and his son singing some nursery rhyme in the den. The nameless fellow didn't seem to mind. While waiting, he walked to the far edge of the veranda in the cool of the evening, a solitary figure in the growing darkness. Many of the leaves had dropped from the trees, yet it was still colorful, a blanket of yellow and red hues.

A few minutes later, O'Neal handed him a white envelope. The stranger took it without saying a word.

"Aren't you going to count it?"

"I did," the dark man said, "and I have." He turned and walked down the six steps from the veranda and across the well-manicured lawn.

What did that mean?

O'Neal watched him disappear into the shadowy trees at the edge of the lawn. O'Neal hated every minute of what had just transpired. These sorts of deals made him uneasy. Once he paid money, he lost control. There was nothing he could do except wait for a progress report. Once he got a report in the form of a paper clipping: *"Samuel Addison dead, killed in a tragic hunting accident. His funeral . . . "* After reading the clipping, he wondered if it was an accident and whether money paid was ill spent.

This could be the same man he'd hired. He was almost sure of it, except this time the fellow was a little more surly. Still O'Neal wondered, thinking that killing some horses was of no consequence, something lost at the bottom of a canyon somewhere. Once he'd heard of a group of cattle standing beside a drift fence. Lightning struck the fence, killed every one. Electrocuted. Already he knew he'd paid far too much for too little. O'Neal regretted having paid the money.

What was I thinking?

O'Neal walked to the veranda railing, laying his big hands on the painted two by sixes, staring into the growing darkness. He wished he could call the man and get his money back. The late fall chill hung in the air. It would frost again tonight

"What could I have possibly been thinking?" he said aloud. "What was I thinking? I overpaid."

Gorman O'Neal immediately wrote off the horse killer he'd hired, dismissing him from his mind. He started looking for other solutions. Yes, the disappearing man was a mistake. He knew it cold as ice. He'd been stupid, too hasty, too interested in getting the job done quickly. For that kind of money, he could have purchased the horses and killed them himself at his leisure.

Ten days later, O'Neal hired a second man, agreed to give him two thousand dollars once the job was finished, paid him five hundred up front for expenses and felt much more in control. He knew this man's name: Loren Peters, a ne'er-do-well from the seedy bars of Lexington, a back-up to an expensive mistake: insurance that the job would be done. And if it wasn't, he'd send someone else. He'd have his way.

Chapter 19

The old man sat on the porch of the Neeley Hotel and General Store in Kane, Wyoming, rocking, deep in thought. The Neeley Hotel and store were both housed in one building: the first floor selling everything from pitchforks to broadcloth; the floor above for hotel guests. He'd been sitting there every morning for a little less than thirty-two months. It was because of his hip. He'd been banged up against a cottonwood, thrown to the ground, stepped on, and kicked by a gruella mustang. The gruella was his. Still, he hadn't sold him; couldn't bring himself to do it though he had thought about it.

It was tough being seventy-three years old and stove up. But that is the way of it and he wasn't complaining. All in all, he felt that life had been damn good to him. It was just the hip. It hurt something fierce, especially in the morning, or when it rained, or snowed, or looked like it was going to rain or snow, or looked like it was going to be morning.

He rose early. He always had--he couldn't help it. Sometimes he tried not to but he just woke up. It was hard as hell staying in bed even though there was nothing to do when he was up except sit on the porch of the Neeley and rock. It was a hell of a way to live but it was all right; his life was what it was. His younger, married sister ran the place where he stayed and she was good to him, fixed him breakfast, and mended his socks, making sure he had what he needed.

A good woman.

But that damn hip just drove him crazy.

A hundred yards in front of the Neeley Hotel stood a wooden fence constructed from the pine trees left from the old burn on the south side of the Big Horn Mountain: dried pine trees baked in fire, roasted in the hot sun for thirty years, and sawed into lumber at the mill halfway up the mountain. Everyone knew the damn fool man that owned the sawmill kept a black bear on a chain, fed it rabbits and cantaloupe, and sometimes a little watermelon and table scraps. To get new lumber, all a man had to do was bring dead fall timber to the mill. Once there the mill man would saw it into lumber. The blacksmith had dragged in good straight logs from the south face, had them sawed, and used the lumber to build the fence that kept the broken down wagons corralled until he fixed them. Pete Smith was his name. He did a good job shoeing a horse, too.

The old man liked him. He'd watch Pete from his window on the second floor: watch him each morning building the fires on the forge: watch the smoke catch the morning breeze: hear him lay the hammer on red-hot steel. The music of the hammer woke Kane, Wyoming up every morning. Old Pete couldn't sleep either, not with the sun coming up over the Horn and horseshoes to bend.

"Mr. Williams?"

Surprised, Henry stopped rocking and turned to the voice that had broken into his morning reverie. Directly behind him, his sister, Ellen, appeared in the doorway holding his morning cup of coffee. She glanced at the girl standing on Henry's left side who'd just spoken to him.

"Hank," his sister said, "here's your coffee. No sugar this morning. We're out." She paused. "Alejendra, how nice to see you. It's been such a long, long time. Several years, if I remember. You are simply beautiful. All grown up. How's your mother? She's one of my favorites, you know. Can she ever make tamales! They are simply the best. Every year I order as many as she can make, poor dear. She works so hard."

"She's fine, Mrs. Neeley. Busy as usual. Has her grandkids. Still making tamales. You must come see her. She'd love it if you would, I'm sure."

Henry nodded his gratitude at his sister, taking the hot cup from her, the strong pounding of the smith, hammer on steel, punctuating the air.

Alejendra? That'd be Manny's girl. The last time I saw her was at Franko's funeral. She must have been about twelve, thirteen. Lord, that was five years ago. She looks about eighteen standing on the porch. No, she is eighteen. Damn, time just gets away."

He wondered what she wanted. Pretty girls didn't seek out old men rocking on a porch; of that he was certain. But this was Franko's granddaughter. The thought of Frank brought a smile to his lips.

Ellen continued. "Hank, I'm cooking pancakes. They're on the grill." Turning to Alejendra, she said, "Dear girl, I have to go inside to keep the cakes from burning. Have you eaten? Please come inside and have breakfast with us."

"Thank you, Mrs. Neeley. I've eaten. Grandmama already fed me eggs and bacon. I just wanted to have a word with Mr. Williams. I could come

208

back. Really, I could. I don't want to be a bother."

"Don't be silly, girl, he's right there. His ears work. It won't be a bother."

Ellen Neeley hustled indoors, her skirts rustling as she hurried on her self-appointed errand to keep the pancakes from burning.

"I'm sorry, Mr. Williams, to bother you so early in the morning. I really could come back if you like," she said as she glanced down the street toward the post office and pool hall, then turned her attention to Henry.

"You're Manny's girl. Met you four or five years ago."

"Yes, sir. At *mi abuelo's* funeral." She paused, looking toward the blacksmith's shop. "Does he always do that?"

"Who?"

"That blacksmith? I mean it's so early. The hammering must drive you crazy."

"Ol' Pete? He's at it every mornin'. Just like clockwork." Henry looked at the girl. He said, "Ain't seen you in a while. Saw your father, three of your brothers ridin' in from the creek yesterday afternoon."

"Yes, sir. I came in the morning so I could see *mi abuela*. I hadn't seen her in a while."

"What can I do for you, sis?"

"Sir, *mi abuela* said that you might be able to help me. And *mi abuelo*, he--."

"Help you what?"

"Well, *mi abuela*--. "

"That'd be Mary Carlos Sanchez Rodriguez," Henry said, nodding his head.

"Yes, sir. How did you know that? I mean . . .

it's just you know her entire name."

Henry smiled at the girl, thinking she looked so much like Anna Marie and Mary Carlos: tall, thin, about five foot seven inches; black hair, braided; dark eyes, olive skin. Her grandmother was hard to forget, as was her aunt--especially her aunt.

"Yes," he said slowly, "I met your grandmother when she and I were young. A long time ago. Fifty years, maybe."

"She said you were a tracker. She said you knew how to look at the ground and read what it tells you better than anyone."

"She did, did she? Your grandmother is some lady. Quite the looker in her day. Always heavy on praise. She made me look twice, the way she looked, the way she said things. A real nice lady. She had a sister that was somethin' else again."

"She was? I mean, she was. Of course she is. How did you know about Aunt Anna? I mean she lives in Mexico."

"Sis," he said, changing the subject, "I have been known to track a skunk across a hard rock. But that was a long time ago. What exactly did your grandmother have in mind?"

Alejandra's hand suddenly came to her mouth. "I'm sorry, Mr. Williams. I'm keeping you from your breakfast. It is so rude."

Henry smiled again. "What did you say you needed?"

"Oh, I'm so sorry. *Mi abuela* said you were a tracker and I need to know how. I need you to teach me. I have a real problem."

"Trackin'?"

"Yes, I need to know how to do that. Could you teach me? What I should look for?"

"I suppose I could, but what about your father? What are you wantin' to track? It ain't like that's a skill you can just take a sugar pill and there you are--the world's best."

"I have eleven mares. They're gone. I told *mi abuela* about my problem and told her that *Papá* was going to find my horses. She said that she loved her son very much but that when it comes to tracking, *Papá* ought to stay at home and chase my mother around the living room. I never heard her say anything like that. It was kind of funny the way she said it. Then she said that if she wanted to track anything she'd want you to do it. I told her that you were broken, I mean that you had a hard time getting around. She said that you weren't always that way--that your leg might be bad, but you weren't blind. She told me to come and talk to you. I am hoping you can show me how to track."

"Well, girl, we did have our times."

"You did? I mean with *mi abuela*?"

"Sis, she wasn't always a short, old Mexican lady livin' on the east side of the railroad tracks. There certainly was a time . . . well . . ." Henry Williams paused, his mind in the distant past. He glanced at the girl. He said, "So you want me to teach you how to track. Horses, you say?"

"Yes, sir. It is my horses. As I said, I have eleven mares. They are all with foal, at least I think so. And they are gone. It's been two days. My *papá* says there isn't anything to worry about. We had to pick up my brother from the train. That's why we are here--to meet my brother. That's why we aren't looking for my mares. I don't know if we can find them. I mean it rained really hard. Something just isn't right, Mr. Williams."

Henry studied the girl, heard Ellen call his name from inside. "Well, girl, let me think it over."

"Please, Mr. Williams. I really need your help. My mares are the best. They wouldn't just run away like that. Not without something causing . . . ." Her voice trailed off.

"I believe you. Manny knows horse flesh."

"You know my *papá* really well?"

Henry smiled again. "Girl, before your grandfather died, I used to know a few people." Henry stared at her. "I am thinkin' there's somethin' you ain't tellin' me. You leavin' somethin' out?" He paused. Alejendra backed up a step on the creaky porch, surprised.

"I don't think so. It's just like something is wrong, Mr. Williams. I saw some horse tracks that I didn't recognize around the corrals and down by the north fence. I think someone is watching me, my horses--maybe all of us. I don't know. I guess it's just a bad feeling. Probably nothing to it."

"Well, that's somethin'," Henry said.

"I don't have much time . . . for you to teach me," the girl said. "We meet the train this afternoon at 2:38. *Mi abuela* told me I should talk to you right away, that you'd know what to do, that I could trust you. *Mi abuelo* said that when he was alive, also. Can you teach me these things, Mr. Williams? I am a fast learner."

212

Henry heard Ellen calling his name again.

"I'll think it over," he said. "I gotta go. Ellen is gettin' impatient."

"Okay," Alejendra said. "Thanks for listening to me, Mr. Williams. I hope you can help."

"Ma'am." Henry watched the girl retreat across the roadway, walking toward the dark red section house and the railroad tracks.

Teach her to track!?

Henry Williams learned tracking young, when his father made him study the ground and tell him what it said, correcting him when he was wrong. It had taken years. He hadn't learned it yet--not all of it.

Teach a girl to track? In thirty minutes? Sitting on the front porch of the Neeley in Kane, Wyoming? How the hell am I going to do that? I'm simply not that good. That ain't gonna happen.

He thought about Frank Rodriguez, glanced east toward the mountain, across the tracks where Mary Carlos lived. Henry heard his name being called again. Slowly he stood, picked up his crutch and braced himself. This was going to hurt.

Teach a girl to track, indeed. Can't even stand up. How the hell can I possibly do that?

With the aid of the crutch, he moved slowly inside, gritting his teeth against the pain of his hip. It would get better with the heat. He'd be able to walk come mid-afternoon. He stopped at the doorway and looked again eastward at the big mountain sitting in the haze. Clouds were hanging low in Cottonwood Canyon. Low Mountain was hidden altogether. Above the clouds he could see the timberline and Mexican hill. It was so named after one of Manny's riders. Poor bastard had been struck by lightning. It killed him, killed the horse, split the saddle.

The damnest thing. A good hand, that rider. Too bad about what happened.

He and Franko had fished with that boy down on lower Porcupine creek what seemed a thousand years ago. Between the three of them, they caught sixteen trout.

Tasted pretty good, too.

By the time he reached the breakfast table, Henry Williams had decided.

Chapter 20

Alejendra Rodriquez's father and her four brothers were already in the saddle and riding; they left at first light to look for her eleven mares. In their absence it fell to Alejendra to milk the Guernsey cow, slop five hogs, and feed and water the late spring heifers in the south corral. It wasn't that she wanted to stay behind but her mother had stressed to her father that Alejendra was an unmarried female, that she had plenty to do without going traipsing all over the mountain looking for horses. That was a man's job. Instead Alejendra helped her mother prepare bread dough for dinner biscuits and went to the garden to see if there were any tomatoes, chili peppers, potatoes, lettuce, and carrots. The frost had gotten all but the carrots and potatoes; they were safely buried underground.

On her way back, she noticed the rider coming up the road from the river bottom. When she saw him the first time, he was at the bend in the road four miles away, but she sensed the horse was moving right along and would be there soon. Even in the distance, it wasn't a pretty horse but it had a certain gait, one that ate up miles. Hustling inside, she deposited carrots and potatoes on the kitchen counter by the hand pump.

"*Mamá*, rider coming," Alejendra said before taking a basket of dirty clothing to the outer room to the wash tubs. Working with her mother was . . . well, she'd rather be doing something else. When she

215

returned, she glanced out the kitchen window again. The rider had drawn closer. The hat was familiar. And the horse? She'd seen both before, or so she thought.

"Oh, *Mamá! Mamá*, it's that Mr. Williams. The one from Kane." She stared out the window. "I thought he was crippled. I thought he couldn't ride."

Her mother came to the kitchen window and looked out at the approaching rider.

"*Mi-hija*, that is Henry. I wonder what he wants."

"Henry? You recognize him?" Alejendra paused. "Oh, no. *Mamá*, do you suppose . . . while we were in Kane to get Alonso I asked him to show me how to track. I didn't think he'd come here to teach me. I didn't mean that."

"Henry doesn't teach, *mi-hija*. Maybe he would show you something . . . the way of it but he won't teach nothing."

"*Mamá*, do you suppose he's--?"

"*Mi-hija*," her mother interrupted, "I have known this man for forever, since before you were born. Your father knew him before we were married. I tell you: He will be at the door in five minutes. He will say he is looking for your horses. He will ask where you last saw them. He will tell you if you are coming, catch up. Then he will be gone. You better hurry if you are going to go with him."

"*Mamá*, should I? I mean, go with him?"

"You asked him, *mi-hija*. He is here. What choice have you?"

"*Mamá*, how do you know all these things? I mean about this man? How he thinks? What he will

216

say?"

"*Tu abuelita* told it to me," her mother said. "*Tu abuelito*."

"*Mi abuelita*? She sent me to him. What's going on?"

"*Mi-hija*, I have no idea. There was something. I do not know what. I asked *tu abuelita* but she never tells. They are like . . . you know . . . *está muy loca*. Nobody talks about it, really. Not your *papá*." Her mother shrugged her shoulders.

"I don't get it."

"Me, either, *mi-hija*, but he is in the yard. Go answer the door. Hurry. Remember what I tell you."

Alejendra Rodriquez stepped out onto the porch and walked to the railing. Henry Williams was sitting astride his gruella, waiting. If he was impatient, she couldn't tell, his eyes mostly hidden under the brim of his hat. He didn't appear agitated or restless, sitting easily in the saddle.

"Mr. Williams. I . . . I didn't expect you." She noted that even his horse was watching her as if she were a person of interest he wanted to know about.

"Missy, I am lookin' for your horses. Where's the last place you saw 'em?"

Alejendra hesitated shocked, remembering what her mother had said. "I . . . I last saw them in the horse pasture. But *mi papá*, *mis hermanos*, they're gone looking, they're . . . I only-- "

"The pasture next to the Two Grey Hills?"

"Yes. How did you know? Yes, that's where, but--"

"If you're comin', catch up."

217

The gruella had turned, the rider barely touching its neck with the reins. Just as quickly horse and rider were moving outside of the yard, down the dirt road, moving toward the mountain on the east and the Two Grey Hills horse pasture.

Her mother appeared at her side. "See what I say, *mi-hija*. Didn't I tell it to you?"

"*Mamá*, I do not understand. I asked him to teach me tracking. I asked him what . . . two days ago while we were in Kane. *Mi abuelita* sent me to him. That's how this happened. I just wanted him to teach me. He's so crippled. He can hardly walk. You know this. He sits on the porch of the Neeley Hotel all day, sometimes. Every day. I didn't expect him to get out of his rocker and come to the creek. He's so old, *Mamá*."

"He was not always that way, *mi-hija*. When *tu papá* was a boy, like thirteen or fourteen, your grandfather went to him, asked him to teach *tu papá* the ways of the hunter, the *caballo*, the *vaquero*. Why, I do not know. An hour later he was in front of *tu abuelita's casa grande* wanting to know where the boy was. Mr. Williams was gone after that with *tu papá* many days, many weeks. When they returned, your father was no longer a boy. I do not know what happened. Your *papá* did not seem to like Mr. Williams, but he never said anything bad about him. Afterwards, always he asked Henry for what he thinks, what he should do. Probably more important, after that time with *Señor* Williams, your father could take care of himself."

"*Mi abuelita* says *Papá* can't track."

"It is not that he can't track, *mi-hija*. He can. He is good at this. He can find his way. It is just that Henry

Williams is better than anyone living. The ground, the marks on it seem to speak to him in a language only he understands. You better hurry, *mi-hija*. This one will not wait." Raquel Rodriguez paused and looked at her daughter. "No. That is not true. One time he waited for your *papá*. It was when your *abuelita* told it to him."

"*Mi abuelita?*" Alejendra glanced down the now empty road. "She told a man who does not wait to wait? And he did?"

Her mother nodded.

"Bye, *Mamá*. I gotta go."

"Get your horse, *mi-hija*. You better hurry. You will lose him. This one will not wait, I think. It is not in him."

Alejendra hugged her mother and ran down the steps toward the barn. Then she sprinted, for the rider was no longer in sight. *Madre de Dios! What is with this man? He's so very old. Old enough to be my grandfather. How does he do this?*

Alejendra kept her bay mare at a fast trot, trying to catch up but the mare was no match for the gruella. By the time she reached the west fence to the Two Grey Hill's horse pasture, he was gone, nowhere to be seen. She, too, studied the ground but there was no trace of him. Instead of continuing blindly, she climbed the west slope of the first grey hill and began to search the fence line with her father's binoculars. Nothing. She began to think her mother was right, that if she missed him she missed him and that was that. Suddenly he appeared outside a stand of cottonwood trees on the east edge of the horse pasture. Looking at him through the binoculars, it was as if he was staring right at her.

219

Finally he waved at her, beckoning her to come to him. She complied, though it was against her better judgment. It was that same feeling she had when she went to first grade in Greybull for the first time and everyone spoke English except her. She didn't want to go after that. Her father said she had to, so she did.

The east fence and the cottonwood grove seemed so far away, but she needed to explain to him that her father and her brothers were now looking for her horses; that she didn't need him to track for her. Not now. She had really wanted him to teach her tracking, not come clear out here on the Creek. It embarrassed her that he'd ridden so far. It was only fair; she had to tell him.

When she reached the grove of cottonwoods, he was not there. It exasperated her. Why didn't he just stand still? Why didn't he just wait? She wondered what her *abuelita* had said--why he waited for her and no one else. She rode the mare into the trees, followed a single horse trail down into the brush, and crossed the creek. But he was nowhere to be seen. After half an hour, she began to doubt that she'd seen him, that he was even there. She found, as if to tease her, that he left more tracks, but they seemed to go nowhere, or maybe everywhere. When she turned around, he was behind her, standing beside his horse, his hat pushed back on his head.

She dismounted.

"Missy," he said, acknowledging her.

"Look, Mr. Williams, I think there's been some sort of mistake. It's my fault."

He nodded his head but was looking at the hill

220

country behind her.

"Mr. Williams, I only wanted you to teach me, to explain to me how it is done. Tracking, you know."

He said, "I showed your father when he was very young. He's west of here, by the way. Up on the north slopes of the Horn. Ten, twenty miles, I'd say."

"He must have followed my mares."

"He followed some horses. Not your mares. They are thataway." He nodded with his head, east toward Shell and the western slopes of the Big Horn.

"How could that be?"

"There are two groups, two bands of horses that were here. He followed the wrong band. He'll find that out soon enough. There was a big rain that muted the tracks. You know that."

"How do you know my horses are east of here?"

"There are eleven head. So that's the right number. They are light. Either yearlings or two, maybe three-year-olds or mares. Mares are light. Don't weigh as much as a stud horse. They are the only ones that are bein' driven. The others are bein' led by a horse, undoubtedly, a stud. Your father is followin' that herd."

"What did you say? 'Driven?'"

"Someone stole your horses, Missy. It don't make logical sense. Why take eleven mares into the Big Horns this time of year? Long time ago before you were born, there was a fellow named Hannon that used to do that over on the Pryor. He'd take 'em across the river at Chain Canyon, drive 'em to the cooley, then take 'em over to Sheridan and sell 'em to the horse traders there. As crazy as it seems, it looks like the man intends to kill 'em. No other reason to take 'em where he's goin'."

"Kill . . . kill them? Why would anyone do that? That's not right. You have to be wrong. No one would harm my horses. They've done nothing."

"Missy, the fellow pushin' 'em has trailed 'em up over the ridge into the canyon country. He has them right on top of the Red Mesa Summit. There's no feed there. There's no water. There are two ways out: one is the way in and the other is a five or six hundred foot drop off the south wall. Ain't no other reason to take them there. He's done a fair job of hidin' his tracks."

"How do you know this? Is that what the marks on the ground tell you?"

Henry Williams paused. "The ground tells me where they are. It don't tell me why they are bein' pushed there. That is a guess. There ain't no other reason. He's pushin' 'em hard and fast. He's run 'em up the mountain onto a mesa with no way out. He ain't tryin' to spare 'em."

"*Mi madre* said that you were the best at reading the signs on the earth."

"Your father ain't bad."

"But he's halfway to Cottonwood Canyon or Medicine Mountain."

"It's an honest mistake. Most of the tracks were washed out in the rain. Hard to read 'em."

"How come you are here and *papá* is someplace else if he is pretty good?"

"Sis, I taught your father. He is doin' what I taught him. He's followed horses from the Two Grey Hills horse pasture. Just the wrong ones. He's trailin' what he can see."

"Why are you defending him?"

"I like your father. He's a good man."

"Oh."

For a moment she didn't know what to say.

"Missy, I waited for you 'cause what comes next ain't easy. To catch those ponies, we'll have to ride hard. Chances are we're gonna have to kill someone, if he don't kill us first. It's either now or never. If I'm right, if the man intends to kill 'em, the moment those mares are dead this fellow is goin' to vanish, disappear. He might kill 'em before we can stop him. If you want to quit, do it now. Avoidin' a fight ain't bad. It's one of the things you can do. It might be the easiest. I waited because they are your horses. I ain't in the mood to kill someone if you don't want him dead. You need to decide, sis."

"Why do you call me 'sis?' My name is Alex."

"It's Alejendra. I like callin' you 'sis.' So I do. What do you want to do? It's time to decide."

Alejendra Rodriquez stared at the old man, seeing his grey beard and grey mustache, his tanned cheeks, the way his hat sat on his head. Mostly, she saw his piercing eyes. She noted that even the gruella, standing behind him, his head up, was staring at her.

"I've never killed anyone," she said.

"It ain't pretty."

"It seems wrong."

"Wrong?" The old man smiled. "Religious folks are into right and wrong. Religion is a pretty picture painted on the wall of some white church somewheres. Trouble is, life ain't no pretty picture. It never has been. Someone is gonna kill your horses. I don't know why. For all I know, they're already dead. You need to decide what you're gonna do about it. You damn well might not walk away from this yourself. You gotta decide if you're gonna allow folks to do this to you, rememberin' this fellow, whoever he is, will most likely be shootin' back."

"Me?"

"They're your horses."

"Yes, they are. They are mine. But . . ." She looked at the old man. "What would you do, Mr. Williams?" she asked.

"Sis, you sure you want to know?"

Alejendra looked at Henry before replying. "Yes, sir. I do," she stated.

"I'd hunt the son of a bitch down and cut his throat. I'd do the same to whoever hired him."

Alejendra stared at him, surprised at how easily those awful words came out of his mouth. What was even more amazing, she believed him.

"Who are you?" she asked in bewilderment.

"I am an old man with nothin' to lose. You, on the other hand, are lookin' at the front end of your life. You're lookin' at havin' a husband, kids, a passel of mares and foals. Maybe you don't want to take chances with it. I don't know what it is that you want, so I am askin' you to decide how you want the bear to run itself over the mountain. Every second we stand here is determinin' the end of the story. This is one of those times when you have to decide and live with it. Whichever way, let's get on with it."

"My horses never hurt anyone."

"I know."

"Let's try and save them."

224

"Say it, girl. Say it out loud. What are we doing here?"

"I want to save my horses."

"And the man?"

"Do we have to kill him?"

"Sis, as long as he's alive, he's gonna be tryin' to kill your horses. My guess is someone is payin' him. He can't quit. He's done signed up. He's done told you what he's gonna do. Look at the ground. 'Less you're blind, it's right there. You gotta decide whether to stop him. There ain't no one else."

Alejendra's hand went to her mouth.

"There you are, girl. Decide."

"Why are you doing this to me?"

"Sis, I ain't doing nothin' to you. You can't lead where you ain't goin'."

He watched her eyes light up as he pushed her.

"All right, Mr. Williams," she said, "let's kill him. Let's put a stop to this. It isn't right." She hesitated. "But, Mr. Williams, if we can, I'd like to catch him and let someone else kill him or put him in jail. Put a stop to this . . . like maybe the sheriff. Isn't that what he's for? I don't want to kill anybody if I can get out of it."

"You're a damn fool, girl."

"Why. . . why did you say that?"

"For one: there ain't no sheriff on the mountain. For another: It's November. We're ridin' up on the mountain and you ain't brought a coat. How the hell do you expect to keep warm?"

"I . . . I didn't think. I wasn't expecting to ride up on the mountain. I didn't know all of these things."

225

"It don't make no difference now. We ain't got no time for you to be runnin' back to the house to get a coat you should have tied to your saddle." The old man stared at her, then shook his head. "Think, girl. Just think. Think. This damn country don't give no second chances. Not to you. Not to me. Not to nobody."

The old man turned to his horse and put a foot in the stirrup. Wincing, he pulled himself into the saddle just as the horse turned into him. "Follow me," he said. "But remember, sis, there ain't no sheriff on that mountain. And there ain't no sheriff gonna stop him from killin' you." Henry Williams reined the gruella around so he could see the girl. "Next time, bring a coat even if you don't need it. 'Cause you never know. Hear me? You never know. By the time this is over, you'll sure as hell wish you had."

"Yes, sir."

She tried to follow him. She tried to remember. What did he mean, "You can't lead where you ain't going?"

They rode all afternoon at a trot, moving due east into the mountains, climbing high and higher with each passing minute. Twice he stopped. The second time, he insisted that she get down and study the ground with him. Why he did this, she didn't know except she'd asked him to teach her. Maybe he thought he was supposed to.

"Now look at this," he said.

"Look at what?" she asked.

He glanced at her briefly, as if trying to collect patience from the sagebrush and juniper. "Sis," he said, "look at the ground. See the tracks? Figure out what they are tellin' you."

"Yes?"

"It's like lookin' at a picture book. And like a picture book, the story starts at the beginnin'. First, look to see the age for the marks you're studyin'. These are old and crusted. Since they were made, there has been a mornin' dew at least once, a light rain from a thunder head maybe. When these tracks were laid down, it was rainin'. That would be the day before you were in Kane."

Incredulous, Alejendra stared at the old man. "How do you know that? Just from looking at the ground?"

"You told me it had rained hard about the time your horses disappeared. It also rained hard in Kane. So I expected to see the proof. And here it is. Look at the crust. Look how it's broken up. See how even the bottoms of the track are crusty and the edges are crisp in places. Note that the hoof marks are sort of muddy, like a stick pokin' into a mud pie.

"After you see the age, then look at the whole picture. See what the hell is goin' on. There's one set that came last. Look how deep they sink into the ground compared with the others. They are shod. Half an inch deeper than the rest. It's a heavier horse. He's either big or someone big is ridin' him."

Alejendra squatted down, staring at the churned up earth.

"Now look at these other tracks. They ain't so deep; they are smaller. If you stare long enough, you'll see there are eleven separate individual tracks. Some are on top of others. And on top of all these tracks is this first one, the deeper set. So you know he's followin'. You know that because his tracks are never covered by the others. It's a saddle horse. For some reason, he's favorin' his right front hoof a bit."

"How do you know that? I mean, favoring his right front hoof? Come on!"

He looked at her, smiled. "I don't know how I know it," he said, "but you'll find out that it is true. There is somethin' there that tells me that and I am not sure what it is. After sixty years, I have learned to listen to the voices. That is why I don't teach trackin'. Some of it I don't know. It just is."

"Wow!" she said. "That's sure something."

He smiled. "Want a corn dodger?"

"I do. I really do. I'm so hungry."

"I'll get you a couple. They'll keep the wolf from the door. You eat and we'll keep movin'. We got some time to make up. We need to hurry, best we can."

Henry Williams kept pushing. He pushed for as long as he could read the earth from the back of the gruella, then he stopped, stepping down from the saddle, loosening the cinch. "No fires, missy," he said. "We wait and see if this fellow builds one. See how much he likes his coffee. Maybe he can't live without it."

"No fire?"

He shook his head "no."

"All right."

The old man smiled. Alejendra wondered why.

Around midnight he woke her; told her it was "her turn." She found his sheepskin coat draped around her shoulders.

"Keep lookin'," he instructed. "You never know when he'll show himself. He might not, but maybe we'll get lucky."

Two hours later, she woke him. "Mr. Williams," she said, "down there under that far ridge--I think it's red--I thought I saw a light. It was just for a second, then it was out. I might have been dreaming. I'm so tired I can't say for sure. But I think so."

"All right, missy. Get a little shuteye. I'll have a look."

Alejendra woke up around four, an hour before first light. She found Henry Williams sitting under a juniper tree, leaning against the trunk, not moving. He was holding the reins to both horses in one hand; he had a canteen in the other.

"You were right," he told her. "Our man smokes. The light you saw was him lightin' a cigarette. Saw the light four times over two hours. Must roll his own. Each time in a different place, so our man is movin'. Your horses must be in front of him. He's takin' his time as if he has a lot if it. I'd say he's takin' 'em to the edge. That'd be my guess. Gonna jump 'em off somehow. I'd just shoot 'em. What's eleven cartridges? For some reason, he ain't. Probably wants to make this horse killin' seem somethin' other than what it is. Probably don't want anyone to know he's here. He ain't actin' like he knows we're watchin'. Probably knows your pa is twenty miles northwest of here. He ain't concerned about your old man. That's fairly evident."

"What are we going to do?"

"Well, sis, I'm gonna go have a look at this

229

character. Maybe get in front of him. Get myself between the horses and the cliff somehow. Maybe I can spook them mares and get 'em to run over the top of him. I am lookin' for surprise."

"That's your plan?"

"It's the only one I got."

"What about me? I don't have one at all. You didn't say anything about me in your plan."

The old man smiled.

It irritated her. "Why do you do that?" she asked. "Why, when I say something, do you just smile like you find me funny?"

"You remind me of your grandmother--well, her sister."

"*Mi abuela? Mi tia?*

"Yes."

"How could I possibly remind you of my grandmother? She's old. She's nothing like me. I've never seen my aunt."

"She is an old lady. And you're everythin' like her. One time long ago, I suggested a plan to her sister and she looked at me just like you did. She said, 'Is that your plan?' Said it like I was some sorta crazy. I told her it was the only one I had and just like you, she said to me, 'I don't have one at all.' I was some sort of crazy. It was a bad, bad plan. Your *abuela* said the same thing."

"And you find that funny?"

"I do."

"Well, it isn't."

"How about ironic?"

"Maybe so. Maybe ironic."

"Anyway, that's what they both said and I laughed when they called me on it. Told Anna Marie to let me know when she came up with somethin' better." The old man smiled at Alejendra. "You got anythin' better?"

"No. No, I don't."

"Ever shoot a Colt, *chiquita*?"

"*Chiquita*? Only my *mamá* calls me *chiquita*. You can't say that."

"Now there's two of us. Ever shoot a Colt?"

She nodded. "A .45 Colt. My *papá's*. They're big, too big for me."

"If you can, it's best to fire from the ground. That way you don't spook your horse. And you don't get throwed off, break a leg."

"You expect me to shoot a Colt? I . . ." She looked over and he handed her his, butt first. She took it.

"Careful," he said. "She's loaded. Ready for bear. Now listen," he said, "you stay here. You watch. If I can, I'll spook them mares. I'll try to get them to run in this direction. Hopefully, they'll run over the top of our man. Sort of a bonus. Once they do, you take 'em. Keep 'em movin'. Stay right on 'em. Push 'em down the trail that brought us here. Keep 'em movin' till you get off this mesa. You know it, so you shouldn't get lost. Find your father. Tell him what you know."

"What are you going to do?"

"After I spook those mares, I'll have a conversation with this here horse killer."

"Alone? Shouldn't you wait? You might need help."

"Sis, once I spook them mares, he'll know we're here, if he don't already. At that point, we become the hunted. If he's any good, he'll kill you before the horses get off this mesa. I figure I better have a conversation with him. Seems the thing to do." The old man paused, looked at the girl standing in the darkness before dawn. "You see this man, sis, you shoot him dead. Don't hesitate; just cut the dog loose. Don't ask permission. Shoot him dead. I'll try to make sure you don't see him. But if you do . . . you know what to do. Sis, kill him. That's what he is goin' to do to you."

"All right."

"Any questions?"

"Mr. Williams, you sure didn't sign up for this. I am so sorry. I didn't . . ."

He smiled at her.

"See there you go again. Smiling. Why do you do that? It isn't right. It makes me feel stupid. Like I'm some dumb girl or something."

'Well, sis, we don't sign up for life. Life just happens. This fellow is either gonna kill me or I'm gonna kill him. That's the way of it. Ain't no pretty picture. As for you feelin' stupid, get over it. I'm gonna do a lot more smilin'. Your *abuelo*--he was damn good at it. Everytime he did, I knew the badger was comin' outta his hole and all hell was 'bout to cut loose."

"Mr. Williams?"

"What?"

"You knew mi *abuelo* well? I mean I saw you when he was dying, when he said if I need anything I was to go to you. Do you remember that?"

Henry nodded.

232

"I remember you at his funeral. Sort of. You were always in the back, didn't say anything. And *mi abuela* was always making sure you were taken care of. You know what I mean?"

Henry nodded.

"And you knew my Great Aunt Anna Marie?" Alejendra looked at the old man. "Did you actually know her? I mean, I guess you did. You said you spoke to her. I mean, did you know her? Was she nice?"

He smiled, nodded his head.

"Mr. Williams?"

"What are you, girl? Eighteen? Nineteen?"

"Eighteen."

"Have a beau? Someone you're sweet on?"

Alejendra rolled her eyes. "I haven't got time for that, Mr. Williams. And boys are so time consuming; downright irritating." She looked at Henry. "It's like I wanted to find a stud for my mares. You know? I just wanted a stud horse. Nothing more. I asked the fellow about his. He doesn't know anything about his own horse But it is some horse. You know, a horse that just looking at him takes your breath away. I asked him what he wanted for stud fees. You know what he wants? He wants my mother's tamales. Six dozen. And the stupid guy spends eleven dollars on my box lunch. Eleven dollars? Can you believe that? I swear that Harris kid has biscuits for brains. What box lunch is worth eleven dollars? And what's so difficult about saying how much he wants for stud fees?"

"Eleven? Sounds like he wants to spend some time with you. Spending that much."

"Well, I'm really not interested."

233

The old man smiled. "I can see that," he said.

"What?"

"I can see you're not interested."

"Mr. Williams . . . ?" Alejendra paused. "I . . ."

"What?"

"Oh, I don't know."

"Me, either," he said, as if wanting to change the topic. Pointing across the mesa, he said, "You ready to open this dance, pick a partner, raise a little hell?"

"Not really."

Henry hesitated. "Well, you keep that Colt handy, sis. I'll spook the mares. You follow 'em. That's all you have to do."

"I can shoot, you know. I've done it before."

"You may have to." The old man stared at her. "Don't you hesitate, missy. Don't you even blink an eye. Just pull back the hammer and let the dog loose. Hear me? There won't be no second chances." Henry shook his head as if reconsidering. "But this time, sis, I'll do the shootin'. You do the hoss chasin'. I'll meet you below. If I don't, you keep 'em movin' till you get home. Okay?"

"All right," she said again, and began to remove the coat from her shoulders. "Here," she said. "What about your sheepskin? Don't forget it. Thanks for letting me use it."

"Keep it, sis. Next time bring your own."

He stood up slowly, awkwardly, as if he were unwinding a spool of waxed threat. Once he had his full height he handed her the reins to her saddle horse, then mounted the gruella. She noted that once in the saddle, he appeared neither clumsy nor awkward. The horse transformed him. Without another word to her, he rode into the darkness, juniper trees on both sides enveloping him in a dark cloak of invisibility.

Chapter 21

The going was difficult. Being careful didn't allow for speed. Henry Williams followed the game trails, riding in the direction he'd last seen a light, considering that the man was moving, or at least had been. The ridge took him to the south edge of the Red Mesa and to a six hundred foot, straight down, drop. The terrain forced him to turn left, following the edge of the mesa, until he worked his way to the bottom of a small canyon. It, too, opened onto the brink of the mesa. He could see where runoff fell over the precipice when, on occasion, a cloudburst dropped its load on top.

Turning from the south escarpment, he rode slowly up the small canyon feeling edgy, feeling like he was getting close to his quarry. But he didn't know. On both sides of the narrow canyon, its walls rose one hundred fifty feet. Juniper and sage grew on the sides and on the floor, making it slow going. Except for three deer and one running horse, nothing had been there in weeks. Across the canyon a rock chuck sat on a boulder watching him. But it hadn't sounded an alarm, perhaps finding him harmless.

A mile up the arroyo, he located the mares. It was then that he saw what he thought the fellow had in mind. He was taking them slowly down the canyon to the mesa's edge. Before he got to the end, he'd start them running. The walls of the canyon would keep them together, so they could only go straight. When they came to the canyon mouth, the end of it at the cliff's edge, they wouldn't be able to stop. Over they'd go.

Lord, why kill these mares? What did that accomplish?

Henry Williams rode into a stand of juniper and scrub cedar and waited. He watched the gruella's ears and those of the mares as they cropped clumps of grass. He waited an hour and studied what was in front of him. Periodically, he checked the canyon walls. He expected the man to come down the canyon floor, keeping the mares in front of him. That's what he had been doing. It occurred to him that the mares were all pregnant–pregnant being the only common factor, other than that they were mares. He hadn't seen it at first; it wasn't obvious, but there it was. *So what?* he asked himself. There had to be something they were trying to tell him, that he ought to be seeing. But he couldn't see it. It made no logical, rational sense. *Why run eleven head of pregnant three-going-on-four-year-old mares off a cliff? One just didn't do that. Well, that was wrong. Somebody did.*

The gruella's ears twitched. He saw the mares' heads come up, turn away from him, their ears pointed, listening, watching.

"Thank God," the old man said softly. "Let's open the ball." The gruella heard him; his ears flipped back, his body tensed. "Where are you, buddy boy?"

Henry pulled the Winchester from the boot. Watching: seeing the mares, seeing them start to move toward him. Then he saw the man. He was wearing a dark green shirt the color of the juniper trees, riding a nondescript horse through the juniper breaks, moving in and out of the trees like a ghost, pushing the mares. Henry smiled.

You've been around, old boy. You're thinking I might be here but you are not sure. So you go slow. Making sure. Not allowing yourself to be in the open, keeping in the shadows. You're gonna make this difficult.

The mares started moving toward the juniper stand that hid Henry.

Ah hell, you're gonna make me take a chance. You're gonna force me to turn them horses 'cause I can't let 'em pass. Damn your horse-killing heart. You ain't givin' me no clear shot.

Henry brought the Winchester to his shoulder, catching a glimpse of his adversary. Briefly, he saw the dark green shirt and part of the horse. Henry guessed where the man had disappeared to and put two shots where he should be. The bewildered mares started to run at him, but Henry jumped his gruella in front of them. Pulling his .45, he fired twice into the morning air, turning them, sending them flying in the other direction, running pell mell, swirling in and out of the brush, barranca, sage, and juniper.

Henry fired the revolver again. The report echoed against the canyon walls like a clap of thunder. Following the dust cloud, he ran the gruella through juniper trees and tall sage, but he saw no one. The rider had disappeared. Startled by the sound echoing against the canyon walls, the mares were racing up the arroyo in the direction they'd come. Henry no longer followed. The rider was somewhere. But where? Henry rode the gruella farther up the canyon, found a small cul-de-sac, and waited. The rider would be looking for him. He wouldn't run unless he was hit. Henry dismounted, keeping the gelding back in the trees, keeping behind sandstone boulders the size of a small house.

He's somewhere. What would I do? I'd pull back and wait. I'd wait for me to show myself. All right, all right. Wait. I'll just wait.

Once Henry saw some black birds, some camp robbers, fly into a stand of juniper against the far wall, then immediately take flight. Henry took note of the place and waited. Nothing. He watched a magpie flying down the canyon veer to the right and keep flying. Henry wondered if he had shot the man.

No. No. I didn't. Two shots into the brush . . . that'd be too good to be true. Nothing could have gotten past me, so he's still in front, probably where the canyon grows wider, its walls farther apart.

A hundred yards away in a stand of juniper, he saw movement; the birds had flown, almost landed, suddenly veering away. It was small; just a branch moving when everything else was still. Could be a ground squirrel. Perhaps a black bird, a crow jumping from branch to branch. It happened again ten feet downwind from the first. Henry pulled the rifle to his shoulder and put two shots several feet apart into the brush, then crawling on his belly, got to the gruella. He moved two hundred yards down the canyon farther south toward the mesa's edge, again hiding the gruella in dense juniper. To make sure he couldn't be blind-sided, he hid his tracks, brushing them away with a branch of sagebrush.

In the shade he waited. He ate a corn dodger,

took a sip from his canteen, reloaded the Winchester, aware that the man would be moving.

No. He wouldn't be moving. He'd take stock. This was no greenhorn. He'd step back to see what had happened, then decide.

One and one half hours later, and maybe a few minutes more, after Henry Williams had left her holding her gelding's reins in one hand and a Colt in the other, Alejendra thought she heard a rifle shot, then, a pistol discharge. Twice. Maybe twice, she wasn't sure. Ten minutes later, nine mares raced past her. She waited until another stumbled by at a walk, trying to keep up, favoring its right leg. Alejendra caught the bay mare. She'd named her Flower. She wasn't trying to evade her and Alejendra looked at her leg. It didn't look broken. She couldn't tell what was wrong. Flower had scrapes along her left flank and a gouge into her right shoulder. She was in pretty rough shape, clearly abused. The leg was most troublesome.

For a moment, she considered shooting her, deciding against it. In the end, she left the mare to fend for herself, to make her way if she could, knowing she probably couldn't. She promised herself to come back for her after she got the other nine to safety.

One more.

The eleventh was nowhere to be seen.

Gotta go.

Alejendra Rodriguez fled across the top of Red Mesa, following the trail of her brood mares. Two hours later, she had the mares walking and was almost off the mesa. She kept looking at her back trail. There was no one. She didn't let the mares stop, except to drink on the creek. It was noon the next day when she walked them into the front yard and put them in the corral, so tired, so exhausted; she was at the edge of collapse. Her mother came running out of the house, throwing her arms around her.

"*Chiquita!* Oh, *chiquita!* Are you all right, *chiquita?* Oh, *chiquita, chiquita.* I was so . . . very worried." Coming right behind her mother were her father and her four brothers. They gathered around her. Her brothers teased her about being the brave *vaquero*, rescuing her own horses, saving the day.

"Not me," she said. "Mr. Williams. He did it, *Papá.*"

"Where is he?" Miguel asked. "Where is the old man? You lost him?"

Perhaps it was the question. Perhaps she was so tired she could hardly think. Perhaps it was the mental image of the old man smiling at her before he pulled back the hammer on his Colt Peacemaker and, in the early morning mist, releasing the hammer again and again. That was just her imagination. She hadn't seen that but . . . . Perhaps she was just hungry, so hungry she could no longer think. Perhaps because she lost two mares--whatever it was, Alejendra Rodriquez started to cry. Tears streamed down her dusty, streaked face. She didn't plan it. She didn't want to cry, but she did, standing in the front yard, her father, mother and brothers all around her, her sides heaving.

"What's wrong, *mi-hija?*" her father asked. "You have your horses--some of them, anyway. Where are the other two? Where is Henry?"

241

"*Papá*, someone stole my mares. Stole them! This was not an accident. He cut the fences in three or four different places. He ran you on a goose chase toward Low Mountain. With you gone, he intended to run them off the cliff, right off the mesa. To kill them." She sobbed uncontrollably. "*Papá*, Mr. Williams is going to kill the man that did this to me. He said he was going to have a conversation with the man, but I know, *Papá*. I know how he intends to converse. I don't think the conversation is going to be very long. *Papá*, Mr. Williams is a very old man. He can barely walk. He doesn't . . . he could get himself killed. *Papá*, I'm so worried. I can hardly stand it."

The teary-eyed Alejendra caught a glimpse of Alonso running to the barn, followed by Tomas and Juan. Miguel hugged her before following them.

"Don't worry, sis," he said. "We'll take care of this. We'll bring the old man back." Then he smiled. "Nice sheepskin coat. Where can I get one?"

She started crying again. "Oh, Miguel, I don't mean to cry. Really, I don't. It's just that Mr. Williams calls me sis, and missy, and *chiquita*. He treats me like a little girl. He's so paternal. It's like it's his job and he likes doing it. Please hurry. Please. There's something about him. He just shouldn't be doing this. He's so old, Miguel. He gave me his coat, let me use it; this is his."

Fifteen minutes later, four Rodriquezes, fully armed, left the compound at a trot, following the fresh trail left by Alejendra and her nine remaining mares. Alonso stayed behind to guard the house and protect the women. He didn't like it much, but he'd drawn the short straw and that is what his father, Manny Rodriguez, wanted.

Chapter 22

Henry Williams did exactly what he told the girl he would do. He spooked the mares. The last he saw of them, they were running pell-mell out of the small canyon and out onto the flat top of the mesa.

In the dust cloud further whipped up by the gusting wind, Henry Williams slipped into a stand of twisted juniper trees and set his gruella in the shade. He listened. He watched. He waited. He kept the gruella in hand, no slack in the reins. Henry was tense, the gruella a bundle of nerves, his muscles bunched and ready. Its ears flipped back and forth from the rider to the canyon, to the sounds that washed up and down the canyon walls. Overhead, a cooper's hawk rode the wind currents, moving in lazy circles. In the west, dark clouds were gathering between the Yellowstone and the McCullough Peaks. Some were much closer. Occasionally, a gust of wind rolled up the side of the mountain in front of him. He waited.

Henry Williams had his rules: The first to move dies; so he watched. Patience carries the hunter to success; so he waited. He listened for unusual sounds, something out of the ordinary: a branch breaking, a rock tumbling, birds fluttering, dodging, suddenly turning. All gave warnings. As he waited, the wind increased in velocity, dancing through the juniper branches, picking up dust as it moved south along the length of the canyon walls. The birds bouncing through the tall sage began to twitter. A meadowlark sang its melody.

Nothing bothered them; nothing set off the usual alarms of an intruder.

Henry waited until the first of the dark clouds was above him. Then, in the gusting wind, the random onslaughts of driven rain, and the darkening landscape, he moved from one stand of juniper to another. He kept low in the saddle, making use of rock and tree, presenting only small glimpses of himself at any one time. He wasn't sure where the man he sought hid himself; he could be anywhere. So Henry hid himself from the line of sight in all directions, as much as possible, slinking through the foliage.

He found the man's tracks, a trail left by his horse. Hesitating, he followed them, taking his time, keeping himself and his horse in shade and shadow. The trail was far too obvious. It wandered through brush, seeming to go aimlessly, drifting northward.

Aimless? No, my man is going somewhere. It just appears that way. It's something else, but what?

Henry thought about it, then returned to the original trail, finding that it actually continued south. He found another trail that branched off, wandering through juniper and sagebrush until it appeared to stop a little farther north. But it didn't. Again, Henry returned to the original trail. He studied it. He studied the first and second spurs and knew he was going to see additional trails wander off in another direction. Maybe. A pattern was emerging. Henry found five different trails made by the same horse and the same rider. All went a ways before disappearing. Except they didn't; the riddle was easy. The rider went a distance, then booted his horse's hooves, probably in some sort of bull

245

hide shoe that covered the entire foot. Then he would return to his original trail and remove them.

This fellow is good.

Each one of the trails required forty-five minutes to an hour to investigate; probably ten-fifteen minutes to make. It was getting toward evening. The sun was still in the sky with, maybe, two hours of light left. Time didn't bother the man he trailed. He was taking his time, committing himself to the picture he was leaving in the dirt. So far, he had not committed himself to a single course of action, a single direction. Instead, he deliberately left clues, hiding others.

There is a rhyme.

The hide and seek ritual played itself out in the late evening, along with horse and rider. Henry found himself on the south side of the mesa, overlooking the sheer drop. Oddly, five of the trails seemed to lead away from where he found himself. Those trails angled north. One trail, and only one, went south, but only a little at a time. Like a hidden piece of a puzzle, five of the trails mostly disappeared. Upon closer examination, they always moved closer and closer to the south rim. This fellow was really good: he'd leave a trail, hide a trail, then return to the original trail. It was the same over and over again. *What was he doing?*

Henry was unaware of any path leading off the south rim. It was steep, falling straight down six, sometimes, seven hundred feet. The sheer cliff walls stood as a barrier, forcing the rider to go back around, getting off the mesa the way he got on it. Yet here he was, right where that fellow didn't want him to be. Or maybe he did.

246

I'll be damned. This is a puzzler.

In the diminishing light, Henry stopped. He built no fires. He didn't even get off his horse. Instead, he studied the rim, running his binoculars over the sheer face over and over again. He'd followed the south bound trail until it disappeared into the jumbled rocks along the edge of the cliff. Somewhere there was a way off the ridge. Henry made a one hundred yard half circle and found a trail, then lost it. He made another larger two hundred yard circle and found it again. Four more times he circled; four more times he lost and found the trail only to lose it again. Finally, he found the passageway off the mesa. But he didn't follow it. It was too dark and he'd be much too vulnerable.

In the late night cool air that drifted off the mesa, he watched the trap unfold. All day it had been primed like a pump with water. He'd found the trail off the mesa, but had not followed it. That would have been too easy. In the distance, about four, maybe, five miles due south, he discovered a fire burning, not too large, yet large enough to get his attention. Instantly, he knew he was meant to find it. Henry reviewed all that he knew, then he went to the gruella, fed him some oats, ate some jerky, drank some water, mounted, and headed north.

If Henry were asked why, he would have been unable to tell you how he knew. He just did. The man he trailed rode north five times, then ended up moving south. He built a fire too large for a pot of coffee, showed light when he should have been hiding, running away. Except he wasn't. The fire was off the mesa, five miles away, designed to mislead. He hid his trail

247

moving south, only to let Henry find it. It was all staged. To follow him south off the mesa was a waste of precious time. Already, the rider he'd trailed was covering his trail better than he'd ever done, probably riding a little south before he started north.

Henry figured if it were him, he'd have a base camp; someplace to reconnoiter from, a place to gather information, to lay a well-conceived plan. There were two such places: one, a line camp about six miles north: the other, a dug-out eight miles farther, once used by a trapper, a long, long time ago. Henry, if it were him, would have chosen the line camp; it had water, a view in three directions. It was hidden along a creek, offering a panoramic view of three approaches: south, west, and north. East was problematic because a forest of pine barred the way, making it impossible to escape eastward. The rest was open.

It took Henry Williams all night because he gave the line shack a wide berth, then came up from behind it on the east. Why look east when that way was barred by trees? In a small park, he picketed the gruella, made himself a crutch, then walked, pain notwithstanding, the half mile back toward the line camp, hiding himself in a stand of pine timber and quaken aspen. There he waited, keeping as low as he could. From his vantage point, he could see part of the small corral and part of the one room log cabin. Of the three options, he guessed at the approach that his quarry would make, and chose the one he'd make. He knew that behind him to the south, the man he trailed was painstakingly covering his trail. His progress would have slowed.

Henry found himself liking this fellow.

It was early in the morning when he first caught a glimpse of him. It was short, very short. The fellow was taking no chances. He came up the trail below the spot where Henry sat on the ground with his back against a tree, grass growing up all around him. The fellow would have had to look right at him to see him. Henry watched. The man decided there was no danger, yet, he remained careful. First, he left his horse in a stand of quaken aspen and walked the last two hundred fifty yards to the cabin. Occasionally, he stopped to have a cigarette, each time looking about, studying the land, just as Henry would do, giving anyone who wanted him time to become impatient, to make an error.

After he had moved past Henry, effortlessly taking his time, patiently watching, and listening, and was nearly to the front door of the cabin, Henry moved to the quaken aspen grove and mounted the man's horse. He walked him nearly two hundred fifty yards, coming up behind his quarry, a pistol in each hand. This game gave Henry the opportunity to cover the distance to the cabin, to assure himself there were no surprises. By some miracle, the stranger was at the door before discovering Henry. He hesitated before opening it, turning into his surprise. There was Henry, an old man, sitting astride his horse, two Colt .45s pointed at his chest. That had never happened before. He was caught dead to rights with no options, at least no options that were any good.

"Mornin'," Henry said. "You're damn good, *amigo*. Thought you should know."

His quarry stood silently, waiting.

249

"I've pretty much decided to kill you. You do somethin' stupid, that'll hurry it along."

Henry threw his right leg over the shoulders of the saddle and slid to the ground, catching himself with his right leg, holding himself steady.

"If you got an idea that you're faster at dodgin' than I am at shootin', go ahead. If I even have an idea, a half-baked thought, that you're goin' for it, or if you're lyin' to me, I'm gonna cut the dog loose. Ain't waitin'. Your bein' straightforward will extend your breathin' a few seconds." Henry paused, staring at the man. "Buster, if I was you, and judgin' from how careful you've been, I'd have several spring guns in that cabin waitin' to surprise someone like me. How many you got?"

"Four."

"Where are they?"

"Chair, cupboard, door, fireplace."

Henry nodded. "Good man," he said. "Extended your life forty seconds. You open the door and disarm 'em. Again if'n you're plannin' anythin' stupid, I am lookin' for it. My intention bein' to put an end to this little waltz we have goin' at the slightest excuse."

The hammers were drawn back on both pistols, the Colts steady in Henry's gloved hands. In such a state of alertness, Henry followed the man through the doorway and watched him disarm the cabin. After he was finished, he told the man to sit down at his table. Henry remained standing, searching the cabin, visually turning over every can, fork, and plate. Finally, Henry sat down in the southwest corner on a wooden box and leaned back against the wall, the pistols trained on the man's chest.

"Name?"

"Chester."

"Only name?"

"I use several."

Henry nodded.

"Well, Chet, you sure as hell had me goin' for a while. Damn fool luck--that's what let me catch on to you. I'd have to say you're damned good."

Chester smiled, his hands on the table, relaxed. "Nice touch. Riding up behind me on my own horse."

"Thought you'd appreciate that, especially after you built that fire down below just for me to see."

"You saw it, then."

Henry nodded. "It was a tad too big. As soon as I saw it, I knew you were leadin' me. Hadn't known about the trail off the south ridge. Decided if you wanted me to go south, I'd go north."

Chester nodded.

"Figured you were hired. Who?"

"Gorman O'Neal"

"Who is he?"

"Owns a thoroughbred name of Impressive Traveler. Real famous. Won some important races: the Derby, the Belmont. Wants to keep the bloodlines clean. Seems the horse got loose out Sheridan way and impregnated a mustang mare some place around Buffalo. Wants to end the line there. Paid me to do it."

"How much?"

"I charged him twenty-five thousand to kill the mares and the stud."

"Lord."

"Yeah, I don't like killin' horses, but that is a lot of money. O'Neal has more money than God, so it didn't hurt him none."

"I saw you got one."

Chester nodded. "Somethin' spooked her. None of my doing, though I would have killed her. She ran down the canyon and jumped. She was alone. Probably a rabbit. Maybe just the wind. The rest didn't follow her. Yesterday you put a stop to me runnin' the others."

"Saw that happen in Mexico once. Horse just jumped to his death. Damnedest thing."

"Mexico? You've been there?"

Henry nodded, noting the man's mustache, his Stetson, his nondescript green shirt, double row of buttons on the front. "I was in Mexico. Just a kid." Henry smiled, not taking his eyes off Chester.

"You ain't asked me to drop my pistols."

Henry nodded. "Go for 'em," he said, "make it easier for me to kill you."

"You're pretty confident."

"Wouldn't you be?"

Chester nodded. "I ain't givin' you no cause. You'll have to do that yourself."

"You'd like Mexico, Chet. Went there when I was nineteen, in 1863. Got any jerky?"

"Can on the cupboard on your left."

Henry glanced at it without moving.

"How old are you?"

"Older than dirt. Old enough to know better. Seventy-three last August."

"You are good at trackin'."

"Thanks."

"Where'd you learn that?"

"Learned it from from my father and from an old man in Mexico. I'm a piker compared to him. He could track a skunk across slate rock, tell you when he last ate and what he thought of it. Now that old boy was good."

Chester sat silently, waiting.

"Where will I find this fellow, Gorman?"

"Kentucky."

"Jesus."

"Yes, a long way. On the Cumberland River due south of Lexington. House is on a rise above the road. Nice place. Nice horse, this Impressive Traveler. Why'd you leave Mexico if you liked it so much?"

Henry smiled. "It was the nicest place I've ever been. Don't get cold like this place. The worst, too."

"How's that?"

"Found a girl. Fell in love but she was marryin' another feller. Good man, too. So there I was lookin' at a gal I couldn't forget, workin' for her old man, a hundred miles north of Mexico City. Her old man raised those black fightin' bulls for the rings in the city. Didn't like me much. They speak Mexican down there. She was a Spanish lass. Her name was longer than my arm: Anna Marie Carlos Sanchez. Her sister was Mary Carlos."

"You remember her name and the name of her sister? That don't sound good." He paused. "I could make a little coffee while you're decidin' when to put a slug in me."

"You could but I ain't thirsty."

Chester sat back in the chair, thinking better of

253

getting up to make coffee. "What happened to the girl, if you don't mind me askin'?"

"Left her in Mexico. Sad story."

"You're gonna have me bawlin'."

"Don't wanna do that. You oughta go to Mexico. I'd let you except you killed one of Alejendra's horses. She'd be Mary Carlos' granddaughter."

"The same?"

"The same."

"Tell you what, Old Timer. I'll pay for 'em. One thousand a piece. You let me go. You'll never see me again. That's gotta be more than they're worth."

"You were hired and paid to kill 'em all."

"I was hired. Obviously, I failed. I'm willing to cut my losses. There's one other thing. There may be others. I don't know it, but there may be. I cut some tracks a couple of weeks ago up by Meeteetsee. Might be nothin'."

Henry nodded. "If I let you go and I see you again anywheres, I'll kill you."

"I expect."

Henry sat in silence, in deep thought, quarter seconds away from pulling both triggers. He shook his head, for there was a time when he wouldn't have even thought about it.

"There's the door, Chet. Put the money on the table."

Chester breathed out. He said, "I'm gonna pull my wallet out of my pocket. My right pocket."

Henry nodded and watched him retrieve the wallet, then count the bills, placing them on the table.

"I'd like to get my things."

254

"Chet."

"On second thought, I don't need nothin'. I'll be leavin'. I'll be walking toward the door. Before I go, there's a question I'd like to ask," he said, waiting. Henry didn't react. "Who are you? Give me that."

"Henry Williams."

"I've never heard of you."

"That'd be good."

Chester smiled. "Yes, it would." He rose to his feet and started walking toward the door, before looking back at Henry. "Did you get the girl? I mean, this Alejendra--she's your granddaughter?"

Henry shook his head "no."

"That is a sad story."

"The sad story is me lettin' you go."

Chapter 23

"*Papá, Papá!*" Alejendra Rodriquez ran from the kitchen, throwing a dish towel on the counter, sprinting toward the front door. Miguel stopped on the stairway, hesitating. Alonso stood up, quickly grabbing the pistol lying on the table. Everyone turned.

"*Papá*, it's Mr. Williams. He's here."

She threw open the door and lunged out onto the veranda, the afternoon rays of the sun casting a warm yellow light on her face, on the chairs and table. Tomas was running from the barn with a pitchfork in his hands. He slowed to a walk when he saw who it was and watched his sister's reaction to the visitor.

Henry Williams sat upon his horse in front of the veranda, looking surprised. His horse backed up several steps, its ears twitching back and forth.

"Damn," he said, drawing it out like it was a sentence of death. "Now this is what I call a reception!"

Manny Rodriquez walked out of the house and stood on the porch in front of the steps, his hands in the front pockets of his Levis. He smiled.

"Hank," he said, "step down. You look like you could use a rest."

Henry nodded his head in agreement, "Sounds like a helluva idea. Except I don't know as I can get off this horse. A while back, got a little close to a tree. Tore the hell outta my leg. Then my damn horse steps on me, and gives me a whack for good measure."

Miguel was down the steps. He said, "I'll give

you a hand, Mr. Williams."

"Sorta catch me as I fall outta the saddle, huh, boy?"

"Yes, sir. Keep you from hitting the ground hard."

"I ain't worried none 'bout hittin' the ground. Just don't wanna bounce." Henry smiled and said, "Well, might as well give it a try. I am a little tuckered."

He put his weight on his left foot and stirrup, swung his right leg over the saddle. Even with his hand tight around the saddle horn, he came off in a rush, a rush broken by Miguel and Tomas. With the assistance of both men, he was hauled up the steps and into a chair. He had to sit a minute to catch his breath.

The first thing he said was, "Manny, I'd appreciate it if you could get that damn horse of mine a bait of oats. Like I told you, he ran me into a tree and damn near kilt me. It's a long way home, so I can't shoot him. Much as I hate that horse, I hate walkin' more."

He turned to Manny as Raquel Rodriguez brought out a tall glass of water and set it on the table.

"Thank you much, Ma'am. I'm drier than a sun-dried snake."

"You are welcome, Henry. Drink that and I will bring you something to eat."

"Damn, this is better than livin' in downtown Lovell in the Palace Saloon."

Manny sat down in the chair beside him. "Henry, where were you? We tried to find you. Every time we found a trail to follow, it petered out. I do not

257

just mean petered out. It disappeared altogether. Finally, we came back here to wait for you. We did not know what else to do."

"Well, Manny, I tracked down our boy. Turned out there was just one of him."

Raquel came back outside with a plate of tamales, some fresh bread, and butter. Henry paused in his telling of the story and looked over the food.

"Ma'am," he said, "I hardly know what to say. Thank you very much. I swear I could eat a full sized horse and chase the rider all the way to hell, I am damn near to starvin' to death. Appreciate the grits. I surely do."

Raquel smiled happily. "You are very welcome, Hank."

By this time, everyone had a chair and was gathered around Henry.

"Well, Manny, I had a talk with this feller. Appears that he's some sorta hired gun from everywhere. Pretty good at what he does, I'd say that. Didn't make too many mistakes."

"You got the drop on him?"

"Sorta. I did figure out where he was goin', went there myself and waited for him to show up. To tell the truth, I went to sleep till he was past me, walkin' to his front door. Woke me up. Spoiled a damn good dream. Caught me a bit by surprise."

"You went to sleep?" Manny sounded incredulous.

"Can't say I meant to. I was all sorts of tired. Anyways, I had a polite conversation with him. Turned out to be a nice young man."

"Henry?"

"Damn truth, Manny. I swear. 'Course he was lookin' at the business end of two .45s and I did tell him that if I even thought he was lyin' to me, I was gonna cut' er loose. Told him if he was to live another fifteen seconds, it'd surprise the hell outta me. Appears he believed me. Course his believin' me wasn't all that hard 'cause I meant it." Henry paused, looked at Manny and said, "*Chico*, do you mind if I eat one of these tamales?"

"I am so sorry, Henry. We're all so interested in what you got to say. Excuse us. Please, don't mind us. Take a bite. Please do."

Henry unwrapped the tamale, setting the corn husk aside. He looked at the tamale as though he was inspecting a horse's hoof; smiled, and took a bite. He chewed slowly, swallowed, and looked at Raquel. "Too damn bad you're married, Ma'am. I swear I'd chase ya clear to Omaha and beg you to let me catch you. This here is the best eatin' I've had since they made sliced bread and a butter knife."

"Thank you, Hank." She looked at her husband. "Why you do not say things like that? Let this man eat. Cannot you see he is so hungry?"

"Manny. Manny," Henry said, "it appears that the short and long of it is that some fellow back east in Kentucky hired this fellow to kill these mares and make it look like some accident. He was also supposed to kill that Harris boy's stud and any mare the stud happened to impregnate. That's why the mares were stolen. He was plannin' on runnin' 'em off that south ridge. You know where I mean. Have 'em fall to their death."

"Did he tell you his name?"

"He did."

"Well?"

"Well, hold on, *chico*. Don't rush me. You'll ruin a damn good story right here in the middle of a damn good tamale. And I ain't had none of this water, yet." Henry took a bite of the tamale, chewed it, then chased it with some water. "Now, *chico*, the difficulty here is that this fellow in Kentucky may have hired a number of these fellows to do this killin'. That's what this fellow said."

"Oh, no," Alejendra said aloud. Everyone turned to her. "Someone's going to kill Harry's stud and he doesn't even know. Someone has got to tell him. Someone has to warn him."

Henry replied, "Sounds like a righteous idea, sis. The fellow back in Kentucky goes by the name of Gorman O'Neal. Accordin' to this fellow, he's got more money than God. He comes well-heeled. Harder to get hold of than black smoke in a strong wind, come midnight and no moon."

"You got hold of this man? You caught him?"

"Well, I got hold of Chet. Not Gorman O'Neal. So, yes, I did, and you're thinkin' that me catchin' him means it weren't all that hard. Before I caught up with him, I followed four different trails; all sorta disappeared before I figured out where he was goin'. So I went where he was goin' and waited for him. He was no slouch. If anythin', he was unlucky and I was lucky."

Manny nodded his head slowly.

"Now, *chico,* if I was you, and I ain't, but if I

was, I'd tighten this here place down. Fact is, if you're watchin', nobody'll get close without you knowin' it. You got these boys to help. You could lay a couple of traps. You know what I mean. You'd catch anybody comin' here before . . . well, I ain't gonna spell it out."

"Where is the fellow you caught? You kill him?"

Henry paused, studied Manny for what seemed a long time. "Manny, I didn't need to kill him. We had this discussion about me killin' him. We decided that he'd like to look at old Mexico before he was real dead. I followed him to Greybull, trailing him about two miles behind. I let him see me every time he got to thinkin' he was alone. I watched him purchase a ticket, load his horse on a cattle car goin' to Billings, then get on board himself. Maybe I'm gettin' old: too much layin' around eatin' cookin' like this here: gettin' soft. But I decided to give the boy a chance."

"Boy? How old was he?"

"I'd say he was twenty-eight, maybe thirty-three or so. Pretty young. Just a kid."

Miguel smiled. "Have another tamale, Mr. Williams. I will get you something a little stronger to wash it down with."

"That's mighty kind of you, boy," Henry said. He looked at Tomas. "Tomas," he said, "ain't seen you in a spell. Hear you got married and have a house full of kids and expectin' another. That's what I hear."

"No," Tomas said. "I mean, I am married but I only have two boys. And my wife isn't expecting."

"Well, good for you. I was thinkin' about you the other day. Remember that time you got on that rank

261

bronc, got yourself bucked off in that cactus? Pulled them spines out of your butt for nearly half an hour. Damn wonder you had kids at all. Those boys of yours: Carlos and Huberto. Did I get that right?"

"How? How did you know?"

"You mean I ain't got that right? I was told they was six and eight."

"No. I mean, yes. How do you know these things?"

"And your wife is beautiful and her name is Soccora. I hear tell she can cook murderous corn bread and boil a coffee bean that'd peel the rust off an old skillet."

Henry smiled and before Tomas could speak again, he turned to Manny.

"Manny," he said, "you keep these boys reined in. I don't want them to kill nobody or be killed by nobody. You keep them home lookin' after you and yours. This is one of those things that can blow over, if you let it. If it don't, we can pull our irons and go to shootin'. But we can do that shootin' on our own terms. We can pick the ground. I'd like to see Tomas alive when those boys of his take to ridin' the green out of them saddle broncs of yours. I'd like not to see Soccora be a widow before her time. I hate funerals. I'm askin' you outta respect for me to let it ride for a week or two."

"Henry, I--"

"No, Manny. Keep them close at home. Watch the back door. You boys are gonna have your hands full just doin' that. I'm tellin' you. Protect the women folk and hold on to what you got." Henry Williams ceased speaking.

There was silence until the silence became uncomfortable: until Miguel brought him a glass of tequila: until Alejendra got up and walked to the end of the veranda: until a gust of wind caught the barn doors and slammed them shut with a loud bang so loud that everyone turned to look to see what had happened.

Manny broke the silence, "All right, Hank," he said.

"Two weeks, Manny. Just two weeks."

Manny Rodriguez nodded his head.

"*Chico*, I have one other request. When I get done gettin' myself around this juice and these tamales, and this here bread, I'd be most grateful if you'd have these boys boost my butt back on that gruella. I got a few places I gotta be and a few gents I need to talk to about a whole string of horses. If you would be so kind. I am not all that sure I can get off the ground without some help. And could you get that damn horse some oats?"

Manny threw his head back and started laughing, "*Mi amigo*," he said, "would you stop, slow down; rest up just a bit? You are driving yourself into an early grave."

"*Chico*, at seventy-three I couldn't hop into an early grave if I wanted to. I figure I'll get all rested up when I'm dead. Remember now, you are givin' me two weeks before you grab the donkey by the tail."

"I will remember, *mi compadre. Dos semanas.* But you, too, please be careful, Hank. You are pushing yourself far too hard. All of my life I have taken advice from you. Take some from me. Slow down. *Por favor.*"

"Even as you say it, *chico*. I'll be takin' it slow."

"Start by staying the night."

"Truthfully, I would, Manny. But if I don't get back on that gruella, I'll be so stiff I can't."

The old man smiled at Manuel Rodriquez, the concern written on his face. "You've done real well, Manny. Take care of this family. Especially this here cook. You don't know how damn lucky you are."

"I do know. It was you who said I should marry her."

"I did? I didn't know I was that damn smart."

Miguel and Tomas went to the barn to get some oats and a feed bag. Alejendra brought a chair up to the table and sat with her father.

"*Bonita*," Henry said, "I see you made it down off the ridge."

"I did."

"Your horses?"

"Nine. Flower had a broken leg. *Papá* had to . . . " The girl's voice got a little shallow. She paused. "I really liked that mare. She was my favorite."

"So, you got nine."

Alejendra nodded without speaking.

"The other is dead, too. Saw her when I came off the ridge on the other side. She fell. Got run off. Damn shame. But that gent felt so bad, he left me some money to give you." Henry reached for his shirt pocket, unbuttoned it, and handed her the bills. "Don't much replace the horse, but there it is."

Alejendra looked surprised.

"What is this?" she said.

"Looks like money to me."

264

"I know, but--"

"That boy felt so bad 'bout causin' you grief that he paid you. You wouldn't have my Colt, would you? I might be needin' it. And that sheepskin? It was a might frosty this mornin'."

For a moment no one spoke, staring at the money. "Yes, yes, I do." Alejendra jumped up. "I'll get it for you." She stood, looking from the stack of bills on the table to Henry Williams. "You're sure full of surprises," she said. "I don't know what to say. That's way over what the two mares are worth."

"Ol' Chet was overcome with grief. Almost started bawlin'."

Alejendra shook her head in disbelief. "I'll get the Colt for you, Mr. Williams." She turned and walked inside the house.

Alonso shifted his weight in his chair.

"*Papá*," he said, "someone should warn the Harris boy."

"Alonso's right about that," Henry said.

Alonso stood up. "I'll go, *Papá*. It's my turn."

"Do you know where to find him?" his father asked. "The Harrises live on the other side of Meeteetsee up against the mountain."

Henry grunted. Everyone turned to look at him. "Alonso, you be careful," he said. "I don't know what's out there, but there is at least one other horse killer. Count on it. That's what I was told."

"I will, Mr. Williams. I'll be careful." Alonso tapped the pistol butt behind his belt buckle. "I'll be real careful, Mr. Williams," he repeated, and started for the steps.

"Alonso," Henry said, "take a rifle, too. You just might have to reach out there and tap someone on the shoulder."

Alonso smiled. "Just like we tapped that black bear, Mr. Williams?"

"Just like it, boy. Just like it. That bear had teeth. Didn't want to get too close."

Chapter 24

Lying in her bed, Alejendra Carlos Rodriguez couldn't stop thinking about Harry Harris. She twisted the sheets until the blankets and her down pillow fell on the floor. She twisted and turned until she had to get up and get a drink of water, unable to stop thinking. For a moment, she stood over the sink full of unwashed dishes watching the harvest moon rising up over Bald Mountain, thinking about the old man Henry Williams, wondering about him. She thought about Alonso; he'd be almost to Greybull. She turned and looked at the ancient grandfather clock but it was too dark to see where the hands were pointing. She didn't care anyway. It was then that she remembered that Harry was working on the Pitchfork, that he'd hired on as a drover, at least through the fall roundup. Harry wasn't at home. He was miles and miles from where Alonso was headed. Harry was in the mountains. That's when she set the glass down and swallowed hard. Harry would never know until it was too late. The horse would be shot dead. It was then that the horrible loss of her two mares seized her heart, holding it in its grasp like iron clamps. Tears of remorse and grief came to her eyes, running down her cheeks.

What had the old man said? "Warning Harry . . . that's a righteous idea."

Alejendra took a deep breath and, with the sleeve of her nightgown, wiped the tears from her cheeks.

I'll need a rifle. Something to eat. Some water. My winter coat for the cold. Riding boots. I'll take Rosie. She can hold up to a long ride.

Her bare feet carried her soundlessly across the hardwood floor to her room, where she dressed. If she had known, she may have taken a little more time, but time was what she didn't have. Even a few minutes could make all the difference in Tapper's life, and whether he was going to have one or not. She had to warn Harry. She had to tell him to run for his horse's life while he had a life.

Alejendra Rodriguez rode quickly. It was hard not to just stick the steel to the mare's underbelly and let her run. But she didn't, knowing that such foolishness would kill the horse, break her wind; that it could happen so fast that she wouldn't even make the river. So she paced the mare at a fast walk, riding into the night, the morning, the afternoon, and the evening of the next day. Three times she stopped for half an hour, letting the mare, drink, crop grass, and rest. It wasn't nearly enough, but she reasoned that it was all she had.

Chapter 25

Henry Williams made it all the way to the Big Horn River and thought he was making pretty good time considering the horse's state of fatigue and his own--he, himself, having been beaten into the ground, worn thin. In a stand of young cottonwood, he stopped and stared at the large moon rising above Medicine Mountain. He turned the collar of his sheepskin up. The gruella was impatient, tossing his head. Overhead, swallows were darting across the dark sky. Somewhere a fish jumped, splashing as it re-entered the moving water. It was quiet. The frogs and crickets were no longer singing, not in November, not in the deep fall of the year, when every night turned cool, leaving frost hanging in the trees.

Henry slid out of the saddle, and got the gruella some oats to eat. He built a small fire, then tended to the horse, removing the feed bag from its nose.

"Reckon we'll camp here, horse. I'm all tuckered. You ain't so spry yourself." He loosened the cinch and removed the saddle. "Take her easy, horse, take it easy," Henry said. "You eat a few oats and you get to thinkin' you're some two-year-old colt. Well, you ain't." Henry paused, listening to the night sounds of the river. "I ain't, neither," he said.

Harry laid out his bed roll on a bed of fallen cottonwood leaves. In the dark, cool evening, he chewed on some jerky, washing it down with water from his canteen. Lying on the canvas that covered his bed roll, wrapped in his sheepskin coat, he tried to sleep but couldn't; not until Orion dropped into the western sky. Somewhere in the night, he drifted away, then awoke with a start, listening, a little disoriented.

In the early morning, before false dawn showed itself, silhouetting the rim of the Big Horns, he got up, checking on the gruella. The horse stood on the end of his picket rope, blowing his nose at him, as if Henry was a bear. Henry smiled. "I know what you're thinkin'. You're wishin' you were home, eatin' Rainbow Harv's timothy hay." Henry stared at the diminishing stars. "It's that damn girl, ain't it? She ain't gonna stay home. She ain't gonna leave well enough alone. It's that damn girl."

The gruella's ears twitched back and forth as he listened to the gravelly voice, to the sounds of the river, to the breeze coming out of Sheep Canyon. Somewhere a lone frog was telling the world about its loneliness. The old man shook his head slowly, resting his hands on the horse's back.

"Well, horse, what would you do if you were a girl in Manny's house, her dad and mother lyin' in bed at the end of the hall? Miguel sleepin' upstairs? Alonso out there ridin' to serve notice? 'Course she ain't set on that Harris boy, yet. She ain't decided that he's the one. That's plain, horse. She gets all irritated with him. He aggravates the hell right out of her."

The old man listened to an owl talking to another; somewhere coyotes were hunting, stopping to howl at the sitting moon, then returning to their incessant yapping.

"Damn it, horse, You see what I see? 'Course

you do. You saw it before I did. Think you're smart, don't you? She wouldn't get so aggravated if she didn't give a damn. So she gives a damn. What a hell of a note. She's already ridin', ain't she? She's got that itch she can't scratch and she don't know it. Well, hoss, I hope you know how to track a lovesick girl in the grey dawn of morning. I sure as hell don't. Trouble is, she's Franko's granddaughter. Guess we better get to trackin'. What the hell you waitin' for, an invite?"

Harry broke camp, saddled the gruella, pulled himself into the saddle with his arms. Taking a deep breath, he nudged the horse forward, looking at the wide expanse of the Big Horn River. "Guess we'll have to swim, horse. That girl could ride clear to Greybull. Use the bridge. Will she?" Henry shook his head "no." "But she won't. She's in a considerable hurry. So, we just need to find where she crossed. So, we'll have to swim. Don't you go dunkin' me, now. Hear? I sure as hell can't walk home. And I can't swim worth a damn."

Henry's horse swam the river a mile above a spot on the map called Spence, Wyoming, a considerable distance beyond Sheep Canyon. Once across, he rode upstream, looking for horse tracks coming up out of the river. Six miles later, he found them. He looked them over, making sure. Several hundred yards later, he was sure. It had him shaking his head in bewilderment.

She's riding a mare looking for a stud horse. That's going to cause all sorts of trouble. Damn fool girl; she doesn't think. Well, who does, riding out in the badlands of northern Wyoming chasing after a boy she can't stand and can't forget? Damn the luck. Nothing

271

like a girl making the morning more interesting than it already is. Don't look like she's all that far ahead of us.

Chapter 26

The cook at the Pitchfork told Alejendra where Harry was working, told her where the line shack was located, and how to get there. By that time, she hadn't slept in more than forty-eight hours and could barely stay in the saddle. But she did, riding the last five miles in a daze bordering on comatose.

Mid-afternoon she rode up to the cabin determined to give the warning, to tell Harry to run; that is why she was there. That is why she'd come. Without getting off her horse, she yelled, "Harry! Harry, are you in there?" She shook her head to clear it. "Harry!" she screamed. "Damn you! Get out here!"

She looked down and there he was. Normally his sudden appearance would have surprised her. Not now. She shook her head again, but it really did no good. It felt like her brain was bouncing in her skull from side to side, that if she wasn't careful her head would fall right off her shoulders and roll onto the ground.

"Alex, what are you doing here?" His hand was on her saddle horn.

"Harry," she said, "Harry, please listen. Someone is coming to kill Tapper. You got to get him out of here. Do you hear me? You got to get him out of here now."

"Lordy, Alex, you look awful. Get down--"

"Harry, I didn't ride for two straight days for you to help me off my horse. Get Tapper and get out of here. Do it now. Did you hear me? Someone is coming to kill him. Now, damn it! Do you hear me?"

"Alex?"

"Now, Harry! Get out of here now. We'll talk later. Please, just go before it's too late."

Never in her life had Alejendra Carlos Rodriguez sworn. Now she had; twice, practically in the same sentence. Mr. Williams, he swore. He swore all of the time. She doubted that he could talk without swearing. That would be impossible, but not her. No, not her.

Harry ran to the corral.

Alejendra slid from the saddle, sat down, then laid back on the ground. She'd had it. She closed her eyes.

Minutes later she saw Harry standing over her, staring at her.

"Alex? Alex, what's wrong? I ain't leavin' you here."

"Harry, please go. They're coming for Tapper. Please go. Save him."

"Alex, who's comin'?"

"Are you listening, Harry? Save your horse. Please, just go."

Harry mounted. "I'm not sure about this. Leavin' you here!"

"Please, Harry?"

Harry rode around the edge of the cabin, looking back at Alejendra sitting on the ground in the shadow of her mare. She waved her hand urging him to go, then buried her face in her hands. It was after he'd disappeared into the pine and quaken aspen behind the cabin that she heard a shot, followed quickly by another. Alejendra jumped to her feet, her hand going to her mouth. She started to run toward the trees but stopped, came back, and pulled the rifle from the boot. She commenced running again. If she could have listened, she'd have heard herself screaming, "Harry! Harry! My God, Harry!" But she couldn't hear herself. She never even felt her feet touching the ground, or noticed the act of chambering a round in the 30-30 Winchester, model 1973.

She found Harry lying in a grove of quaken aspen. He was on the ground, the reins wrapped around his right wrist. The stud was pulling away from him, half dragging him. She grabbed the reins and released his wrist from the twists. Quickly, she got Harry to his feet, and helped him limp to a log, sitting him on the ground. He'd been shot through the left forearm and the leg. He was bleeding profusely.

"Geez, Alex. I've been shot."

"Be quiet, Harry. I'll be right back."

Alejendra ran to where the stud was ground hitched and led him back into the stand of pine and quaken asp, tying him to the limb of a fallen tree. Carrying her rifle, she rushed back to Harry. He was white, his face ashen and bloodless. Laying the rifle down, she quickly examined Harry's leg and arm. Blood was leaking everywhere. She tried to remember what she should do, but her head wasn't working. In the middle of it, she heard a shot. She picked up her rifle and fired back at nothing.

"Why'd you do that?" Harry whispered. "Now, they'll know where we are."

"And they'll know we aren't going to die easily."

"You might not, but I don't know about me. I'm bleedin' all over the place."

"Shut up. I'm trying to think."

"Thanks for comin', Alex. I mean it. Thanks."

"Would you please shut up? I'm trying to think of what to do. I gotta do something."

Harry stared at her. "It's all right, Alex. You've done what you could."

"Shut up, I tell you." She was inches away from crying.

"I'm shot, Alex. I'm shot bad. Look at the blood. There's nothing you can do."

"What the hell is goin' on here?"

In the fog of her overstressed, exhausted brain, Alejendra looked up, knowing she was dead; she'd been caught; her life was over. Then it dawned on her that she had heard the voice before. Recognition was coming, but it wasn't there yet. Four seconds had ticked away since the question "What the hell is goin' on here?" had intruded into her thoughts. *What*?

A man--the shadow, the voice, the sheer strength of him--was stepping down from his horse, a gruella. He grabbed her by the shirt and literally jerked her up by the collar, standing her on her feet. He slapped her across the face, a hard stinging blow. Her head was immediately clear, and she was, oh, so angry.

"Girl," the voice said, "wake up. This boy needs you now. Take his belt. Wrap it around his leg. Tight. Hear me? Cut the bleeding. Take your bandana and tie it tight around his forearm. Stop the bleedin'. Get him on his horse and get him some help."

"Mr. Williams, I'm so tired. Someone shot him. Can't you see?"

"I don't give a damn if you ain't slept in a year. Get to work. Do it now. Give yourself no excuses. Get him in the saddle before he's dead. Remember who you are."

"I can't. How can I?"

"If you have to cut him in pieces and stick him in his saddle bags, get it done. Hear me? Remember who you are!"

"What about the--?"

"Don't you worry your head about nothin' else. I'll have a talk with this fellow."

Abruptly, he turned and mounted his horse in one sweeping action. She saw his face and realized he'd just done what he could never do; then she knew what he meant. When she looked again, he was riding out of the clearing on the back of a gruella.

My God, she thought, her face stinging, her ears ringing.

She looked at Harry.

"Who was that?"

"I don't know, Harry. I'd say he was my father's father except my grandfathers are both dead. He was at my grandfather's funeral. Stayed in the back. Didn't say much. In fact, he didn't say anything at all. He sure isn't cutting me any slack, is he?" Alejendra turned to the wounded man, "Now, Harry, I am going to take your belt and wrap it around your leg and stop the bleeding. I am going to wrap my bandana around your forearm tight to stop the bleeding. Then I am going to get you on your horse."

Harry nodded.

Alejendra took a deep breath. "And after that I am going to walk on water."

Harry smiled in spite of himself. "I believe it. But who was that?" he asked again. "He really popped you hard."

"Henry Williams."

"I ain't never heard of him."

"You have now."

Alejendra knelt down beside Harry and began working his belt from its loops and from around his waist. He was watching her, trying to help, his hands getting in the way of her efforts.

"I can tell you one thing, Harry," Alejendra said as she got the belt loose, "Henry Williams always walks on water."

Chapter 27

Henry Williams had trailed the girl. It wasn't hard. She wasn't trying to hide her tracks. She rode west right up the Greybull river toward Meeteetsee, then she kept to the north, still riding in a westerly direction. He discovered the places she'd stopped: where the mare had cropped grass: where Alejendra had grained her, dropping the oats on the bare ground.

The gruella was efficient. He'd done this before, walking steadily, effortlessly. When they stopped, he cropped grass, chewed a bait of oats on a piece of canvas Henry rolled out on the ground. Every hour they stopped to rest, then moved on, walking up the river bed following the trail of the Rodriguez girl.

A few minutes after noon of the second day, Henry reached the Pitchfork home ranch. The cook house, bunk house, and main house were adobe structures. The buildings were settled in a small valley, built around a creek decorated with leafless cottonwood trees. Beyond the valley, both north and south, the land was dry and arid. Further west, the Absaroka mountains raised their snow-covered peaks into the sky. Beyond them lay the valley of the Yellowstone. Henry happened upon a fellow he knew only as Mack, standing by the horse corral. Several hands were working the green out of the rough horses; he was helping hold them down as the rider mounted.

"Hank? What are you doin' here? Ain't seen you much. Figured you were dead."

"Been around, Mack. Still suckin' in and breathin' out. Settin' on the porch, mostly. I'm lookin' for a girl."

"At your age? You oughta be lookin' for a couch. Not chasin' skirts."

"Ain't that the damn truth."

"Would that be a Mexican girl? Good lookin' as sin? Ridin' a young mare with sore feet? Pretty much done in?"

Henry nodded. "That'd be her."

"Went through here maybe an hour ago. Lookin' for that Harris boy. He's workin' fence up in the line shack on the north ridge a couple miles this side of Franc's Peak. Know where I mean? Five or six miles from here, then a short jog to your right. She talked with Jim-Bob, so I'm short on all she said."

"I've been there. A long time ago. Reckon it ain't moved."

"Naw, it's still there."

"See anybody else? Be an easterner, I suspect. Somebody out of place. Won't be sayin' much."

"Can't say that I have. Jim-Bob mentioned that he came across some strange tracks a day or so ago east of here. Not long. Come to think of it, it was yesterday mornin'. Think that's what he said. Said he didn't recognize the horse from the tracks. It was nobody, I reckon. Jim-Bob, he ain't here or you could ask him. Trouble?"

"I expect. I'll be goin', Mack. Gotta track that girl down before she gets herself shot all to hell."

"See you around the farm, Hank."

"You too, Mack. Keep the wind at your back.

Don't step in no gopher holes."

The gruella, given his head, moved out. Henry cut the trail that Mack had mentioned to him. The tracks were fresh. It was a horse riding heavy, meaning, either it was a big horse or a big man on a normal sized horse, or both. The ground didn't tell Henry which. It was clear the man he tracked was following the mare; the larger horse's tracks covered those of the mare, and, in some places, destroyed them altogether. About four miles up the canyon, the trails diverged, the larger, weight-bearing horse turning more to the right into the sparse timber. Henry followed the bigger horse, minutes behind him.

The fact that the traveler's tracks covered Alejendra's was worrisome to Henry. His concentration was interrupted by two rifle shots in quick succession. They were fired close together; someone was doing his best to pump a lever action Winchester. The repercussions were loud, close at hand. Henry pulled his revolver and walked the gruella forward; he passed through a clearing, over a rise, and into a meadow.

He found the horse but no rider. He did see where the man had dismounted and walked to the rise. Henry dismounted and hobbled up the trail to where the rise overlooked the line cabin that he'd been seeking. To his right he saw the outline of a man lying down in the brush, peering into the small basin below. Henry moved closer, slowing himself way down so as not to make any noise.

Out on the rim's edge the wind picked up, tugging at his jacket. When he was twenty feet away he could see what the shooter was looking at. Below him Alejendra's mare stood at the door of the log cabin. To his right he could see her sprinting up the small creek through some pine trees and a few quaken asp. Ahead of her he could see part of the Harris boy's stud horse standing in the clearing and the Harris boy himself lying on the ground, his torso partially hidden behind brush growing along the creek.

The shooter was cocking his rifle, unaware of Henry watching him, his .45 Colt in his left hand.

"How's the huntin'?" Henry said to him. "Shoot any girls, lately?"

The effect of Henry's voice was electrifying. Immediately, the shooter sprang to his feet, trying to bring his almost cocked rifle to bear on the intruder. Henry watched, fascinated. As the rifle came up, about to be brought to bear, Henry calmly shot him in the stomach. Henry's shot was followed shortly by a rifle shot from below and the big fellow falling over, grabbing his stomach with both hands.

The man looked at Henry, then down at the blood leaking from his stomach wound. "My God, you gut shot me," he said, as if what he was seeing was a surprise to him.

"I did," Henry said. "What did you expect, you tryin' to put a hole in me, yourself?"

The rather large man rolled on the ground, trying to assess his wound. "My God," he said, "I think you done kilt me."

"You shouldn't have throwed down on me."

Henry stood over the wounded man, watching him closely. Out of caution, he picked up the man's

Winchester, smashed the stock, and cast the barrel and locking mechanism off to the side. "I'll be back," he told the shooter. "Gotta see what you did to those kids. Shootin' like that from this distance, downhill and all. God only knows."

"You're leavin' me here?"

"Damn right."

Henry Williams hobbled back to his horse, mounted, and rode down the hillside at a run. He rode past the cabin, Alejendra's mare, and into the small basin where he came upon the pair. Alejendra was bending over the wounded Harry Harris. He could see the boy had been shot in the arm and the leg. His leg was bleeding profusely. The stud horse was standing back in the grove of aspen. It was apparent to Henry that Alejendra was too overwhelmed to act, to take control of the situation. He stepped down from the gruella and walked up behind her and broke the silence.

"What the hell is going on here?" he said louder than he wanted.

A dazed Alejendra looked up and stared vacantly at him, blinking her round brown eyes, working her jaw as if she were about to say something. But she didn't.

This is no good. He reached down, seizing her by the collar, and yanked her to her feet, slapping her across the face. "Girl," he said, his face right in hers, "wake up. This boy needs you now. Take his belt. Wrap it around his leg. Tight. Hear me? Cut the bleeding. Take your bandana and tie it tight around his forearm. Stop the bleeding. Get him on his horse and get him some help."

"Mr. Williams, I'm so tired. Someone shot him. Can't you see? I'm--"

"I don't give a damn if you ain't slept in a year. Get to work. Do it now. Give yourself no excuses. Get him in the saddle before he's dead. Remember who the hell you are."

"I can't. How can I?"

"If you have to, cut him in pieces and stick him in his saddle bags. Get it done. Hear me? Remember who you are! Save his life."

"What about the--?"

"Don't you worry your head about nothin'. I'll have a talk with this other fellow."

"One other thing. Don't ever shoot 'less you know what it is you're shootin' at. You coulda kilt me and I ain't likin' that idea. Hear me?"

"Yes, sir."

Abruptly, he turned and mounted his horse in one sweeping action. *Damn, that hurts like hell. Stupid kid."*

He rode the gruella out of the glen and around the side of the hill overlooking the cabin. He had to hurry; he didn't know how long the shooter would last and he wanted to ask him several questions. There certainly wasn't much time, not as much as he wanted.

He found the man. He wasn't dead but time wasn't waiting. Henry could readily see this fellow was marching with the grim reaper, matching him stride for stride, the second hand racing toward the end one heartbeat at a time. When the man saw him, he spoke in a rattling, hard breathing manner. It was difficult for

284

Henry to understand him.

He said, "I didn't think you were comin' back."

"Had some questions I wanted to ask."

"Did I get that stud horse?"

"No, you missed him. Got the boy, though. Shot him in the leg and arm. Why did you go do a fool thing like that? You oughta know better."

The dark complected man was having trouble lifting his arm so he let it lay uncomfortably on the side of his chest just above his stomach wound. Blood leaked down his stomach wall, staining his blue cotton shirt like so much fresh red paint running down a wall.

"Who hired you to kill that horse?"

The wounded man took a deep breath as if he wondered whether or not to answer the question. Finally he said, "O'Neal."

"That'd be Gorman?"

"Yes. How did you know that?"

"He hired another, a feller that was a lot better than you."

"Oh."

"Does this O'Neal live in Kentucky?"

"Yes."

"Same fellow, then."

The man lying on his back didn't answer, his hands gripping the bloody shirt that covered his abdomen.

"What do you want me to do with your horse?" Henry asked.

"Turn him . . . loose. But don't go. I don't want to die alone."

"You shoulda thought that 'fore you tried to kill

285

me." Henry glanced at the dying man, thinking: *Everyone dies alone. Can't be helped. Even Franko, with all of those folks standing around him willing him to live, died alone. And Franko didn't try and kill nobody, not that didn't deserve killing.*

Henry had difficulty sympathizing with the man who shot the Harris boy, having taken money to kill a horse. Silence prevailed momentarily. Henry looked at his gruella. The horse killer saw him and protested.

"Don't go," he begged. "Please. I don't want to die alone."

Henry sat down slowly, leaning against a piece of granite rock and the embedded remainder of a dead pine tree that hadn't felt sap creeping up its trunk for years and years.

Why not wait? The damn tree had died just like this man is going to die. What the hell?

"Mister?"

"I'm right here."

"It was good money. I mean twenty-five hundred dollars to kill a horse."

Henry nodded and asked, "Got a wife and kids?"

"No."

"That's good."

"Is it, mister? Is it really good? I could have had a wife and kids."

"Instead, here you are dyin' on a tree-studded ridge in Northern Wyoming. Hell of a note, ain't it?"

"I never expected it."

"Nobody does," Henry replied, "except old Franko. He expected it a long time before he got

286

pneumonia. Made me promise to take care of his woman. Made me swear. Damn his hide. Guess it don't make no difference. I'd a done it even if he didn't have me promise. I wonder why he was so damn worried about that." He paused, shaking his head at the thought. He said,"We were fishin' up on Trout Creek. Me, Franko and this Indian, Fleury. Been there two weeks just gettin' good and drunk, and Franko starts in on this talk. Fleury said 'Franko, you're damn crazy.' But Franko insisted. So I promised."

"I wish I was fishin'."

"Stop your damn whinin'. You got yourself into this. Now you gotta live with it. It's your own damn fault."

"You're right, but I don't have to like it."

"No, I guess you don't."

The shooter died later in the evening, about the time the moon was settled over the Absaroka Mountains. Next morning Henry didn't bother burying him. He didn't have a shovel and saw no point in working up a sweat piling rocks on the corpse. The coyotes would get at him anyway. Besides there weren't any rocks to carry. He fed the dead man's horse a bait of oats and turned him loose. He left his saddle, bridle, an old Navy Colt, and the rifle with the broken stock. He claimed as his own the thirty-six dollars in folding money the fellow had in his pocket.

By the time Henry made it off the ridge and headed east to the Pitchfork Ranch, the buzzards were circling the corpse. Several had settled in the nearest trees and the magpies were pulling him apart, picking at his lifeless eyes. Ironically, the coyotes wouldn't have anything to do with him because he smelled too much like a man. By the time they'd built up some courage, there was nothing left to eat

Henry checked on Manny's girl before he started home.

Mack was standing in the yard, leaning against a double bladed ax handle, watching him as he rode in. To his left was a pile of split firewood he'd been working on. Behind him was a cross-cut and a stack of pine logs waiting to be sawed.

"Mack, how the hell are you?" Henry said as he slid from the saddle.

The two men shook hands; Henry studied the stack of logs.

"Looks like you've got your work cut out for you."

Mack smiled. "Yeah," he said, "this is the part of cowboyin' I ain't too excited 'bout. But it does work up an appetite."

"That gal make it down offa' the ridge?"

Mack nodded. "That Harry, too. She's over'n the bunk house sacked out. I'd say that girl was wearin' it at both ends. She was plumb tuckered. Harry all shot ta hell. Looks like he'll make it less he gets some sorta infection."

"That's good."

"How'd Harry get that way?"

"That feller you told me 'bout shot him tryin' to kill that stud of his. Musta been damn near blind. Couldn't hit a rat in a can with a stick."

Mack looked at Henry.

"Don't you worry. That feller had himself a real

bad day. Reckon I'll have a look at that girl and get on down the road."

Mack picked up the ax by its handle and looked at the wood he was splitting.

"Mack, you keep the wind at your back. Don't be takin' no wood nickels."

"You too, Hank."

Henry took up the reins of the gruella and started limping toward the bunk house to look in on Alejendra. She was asleep, wrapped in a wool blanket, her head buried beneath a feather pillow. For some reason not entirely clear to him, he was pleased she didn't know he'd been there, standing over her watching her breathe.

Chapter 28

After Alejendra Carlos Rodriguez had pushed Harry into the saddle, she led Tapper out of the trees and to the cabin where her mare was standing, resting, her head down, her butt turned to the sun. Alejendra looked at the horse and shook her head. *No, I shouldn't do this*, she thought, but she climbed onto the back of her mare anyway. It wasn't a good thing to do; one look at the mare told her it was a mistake, but she had to ask. She had no choice. She had to get Harry help or he would die.

"Here we go, girl," she whispered. "Just another five miles. What's that to a mare like you?"

The mare was willing. Alejendra kept the mare tight against the taller stud horse, literally holding Harry in the saddle. Several times he came close to falling but there she was pushing him back, keeping him upright. When that no longer worked, she stood up on her saddle and jumped onto Tapper's back, settling herself behind Harry. She held him upright with one hand, securing the reins with the other. She left Rosie standing in the knee high grass.

Alejendra thought about running the stud, but decided against it. Control was the important factor. Harry weighed much more than she. Compared to her one hundred twenty-two pounds, he was too large. To run the horse and keep Harry in the saddle at the same time was impossible. Instead, she kept the stud at a brisk walk, urging the horse onward whenever he slowed. It took her a little less than two hours to cover four miles and it was four miles before she could see the ranch buildings and know exactly where she was going, where she wanted to be.

With each step she kept her hand on Harry's back, gripping the back of his shirt in her fingers. When he began to slip, she pulled him back. Toward the end he was unconscious, his chest leaning over the saddle horn, his arms drooping. Somewhere in the midst of her efforts, riders found her. There were three. A man called Rick told her to stop. She didn't want to. She was aware of him jumping off his horse and grabbing Tapper's reins.

"Get down," he said. She stared at him. "Get down," he ordered again, his voice insisting.

It was no use. She gave up. Sliding to the ground, her knees buckled. But for Rick grabbing her arm, she'd have collapsed onto the sod completely. Weakened by lack of sleep, from fighting with Harry and gravity, and continually urging the stud on, she barely maintained her equilibrium. Physically, she'd reached the point where no matter what she asked of herself, her body ignored her requests. Emotionally and mentally she'd checked out, left the rodeo, operating on sheer will and perceived need, unable to keep her thoughts trained on Harry, or the horse, on anything.

The lithe rider swung up behind Harry without using the stirrups. Holding Harry in front of him, he stuck the steel to the thoroughbred and was off like a pony express rider delivering the mail. The stud took the last mile at a dead run, Rick and Harry on his back, Rick jabbing his sides while keeping Harry in the saddle.

Alejendra watched, wanting to cry, barely able to hold herself together, wanting to fling herself onto the sod. "Flinging", however, was out of the question. Collapsing had become her only option.

"Ma'am."

She looked up at the second rider, blinking her eyes, awash in confusion. The horseman was reaching for her. She stared at him, at his offered hand.

"Ma'am, take my hand. Stick your foot in the stirrup. I'll help you up behind me. Old Sal rides double. Give me your hand." The rider looked at her.

Alejendra shook her head "no." She wasn't going anywhere. She couldn't think why not. It didn't matter. She said "no" by shaking her head, teetering, almost falling to the ground.

"Mack, I need a little help."

She was conscious of someone behind her. Whoever it was, picked her up and placed her behind the saddle. She thought she was heavier than that: that the horse was taller: that this fellow Mack was too short: that it couldn't be done. She grabbed hold of the rider's waist to keep from falling off the horse.

"That's it, Ma'am. You hold on. We'll take her easy, get you down the hill."

Apparently, he got her down the hill but she wasn't entirely aware of it. She kept wanting to remember who she was, and avoid giving herself any excuses. Who was Henry Williams? Who was he?

Alejendra woke up in a bunk, her legs and arms tangled in three blankets and a pillow. It was like

292

waking up in the dark, except she could see everything. The sun was up. It was bright outside; the curtains were dirty and needed washing. She noted that the door going outside was open; the fall air was cool, but fresh; chickens were pecking in the dirt, clucking. Someone was leaning against a cook stove with no fire in the firebox. Yet, she remembered nothing: not even how she got there, or why, or when. She blinked her eyes. She was aware of a voice speaking.

"Say, Mack, we gots ourselves a visitor. Looks like she's joinin' the livin'."

Suddenly, two men stood in the light, looking down at her, their heads dwarfed by huge hats, two days' growth of whiskers on their sunburned faces.

"You alive, Ma'am?" the cowhand on the right asked. "Get her a glass of water, would you, Mack, and a cup of coffee."

It came flooding back in a rush of mental images. She jumped up and nearly fell back onto the bunk.

"Wal, I'll be danged, Mack. She is alive."

The cowhand handed her a cup of hot coffee. "Get yourself around that coffin varnish, Ma'am. Ya might stand up slower so's not to kill yourself."

She took the cup but immediately set it down, her fingers burning.

"Damn it, Mack, ya gotta cool it down some."

Mack retrieved the steaming cup and somehow cooled it before handing it back. This time she could hold onto the metal handle. It was still a little warm.

"Harry?" she asked. "Is Harry all right?"

"The kid? He's restin' easy. Damn near died,

293

but nothin' can kill him. Want somethin' to eat? Mack, get this gal some of them biscuits and some of that gravy. Any of that side pork left? Get her some of that. Get her a fork, too."

Alejendra took another sip of the coffee and remembered Henry telling Tomas that his wife could boil a coffee bean that would peel the rust off an old skillet. *Was that it? Something like that?* She smiled.

"Mack, the girl--she's smilin'."

Alejendra looked at her two benefactors. "I'm so sorry," she said. "I owe you two. I'm just not thinking. I was remembering a friend of mine telling my brother that his wife could boil a coffee bean that would peel the rust off an old skillet. I remembered that drinking this coffee, not that it's bad. I just remembered it and it made me smile. Really, thank you so much. I'm not myself." She paused. "I really don't know who I am."

"That pretty much describes the cook's coffee. Pretty much says it," Mack replied.

"Pretty much," the other hand repeated.

"Is he going to live? Harry, I mean. Is he going to be all right?"

"Why don't you get your feet on the floor and up to the table, eat a bit, and we'll take you to him? I would say that he's been better. He's havin' himself a rough patch."

"Rosie?"

"Who?"

"My horse, Rosie."

"Got her in the corral. Now, she's plenty played out, Ma'am. Oughta let her rest a day or two. Walkin' like her legs are a little sore. Not movin' much. I'd say she's felt better. Wind ain't broke. She's breathin' all right. Shin splints--I reckon she's got a case of those. Legs been poundin' that shale. Ain't used to it. Front shoe a little loose. Holdin' her head up this mornin'. Got a good look in her eye. I'd say that horse will do fine."

Alejendra stood, uncertain if she'd stay standing. She did. She ate biscuits and gravy, not realizing how hungry she was, nor how thirsty. Even so, she was surprised at how little she could eat and how little she could drink.

Harry was laid up in the main house, his body resting on a ticky mattress in a sparsely decorated room all to himself. He wasn't awake when Alejendra was brought to the room by someone in a worn and tattered red wool shirt with two rows of brown buttons. All the tears were neatly sewed with white thread and the shirt looked clean. The upper portion of the rider's face was white while the bottom was tanned a rusty brown. He was clean shaved, his legs slightly bowed, his boots worn down at the underslung heels.

Inside the room, she was left alone with Harry. She stood in a shadowed silence punctuated by Harry's shallow breathing and the ticking of an old clock. After a moment passed and realizing he was asleep, she walked across the hard wood floor and stood by his bed and stared down at him. She wasn't sure what she'd find. The last time she'd seen him he'd been ghostly grey and unconscious. In the quiet she watched the rise and fall of his chest. The color had returned to his cheeks.

Harry had the familiar two-toned face, his forehead white where it had been covered by his hat, the lower cheeks and jaw tanned where it had been exposed to sun and wind. He moaned in his sleep, his wounded arm resting on his chest. It hadn't been moved in deference to the pain moving it would cause. His left arm hung in space off the mattress. Alejendra moved it back onto the bed. It surprised her how calloused his hands and fingers were. She hadn't noticed when she'd danced with him. *Twice--no--three times. If you called that thing he did dancing.*

It was quiet except for Harry's breathing. He looked so different from the first time she met him at the box social in Greybull. At the dance all he had wanted to do was talk. Alejendra smiled. It occurred to her that Harry had been nervous, that her presence made him anxious and uncomfortable. She remembered his comment that he'd never been to a dance in the Community Hall. She nodded her head, realizing that he had been in a place he was not used to, dancing with a girl he wasn't sure about. Dancing? He certainly hadn't done that before. In a place where she was comfortable, he had been entirely out of his element: no horses: no sun: no rain: no snow: no wind: no cows to complain about: no pistols to shoot rattlesnakes and gophers: no ropes to hurl: no spurs and jinglebobs scraping across the floor. It all began to make sense. All of his motherless life Harry, his father, and Janille had lived alone with four horses, some laying hens, and a couple hundred head of mixed cattle.

What a picture.

Alejendra reviewed Harry Harris: his life. From

the time he was three there had been no women in his life except for a kid sister. A baby sister really didn't count. There were girls where he went to grade school but not that many. She remembered that he'd barely made the eighth grade and wasn't interested in the ninth; he had to make a living for his father, for Janille. She remembered him standing across the large room watching the dancers, alone.

Oh my, Harry stood alone because he was alone.

When he rode that saddle bronc in Greybull, he'd ridden him to a standstill with all those people cheering. That ride hadn't been done before. She remembered him walking away from the mustang, smiling, pleased with himself for doing well, yet embarrassed by the acclaim.

Doing well was not the same as showing off. Not like I thought. He didn't even know he was good. He thought himself lucky. That's what he said, "I was just lucky he bounced the way he did." It never occurred to me that he meant it. Oh my God! He was trying to impress me. He was doing the only thing he knew how to do to get my attention. I sure gave him some of that.

"Oh boy," she whispered, "I sure got this one wrong." Henry William's words came rushing back. "Remember who you are." He'd said it twice. "Remember who you are."

Remember who I am? *Yes. I'm Alejendra Carlos Rodriguez. My father is Manny Rodriguez. We have four hundred cows, eighty bulls, three hundred eighty-three yearlings, and sixty head of horses, nine of which are mine. We have ten thousand acres of graze standing*

297

up against the western flanks of the Big Horn Mountains. I thought I was somebody that night with this boy holding my mamá's box lunch, with its pint of watered down tequila, twelve tamales, and a baked fool's hen: all made to impress, none of it mine. And I have four brothers and they love me. And all Harry did was be himself. He had no one. I should be embarrassed.

And every time I came near him, this fool stood up; he took his hat off, holding it in front of him like a school boy. He'd been taught that. Besides, once he had it off his head he didn't have any place to put it. He was so nervous he held it in both hands. Did I ever mistreat him. It will be a wonder if he'll even speak to me. Did I ever have this one wrong, so very wrong. He must think me a fool. He was shot and I didn't even know what to do, I was so flabbergasted. If it wasn't for Mr. Williams slapping my face–oh, that really hurt–but I needed it. He sure woke me up. "Remember who you are," he said. "Give yourself no excuses."

Alejendra stared at the sleeping man, watched the rise and fall of his chest. He seemed so pitiful, so vulnerable. She didn't like him that way. That's not the way she wanted to remember him. All of it made no sense. Yet it did. She buried her face in her hands and wept, hardly able to breathe. She'd been so wrong.

A rough, calloused hand, with long, hardened fingers touched her arm and so startled her she jumped.

"What's wrong, Alex?" Harry whispered.

"Harry. My God, you're awake, you're alive," she sobbed, embarrassed, wiping her nose with her sleeve.

"What's wrong? Why are you crying?"

"Oh, I'm just feeling sorry for myself," she said, wiping the tears from her eyes and cheeks. "I was cussing myself. I should have ridden faster or left sooner or . . . if I'd just got there somehow, even a few minutes earlier, you wouldn't have been shot. If I'd just thought." Again, Alejendra wiped her eyes. "Harry, I'm so glad you're not dying." She wasn't sure that sentence came out right, or even if it were true.

"You sure got yourself a set of broad shoulders, girl. If a man is gonna shoot at me, he is gonna shoot at me." He paused, looking at her. "What? You gonna stop him. Is this you walkin' on water?"

She smiled, nodding. "I'd stop him all right, I would."

"I believe you," he whispered. "I believe you." He closed his eyes. When he opened them, she was standing hovering over him.

"You're going to be all right? You are, aren't you?"

"I sure hope so." He grimaced as he moved his right arm, resting it on his chest. "I gots some big plans."

"Am I in them?" She said, immediately regretting having said it, wishing she could slap her own face.

Harry Harris smiled at her and through pale lips and a grimace said, "You sure are."

"Oh, yeah? Are you going to let me in on them?"

"I sure am."

All she could do was smile.

299

Chapter 29

Henry Williams made it home two days later. He'd taken his time--what there was of it. Before going to the hotel, he'd made his way along the south side of the tracks and stopped at the long log cabin of Mary Carlos with its low roof, its multiple windows, its porch wrapped tightly around it. He had the gruella stand in the extra cool shade of the yellowing cottonwoods, giving him time to convince himself that he should step down from the saddle. He wanted to but he didn't want to feel the pain that would come once his right foot gained purchase on the hardpack, taking his weight. So he studied the logs that he and Franko had snaked off the mountain below Five Springs. A long time ago there had been a fire and it had left a lot of tall pine standing: needleless, black trunks pointing into the sky. Good logs, too. Eventually, he held his breath and slid to the ground, wincing. Then he hobbled to the steps of the enclosed porch. For a moment he stared at the steps he had to climb, steeling himself again, aware of the protest his tired body would make. He looked up.

Standing above him was Mary Carlos Sanchez Rodriguez. Her presence surprised him.

"*Madre de Dios*," she said, "you look awful. Just terrible. When was the last time you ate? You cannot do this to yourself, Henry. What is wrong with you? You have not got the sense God gave my mother's tamales. Are you trying to kill yourself?" On and on she went without stopping, stepping down the pine plank steps.

Suddenly, she was beside him, supporting his weight from the left side. "Let me help you," she said. "Let us get you inside into Frank's chair."

Henry smiled. "Let's do that," he said, gritting his teeth. They made it up the four steps to the front door and the threshold--he, leaning on the small woman for support, she, taking more of his weight than he thought possible.

"You, first," she said.

He grabbed the door frame.

Somehow, Henry Williams made it to the chair, the ordeal ending with Mary Carlos propping his legs up on a leather-covered ottoman scarred from the rowls of Mexican spurs.

"Damn," he said, once she had him settled in the chair. "Could you get me a drink of water, please? I'm a bit dry."

While she was in the kitchen getting a glass, filling it with water, buttering some bread, the old man fell asleep. When she returned, his chin was resting on his chest; he was breathing heavily through his nose. His hat had fallen on the floor. She picked it up and hung it on the peg next to Frank's. Mary Carlos stared at Henry Williams, then went outside to unsaddle the gruella. She removed the blanket, saddle bags, rifle, scabbard and riata. She stacked those items on the porch. Afterwards, she led the horse across the tracks, taking him to Rainbow Harv's Livery. Henry was still asleep when she returned. In the twilight, she covered him with a wool blanket, trimmed the lamp, and went into the kitchen. Henry slept the night through without moving.

The sounds of a dog barking, the smell of frying bacon, coffee boiling, and potatoes frying in a black skillet awakened him. Without moving, he took a deep breath and felt the pleasant heat from the sunlight streaming through the east windows. Beyond the porch, he could see the river and the mountains towering in the distance.

Mary Carlos came into the room with a plate full of eggs, bacon, and potatoes.

"Damn, I was tired," he said to her, taking the plate.

"You were," she answered.

"You were right, you know," he said.

"I was?"

"It was more than horses runnin' through an open gate. A fellow hired some people to kill them mares." Henry told her all that had happened.

"What now?" she asked after he'd finished.

"I need to have a word with him."

"*No es posible*."

"Mary Carlos, I don't see any choice. He's gonna keep sendin' these folks. Someone is gonna get killed. Someone already has. Next time, it will be someone you know."

Mary Carlos stared at him. "But, Henry, you cannot do this."

"You're right. I can't, but there ain't no one else."

"I will send for Manny. We will talk about what is best."

"And what will Manny do, Mary Carlos, besides get himself and those boys of his killed? You know, before he died, Franko told me that something bad was gonna happen. He said it right in that room. And here it is: somethin' bad."

"There has to be another way," she said, setting the glass of water on the arm of the easy chair. She proceeded to walk back and forth across the floor, one arm across her waist, the other hand supporting her chin, deep in thought.

Henry didn't say another word. She was still walking across the floor when he finished the last forkful of eggs and fried potatoes.

She looked at him.

"I'll leave tomorrow," he said.

"You will not. You will kill someone. I do not want you to kill anyone. You and Frank killed enough people."

"Maybe I'll get myself kilt. Ever think of that?"

Mary Carlos shrugged that off. "You won't," she said. "Nothing can kill you."

Henry smiled. "Hope you're right," he said.

"I am."

"Mary, don't bother yourself with this matter. This horse is saddled."

"Well, take the saddle off."

"Can't. Say, do you think Anna Marie is still alive? In all these years have you ever heard from her? I've been thinkin' about her lately."

"You are always thinking about her."

"Not always."

Mary Carlos stared at him. "When are you not

303

thinking about her?"

He laughed and said, "When I'm thinkin' about you."

She wadded the dish towel up and threw it at him.

Chapter 30

Henry Williams watched the train slow down and come to a stop. Puffs of white steam billowed from around the huge iron drivers, evaporating like smoke blowing in the north wind. The engineer nodded at him from the cab, waving his gloved hand. In return, Henry touched the brim of his Stetson, then glanced down the long brick platform as the conductor stepped down onto the platform, the flat rows of brick and mortar that covered the railroad cistern.

After the passengers for Kane had disembarked and the conductor had stepped to the side, he hefted his saddle and bridle and mounted the steps of the Pullman car. He turned left at the top and walked down the aisle. He found a seat on his left, next to a window, depositing his gear in the aisle seat. Sitting down, he looked out on the milling people that had disembarked before he got on: some waiting, some collecting their luggage. Standing at the corner of the station house he saw the diminutive Mary Carlos Rodriguez. Her hand went to her mouth when they made eye contact. He smiled. He watched her lips as she mouthed the words, "Hurry home. We miss you already." He nodded his head. She smiled, and for a moment was hidden from his view by a man arguing with the station master; apparently he'd lost his baggage. Something certainly wasn't right. When the matter was resolved, the two men moved toward the section house. He looked for her, but Mary Carlos had disappeared.

It is approximately fifteen hundred miles from the section house in Kane, Wyoming to the depot in Lexington, Kentucky. Henry Williams rode the rails all the way. He had to get off and get on several times, but he made it. It took him forty-two hours and thirty-nine minutes. It wasn't a straight shot. He had layovers and hook ups and more layovers, but that's how many hours he rode the train, stopping in Chicago, waiting in Cincinnati. Finally, at 2:44 in the afternoon, he was standing on the platform in Lexington, Kentucky.

It was an uneventful trip except for an exchange he had with a four-year-old girl who wanted to know if he was a grandpa. He said that he was not. She wanted to know why not; he said he didn't have any kids. She wanted to know why not, and he said because he wasn't married. She wanted to know why not; he told her because someone else married his girlfriend and stole her away from him. She looked at him a long time then, and finally asked what he did about that. He was rescued from answering the last question by the child's mother who'd misplaced the child and was angry with him for answering all of her questions.

He answered her by saying, "Pardon me all to hell, Ma'am." The lady and her little girl went away, the little girl waving, and her mother, still angry, glancing back at him over her shoulder.

Chapter 31

"My *papá* is here, Harry. He's come to get me . . . to take me home."

Harry looked at Alejendra from the bed, his head resting on pillows. "Who?" he asked.

"My brothers. Alonso. Miguel. Tomas. They are all here. My *papá*. Not Juan. He stayed home. They're pretty upset, actually. I left in the middle of the night without telling anyone."

"You're in trouble?" he asked.

"Yes, a little." Alejendra paused, smiled. "Maybe a lot. My *papá* is beside himself. But don't worry yourself. I will handle it. My *papá*, he worries," she explained. "I should have told him. I didn't."

"Alex," he said, looking at her, "thanks for everything. I mean, really."

Alejendra stared at him. "How? I mean . . . you and I? How is this going to work?"

"I don't know. We need to talk about it."

"We are talking about it."

Harry smiled at her. "Yes, I guess we are," he said.

"Do you know what Henry Williams said?"

Harry looked at her, waiting.

"He said 'You can't lead where you ain't going.'" She smiled at Harry. "I didn't know what that meant until now. We need to know where we're going."

Harry started to swing his legs out of the bed, to put his feet on the floor.

"What are you doing?" she asked alarmed.

"Gotta sit up."

"Why? What do you need? I can get it for you."

"You said your *papá*, your brothers were here. They're gonna take you away. They're upset. You said we need to talk. I'm trying to sit up so we can talk. I need to explain to them what happened."

"You can lay down and we can talk. I will explain to my family."

"It's too important," he said. "I gotta sit up so I can think." Harry shook his head, a little woozy. "I guess I'm still a little weak. I feel dizzy."

"Harry, you were shot three days ago. You lost a ton of blood. What do you expect?"

"I don't know," he said, shaking his head again: the cobwebs wouldn't clear. "I ain't never been shot before." Harry made no additional attempt to move from the bed.

She said, "I'm thinking we just need to know where we are going, so we can get there." She paused. "Harry, I'm going home. I have to. I have to find Henry Williams. I need to talk to him."

"What for?"

"He'll know what to do." She paused. "*Mi abuelito*, he told me a long time ago to go to Henry Williams when I need help. Someone shot you, Harry. They tried to kill your horse."

"Don't you think we can figure it out?"

"I would think so. But maybe we can't. I need to talk to him. He'll know what we should do."

"This Henry Williams casts a long shadow. How do you know him? I mean, really?"

"I didn't use to. I didn't really know him until about ten days ago. But *mi abuelito* told me that if I needed anything I was to go to Mr. Williams. I was thirteen. I barely remember. I didn't think I would ever need anything. It was so sad. He was dying. Besides he was old. I thought he didn't know what he was talking about."

"Who was dying?"

"My grandfather." Alejendra paused, looking at Harry. "Does that make sense? I hope it does."

"Yes," Harry said and laid back on his bunk. "Damn," he said. "I'm so weak. I can hardly move."

Alejendra smiled. "I told you so," she said. "A few days ago, Henry Williams showed up at our place. He found my horses when no one else could. Before he got down from his horse he made *Papá* promise him that he'd have my brothers help him back on his horse."

"Back on his horse? What was that all about?"

"He has a bad leg. He can hardly move except when he's on his horse."

"What happened?"

"I don't really know. Juan told me his horse ran him into a tree, threw him off, stepped on him, and kicked him."

"I saw him get on his horse the other day when he picked you up and smacked you. He seemed to be able to do that then."

Alejendra laughed. "He sure made me mad. But did you see his face? When he got on his horse, I mean, did you see it?"

"I'm not sure I could see anything. I saw your face."

"He was so determined. Harry I think he could have done anything. He was in so much pain, but nothing could stop him. That's what he told me. He said you have to want it."

"I didn't hear that."

"He said 'Remember who you are.' He said get the job done because it needed doing. He told me not to make any excuses for myself. You know, I never thought about it until now, but there was nothing he could have done to help you. Not that I couldn't do. He told me that, and I never heard him until right now. Twice he told me to remember who I was."

Alejendra Carlos Rodriguez nodded her head in understanding. "*Madre de Dios*," she said looking at Harry. "How badly do you want me, Harry? I think we can be happy, you and I. But whatever it is that you and I can be together, we have to both want it as badly as he wanted to get on that gruella. We have to be willing. We cannot make any excuses for ourselves. We have to see what needs to be done and do it."

"Whoa, Alex, that's heavy. That's really deep."

"It is, isn't it?" Alejendra looked at Harry. "How badly do you want me, Harry? How important am I to you?"

Harry took her hand, holding it. "I'll do anything, Alex. Anything at all."

"All right," she said. "I have to go, Harry. They're waiting." She started for the door, stopping when she reached it. "That was the right answer, Harry." She smiled at him, then disappeared from his sight into the bright sunlight.

Chapter 32

The old man stepped down from the rental horse, wrapping the reins around the hitching rail. He stretched his muscles and, at the same time, looked right, then left. Favoring his left hip, he stepped up onto a boardwalk, then followed it to the front door. Henry paused and looked out on the trees of the river bottom, finding glimpses of the river. It was a cold fall with a lot of humidity, something he wasn't used to. The leaves were a brilliant red, yellow, and orange.

Casually, he released the leather latch from the hammer of the SAA 1873 Colt, thinking that he'd been packing that gun a long, long time. He'd known a fellow once who favored an 1850 Navy Colt, never took it off his hip; the fool kept using paper cartridges, preferred them to brass. Henry thought about the man, trying to remember his name, but he'd forgotten. He wondered whatever happened to him. A flock of dark colored black birds fluttered by, landing in the magnolia tree that during the summer shaded the southern exposure of the weathered house. They were black, but they weren't blackbirds. He'd never seen this variety before.

Henry knocked on the door, then stepped back and waited, his mind focused on the door and the sounds around him, especially those coming from within the structure. Behind him, his horse shook itself, breathing out loudly.

Odd how the prospect of danger seems to make

sounds louder, easier to hear, the mind clearer.

The door opened, framing a nine-year-old boy in a shirt that needed to be re-buttoned, hair that could use a brush.

"Boy," Henry said, "I need to talk to your old man."

"My what?"

"Your father. I'd like to speak with him."

"Oh. Okay. Would you like to come in? I'll go tell him."

Henry followed the boy inside, closing the large oak door behind him. Inside, it was pleasant and cool. Somewhere close by someone was baking bread; coffee was boiling; there was a hint of cured bacon frying.

Presently, the boy brought a man into the living room. Henry didn't like the way his face was framed against the windows, initially making it hard to see him. The man and boy moved away from the light into the center of the room. The man was laughing at the boy.

"What? What? What's going on, Roger?" he said. "Where are you taking me?"

"Him," the boy said, looking at the older man. "He wants to see you."

Gorman O'Neal looked at the old man, an expression of surprise on his face. "Oh," he said, "what are you doing here?" The voice turned cold, menacing, leaking with condescension.

"Mister," Henry said, nodding, "I've come to see you about a horse."

"A horse! You go to the stables, to the horse barn for that. Not to my house. You get out of here. You get out right now."

312

Henry tossed the bag toward the man. It landed at his feet, on the edge of a braided rug, with a thump.

"What's that?"

"Gonads." Henry paused for effect. "Horse gonads."

"So? Why bring them to me?" O'Neal's voice turned incredulous. He paused. "You castrated a stud? My stud? You brought his nuts here?"

"The boys said you were right smart. That would be a six-year-old stud. Gots his teeth. Looked like a thoroughbred. Looks like he was with a good lookin' mare."

"Six? Did you say six?"

"I did."

Rage suddenly possessed Gorman O'Neal. He stepped forward, intent on wrapping his fingers around this stranger's throat, on doing great bodily harm, killing him, regardless of age or social standing. The passion washed over him like a hot, dry wind. He found himself looking down the seven and a half inch barrel of a .45 Colt Peacemaker. The bore seemed larger than he remembered it. The sudden appearance of the pistol brought him up short, stopping him where he stood, his son by his side, looking on. Rage continued to burn in the core of his being. O'Neal immediately took stock, sizing up the situation. He hadn't become a captain of industry by running from every conflict that happened to step through the doorway of his office.

"Roger, go to your room."

"Leave the boy be. I reckon he should get a good look at his old man, should know just what he's made of."

"Mister, you brought a pistol into my home," O'Neal said, speaking slowly, drawing his words out. Then looking at his son, using a softer voice, he repeated, "Roger, I told you--"

"No. Three pistols. You get to see two."

When O'Neal looked back at the speaker he indeed found himself looking at the bores of two .45s. The barrels did not waver in the old man's hands. Consciously, O'Neal recognized that small fact. Heavy though they were, this old man was having no difficulty at all holding them steady.

"All right." O'Neal paused. "Don't you think it's best for you and I to talk without the boy?"

"Perhaps you didn't hear me. I said, 'leave the boy be.' Besides the chances of you livin' another thirty seconds ain't too good."

"Why would you do that?" Gorman O'Neal pointed at the dark red sack on the floor. "Why? Why come to my house? Injure my horse, I mean--good God, man! It's you who won't live another thirty seconds."

"Maybe. You move a hair and we'll see just how short your thirty seconds is gonna be."

O'Neal felt a rush of raw frustration. He didn't immediately recognize the experience. In a short second he was inundated by helplessness, anger beyond control yet awash in futility, his horse dreams shattered, running from him. "What do you want?" he finally asked. "Do you want to kill me in front of my boy? Is that it? What have I done to you?"

"It seems you hired a man to kill some mares. That boy wasn't all that good."

O'Neal felt the air go out of his lungs.

"It seems you hired another man to shoot a stud horse. Shot a boy instead. Seems your man don't know the difference in a stud horse and a boy ridin' a stud horse. That one wasn't all that good, either. Both of these gents said it was you who did the hirin'. Paid one feller a hefty sum, the other not so much." Henry paused and said, "Which brings us to the last fifteen seconds of your life."

"Jesus," O'Neal said.

"Reckon you'll be meetin' him soon."

"You'd shoot me in front of my son?"

"Your man shot a boy in front of an eighteen-year-old girl. What kind of horseshit was that?"

O'Neal's mouth dropped open, but he didn't say anything.

A female voice came from another part of the house, just entering the room.

"Hello," she said, then she saw the pistols. "What's going on?" the woman demanded.

Interrupted, O'Neal and the boy turned to the woman's voice. The old man didn't.

"Oh, God," O'Neal said softly.

Henry answered the questions. "It seems, Ma'am, that your husband has taken on religion. It seems that he's about to be dead or he's gonna decide to make it right to an eighteen-year-old girl. Sorta death bed repentance, considerin' we both agree I'm gonna shoot him dead."

"Yes. Yes," O'Neal said.

"Gorman?"

"Please be quiet, Evelyn. Please, not now."

O'Neal had never been beaten in a war over

315

money and power; never lost once. Yet he found himself staring at another undefeated yet old man standing in his living room with two unwavering Colt .45s in his hands. "What is it that you want? What is it?" he asked.

The old man was thinking, looking at the boy standing by his dad's side. It would have been so much easier just to shoot O'Neal. That certainly was his intention. But the boy? The woman? That made difficult more difficult and he didn't like it. He remembered Mary Carlos saying that he and Franko had killed too many people.

"How do I make it up to this eighteen-year-old girl? Is that what you want?"

"I am not a believer, Gorman. I can't see you willingly doin' right. Seems you need to be forced more than you need to be asked. Seems I need to get your attention."

"Good God. You're standing in my living room with two pistols pointed at me, my boy, my woman. You've castrated my stud. I'd say you had my attention. I'd say you had more of it than you could possibly want."

"No, I want it all." He paused. "Tell you what, in three weeks, I want you to personally take that stud horse of yours to Greybull, Wyoming. I'm talking about Impressive Traveler. I want you to take him to a girl named Alejendra Rodriguez and offer to sell her the horse for fifty dollars. If she ain't got fifty dollars, I expect you to lend her the money to pay for the horse. Do you understand? Have I made myself clear?"

"Fifty dollars? Me? That horse is worth . . . a lot

more than that." O'Neal's voice fell off.

"Yes. He is. But not to you."

"Three weeks. Why three weeks?"

The room erupted in gunfire--two shots close together. In the quiet that immediately followed, the sound of two hammers being drawn back was heard. The woman screamed. The man was knocked to the floor. The boy jumped on him, yelling, "Daddy, Daddy, Daddy." The woman ran to the fallen man, kneeling by his side. Gorman had grabbed his legs, raising them from the floor. Blood was forming in two patches over his shin bones. He'd been shot in both, as suggested by a hole dead center in the legs of his cotton pants.

O'Neal screamed, "Why? Why? I told you 'yes.' Please? What more?"

The old man answered the question. "Because it is goin' to take you three weeks to be able to walk with a couple of sticks, this here woman and the boy helpin' prop you up. Understand this, you miserable pile of horse turds, you've just traded your life for a piece of horse flesh. I'd of killed you straight away but for this boy and his mother. You take advantage of my weak moment and you won't be so lucky. You hear me?"

"I hear you," O'Neal said. "I hear you."

"You bastard," Evelyn O'Neal said. "If I were a man--"

"Evie, please. Not now." O'Neal gasped.

"If you was a man, lady, you'd be dead. So would this miserable excuse for a husband." The old man paused before resuming. "He'd be dead and he wouldn't need to hire nobody to shoot up a boy and run no mares off the side of a mountain." He stared at

317

O'Neal. "You got any questions? Things crystal clear in your head? Three weeks. Fifty dollars. Alejendra Rodriguez, Greybull, Wyoming. I don't advise being late."

Gorman O'Neal shook his head "no," his face contorted, grimacing. "I understand," he said.

The woman was looking at the bloody sack lying on the braided rug. "What's that?" she asked.

"Evie, please don't," O'Neal gasped.

"Horse gonads," Henry answered.

"Oh, my," Evie said. "Oh, my. Do I dare ask which horse?"

"I have no idea, Ma'am. Picked 'em up outside of Lexington at a processing plant. Thought you'd like to cook 'em up for supper. If not, dogs like 'em."

The old man touched the edge of the brim of his hat. He paused and looked at Gorman O'Neal. "Ma'am," he said, "I'd have a vet look at that man's legs. Be a shame if he got gangrene and had to cut 'em off."

Again, he looked at the man on the floor. "Listen, O'Neal. I don't give second chances. It ain't in my nature. This here ain't a second chance. Me lettin' you live ain't no chance at all. If you don't show up like I told you for any reason, or no reason, I'll be back. I'll put a couple of rounds through your chest and I'll burn this house to the ground. I'll run off all your stock and I'll kill your dog. Then, I'll get serious. You hear me? I'll skin the hide off'n your back with you in it. You understand?"

The room had turned silent.

"Do you hear me?"

"I hear you."

"All right, then. I'll be leavin'."

The woman and the grim-faced Gorman watched Henry Williams retreat, slowly limping from the room. He let himself out, closing the door behind him. For a moment the room was silent, then the silence was broken by Gorman O'Neal groaning. The woman turned her attention to O'Neal, shaking her head.

"What just happened, Gory? Do you want to tell me what just happened?"

Chapter 33

The buggy, with a tall, lean, thoroughbred horse trailing behind it, stopped in front of the Rodriguez ranch house on the west slope of the Big Horn Mountain. Alejendra was standing on the porch, cradling a rifle in her arms, her finger resting on the trigger, the hammer pulled back and locked. Across the hardpack, the barn door that had earlier been opened was closed. In the loft above the door, she could make out someone standing in the shadows, also with a rifle. The buggy was a two seater. In the front seat was a middle-aged man, obviously in some pain, holding two crutches braced in his right hand. The driver she recognized from the Lancing Stables in Greybull. In the second seat, closest to Alejendra, was a slender, well-dressed lady holding a parasol. Next to her was a young nine-year-old boy. No one was carrying a weapon that she could see; not that she breathed any easier, for she recognized only the driver. Strangers in a small town sometimes meant trouble.

The man sitting next to the driver spoke to her. "I'm looking for Alejendra Rodriguez," he said.

Alejendra was slow to respond. *Who are you?* she thought. When she did respond, she said, "I am she."

"I am here to sell you my horse, Impressive Traveler," he said, nodding toward the exquisite horse standing behind the buggy, ears pointed toward Alejendra, his eyes studying her. Impatiently, he stomped his feet, blowing his nose.

"Sell him to me? What makes you think I want to buy him? I am a little horse poor." She said those words cringing, knowing that not a hundred feet from where she was standing was the leather pouch containing the two thousand dollars Henry had given her. Still, she didn't want to part with it; money was hard to come by.

Alejendra stepped to the edge of the porch and looked at the horse. "Why would you want to?" She asked. "A horse like that?"

The woman interjected, answering her question without being asked. "Because Gory will be shot if he doesn't. He's already been shot twice."

"Shot? Who shot him?" Alejendra turned to the man. "Someone shot you? Why would someone shoot you?"

The middle-aged man interrupted, not answering her question. "Fifty dollars. I want to sell him for fifty dollars."

"Fifty dollars? That horse? He's worth . . ." She paused, looking at the horse again. "Well, many times that. Is something wrong with him?"

"Nothing is wrong with him. And he is worth more than that. Fifty dollars is, however, my asking price."

"I haven't got fifty dollars." *Not to spend on another horse,* she thought suddenly being very cautious.

The woman hit the man sitting in front of her on the back of the left shoulder. "Gory," she said.

"I'll lend you fifty dollars, if you do not have

fifty dollars." He paused, staring at her, his face tightening up, obviously overcome by some pain. He acted as if the horse was sold; that she'd purchased him, that she'd paid for it, and the transaction was complete. He confirmed it by sarcastically saying, "Thank you for the payment. Roger, do what I told you. Give the girl the papers. Untie the lead rope and hand it to her. Let's get out of here." He turned to look at the boy. "Now, Roger."

The boy popped off the seat, leaped to the ground, ran behind the buggy, and proceeded to untie the lead rope from the back of the conveyance.

"Hey! Mister! I am not buying that horse for fifty dollars," Alejendra said. "You probably stole him. Now get out of here." The rifle was no longer cradled in her arms, the butt now held loosely at her shoulder.

"What do you think he's worth?" O'Neal asked her.

"I don't know. He looks like he's worth more than ten thousand. I know that. A lot more."

"You don't have fifty dollars, so you don't have ten thousand dollars? Am I right?"

"No. I don't have fifty dollars or ten thousand dollars and I am not buying your horse." The harder the man pushed, the more she resisted. Sure, she had fifty dollars. Yes, she could pay it. But no, she didn't want to pay it; especially when it wasn't her idea. Besides something was wrong.

"I'll lend it to you. Roger?"

"What's wrong with you? Are you deaf? I don't want to buy him."

The woman sitting primly in the back seat

turned to her, smiled. "Nothing is wrong with him, dear other than that crazy old man shot him in both legs and he can't walk. If he doesn't sell him specifically to you for fifty dollars, the old man is going to kill him. So, nothing is wrong with him. He's just scared of some old man."

"What old man?"

"I thought he was your father or grandfather or something. But he was a white man, and you look like a Mexican or a Spaniard, or maybe an Italian. So I don't think he's your grandfather or father, but he was plenty serious, so take the horse. We got to get out of here."

The boy had taken the lead rope and tied it to a stay in the veranda railing. He'd dropped a white envelope on the porch floor, then climbed back into the buggy sitting beside the woman.

"I am not buying that horse," Alejendra insisted. " I can't--well I can, but I don't want to. I am not buying your horse."

"Aren't you sweet, dear."

The man in the front seat told the driver to "go." The woman smiled and waved from beneath the parasol.

"Hold it," O'Neal said to the driver. The buggy hadn't moved. He turned to Alejendra. "Listen, girl," he said, "you tell that old son of a bitch that if I ever see him, I'll shoot him on sight. I'll find him. I'll kill him. You tell him that. He stood in my living room and shot me in both legs. I'll get him. You tell him that. You tell him I'd kill him right now except I can't get out of this buggy."

"Gory!" the woman exclaimed, turning to the

girl standing on the porch. "He didn't mean it. He didn't mean it at all. Let's go, Gory. We've been here long enough. Driver," she said, "let's go back to that dirty little town."

The driver immediately slapped the team of blacks on the butt with the ribbons, yelled 'haw' and turned the buggy smartly around in the yard, the shiny wheels cutting into the hardpack.

Miguel came out the front door and moved to where Alejendra stood on the veranda holding the Winchester rifle, staring nonplussed at the retreating buggy.

"What's going on?" he asked, seeing the chestnut horse. "That's some horse."

"Those people just tried to sell me a horse that I don't want to buy; that I told them I wouldn't buy."

"I didn't know you had any money."

"Well, I do, but I don't want to buy a horse." She turned to her brother. "Miguel, did you hear him? He said that some old man shot him in the legs and told him to sell me the horse for fifty dollars or he was going to kill him. That's what he said. Can you believe it?" Alejendra stared at her brother then looked at the retreating buggy.

Her brother was standing beside her, his face a picture of disbelief. "Here we go again," he said softly. "Wait till *Papá* hears this." He smiled. "How many old men do you know, Alex?"

Their mother joined them on the veranda staring at the long chestnut horse tied to the veranda railing. "Whose horse, *mi-hija*? He's pretty. *Es muy bonito.*"

"That's Alex's horse, *Mamá*," Miguel said,

324

laughing. "She just bought him from a man sitting in a buggy . . . on credit, no questions asked, no payments due. Get this, *Mamá*, he said an old man shot him in both legs."

"An old man?"

Miguel stopped laughing. "Do you think that Henry Williams shot him *Mamá*? Who else could it be if it wasn't him?"

"Maybe," Raquel answered.

"But that can't be. He didn't even shoot that fellow that wanted to kill Alex's horses. He let him go. What makes you think he would all of a sudden shoot somebody sitting in their house a thousand miles from here?"

"What makes you think his house is a thousand miles away?"

"Weren't you listening? He called the horse Impressive Traveler. We're talking Kentucky. That's where that horse is stabled. Alex. Impressive Traveler? The race horse?" Miguel looked at his sister. "What about the guy who shot Harry Harris? Did Henry Williams kill him?"

Alejendra smiled. "I don't know," she said. "He may have. No one told me. I didn't ask."

"Well, for Henry Williams to shoot this fellow at his house in Kentucky, he'd have to travel there. Do you think he could? He's so busted up he needs help getting on his horse."

Alejendra pursed her lips and stared at her brother, remembering Henry Williams swinging up on his horse. She thought about his questions, but did not answer him. *You might be surprised, Miguel,* she thought. *Henry Williams can do anything. He may have killed that fellow that shot Harry. He said he was going to have a conversation with him; he may have killed him. I just don't know.*

Chapter 34

The next day--the day after the "horse" was delivered--Alejendra found herself standing in front of the kitchen window looking across the hardpack at the thoroughbred stud standing in the horse corral. She couldn't help but think he was a good looking horse. Yesterday she had looked at each hoof: they were shod and in perfect order. She'd opened his mouth and studied his teeth: he had them all.

Her hands were worrying a water glass partially full. She glanced at it, sloshed it around, took a sip, swallowed though she wasn't thirsty.

"*Mamá*," she said. "I think I will go visit *mi abuelita*. While I'm there I'll talk to Mr. Williams about this horse." She turned to her mother. "I can't believe it! I got Harry. I got this horse--everything all at once. First, I need to figure out what to do with this horse. My keeping him just seems wrong. Fifty dollars for a horse maybe worth ten thousand. That's just not right. *Papá* thinks so, too. He sent for the sheriff to look at him. To see if he's stolen. I don't know what to do, so I'll talk to Mr. Williams, strange as that may seem."

Alejendra shook her head in disbelief and looked at her mother. "You know, Miguel is probably right. It's impossible. An old man who can't walk going clear to Kentucky to shoot someone in the legs! Why would he do that? It couldn't have been him." She paused, setting the drinking glass on the counter. "But I won't know unless I talk to him and ask."

Raquel was busy wiping the counters, wringing out the dish rag in her hands. She turned to her daughter. "What is it your problem is? This Harry Harris or the big horse?"

"*Mamá*, it is not Harry Harris. I know what to do with him. But the horse-- I don't understand exactly why I have him standing in our horse corral. I want to tell *mi abuelita* about Harry. I think she will be happy for me. Besides, *Mamá*, Harry will be here as soon as he can travel. Then I'll have no time."

"So you have this Harry all worked out? *No problem*? No questions? No doubts in the head?"

"No, *Mamá*, no doubts in the heart. I have doubts in the head, but not about Harry. I don't know how it is going to work. I just know that if we work at it, it will. In my heart, it is good." She glanced at her mother. "At least I have two thousand dollars and nine mares."

"And he is handsome. Yes?"

"Yes, he is that. And he wants me. He said so. I want him. What else is there? No one knows for sure how things will work out. They just believe they will."

Raquel looked at her daughter and smiled; she patted her cheek, brushed the hair from her eyes. "It is good, *mi-hija,* Go see *tu abuelita.* She will be happy for you I think also. It is the same for her, for you, for me. That is what I think."

Alejendra stared at her mother. "*Mamá*," she said, "you make it sound as if choosing a husband was the same for you. You had no difficulties with these things? Truthfully, I didn't know until I saw Harry lying on his back, shot full of holes that I was in love with him. I practically had to be hit over the head. You know Henry Williams picked me up off the ground and slapped me. Knocked some sense into me."

"With me, not so much. With your father, this is so."

"What?"

Raquel smiled. "*Mi-hija,* your father's father, he not like me so much, I think. He wanted your father to marry with another--a nice girl from Mexico with a large family. Very wealthy, I am told. He was strong this way."

"Really? This is true? But *Mamá,* what about *mi abuelita*? Did she think this also?"

"*Tu abelita* did not agree. She refused; she would not say. She told your grandfather it was not his business to say this. She said that this was the old way and the old way was not good way. That he should keep his opinions to himself about this. He was very angry *tu abuelita* talks this way to him."

"What did *Papá* do?"

"You will never believe it what he did."

"*Mamá?*"

"Your father went to talk to Henry Williams."

"No, *Mamá. No es posible.* Why did he do that?"

"I think maybe *tu abuelita* tell it to him. I think maybe so."

"What did Mr. Williams tell him?"

"I tell you, *chiquita*, but you must never repeat this."

"*Mamá?*"

"Never, *mi-hija.* Never."

"*Mamá*, aren't you being a little dramatic? What could it matter?"

"Between you and me, I think it is why your father, he marry with me."

"What did he say?"

"*Mi-hija*, never. You cannot repeat what I tell you."

Alejendra stared at her mother, not sure whether to laugh or give in. "All right, *Mamá*, all right. I swear, cross my heart."

"You better, *mi-hija*. Your father does not talk about it."

"Okay, so what did Mr. Williams say to *Papá*?"

"At first, he laughed. He said he was not the one to talk to when it comes to women. Then he asked him if he really wanted to hear what he thinks? If he was really that crazy in the head? *Tu papá* tell it to him: yes, he says."

"*Mamá*, why are you dragging this out? You're killing me. What did he say?"

"First, he say that he was not to repeat him to anyone. Then he say that when it came to deciding who he was going to marry he must answer one question *solemente*."

"One question *solemente*? *Mamá,* what is it?"

Raquel paused. "*Chiquita*, the old one, he says to *tu papá*, he says that the question for *tu papá* to answer was who it is that he wakes up in the morning to think about? He says this one should be the girl that when he sees her, he can think of no one else. That he sit around the table with this one, sip the tequila, laugh much, make secret plans much. That when he does not

330

see her, when he not with her, he can think of no one else. That their secrets, their plans were their plans and no one else's plans. Who, when it is between them, it is between no one else; who, in the crowd, they are alone together, their hearts and thoughts always of the other. That is what he said. He told it to him that would be who he should marry and none other. That is the question *solemente* he told *tu papá* to answer it."

"*Mamá*, that is so so sweet. Was that so hard? Why do you make a secret of this?"

"It is important that *tu papá*, his friend the Henry Williams, *tu abuelita* not have--how do you say it?--the red face about this one."

"Embarrassed? You think they will be embarrassed? *Mi abuelita*? What does this have to do with her?"

"Embarrassed, yes. They should not be this way. Especially *tu abuelita*."

"Why her, *Mamá*?"

"*Tu abuelita* sent your father to *Señor* Williams, *mi-hija*. She sent him to him against the will of your grandfather. It made *tu abuelito* very angry. I think this is so."

"Weren't *mi abuelito* and *Señor* Williams good friends?"

"*Si, mi-hija*. They are the very best. They were like brothers. They would die for each other. They fight the war. No question. *Es la verdad*." Raquel looked at her daughter, nodding as she spoke. "Now, go get the eggs. We have much to do. You need to tell your father you are going."

331

Her father had other concerns about her going to see his mother. Something is wrong," he said. "The horse deal isn't right. Men with money don't give away horses, not like that. Not that horse. If it is that horse.

Alejandra explained to her father. She said, "I need to speak with *Señor* Williams. Maybe he'll know what to do with this horse."

"This is good," Manny said, "I suppose you should. Yes. You do need to tell Henry about that horse. You should do that right away. I do not know. I . . . go get Miguel for me, would you?"

Before she had gone to the hen house and had finished gathering the eggs in her basket, all of her brothers were gathered around her father in the barn by the double doors. Her father stopped her.

"Listen," he told her brothers, "take your sister to Henry Williams. Henry needs to know about that horse. He will be expecting trouble. You can expect it, also. If there is trouble, it will come at him sideways. I do not know that it will, but with Henry that is always the way it comes. So without being in plain sight, look around while your sister speaks with Henry. See if anyone new is there. Keep an eye on her. That horse is going to be trouble. Henry will have a plan. It will not seem like it, but he has one or will get one. Keep your sister and my mother safe. Especially watch out for your sister."

Miguel looked at his father. "And the old man, *Papá*? Should we look after him, also? What about Henry Williams?"

Manny shook his head and smiled. "I know you will find this hard to believe but he will be looking out for you. Of him, you never need worry."

Alonso looked at his father. "He is old, *Papá*, and broken. He can barely look out for himself." The four brothers nodded their heads in agreement. "I think we should look out after him, too."

"Okay," Manny said shaking his head. "I will tell you boys this. My father and this old man and my mother--they had something. It was like some secret. I do not know exactly what. I do not know why. I do not know how. All my life, when there was trouble, Henry showed up. When your grandfather was alive, it was both of them. Not just once, but every single time that I can remember. I have not really told you much about him."

Manny laughed, wistfully. He continued. "You might think I'm crazy. I have never told anyone this story. It is too unbelievable. It was one time of many. When I was five, maybe six, I was riding behind your grandfather on his horse, a big horse. I do not remember where we were going. I was young. We came over this rise and below us was a wagon and a fight was going on down there. Many men. There must have been ten or fifteen. Henry was right in the middle of it. I think they were trying to kill him. He was fighting back.

"My father lifted me off the horse. He threw me into a bush, pulled both of his pistols, and spurred the horse. He came down on them, shooting. He did not hesitate. He did not think about it. He simply tossed me in a bush and put the steel to that horse's belly. Men were running, dodging, swearing, screaming. When he ran out of bullets, he was off the horse and using his rifle as a club. Those two were the only ones left when

333

it was over. They piled the bodies in the wagon, all of them, and sent it down the road, no one holding the ribbons."

Tomas studied his father. "The ambush at Layout. Some said it was the Crow."

Manny nodded.

"That was them? *Abuelito* and the old man?" Juan asked.

"There were actually three, Juan. The other man was an Indian. He was big like a wall is big. Made a big horse look small."

"What was it about, *Papá*?" Tomas asked.

"I don't know. Sheep? Cows? Water? Rustlers? Land grabbers? Maybe something else. I was so small. And they never spoke of it. But that is why I know that Henry does not need to be taken care of. Do not mention it to him. I do not know how he would react. Your grandfather and Henry were something people talked about without even knowing it." Manny paused.

"*Papá*, you said there was a third? An Indian?"

"Yes, I know it was an Indian because afterwards, he picked me up, holding me by the butt in one hand. He looked me over. He said to your grandfather 'This one yours?' Your grandfather said 'yes.' 'He is very pretty, this boy. I like him very much.' And Henry said, 'It is because he has a pretty mother.' And the Indian said, 'And no doubt he has a pretty Auntie. Yes?'

"They all three started laughing like it was some joke. I didn't think it was all that funny. That was when I learned I had an aunt named Anna Marie." Manny laughed. "I didn't know before that," he said.

"Afterwards, Mother told me all about her, about her sister. I said I wanted to go see her. She said, 'Be sure to take Henry with you.' And then she started laughing. I still do not understand what was funny."

Manny Rodriquez was still for a long moment, deep in thought, staring at the ground at his feet. "You are all right. Henry is old. He is very old. He can hardly move. My *papá* is no longer alive and Henry is all alone. He no longer has my *papá*. Whenever you can, help him. He may need it. He deserves all of our care, all of our attention. He would do anything for any of you, anytime, anywhere. Yes, he deserves it, *mi-hijos*. He earned your respect a long, long time ago."

Chapter 35

Alejendra Rodriguez and her brothers reached the east side of the stockyards in Kane, Wyoming in the late afternoon, and found no one at the home of their grandmother. The chickens were busy in the yard, clucking and picking in the dirt for rocks, weed seed, and an occasional grasshopper. The mule was in the corral scratching himself against the snubbing post, looking at her in disinterest, twitching its ears. The hogs were lying in their bed in the cool of the shade shed grunting as they tried to find a more comfortable place to lie, a cooler place to stretch. Out in the five-acre pasture, she could see her grandmother's sheep and goats, but no grandmother.

Miguel said he was going to repair one of abuela's chicken coop doors that failed to close. Alonso went to talk to the blacksmith; he had a horse that needed shoeing. Oddly, he left his horse in the horse corral. Tomas went to talk to the railroad master at the section house. Juan wanted to see who was drinking at the Big Horn Bar; then he was going to walk over to the pool hall. There was someone there he needed to speak with; Alejendra couldn't imagine who.

After an hour and a half of waiting, she began to worry, questioning herself. Finally, tired of walking in and out of the kitchen and looking out the window by the sink, she crossed the tracks and went to ask around. She stopped at the Kane General Store and found it empty, except for the clerk, a young fellow named Bill

Scott. He was busy reading a dime novel, but looked up to ask her if she needed any help. She didn't. Next, she visited the livery. An older man–she didn't know his name--told her he hadn't seen her grandmother. Lastly, she stopped at the post office. Janey Jones had not seen her grandmother, either. It was afternoon and she suggested that Alejendra go to the Neeley, noting her grandmother had been over there a lot lately. It seemed that Henry Williams had been on some trip and wasn't in too good of shape.

Janey added, "Of course, he hasn't been in good shape for three years. So what was new? I mean, really."

On a trip? Do you know where?

"Nope," Janey said. "Back east. That's what I heard."

The improbable was true.

She also learned that last summer the Porter boy had drowned swimming in the Big Horn River: that the Clarkes were living up next to the mountain and had built themselves a nice house; painted it white. She learned that just last week the Lowes and Smiths had been to the Kane store to buy groceries and supplies for the winter: that they were expecting a real cold one this year and had filled both wagons with flour, corn meal and two hundred pounds of potatoes. The basis for their prognostication was the length of hair on their mule's back.

Janey had seen it. "Truthfully, that mule's hair is really long."

She'd have learned a lot more except she grew impatient, excusing herself. After picking up the mail,

Alejendra walked down the street to the Neeley to see if Mrs. Neeley had seen her grandmother.

She pulled her jacket around her shoulders. There was an odd sort of chill in the air. If you were standing in the sun, it felt all right, mostly, but if you were in the shade, it was chilly. She'd noted that the postmistress had a fire built in her heating stove. Winter was coming on. From the looks of the clouds hiding Low Mountain, it would be soon.

There was no reason it should have surprised her, but it did. When Alejendra rounded the corner, stepping up on the hotel porch, she found Mrs. Neeley sitting in a chair in the shade, a shawl wrapped around her shoulders to ward off the late fall chill. Mr. Williams sat in his rocker, moving slowly back and forth as he busied his hands removing corn shucks from tamales. At his feet was a Mason jar of apple juice. Seeing that apple juice, thinking of her mother, it suddenly dawned on her where her mother got the recipe. Eighteen was old, old enough, but her mother was twice her age, more. And her *abuela* was three times, maybe more. The recipe for apple juice and some tequila was probably older than them all. What was suddenly so surprising was the thought that these people had lived real lives a long time before she was even born.

Alejendra didn't see her at first, but when she stepped up on the porch to greet Mrs. Neeley, she discovered her grandmother sitting on a wooden box, a red blanket wrapped around her legs. She was sitting in the sun, leaning up against the pole that supported the porch overhang.

"*Mi-hija*, come sit down," she said. "We were watching Henry eat tamales. Do you want some?"

"I . . ."

"Come sit by me. I will scoot over. Make you some room."

Henry Williams looked at her. He said, "Alejendra, how are you? What a pleasant surprise on a fall afternoon. We were just talkin' about you."

"About me?"

"Sure, sugar," Ellen said, smiling. "These two had you married to that Harris boy you're so fond of, living in a log house on the Big Horn Mountain with six kids and a dog."

"Oh my goodness, I never even imagined that," Alejendra said, which was a lie. She'd thought about it a thousand times. Other than that stud, it was all she thought about.

Henry looked at her, smiled. "Yeah, Alex, you've never thought of that Harris boy, not once."

She watched Mr. Williams reach down, take the Mason jar in hand, and sip the apple juice. He swallowed, smacking his lips, then set the jar back down beside the rocker.

Alejendra seated herself by her grandmother, who patted her on the knee. It was comfortable and warm.

"Does that have tequila have apple juice in it, *Abuelita*?"

"What else?" Her grandmother replied.

"That's my *mamá*'s recipe. She get it from you?"

Henry nodded. "I was introduced to that recipe

339

by Franko, himself. His mother made it. Kept jars of it in the root cellar." He smiled as he thought about it.

Alejendra said, "Franko? Who is Franko?"

All three of the older people stared at her.

It was her grandmother who broke the silence that had ensued. "Francisco Rodriguez, *chiquita*."

"My grandfather? You're just saying it. You drank tequila with my grandfather in Mexico? I didn't know you were in Mexico. I didn't know Franko was his name. I've never heard him called that before."

"The very same," Henry replied, softly.

"That's not all they did," her grandmother said. "That is not even a beginning."

Henry Williams handed Alejendra a tamale. "Eat, girl," he said. "You're too damn skinny. Your mother needs to fatten you up. Come a windstorm, you'll blow plum away."

"Do you know my mother, Mr. Williams? She came from Baja, California. Do you like her also?"

"I do, to both questions. Why do you ask such a damn fool question?"

"She told me what you said to *Papá*." Alejendra's hand immediately covered her mouth. "Oh, *Madre de Dios*, I wasn't supposed to say that. I promised. And I'm not supposed to swear."

The three older people burst into laughter. Mr. Williams glanced at her with a raised eyebrow, a wry smile on his face.

"That damn Manny. I made him promise, too. I should have known."

Her grandmother hugged her. "I never knew it. What did Henry tell your father, *chiquita*?" Her

340

grandmother asked. "Tell me."

"*Abuelita*, I . . . "

"Mary Carlos, you know damn well what I told that boy of yours. You sent him to me."

"I sent him, but Manuel never told me what you said. He refused. He said you told him not to. I want to know."

Henry chuckled. He said, "I suppose it don't make no difference, Not now. Franko's dead. Can't shoot me. Can't go fishin'. Can't get drunk with that Indian Fleury. Why'd he ever get that pneumonia? Damn his worthless hide." His voice nearly cracked. He glanced at the three women, took another sip from the Mason jar, smiled, and said, "A good cry never hurt nobody. Not much."

"You and my grandfather got drunk with an Indian?" Alejandra said.

"Damn right we did, girl. Every year, second week in August."

"*Mi-hija*, you are changing the subject. Tell me. I am waiting."

"Tell her, girl. I'll never hear the end of it."

"But--"

"Go on. Tell her. It's okay. Ol' Franko can't shoot me."

She looked at her *abuela*, still hesitating, then, speaking softly, unsure of herself, she began, wondering what her mother would say if she ever found out.

"*Abuelita*, he said . . . he said that *Papá* needed to answer the 'who' question. He told *Papá* to ask himself: Who is the girl he wakes up thinking about in the mornings? Who is the girl that when he sees her, he can think of no one else? She should be the one he sits with at the table, maybe sipping apple juice and tequila, laughing, making plans for their future and loving every minute he spends with her. Who is the girl that when he's not with her, he can think of no one else? Who is the one that even when they are in a crowd, they are alone together, that their hearts and thoughts always are for the other? That is what he said. He said that when *Papá* answers that question he will know who he should marry. He told *Papá* to marry that girl. That is the 'who' question he told *Papá* to answer. And he did. *Papá* married *Mamá*."

Henry smiled, "He sure as hell did, sis, and Franko didn't speak to me for damn near a month. 'Course he was workin' down south."

"You said that to Manuel, Hank? This was a good thing you said. You should have told me. My sister does not know what it is she missed."

It was then that Alejendra noticed the rifle leaning against the porch railing, the wooden handled pistol resting easy in the old man's belt, the gunbelt hanging from the back of the rocking chair where it moved slowly back and forth as the chair rocked. She noticed the old man's restless eyes covering everything in front of him and to the sides as he moved back and forth in the rocker.

"What are you doing?" she asked him. "Why do you have all of these guns? What are you looking for?"

"Keepin' the rattlesnakes off the porch." Henry Williams paused and glanced at Alejendra. "So far it's been workin'. I ain't seen a one."

Alejendra Rodriguez remembered later how her

grandmother chided the Mr. Williams about speaking straight, about not talking in riddles. She remembered how she realized that Henry Williams never rested, never sat still, and she thought how sad it was to never rest.

"*Mi-hija,* this one is concerned because he shot someone and he is thinking that he will send someone to shoot him."

Alejendra looked at Henry. She said, "Mr. Williams, don't you realize that you are old, that you shouldn't be doing these things?"

"Oh, I realize it only too well, Alejendra."

"Mr. Williams, I think the someone you shot came to our house three days ago. He came in a buggy with a woman and a boy. He asked for me. I didn't know who he was so I didn't answer him right away. He had a beautiful horse trailing behind the wagon. Both of the man's legs were bandaged. He had crutches. He'd been shot in both shin bones. He was very angry. He tried to sell me a very valuable horse for fifty dollars. I didn't have fifty dollars that I wanted to spend on a horse, so he lent me fifty dollars. I didn't ask. My father, he says the horse is worth far more than ten thousand dollars, if the papers are right. Both my *papá* and my *mamá* agreed that I should talk to you about this horse. My brothers brought me here. They're not supposed to let me out of their sight. *Papá* said for them not to. I . . . " she paused, thinking that the old man was staring at her. He wasn't. It dawned on her then that he was looking at her grandmother.

It was her grandmother who stood up and walked to where the old man was rocking, one hand

343

resting close to the pistol butt, the fingers playing with a corn husk that had once wrapped a tamale.

"He brought the horse. Do you think it is over?" the old woman asked Henry Williams.

"No," he said. "I'd like it to be over but I don't think I'm that lucky." The old man seemed to take a deep breath. "Listen, *chiquita*," he said to Alejendra, "listen to me."

She listened, thinking later how much she had grown to adore him calling her that, like her grandmother and her mother. His eyes seemed to see her, to watch over her, to hold her away from the evil that walked everywhere, like her *abuelito*.

He said, "I want you to go over there to the section house and telegraph that man. I want you to send him a telegraph, usin' your name. Ellen will give you his name, his address. I want you to offer to sell him that horse for ten thousand dollars. We got a paper around here somewhere. It's got all of this stuff on it. Tell him to send the money and come and get that damn horse. That's all. Understand? We'll see what that horse is worth, if it's worth anything."

"Yes, but--"

"Sis, you don't want that horse. He's nothin' but trouble, a black sin waitin' to happen. Tell him to come and get him and bring the money. I told the folks over at the telegraph you'd be comin'."

"You did?"

"*Mi-hija.*" Her grandmother was fumbling in her pocket. "Here is the message you send." The old woman handed her a slip of folded white paper.

"But what am I going to do--?"

344

"*Mi-hija*, the money--if he sends it--it is for you and that Harris boy."

"But, *Abuelita*--"

"*Mi-hija*, go to the telegraph. Do what Henry said. You don't want that horse."

Alejendra stood up.

"Wait," Henry said sitting up, his eyes holding her on the porch. "Before you go, Alejendra, I want you to tell me everything he said to you. Leave nothing out."

She did. He listened.

"Describe this horse to me."

She did.

"Your father have a look at him?"

"Yes."

Henry nodded, thinking. He said, "Did you say this horse had a white blaze and white hair around his left front hoof?"

"Yes. Not much, though. Hardly any."

"Did you bring the bill of sale?"

"Yes." She handed it to him.

He unfolded the document, looking it over twice; then refolding it, he handed it back. His eyes were narrow, his features hard to read.

Henry took a breath, keeping his thoughts to himself. "All right," he said, "go send that telegram. See if we can't coax this fox outta the hen house."

She remembered walking away, stepping from the porch and crossing the street to the section house. She remembered Mr. Williams saying to her grandmother "Those damn grandkids of yours are goin' to be the death of me. Can you believe that damn

Franko? He died of pneumonia. He wouldn't let them grandkids kill him. You gotta admire that." She remembered the telegraph agent taking the white piece of paper and looking up at her. He asked, "Are you all right?"

Tears streamed down her face. She couldn't stop them. She didn't try. She said, "Yes. Yes, I'm all right."

"Why are you crying?"

"Those people over there." She pointed with her hand at the Neeley Hotel. "They love me."

The telegraph operator shook his head, looked at the piece of paper, and began tapping on the key. "I suppose they do," he said.

Chapter 36

Henry Williams' eyes followed the diminutive girl as she walked across the street, watching as she glanced back at him and the women standing beside him. She waved her hand, smiled, then continued her journey to the telegraph office.

In response, he lifted a hand, then looked at his gnarled fingers, thinking.

Nothing good ever happens this easy. No. It doesn't. Even bad things don't happen without considerable fuss. O'Neal brought that girl a horse. Which horse? If it were Impressive Traveler, O'Neal wasn't the type to slip easily into the night. That's a pipe dream. Three days ago he was at Manny's. Three days. Today he'd be on the train back to Kentucky. Maybe he'd already be there. But what did he do before that?

Henry glanced toward the livery and saw Juan Rodriguez standing at the door talking with Rainbow Harv, armed with a rifle and a six-shooter. He turned and glanced across the fence into the blacksmith shop and the rows of broken wagons awaiting repair. In the shade of the lean-to, Alonso stood cradling a rifle, talking to no one. That meant that Miguel and Tomas were somewhere nearby. Maybe Manny knew something he didn't.

A gust of wind blew up, swirling around him. It was sharp and cold, leaving him blinking. He coughed, thinking of Frank.

347

Henry thought about Gorman O'Neal, remembering his eyes, the way he spoke. Even when he was retreating, he was taking the offensive: always insisting on having his way, no quarter ever. Everything was always a war, someone to conquer, someone to destroy. Never retreat.

A dark, cold feeling washed over Henry. He'd had that feeling before. He knew what it was with a certainty borne of experience. The first time was so long ago. Yet it seemed like yesterday. He had been nineteen. Through the window of the adobe bunkhouse, he'd been watching Mary Carlos Sanchez before she was a Rodriguez; she was walking slowly across the Sanchez compound toward the bunkhouse that housed the *vaqueros*. Mary Carlos Sanchez had her arm around her sister; Anna Marie's head was down. Anna Marie was sobbing, her shoulders shuddering as she walked. That was a bad day, the worst of his life.

The second time was when he was looking out the window of the line shack on the back of the Big Horns. He had been watching the horses in the horse corral. Their heads were suddenly up. They were moving nervously, blowing through their nostrils, all staring in the same direction. He remembered he hadn't yet seen what the horses were looking at but the dark, cold feeling had welled up in him so strong that he'd nearly choked. "Franko," he said, "grab a rifle, we got trouble." That, too, had been a very bad day, a dark day, one that he chose not to remember.

My God. Mary Carlos was right. I should have killed that son of a bitch-- woman or no, piss-ant son or no.

348

"Ellen," he said, "Ellen, what time does the next train roll in? The next one to stop here?"

The two women were standing at the edge of the porch wrapped against the cold breeze with a blanket and a shawl. Across the wide street, Alejendra had mounted the stairs by the section house and was walking across the platform.

"Ahh, it comes in at 4:44. In fifteen minutes, Henry. Why?"

"Passenger train?"

"Yes."

"Ellen, you and Mary Carlos, go get that damn girl. Right now. Get across the tracks. Take her down in that cottonwood grove below the house. Don't stop until you get on the other side of that goat pasture. Do you hear me?"

"What?"

"Damn it, Ellen. Get movin'. Mary Carlos, when you get to your house you'll find one of Manny's boys there. Send him to me. Hurry! Tell him to bring Franko's ten gauge and a rifle."

Henry Williams turned back to the women. They were still standing, looking at him. "Damn it, get movin'. Get that girl outta that telegraph office. I ain't got time to explain." Henry paused. He looked at Mary Carlos. "Mary," he said, "when you go through your house, arm yourself. Do you understand? Then, get out of there. Go to that cottonwood grove below the goat pasture. Stay there until I come to get you."

They still hadn't moved.

Henry took a deep breath. "All right," he finally said. "That horse of O'Neal's, the one that won them

349

races, he was a pure chestnut bay. No white. That ain't no Impressive Traveler standin' in Manny's horse corral. O'Neal ain't sellin' that stud. He ain't makin' peace. He's declarin' war. That girl said that if O'Neal saw me, he'd kill me. He won't do that. He'll send somebody. More'n likely he'll send several somebodies. He never does any of the killin' himself. I reckon they're comin' in on that train. So, get that girl and get outta here." Henry paused, staring at the two women. "Please," he said.

The two women didn't say anything in response to his plea. They were already in motion.

The old man had risen to his entire height--all five-feet-eleven inches. As the women scurried off the porch, he checked the loads in one pistol, then, taking up the holster from the chair back, he strapped on the belt and holster, checking the loads in the second. No longer did he pay any attention to the running women. He did not watch them cross the street, the dust puffing up with each footfall. He glanced at Alonso standing in the shade of the blacksmith's lean-to, and beckoned for him to come to him.

By the time Alonso had reached his side, he'd picked up the Winchester, fed the first cartridge in the magazine into the firing chamber, and added another to the magazine. It was fully loaded.

"Mr. Williams," Alonso asked, "what's going on?"

Henry glanced at Alonso, seated his Stetson on his head, pulling it down over his forehead by the brim.

"In a few minutes, boy, the passenger train is goin' to pull into the station. I expect some men will be gettin' off. Don't know how many, but a few. Don't know what they look like. Don't know if they will actually get off. But I expect they will. They're comin' to put an end to me, to the Rodriquezes, to that damn Harris boy, and his stud horse. Get your brothers. I see Tomas is down at Rainbow's. Which one is at Mary Carlos' cabin? "

"Miguel."

"Mary Carlos will have him come here. We got less than ten minutes. Hurry. This ain't gonna be pretty, boy."

If the old man felt any pain, it was hidden behind a stoic face, a slow pounding heart, and the urgency of the moment boiling over into the very air he breathed. It was an urgency born of certainty, a feel for the texture of danger as it grows and festers, clouding sky and field, shadowing everything that moves, weighing down on the heart like an anvil of steel. Indeed, he had felt it before.

A little over three minutes later, Juan, Alonso, and Tomas stood on the porch with the old man. Miguel was sprinting across the street from the shadows of the section house, carrying a rifle in one hand and a shotgun in the other. His pockets were loaded with ten gauge shotgun shells. The four men watched him. When he arrived, the four boys, their faces somber, turned their attention to Henry Williams, the parting words of their father ringing in their ears.

Henry explained, "In a few minutes the 4:44 will be rollin' in. There will be a number of men gettin' off. I don't know what they look like or how they are dressed. You'll recognize 'em though. They will be gunnin' for me, for the lot of you, for your father, for your mother, for Alejendra, for that Harris boy, and for that damn horse of his. If they don't get off this train, some or all of 'em will have gotten off in Greybull. In that event, your father is already dead, your mother, too, and your damn dog will be runnin' for the timber, if he ain't dead."

Henry stopped talking, then started quickly explaining. "We're goin' to catch 'em at the depot. Alonso, take the corrals. Get behind those timbers so when the train is standin' still, you can see down the east side of the tracks. Miguel, you hotfoot it over and sit yourself behind that stack of railroad ties on the southeast side. Keep low. Keep behind 'em. Be inconspicuous. Do not stand up. Don't give these bastards a target bigger than a half dollar standin' sideways. Both of you: don't do nothin' till after the train pulls away. Hear me? Let the train go. See who's left. I will open the ball. Once I do . . . shoot to kill. We get no second chances. They'll be comin' loaded for bear." Henry paused, and looked at Tomas. "Tomas, take the north end of the platform. Shoot from cover. Juan, take the south end of the platform. There is some old ML boxes and crates stacked over there. Stay behind 'em. Look drunk. Shoot straight. Questions?"

No one responded to his query. Henry Williams looked at the young men, shaking his head, wondering about the promise he'd given their grandfather, wondering why the bear took the time to go over the mountain, wondering what he saw once he got there.

"Boys," he said, "don't give these bastards nothin' to shoot." Henry paused, trying to think of what

352

he didn't remember to tell them. He said, "Shoot to kill, dead center of the chest."

They heard the train whistle blowing as it came out of Sheep Canyon. Henry Williams smiled at the four somber faces. "Five minutes," he said.

"Where are you going to be, Mr. Williams?" Miguel asked.

"I'm gonna go sit on that green bench on the railroad platform."

"But you'll be in plain sight."

"I will. Nowhere else for me. I'm too damn old to outrun a bullet. I want 'em to see me. I want 'em to hesitate just that much before they grab their irons. When they do, I'm hopin' you'll shoot straight and often. Do not hesitate, for they'll be carryin' an arsenal of death. They'll be packin' six shooters to back up six shooters." Henry stopped speaking. "All right, boys, let's get to movin'. The devil ain't waitin' for no holiday."

The four young men nodded, running across the street, heading for the railroad platform.

Henry Williams took a deep breath and let the air out slowly. He had no illusions; he figured himself dead. As he said, he couldn't run, he could hardly walk, and he couldn't dodge a bullet.

What a helluva note, he thought, laughing at himself. *Well, Franko, keep a chair empty at the dinner table; and a fishing pole, the hook baited and ready to go; maybe some apple juice and a bottle of tequila. I figure to be joinin' you soon. And no more promises, Franko. None at all. These promises are heavy to carry. They don't go away.*

353

To the north, clouds hung low on the barren slopes of the Mountain. There was a bite in the wind. He could smell the promise of snow. To the south, the sun was still shining. In the west, the clouds were dark, foreboding. *Storm coming*, Henry thought. *Be the first snow of the year, the way she looks.*

As he turned toward the station house, the four boys were across the street, climbing up on the platform. From there, they walked to their assigned destinations. Miguel, still carrying the shotgun and the Winchester, glanced at him, then disappeared behind the section house.

God, they are so young. Franko, I'm so sorry. So very sorry. Hope you're seein' this. Hope you understand. If you ain't too busy, I sure could use some help. Where do you think that damn Indian is? I do believe I need him.

Using the rifle as a crutch, Henry made his way across the street. "Goin' to be a warm one today," he said to himself, laughing because it felt anything but warm. He wondered if the women had secluded themselves in the cottonwood grove, hoping they had. He made his way up the steps of the brick platform and made his way to its edge. He looked down the long steel ribbons that served as railroad tracks. He could see the small black dot of the engine with white smoke and steam blowing out of the stack. A small girl and her mother who had been sitting on the green wooden bench got up and walked down the platform as they became aware of the approaching train. A cold breeze swirled around, pushing them. Henry Williams sat down, his hip complaining vigorously. He leaned the

354

rifle against the bench, reseated his hat, then tugged at his soft leather gloves on either hand. Deep in thought, but not thinking, he pulled the SAA pistol with the walnut grip from his waist belt, pulled back the hammer, listened to it click. He did the same with the holstered pistol, holding one in each hand. There were no empty chambers. He'd checked twice. Taking a deep breath, he leaned back against the bench and waited.

An eight-year-old boy standing behind his mother's billowing skirts with his younger sister stared at him. Henry winked. The boy smiled. Everyone on the railroad platform was now looking at the approaching engine. Henry smiled.

Damn it, Franko. When I really need you, where the hell are you? In a pine box resting on a hill in Iona, that's where. Why did you have to go do that?

The train, pulling five cars, rushed in, steam belching from the tortured brake cylinders; the front drivers appeared to reverse themselves ever so slightly. From the cab of the standing locomotive, the engineer looked back down the platform. The conductor was dismounting from the steps of the third passenger car. Sixteen people got off the train that afternoon. There were glad hellos, hugs, smiles, and one grim, "get the hell out of my way." There were two boys running down the platform to the south end, leaping into their father's arms; a smiling woman following them. Lastly--he didn't see them at first--there were seven grim-faced men: four dressed like range cowhands, one all in black like a sextant going to a funeral, two wearing leather jackets, one with fringe, and one without.

Henry Williams remained seated, wondering

who and how many were getting off on the other side. The men climbed down the steps from the passenger cars packing saddles, saddle bags draped over their shoulders. All of them had rifles, some in scabbards. All wore broad brimmed hats. From the looks of their jackets and coats, they were also armed with additional pistols, pistols to back up pistols. One had a long Bowie knife stuck in his belt. One paused and looked back up the steps of the passenger car. He was talking with someone on the steps. He smiled.

Passengers began boarding. There weren't as many as had gotten off. Soon the conductor was looking both ways. He waved his arm to the engineer, signaling that boarding was complete. The train began to move, sluggish at first. The drivers engaged, turning slowly, slipping momentarily on the rails; the cars clanked as the slack was pulled out of each of the attached cars. The conductor stepped aboard the moving car. The drivers were squealing; steam was coming in gusts, billowing from the engine. The platform was beginning to clear. Three minutes had passed; the second hand was working on a fourth. The men who'd gotten off last were beginning to pick up their gear as the last passenger car was pulled down the tracks past the bench where Henry sat. He noted that three men had gotten off the train on the east side. They were looking toward the corrals, collecting their things, their backs to the railroad tracks and the section house.

Henry Williams stood, one foot slightly in front of the other, his feet spread so that there was eighteen inches between them. He smiled, thinking of Frank.

This is all such a bad joke. Such a circus: a

bunch of damn apes, no drummer, no organ player. Just some clowns.

The train was gone, taking the roar of steam, the high pitched squeal of steel pushing steel. Somewhere over toward the post office a dog was barking.

"You boys lookin' for me?" Henry drawled.

The only man of the seven to hear those five words was the fellow dressed in black broadcloth standing beside the open window of the telegraph office. He had asked the telegraph operator where the hotel was located, where he could find this Henry Williams. The gravelly voice interrupted him before he could get the words out. He glanced at the old man standing thirty feet away from him on the platform, a bench behind him, a rifle leaning against it. He held two Colts, one in either gloved hand. There was no doubt in the stranger's mind that the hammers were pulled back and locked.

Six days before, Gorman O'Neal, using crutches to stand, speaking slowly, had said, "Gentlemen, the one you are looking for--he's an old man, looks like death eating a pickle. His hair is mostly grey. He's always in pain, slightly bent over like his back is aching. He wears a big Stetson hat and a worn out insulated denim jacket. He can hardly walk, favors his left hip. Lastly, and remember this: he's good, he's very good. If you see him and he knows you're coming, it's too late. He's successful because he plans everything. Take nothing for granted. Take no chances. He won't."

The sextant had looked at his nine companions, studying them. Shooting an old man sitting on the porch of a hotel in a one horse town didn't sound all that difficult. Certainly not for ten men. Any one of them could do it easily. Ten men? The man dressed as a sextant had wondered what had scared his employer so much. What was there about a crippled, old man?

It was as though Gorman could read all of their minds. "There are ten of you." He paused. "If I could find them, I'd send fifteen. Hear me. Everyone I've sent is dead. Do you hear me? Dead. I'm not taking any more chances."

Priority was stressed. "Get the old man, first. Hear me? Before you do any of the other things, you get him. Dead, he has to be dead, understand?" The man with the money stopped talking.

Then he explained how he wanted them to arrive in that town after he was there and gone. "Give me three days," he said, stressing that he was leaving that day. "I'll be there and gone in seventy-two hours. Six days from now I want you boys to be getting off the train. I want him taken care of first." Gorman had paused, then repeated himself. "It is important that the old man be taken care of first." They had nodded, expressing their collective understanding.

That is what the middle-aged eastern man wearing a derby hat had told them before he boarded the train in Lexington, Kentucky six days before.

The arrangement seemed ludicrous to the sextant. It made no sense; it certainly did not justify the expenditure. *Kill a man, kill nine mares, kill a stud horse. Any one of them could do that. Ten men,* the sextant thought. *Ten. What wasn't being explained? What was missing?*

Three days later they had boarded the train, not looking forward to riding the rails. But the money was good; the risk was low. The sextant had listened to the comments of the others as they mused about the circumstances. Someone wondered why so many for an old man. Another had commented that it was odd how a man has a reputation and after a while everyone knows what it is and even if he tries he can't get away from it.

The speaker had smiled. "You boys ever heard of Henry Williams?" Everyone said "no." "I have," he said. He didn't say anything more. The sextant had asked him. "I've just heard the name. I was told that he could track pretty good. That's all."

The sextant man saw Henry. He said, "Jesus," dropping his saddle, his saddle bags and rifle, grabbing for an unseen revolver, all with the old man watching him, a slight puzzled smile on his lips.

Henry waited, cursed himself for doing so, and then shot the man through the chest as his pistol came up.

"Guess you are," Henry said, answering his own question, then he stepped forward, shooting at anything that moved or looked at him sideways.

Henry had never thought he lived a charmed life. Fact was, there was nothing charming about it. It was just the life he knew. One round ripped through his hat and peeled back a layer of his scalp. Another cut the fleshy inside of his left leg. One struck his heel and knocked him to the surface of the brick platform. It saved his life.

The Rodriquez boys followed his initial

instructions, taking their first shots from cover; after that they ignored him altogether. They were running, firing their rifles as they moved, trying to get to the platform and save the old man from getting himself killed. It helped that there were five down after the first volley.

Once alarmed, the remaining gunmen jumped for cover or crouched on the brick platform. The old man somehow got to his feet with all of this going on, shots pouring in from all sides, amid the loud percussion of discharging weapons. He simply limped steadily toward his adversaries, firing with each step, until the bullet clipped his boot heel. It was simply the only way he knew.

Before he left the bench, Henry knew he was facing experienced gunmen. It did not surprise him that, after the first exchange, some were on one knee, firing at whatever was firing at them, not realizing that the quarry they sought was right in front of them, seeking to kill before being killed. By the end of the second exchange, the old man was down again, shot through the lower leg, the heel of his boot knocked off. Two of the men never saw him at all. Miraculously, two of the seven that got off the train on the west side survived the initial exchange, though they could barely move, having been shot several times at close range. The others were not so lucky. One of the two survivors soon died from his wounds; the other was laid up for the better part of two months. One day the doctor looked in on him and he was gone. He had disappeared. No one knew what happened to him.

The firing stopped abruptly. The old man sat up.

Getting to his feet, he immediately ejected the spent cartridges onto the brick platform, filling the magazines from the cartridge belt. Warm blood ran down his face from the scalp wound; his left leg stung like crazy, his pant leg soaked in blood.

Tomas took a round in the shoulder through the deltoid muscle. Juan was shot just above the hip bone. The other two Rodriguez boys escaped unscathed.

Juan later told his father, "*Papá*, the old man didn't look so good. He was all shot up. I tell you, *Papá*, I don't know how he could even move, blood running down his leg, his head matted in it. He still had those pistols, one in each hand."

"Alonso," Henry said quietly, his hand around the young man's shoulder, steadying himself, "you and Miguel get some help for Juan, for Tomas. Old Doc Thompson. He's around here some place. When you're finished, get the ladies from the cottonwood trees. After you've done that, if I were you, I'd get your horses. You'll be needin' to get home. No tellin' what's happenin' there. I don't expect this is over."

Chapter 37

Six days later on Friday evening, the old man let himself in the beautifully furnished house by using the heavy oak door. He'd let himself in without knocking and he sat on the overstuffed couch in the living room of Gorman O'Neal. His scalp wound was healing up, but the wound on his leg was troublesome. It seemed unduly sore. Fact was, he could barely walk, but what was new?

The boy walked into the overly decorated room and found the old man watching him from the overstuffed couch, his hands appearing to be in his lap.

The boy stared momentaily, hesitating, then said, "I don't think my Dad likes you much."

"I know, boy. Life is that way."

"I think maybe he'd want you to go."

"I reckon."

"Did you shoot my dog?"

"No, I ain't. Figured you might need him."

"I do. I like him. Are you going to go?"

"In a minute."

"Are you going to shoot my dad?"

"Boy, why don't you sit right there in that chair."

"Why?"

"I guess I don't know why."

"Are you going to shoot my mom?"

"Not if I can help it."

The old man stared at the boy, thinking, then he

362

nodded his head as if he came to some decision. He said, "Sit right there, boy. I'm gonna call your father out here where I can talk to him."

"You are? I don't think he will listen. He doesn't listen to anybody." Having said that, the boy sat down in the easy chair with his back to the windows, staring at the old man. He sat upright, not leaning back.

"I expect you're right," the old man replied. "You might want to cover your ears. This will be kinda loud." Whereupon the old man discharged his .45 in the confined space, blasting a small hole in the ceiling. The blast was incredibly loud. It was then the boy discovered that each of the old man's gloved hands held a revolver, same make and model.

The effect was instantaneous.

Gorman O'Neal came limping down the hall trying to hurry. He entered the room, his eyes immediately focusing on his boy holding his ears and then the old man slouched on his overstuffed sofa, a smoking pistol in his left hand. Gorman O'Neal's shin bones hadn't completely healed; they still ached horribly, especially when he walked. Blood, once in a while, leaked from his left leg where the bullet hadn't entered straight away, cutting a groove to the left as it had exited the back of the bone. Sometimes he could hardly stand. This wasn't one of those times.

When Gorman O'Neal saw the old man, he forgot his son. He cried out "Oh, my God!" in stark disbelief and leaped for the rifle rack that hung on the wall on his immediate right. He found a twelve gauge double barrel shotgun and jerked it from the rack, falling to the floor as he tried to find refuge from the old man's fire.

It never came.

Suddenly it was silent, except for O'Neal cocking the hammer on one of the barrels.

"Dad?" the boy said to the man hiding behind the other sofa.

"Roger, get to your room."

Roger glanced at the old man who shook his head "no."

"This old guy wants me to sit here."

"Roger, get to your room. Do what I say."

Again, the boy glanced at the old man who shook his head "no."

"He wants me to sit right here. What do I do, Dad?"

Gorman O'Neal peeked above the sofa he was hiding behind. The old man hadn't moved.

"Let my boy go," he demanded.

"I ain't got a hold of him, Buster. But I do have a hold of you."

Buster? "What? You son of a bitch." He brought the shotgun up and over the back of the couch. The old man shot him through the chest and once through the head. The shotgun discharged, blasting a hole in the hardwood floor. Gorman O'Neal, the financier, the coal man who owned thirty-five deep draft ships, the owner of Impressive Traveler, was shoved backwards against the wall, rolling on the floor behind the couch.

The boy remained in the chair, his hands over his ears. Henry glanced at him. He said in a tired voice, "Boy, I'm sorry you had to see that. I wish you didn't."

"What did he do to you?" the boy asked, tears

364

beginning to run down his ruddy cheeks, streaking his face, still not moving from the chair, his hands still clamped over his ears. "I'm going to kill you."

"You may try. Won't be the first time. I was forced to put an end to it. You probably don't understand this, but your father was evil: killin' horses, killin' men, runnin' roughshod over what wasn't his. Maybe you'll understand that someday. Maybe you won't."

The old man stood, groaning as he gained his full height, holding steady against the pain.

"What's wrong with you?" the boy asked.

"Some of those men your dad sent got a bullet or two in me."

"Where are they?"

"They're havin' supper in hell."

A woman came running into the room. He recognized her. The boy still hadn't moved from the chair. She looked at the old man, then at her husband on the floor, the shotgun near to hand.

"Ma'am, if you are of a mind, you can pick up Mr. O'Neal's shotgun. There is one chamber left unfired. I'll let you pull back the hammer, if you are of a mind. Give her a go."

She stared at him, hesitating, seeing the pistols in each hand.

"Momma, don't," the boy pleaded. "He'll shoot you dead. Momma, please."

"Roger, hush."

"Go ahead, Ma'am. I'll let you pick it up. The boy is right. That is all I'm gonna let you do."

She did not move toward the shotgun.

"Ma'am?"

"Please leave."

"You sure?"

"Yes. Please leave."

"All right. If you're sure." He holstered the pistol in his right hand, shoving the second behind his belt buckle. He turned, looking at the front door. It was then she noticed the third hidden in the folds of shirt in the small of his back. He glanced back at her, then limped to the corpse of Gorman O'Neal. He hefted the shotgun from the floor, breaking it open. He winced as he bent over, gasping; the pain so intense, he was forced to hold still. All the time, he watched the woman. He removed the remaining shotgun shell and dropped it in his pocket, then reseated both hammers and set the shotgun in the empty space in the wall rack.

"Ma'am?" he said.

"What?"

"Your late husband sent twelve men on and off to threaten and kill me and the Rodriguez family, not to mention Alejendra's horses and that Harris boy. If I even smell, even wake up in the morning in a sour disposition, and think you might be tryin' to finish what your husband started, you'll find me on your doorstep. I'll have no mercy. Understand? I'm lettin' you choose how you want this story to end. Ma'am," he said, pausing, "it would be a mistake if you didn't think I can get to you."

"All right. It's over. I understand. Please, please just leave."

"If I even smell someone on my back trail--"

"I heard you. You'll not find me doing what

Gory did."

"That is what Mr. O'Neal said, but he done forgot."

"Please, just leave. Believe me, I won't forget."

"All right," he replied, turning to Roger. "Boy, you got anythin' to say?"

"Are you going to shoot my dog now?"

"No, I ain't got nothin' against your damn dog."

The old man stared at the boy momentarily, then started limping toward the front door.

As he did, air rattled from Gorman O'Neal's lungs. Evie jumped. The boy came to his feet, staring at the dead man, tears still running down his cheeks. His mother ran to him, gathering him in her arms, hugging him, holding him close to her bosom.

"Momma?"

"What, sweetie?"

"Why didn't Poppa just leave the old man alone?"

"I don't know. Your father couldn't leave anything alone."

"Are we going to leave the old man alone?"

"I pray to God we never see or hear of him again."

"Me too, Momma. I hope he doesn't kill my dog."

The old man walked slowly, painfully to the front door. Turning the brass knob, he opened it and stepped out into the dying light. Painfully, he made his way to the rented horse and pulled himself into the saddle, using the strength in his arms and shoulders. He sat there for a moment, gathering himself, watching the sun set in the Appalachian hills. The trees had lost their leaves weeks ago. In place of brilliant color was winter brown: tree skeletons pointing into the evening sky. The breeze was sharp and cold. He turned up the collar on his sheepskin, then reined the horse around. Taking his time, he walked him to the county road thinking he'd like to ride clear to Mexico. He could live in the shadow of some palm tree where it was warm, where life wasn't nearly so complicated, maybe soak his head in a bucket of tequila and snack on some very hot tamales. Wouldn't it be something to meet Anna's sons and daughters, her grandchildren? He wondered if he could talk Mary Carlos Sanchez into going with him.

"Probably not," he said. "Probably not."

But he did.

The End

Introducing G.R. Howe's
upcoming Western novel:

HACK

CHAPTER 1

Jacob Tallasinius sat his sorrel horse, conscious of its telltale signs of impatience: the shifting of its weight from one leg to another, walking sideways on the prairie sod, sometimes prancing, sometimes dancing, its ears laid back, listening, as it wondered about the rider's hesitancy to move forward. In spite of the sorrel's nervous impatience, Tallasinius continued to rein him in. He studied the ridge that rose on his right--not high, just five to ten feet higher than the creek bed--extending north for a quarter of a mile. Beyond that, the land leveled out until it reached the canyon country and the dark blue range of mountains beyond. He took a deep breath, something, somehow wasn't adding up. It was too quiet, for one thing. Nothing moved, for another. It was if the world was holding still, full of apprehension, waiting.

He saw some prairie chickens take flight a hundred yards up the ridge line. He heard a rock dog chirping incessantly. Behind him, he was conscious of the wagons lining up, all twenty-four, readying themselves for another day's journey, another ten to fifteen miles, if all went well. To his right, along the ridge, on a flat red rock, a chipmunk was doing its herky-jerky movement, suddenly holding himself still, eyeing him; then its tail started bouncing and bobbing.

If. If. If. That was just it. If. If all went well. But something . . . He could feel it but he was just not able to put a finger on it, his restless nerves rattling around

371

in his head. His nephew, Hack, had left early, long before first light, scouting the trail north of them.

Before he left, he'd stood with Tallasinius on the north edge of the night camp, holding the reins to his bay horse while both studied the lay of the land, gazing at the stars that sprinkled the night sky. It had been quiet then, too.

"I don't know, Uncle Jake," Hack had said. "I just don't know."

"Me, either," Tallasinius replied, pausing. "Well, be careful, Boy. Extra careful. I feel the same thing you do."

As he had listened, he had heard the high pitched sound of a killdeer; wondered what a killdeer was doing singing that early in the morning. Standing there with a false dawn creeping up over the mountains, Hack had smiled, musing.

"Uncle," he said, "it's sorta like waitin' for the bronc to get himself uncorked; you sittin' in the middle of him, the bronc restin' in the shade of a cottonwood, barely movin' a muscle, yawnin' like he ain't got no care. You know it's gonna happen, just not when, just not where. But you know."

Tallasinius had nodded. "I know, I know. Somethin'. Just somethin'. Don't know what it is. Better get, Boy. See what you can see. Maybe we can figure this out 'fore it buries us."

Tallasinius stepped away from the boy and his horse, moved a short distance into the cool of the night, breathed in the dank, night air through his nose, then looked back at the boy. "I'm goin' to alert the night watch. Now you be careful, Hack. See you this evenin'. If ya can, bring back a couple a mule deer."

The boy had mounted the bay horse, swinging into the saddle, finding the stirrup with his off foot. He had glanced at his uncle, touched his hat with his gloved hand in acknowledgment, and nudged the tall bay horse into motion.

That was three and a half long hours ago.

Tallasinius relaxed the tension in the reins, allowing the sorrel to step forward, at the same time motioning for the lead wagon to follow, to start moving. He heard the teamster walking alongside his wagon start talking to his oxen, heard the wagoneers behind put their teams in motion. Whips cracked. Wheels squeaked. Wagon boxes creaked as teams leaned into their harnesses, the slack taken out of the trace chains. Tallasinius rode out front, suspiciously studying the edge of the ridge, the creek bed, and the country beyond. Somehow it was lying to him and he knew it. The company of emigrants began to stretch out along the lee side of the red ridge, moving between it and the brush that hid the creek. A breeze picked up, bending the grass in brown waves. Tallasinius turned in the saddle, looking back at the wagons, watching them falling into line and moving forward.

It was then that he saw them: armed men advancing out of the creek brush, moving on foot, suddenly running toward the creeping wagons, and the unsuspecting settlers. Without actually seeing them, he knew others were coming off the ridge on the other side of the wagons. It was a trap, sprung in the morning mist, with the dew clinging to the drying grass. The first wave of insurgents was already to the wagons. It was happening so fast. Tallasinius pulled his navy Colts from their holster, fired a round at the attackers, spurring the sorrel, yelling, charging the nearest attacker, killing him--at least stopping him if he weren't dead. He heard a shrill scream edged with panic, saw men in the seats above the jockey boxes turning, reaching for weapons, focusing their attention on the commotion; he heard weapons discharging up and down the line of wagons.

Tallasinius rode the second man down, shooting him in the head, his horse's forward movement knocking him sideways. An arrow caught the horse in the chest through the saddle cinch. He reared. Tallasinius stepped down from the horse as it rolled, kicking frantically. He clubbed an attacker over the head with a pistol butt, shooting the man behind him with the pistol in his other hand. He felt an arrow drive deep in his chest, realizing there wasn't ever going to be "no never mind," that this was it, that he wasn't walking away from this one. He fired his revolver from his knees, shooting again and again, feeling the light steadily drain from him, and someone club him over the head with a glancing blow. Turning to the man wielding a club, he stabbed him with his long knife, driving it into his assailant's body, burying it deep in his abdomen. Dimly, as if seeing through a glass darkly, Jacob Tallasinius saw two warriors advancing toward him, both running, one firing an old Colt dragoon. He felt the molten lead pierce his body, driving him backwards. He got off two more shots, shooting at forms and shadows before the light of his soul went out and he surrendered himself to grey oblivion.

G. R. Howe was raised in Kane, Wyoming. He graduated from Brigham Young University and received a law degree from John Marshall Law School in Chicago. He began practicing in Ventura, California in 1976 and pursued a career in law for the next thirty-four years, after which he and his wife, Joy, retired to Wyoming and began writing western novels. He is an associate member of Western Writers of America.

www.ingramcontent.com/pod-product-compliance
Lightning Source LLC
Chambersburg PA
CBHW061304170626
46817CB00001B/47